AMERICAN BORN CHINESE

B/T

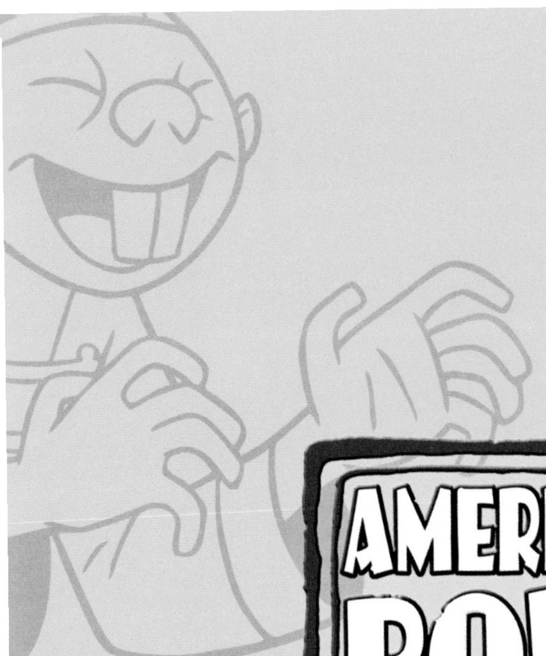

AMERICAN BORN CHINESE

Gene Luen Yang

Color by Lark Pien

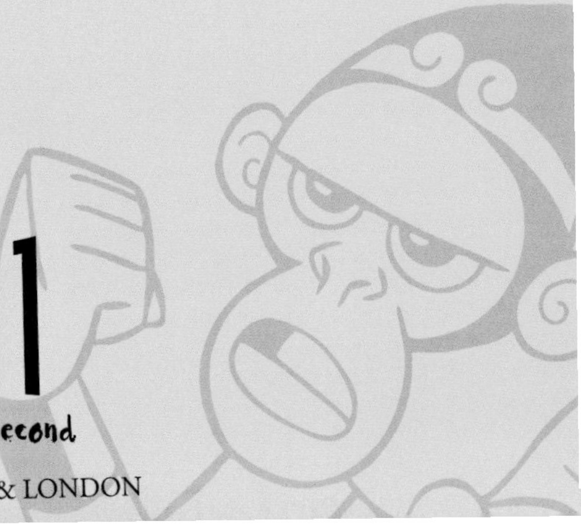

First Second
NEW YORK & LONDON

To Ma,
for her stories of the Monkey King

And Ba,
for his stories of Ah-Tong, the Taiwanese village boy

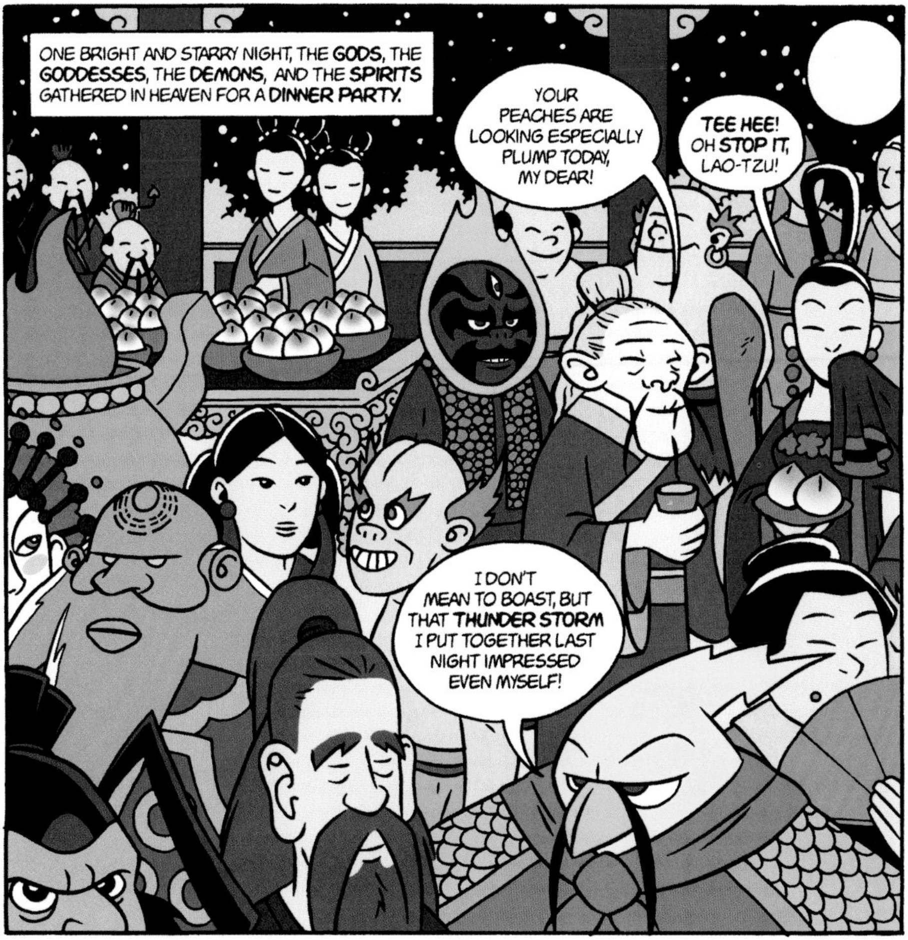
ONE BRIGHT AND STARRY NIGHT, THE GODS, THE GODDESSES, THE DEMONS, AND THE SPIRITS GATHERED IN HEAVEN FOR A DINNER PARTY.
YOUR PEACHES ARE LOOKING ESPECIALLY PLUMP TODAY, MY DEAR!
TEE HEE! OH STOP IT, LAO-TZU!
I DON'T MEAN TO BOAST, BUT THAT THUNDER STORM I PUT TOGETHER LAST NIGHT IMPRESSED EVEN MYSELF!

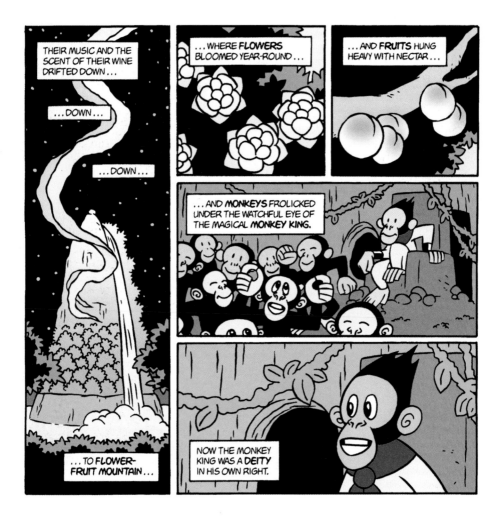

THEIR MUSIC AND THE SCENT OF THEIR WINE DRIFTED DOWN...

...DOWN...

...DOWN...

...TO FLOWER-FRUIT MOUNTAIN...

...WHERE **FLOWERS** BLOOMED YEAR-ROUND...

...AND **FRUITS** HUNG HEAVY WITH NECTAR...

...AND **MONKEYS** FROLICKED UNDER THE WATCHFUL EYE OF THE MAGICAL **MONKEY KING**.

NOW THE MONKEY KING WAS A **DEITY** IN HIS OWN RIGHT.

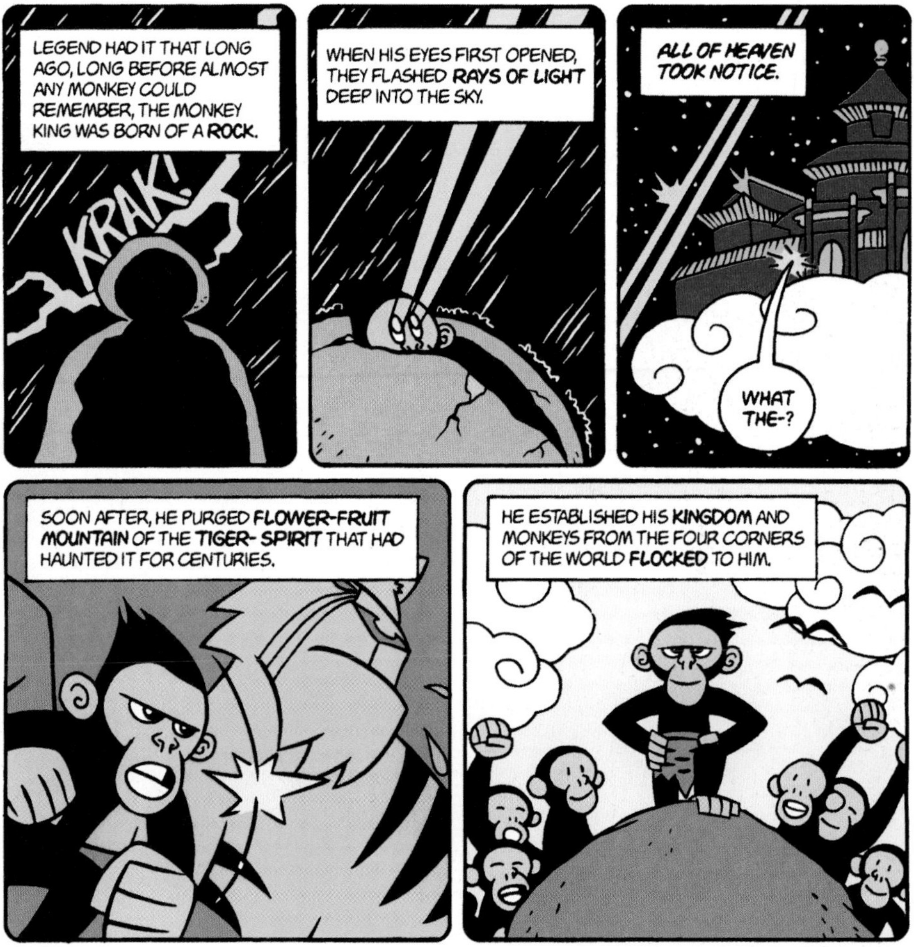
LEGEND HAD IT THAT LONG AGO, LONG BEFORE ALMOST ANY MONKEY COULD REMEMBER, THE MONKEY KING WAS BORN OF A **ROCK**.
KRAK!
WHEN HIS EYES FIRST OPENED, THEY FLASHED **RAYS OF LIGHT** DEEP INTO THE SKY.
ALL OF HEAVEN TOOK NOTICE.
WHAT THE-?
SOON AFTER, HE PURGED **FLOWER-FRUIT MOUNTAIN** OF THE **TIGER- SPIRIT** THAT HAD HAUNTED IT FOR CENTURIES.
HE ESTABLISHED HIS **KINGDOM** AND MONKEYS FROM THE FOUR CORNERS OF THE WORLD **FLOCKED** TO HIM.

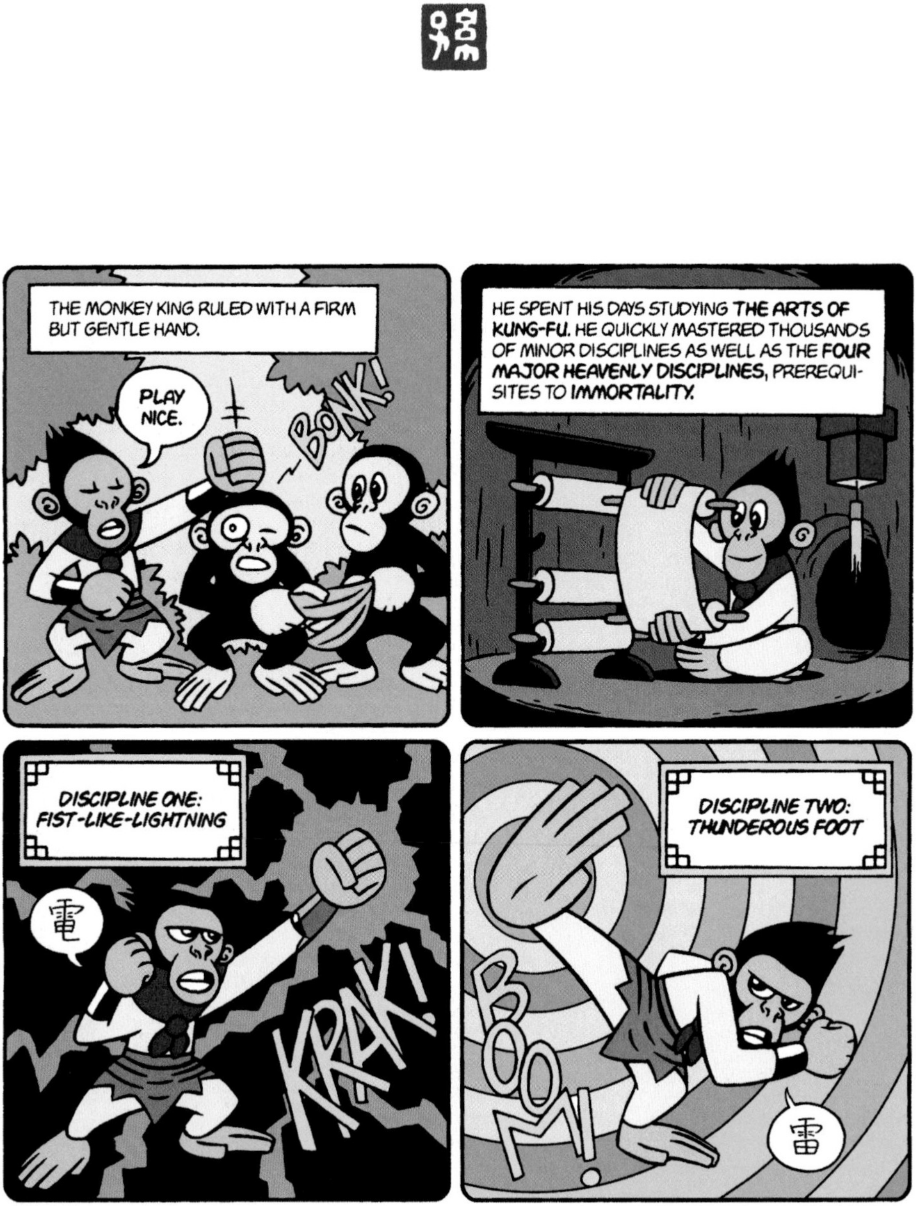
THE MONKEY KING RULED WITH A FIRM BUT GENTLE HAND.
PLAY NICE.
BONK!
HE SPENT HIS DAYS STUDYING THE ARTS OF KUNG-FU. HE QUICKLY MASTERED THOUSANDS OF MINOR DISCIPLINES AS WELL AS THE FOUR MAJOR HEAVENLY DISCIPLINES, PREREQUISITES TO IMMORTALITY.
DISCIPLINE ONE: FIST-LIKE-LIGHTNING
電
KRAK!
DISCIPLINE TWO: THUNDEROUS FOOT
BOOM!
雷

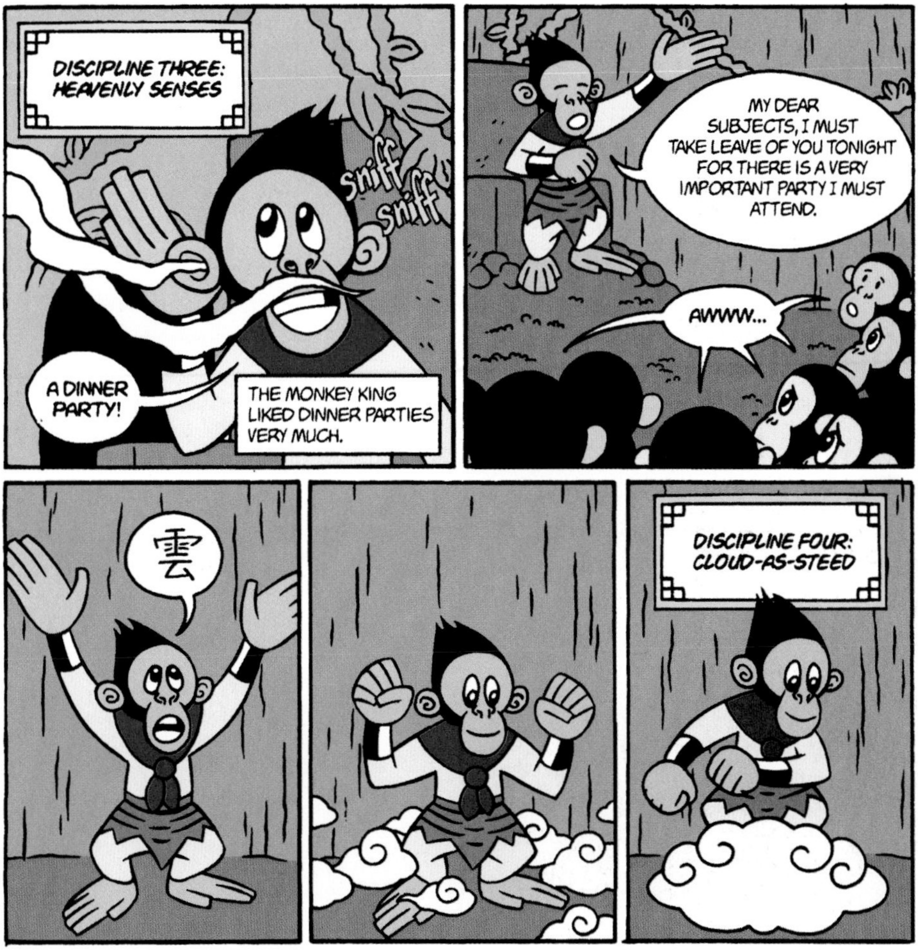
DISCIPLINE THREE: HEAVENLY SENSES
sniff sniff
A DINNER PARTY!
THE MONKEY KING LIKED DINNER PARTIES VERY MUCH.
MY DEAR SUBJECTS, I MUST TAKE LEAVE OF YOU TONIGHT FOR THERE IS A VERY IMPORTANT PARTY I MUST ATTEND.
AWWW...
雲
DISCIPLINE FOUR: CLOUD-AS-STEED

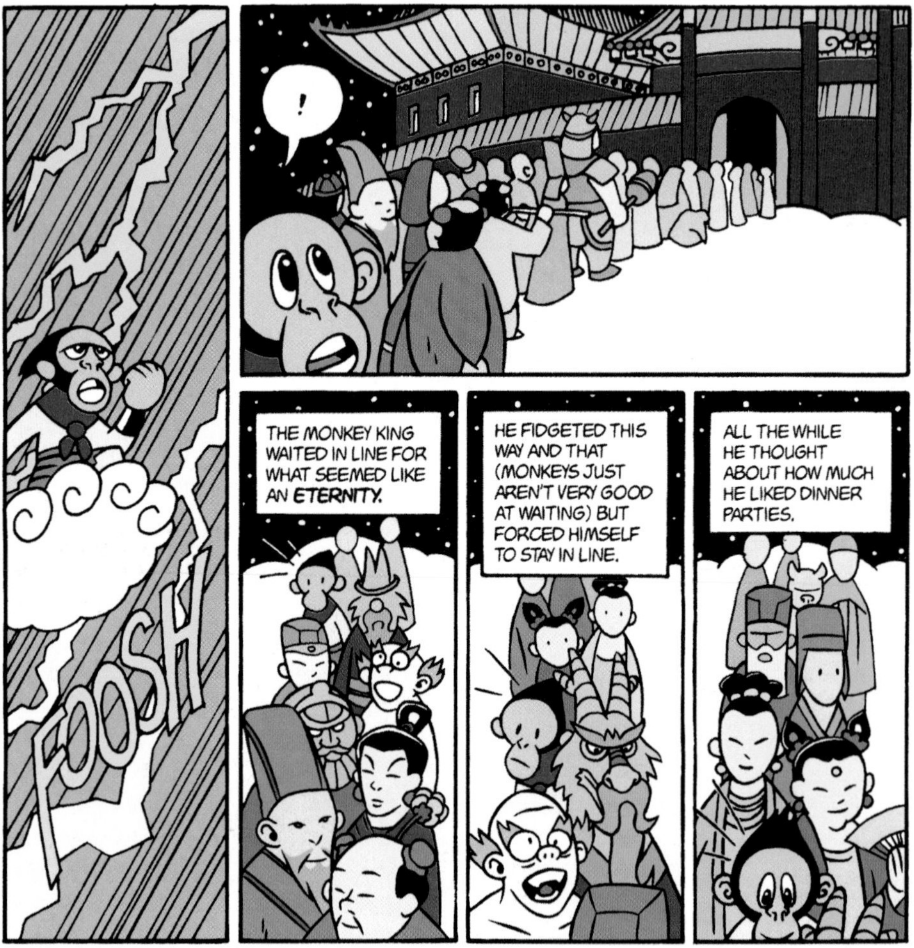
!
FOOSH
THE MONKEY KING WAITED IN LINE FOR WHAT SEEMED LIKE AN **ETERNITY.**
HE FIDGETED THIS WAY AND THAT (MONKEYS JUST AREN'T VERY GOOD AT WAITING) BUT FORCED HIMSELF TO STAY IN LINE.
ALL THE WHILE HE THOUGHT ABOUT HOW MUCH HE LIKED DINNER PARTIES.

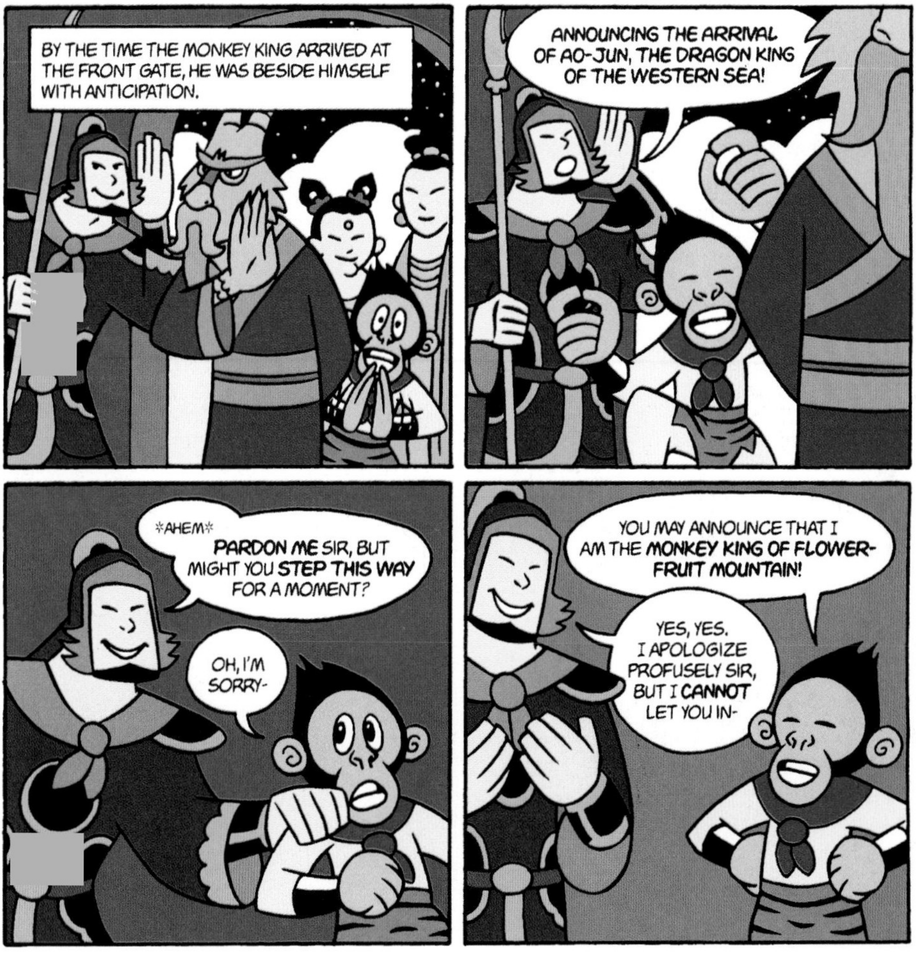
BY THE TIME THE MONKEY KING ARRIVED AT THE FRONT GATE, HE WAS BESIDE HIMSELF WITH ANTICIPATION.
ANNOUNCING THE ARRIVAL OF AO-JUN, THE DRAGON KING OF THE WESTERN SEA!
AHEM PARDON ME SIR, BUT MIGHT YOU STEP THIS WAY FOR A MOMENT?
OH, I'M SORRY-
YOU MAY ANNOUNCE THAT I AM THE MONKEY KING OF FLOWER-FRUIT MOUNTAIN!
YES, YES. I APOLOGIZE PROFUSELY SIR, BUT I CANNOT LET YOU IN-

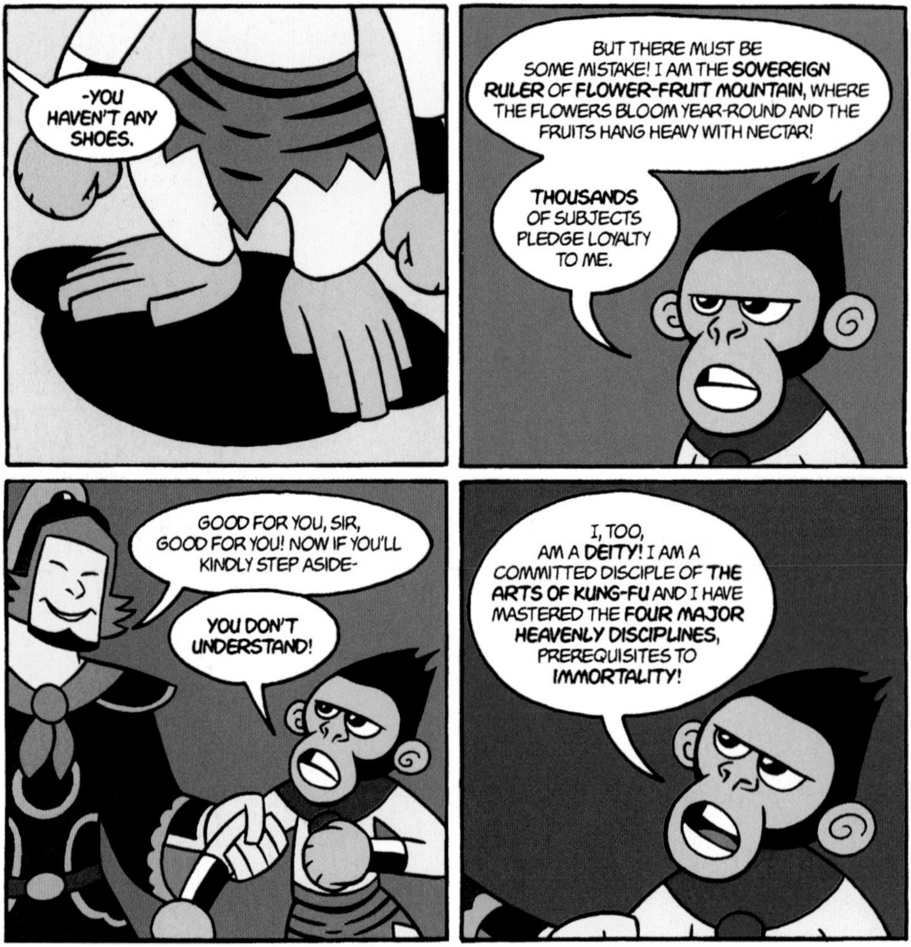
-YOU HAVEN'T ANY SHOES.
BUT THERE MUST BE SOME MISTAKE! I AM THE SOVEREIGN RULER OF FLOWER-FRUIT MOUNTAIN, WHERE THE FLOWERS BLOOM YEAR-ROUND AND THE FRUITS HANG HEAVY WITH NECTAR!
THOUSANDS OF SUBJECTS PLEDGE LOYALTY TO ME.
GOOD FOR YOU, SIR, GOOD FOR YOU! NOW IF YOU'LL KINDLY STEP ASIDE-
YOU DON'T UNDERSTAND!
I, TOO, AM A DEITY! I AM A COMMITTED DISCIPLE OF THE ARTS OF KUNG-FU AND I HAVE MASTERED THE FOUR MAJOR HEAVENLY DISCIPLINES, PREREQUISITES TO IMMORTALITY!

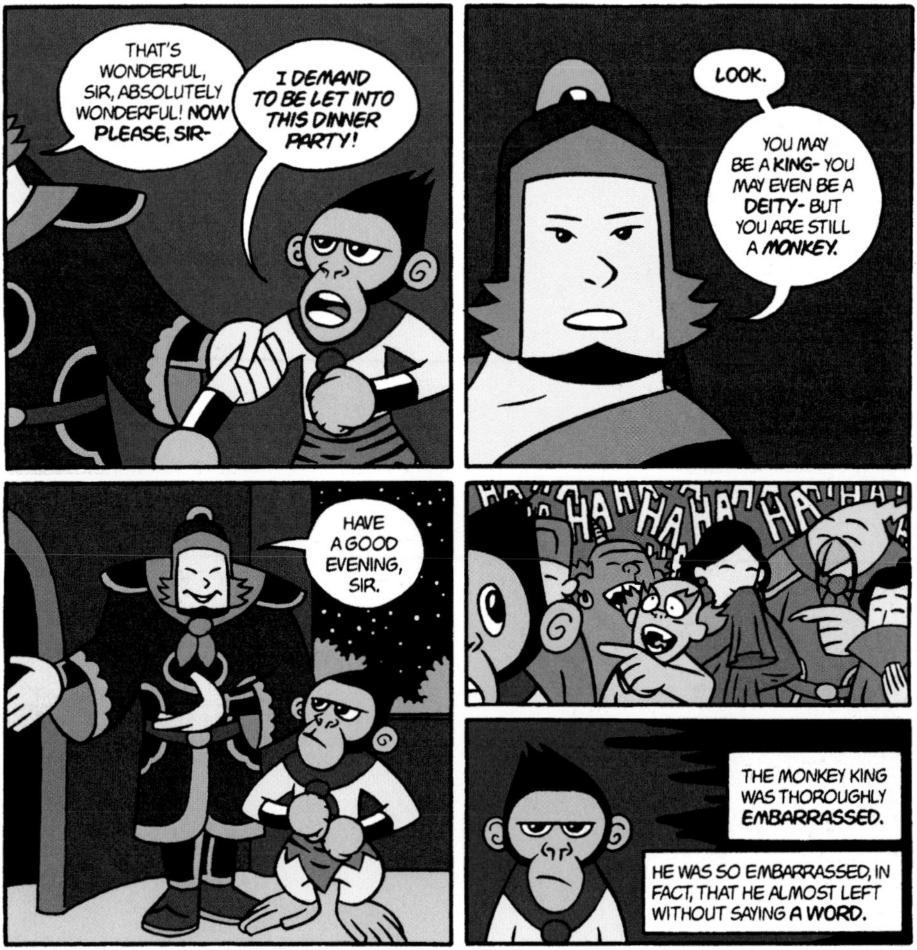
THAT'S WONDERFUL, SIR, ABSOLUTELY WONDERFUL! NOW PLEASE, SIR-
I DEMAND TO BE LET INTO THIS DINNER PARTY!
LOOK.
YOU MAY BE A KING- YOU MAY EVEN BE A DEITY- BUT YOU ARE STILL A MONKEY.
HAVE A GOOD EVENING, SIR.
HA HA HA HA HA
THE MONKEY KING WAS THOROUGHLY EMBARRASSED.
HE WAS SO EMBARRASSED, IN FACT, THAT HE ALMOST LEFT WITHOUT SAYING A WORD.

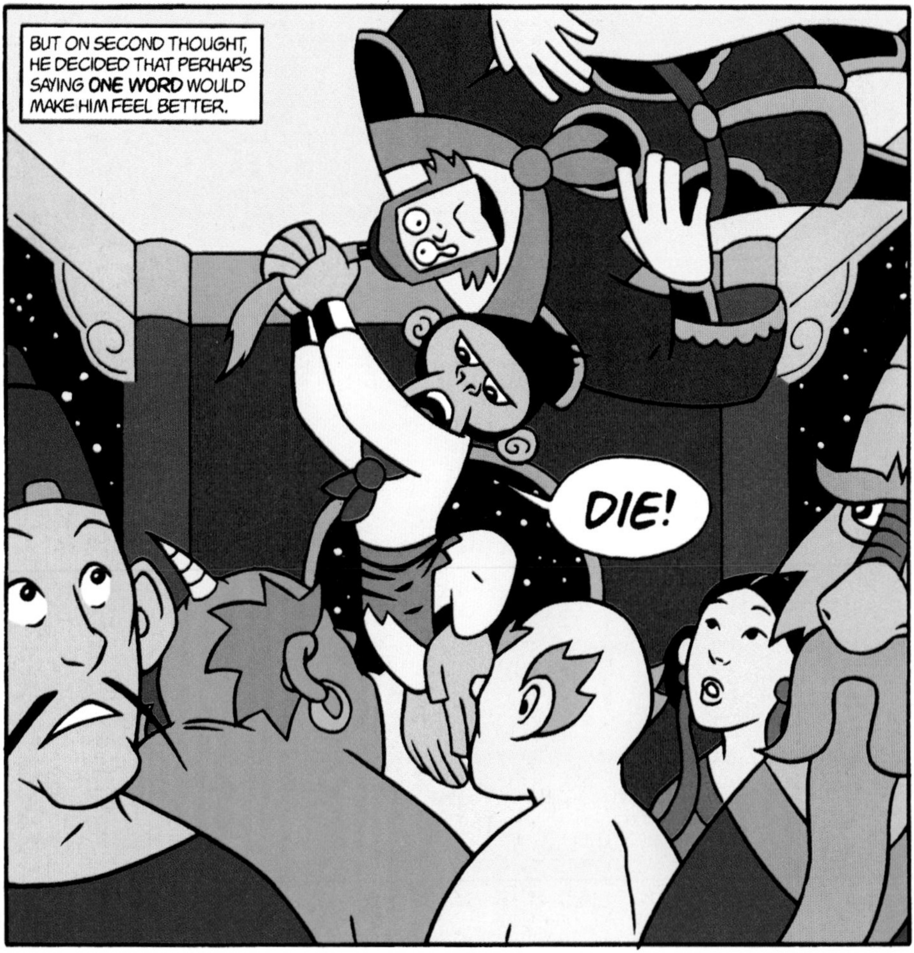
BUT ON SECOND THOUGHT, HE DECIDED THAT PERHAPS SAYING ONE WORD WOULD MAKE HIM FEEL BETTER.
DIE!

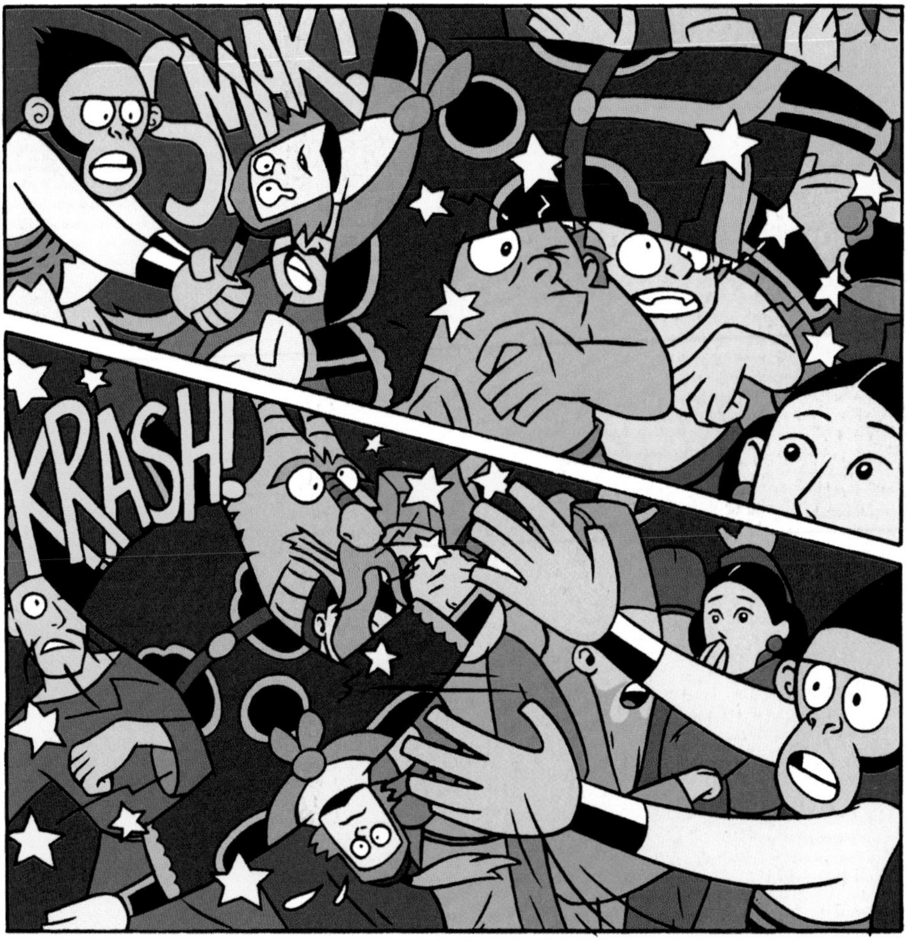
SMAK
KRASH!

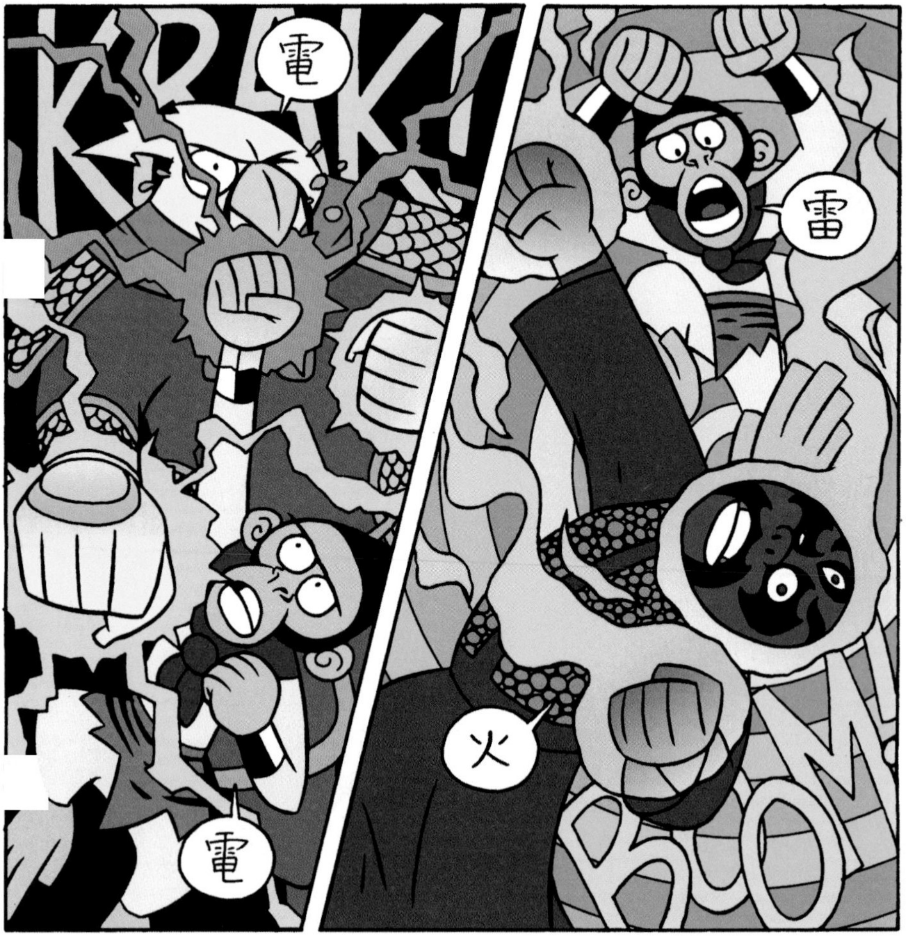
電
電
雷
火
BOOM!

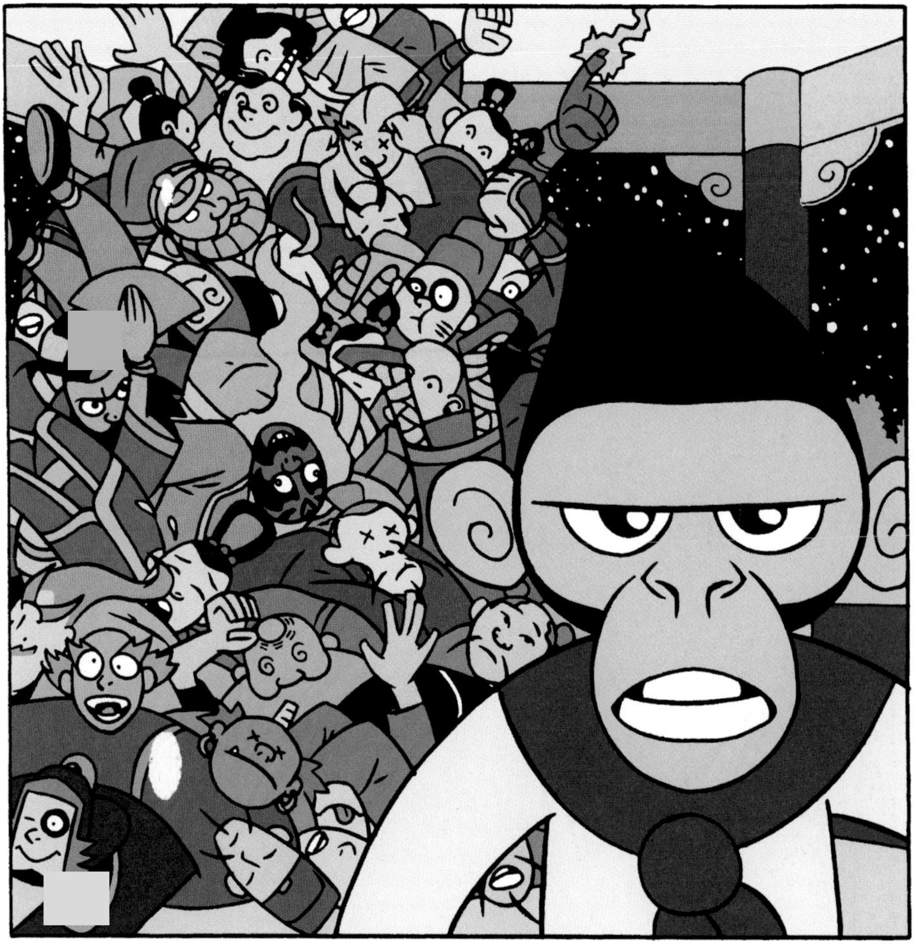

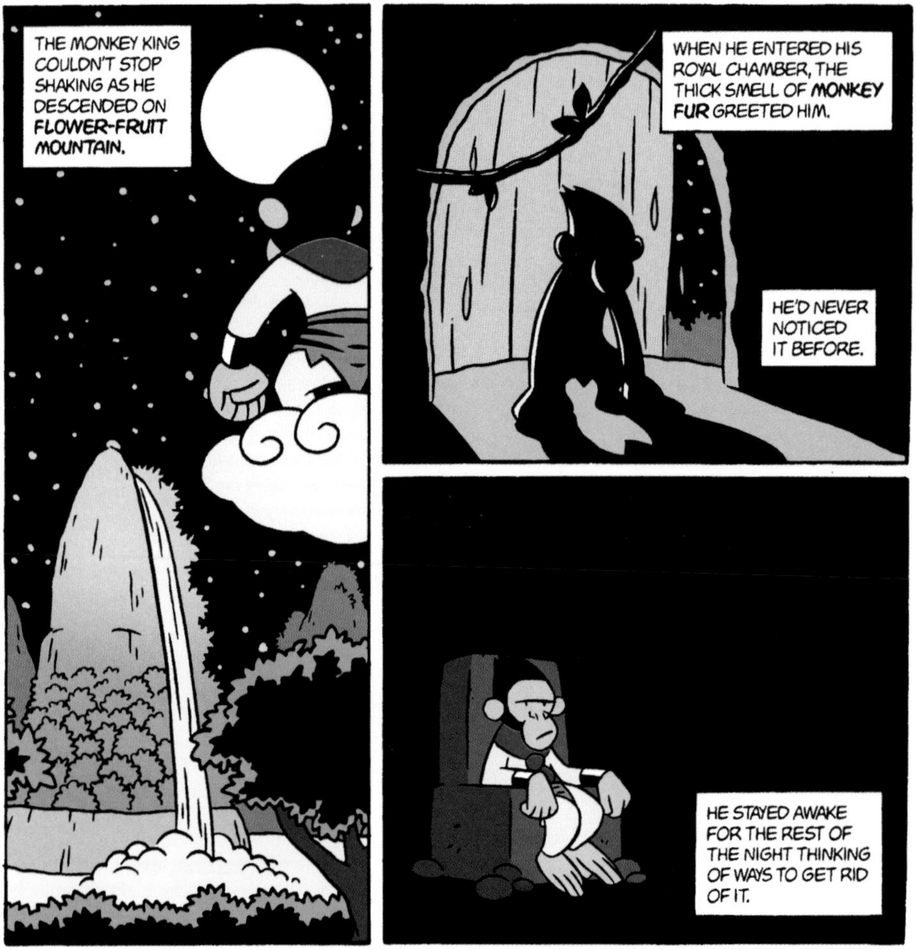
THE MONKEY KING COULDN'T STOP SHAKING AS HE DESCENDED ON FLOWER-FRUIT MOUNTAIN.
WHEN HE ENTERED HIS ROYAL CHAMBER, THE THICK SMELL OF MONKEY FUR GREETED HIM.
HE'D NEVER NOTICED IT BEFORE.
HE STAYED AWAKE FOR THE REST OF THE NIGHT THINKING OF WAYS TO GET RID OF IT.

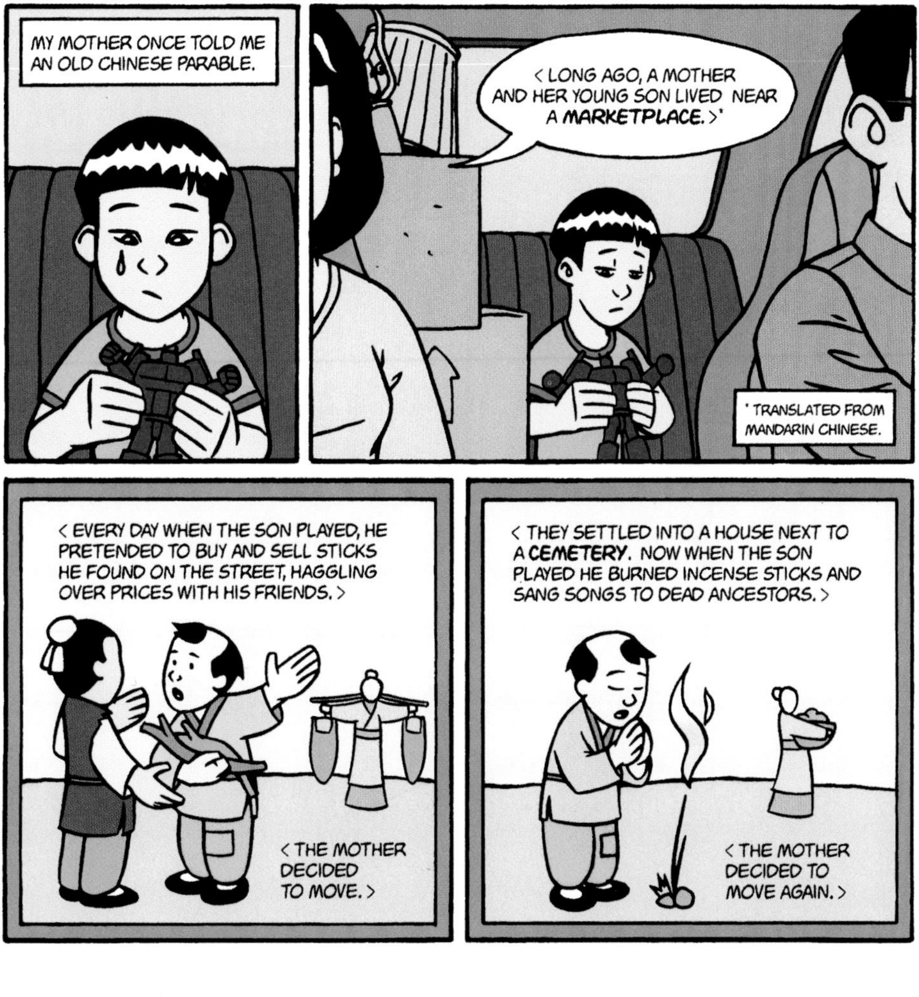

MY MOTHER ONCE TOLD ME AN OLD CHINESE PARABLE.
< LONG AGO, A MOTHER AND HER YOUNG SON LIVED NEAR A MARKETPLACE. >*
* TRANSLATED FROM MANDARIN CHINESE.
< EVERY DAY WHEN THE SON PLAYED, HE PRETENDED TO BUY AND SELL STICKS HE FOUND ON THE STREET, HAGGLING OVER PRICES WITH HIS FRIENDS. >
< THE MOTHER DECIDED TO MOVE. >
< THEY SETTLED INTO A HOUSE NEXT TO A CEMETERY. NOW WHEN THE SON PLAYED HE BURNED INCENSE STICKS AND SANG SONGS TO DEAD ANCESTORS. >
< THE MOTHER DECIDED TO MOVE AGAIN. >

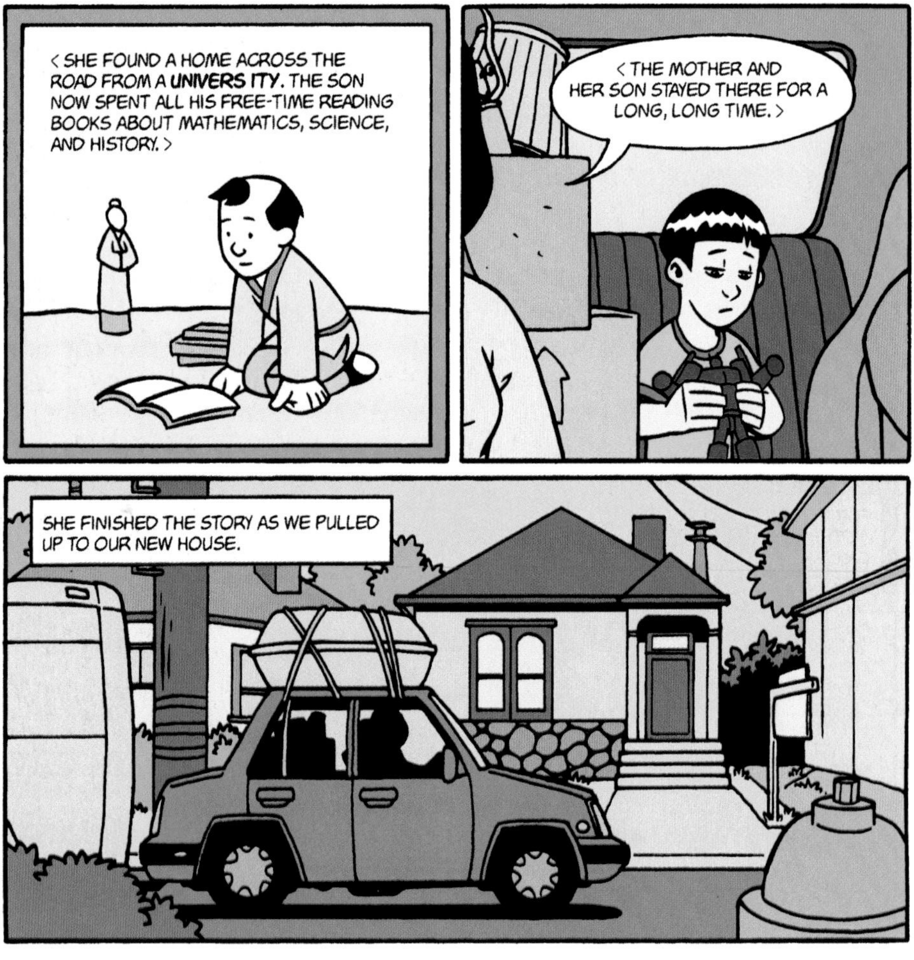
< SHE FOUND A HOME ACROSS THE ROAD FROM A UNIVERS ITY. THE SON NOW SPENT ALL HIS FREE-TIME READING BOOKS ABOUT MATHEMATICS, SCIENCE, AND HISTORY. >
< THE MOTHER AND HER SON STAYED THERE FOR A LONG, LONG TIME. >
SHE FINISHED THE STORY AS WE PULLED UP TO OUR NEW HOUSE.

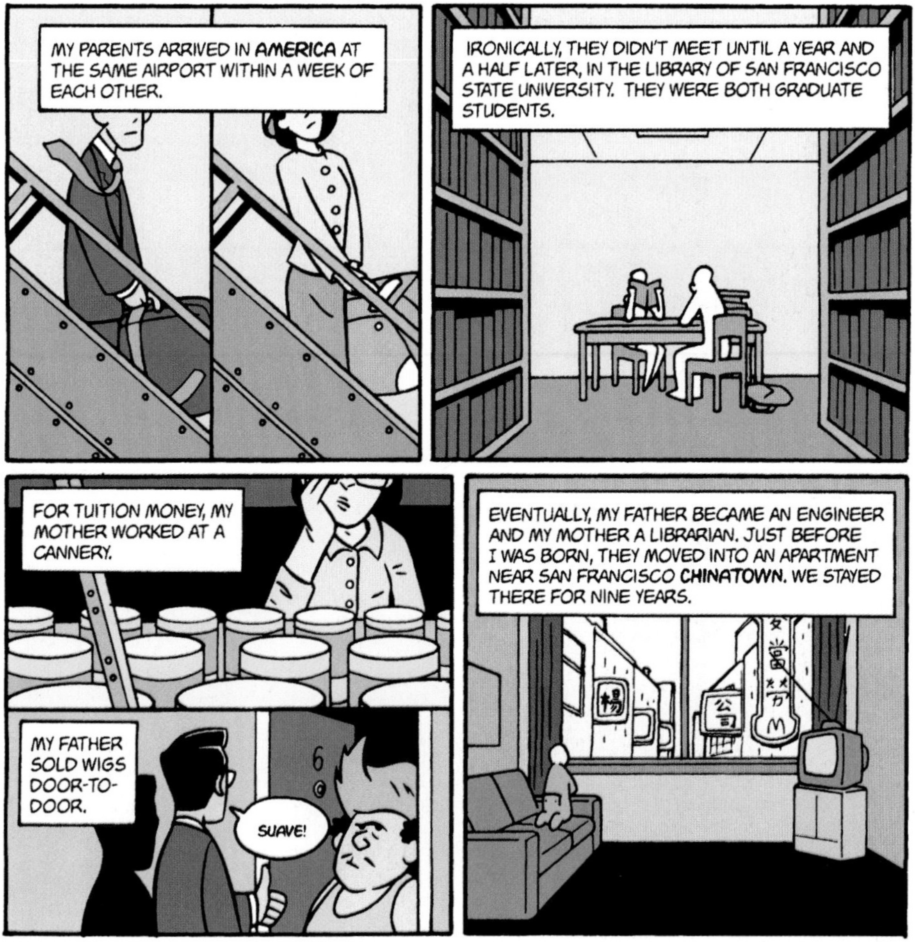
MY PARENTS ARRIVED IN **AMERICA** AT THE SAME AIRPORT WITHIN A WEEK OF EACH OTHER.
IRONICALLY, THEY DIDN'T MEET UNTIL A YEAR AND A HALF LATER, IN THE LIBRARY OF SAN FRANCISCO STATE UNIVERSITY. THEY WERE BOTH GRADUATE STUDENTS.
FOR TUITION MONEY, MY MOTHER WORKED AT A CANNERY.
MY FATHER SOLD WIGS DOOR-TO-DOOR.
SUAVE!
EVENTUALLY, MY FATHER BECAME AN ENGINEER AND MY MOTHER A LIBRARIAN. JUST BEFORE I WAS BORN, THEY MOVED INTO AN APARTMENT NEAR SAN FRANCISCO **CHINATOWN**. WE STAYED THERE FOR NINE YEARS.

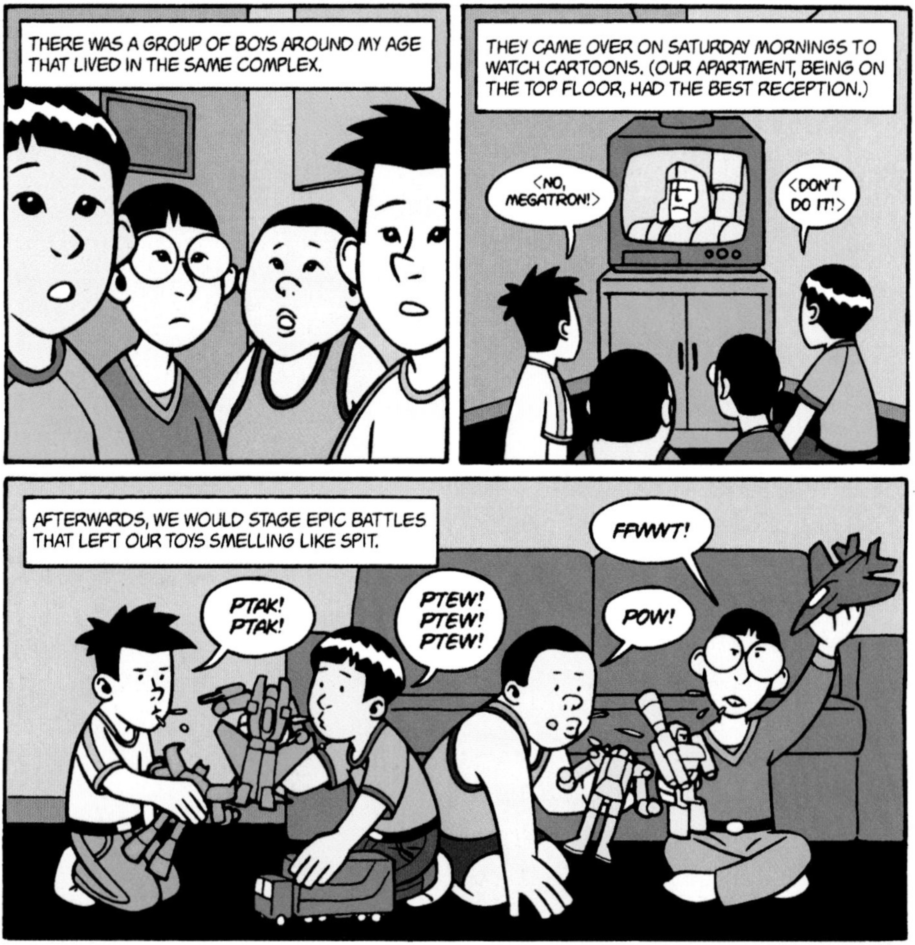
THERE WAS A GROUP OF BOYS AROUND MY AGE THAT LIVED IN THE SAME COMPLEX.
THEY CAME OVER ON SATURDAY MORNINGS TO WATCH CARTOONS. (OUR APARTMENT, BEING ON THE TOP FLOOR, HAD THE BEST RECEPTION.)
<NO, MEGATRON!>
<DON'T DO IT!>
AFTERWARDS, WE WOULD STAGE EPIC BATTLES THAT LEFT OUR TOYS SMELLING LIKE SPIT.
PTAK! PTAK!
PTEW! PTEW! PTEW!
FFWWT!
POW!

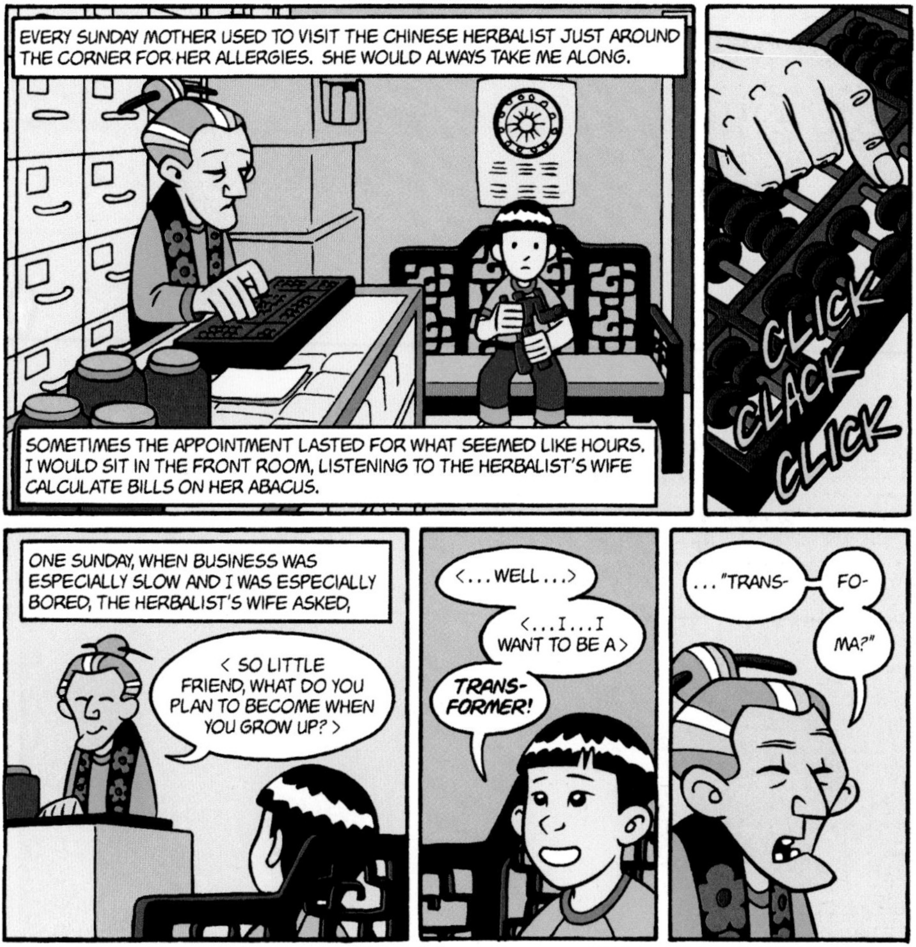
EVERY SUNDAY MOTHER USED TO VISIT THE CHINESE HERBALIST JUST AROUND THE CORNER FOR HER ALLERGIES. SHE WOULD ALWAYS TAKE ME ALONG.
SOMETIMES THE APPOINTMENT LASTED FOR WHAT SEEMED LIKE HOURS. I WOULD SIT IN THE FRONT ROOM, LISTENING TO THE HERBALIST'S WIFE CALCULATE BILLS ON HER ABACUS.
CLICK
CLACK
CLICK
ONE SUNDAY, WHEN BUSINESS WAS ESPECIALLY SLOW AND I WAS ESPECIALLY BORED, THE HERBALIST'S WIFE ASKED,
< SO LITTLE FRIEND, WHAT DO YOU PLAN TO BECOME WHEN YOU GROW UP? >
<...WELL...>
<...I...I WANT TO BE A>
TRANSFORMER!
..."TRANS- FO- MA?"

< YEAH! > A ROBOT IN DISGUISE! < LIKE THIS ONE! >
< HE CHANGES INTO A TRUCK . . . >
CLICK
CLICK
CLACK
< . . . SEE? > MORE THAN MEETS THE EYE!
< IN THE CARTOON, HE'S ALSO GOT A TRAILER THAT MAGICALLY APPEARS WHENEVER HE TRANSFORMS, BUT ON THE TOY IT'S A SEPARATE PIECE. >
< SO YOU WANT TO BE A . . . A . . . > "TRANS-FO-MA," < HUH? >
< YEAH . . . BUT MA-MA SAYS THAT'S SILLY. LITTLE BOYS DON'T GROW UP TO BE > TRANSFORMERS.
< OH, I WOULDN'T BE SO SURE ABOUT THAT. I'M GOING TO LET YOU IN ON A SECRET, LITTLE FRIEND: >

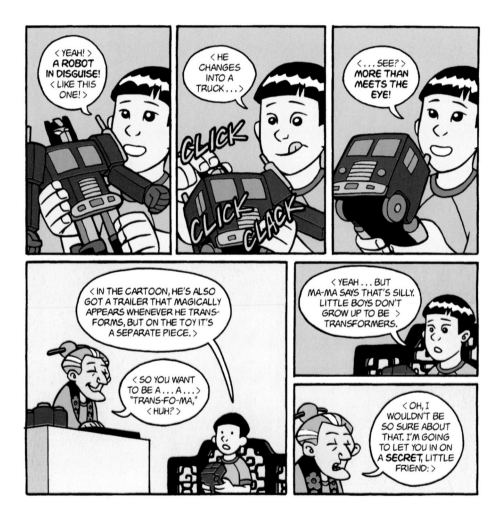

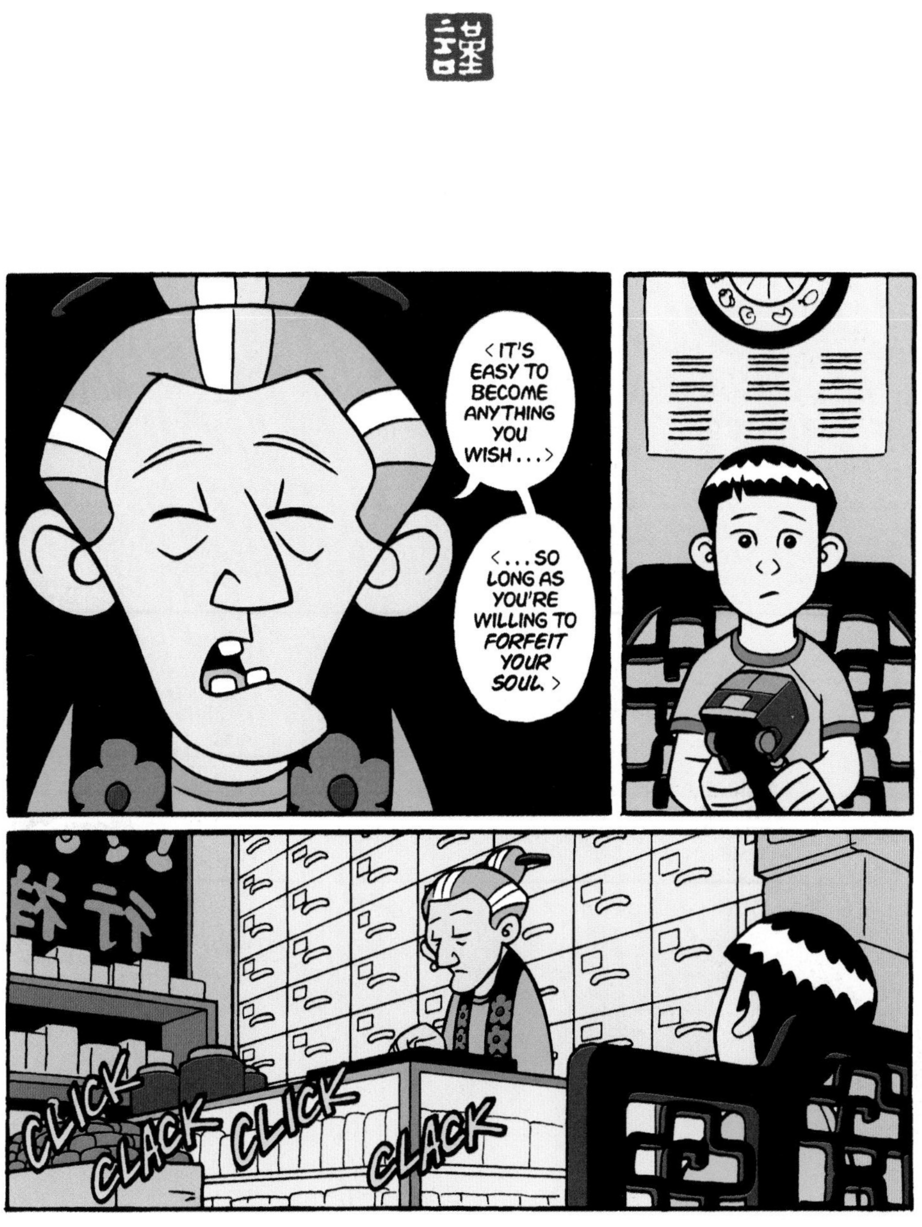
<IT'S EASY TO BECOME ANYTHING YOU WISH...>
<...SO LONG AS YOU'RE WILLING TO *FORFEIT YOUR SOUL.*>
CLICK
CLACK
CLICK
CLACK

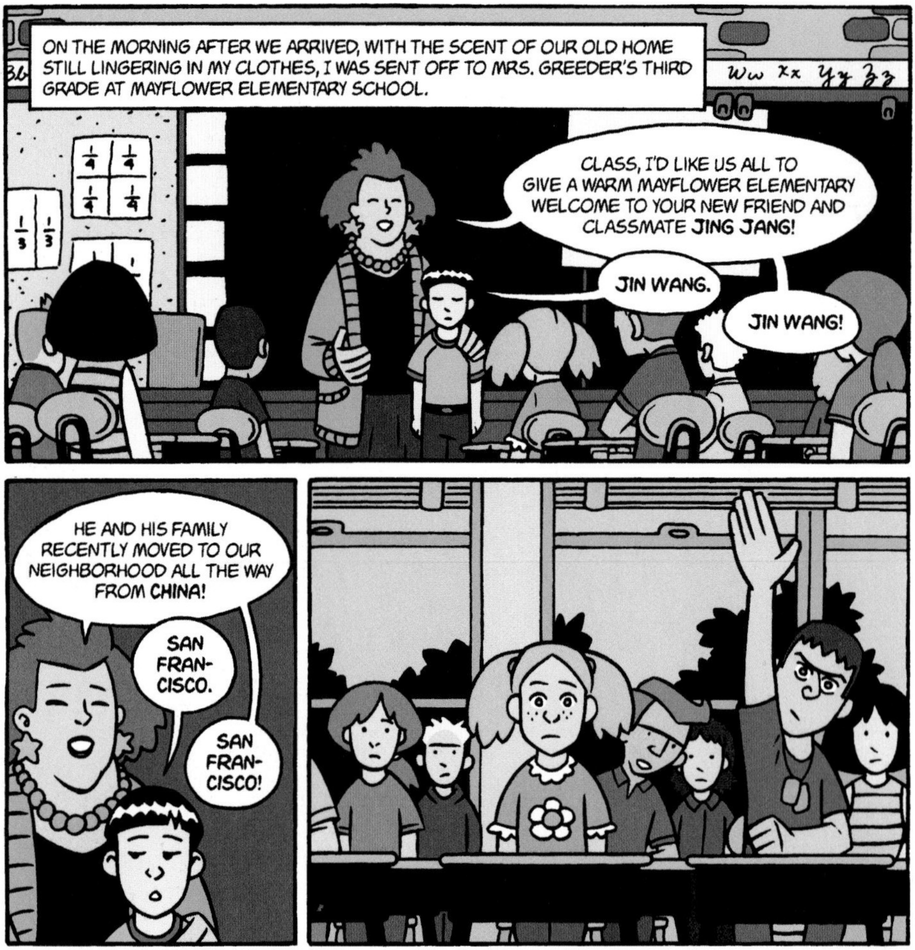
ON THE MORNING AFTER WE ARRIVED, WITH THE SCENT OF OUR OLD HOME STILL LINGERING IN MY CLOTHES, I WAS SENT OFF TO MRS. GREEDER'S THIRD GRADE AT MAYFLOWER ELEMENTARY SCHOOL.
CLASS, I'D LIKE US ALL TO GIVE A WARM MAYFLOWER ELEMENTARY WELCOME TO YOUR NEW FRIEND AND CLASSMATE **JING JANG**!
JIN WANG.
JIN WANG!
HE AND HIS FAMILY RECENTLY MOVED TO OUR NEIGHBORHOOD ALL THE WAY FROM **CHINA**!
SAN FRAN-CISCO.
SAN FRAN-CISCO!

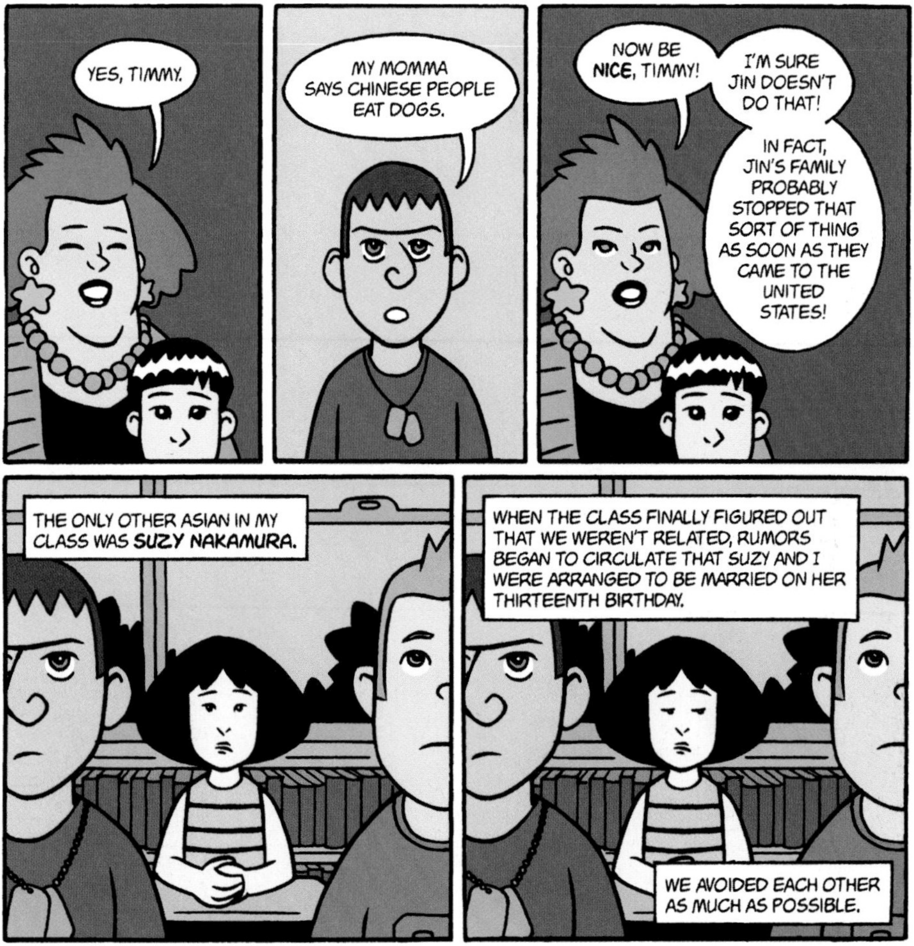
YES, TIMMY.
MY MOMMA SAYS CHINESE PEOPLE EAT DOGS.
NOW BE NICE, TIMMY!
I'M SURE JIN DOESN'T DO THAT!
IN FACT, JIN'S FAMILY PROBABLY STOPPED THAT SORT OF THING AS SOON AS THEY CAME TO THE UNITED STATES!
THE ONLY OTHER ASIAN IN MY CLASS WAS SUZY NAKAMURA.
WHEN THE CLASS FINALLY FIGURED OUT THAT WE WEREN'T RELATED, RUMORS BEGAN TO CIRCULATE THAT SUZY AND I WERE ARRANGED TO BE MARRIED ON HER THIRTEENTH BIRTHDAY.
WE AVOIDED EACH OTHER AS MUCH AS POSSIBLE.

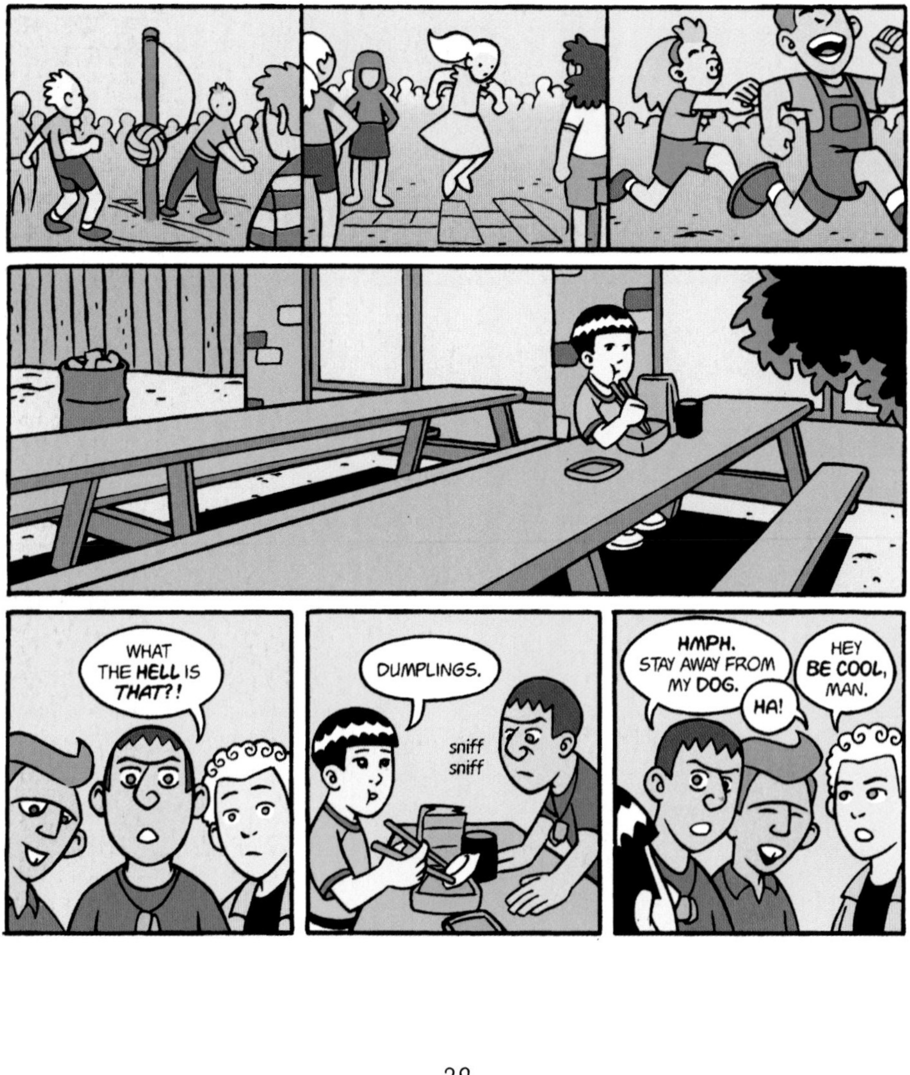
WHAT THE HELL IS THAT?!
DUMPLINGS.
sniff sniff
HMPH. STAY AWAY FROM MY DOG.
HA!
HEY BE COOL, MAN.

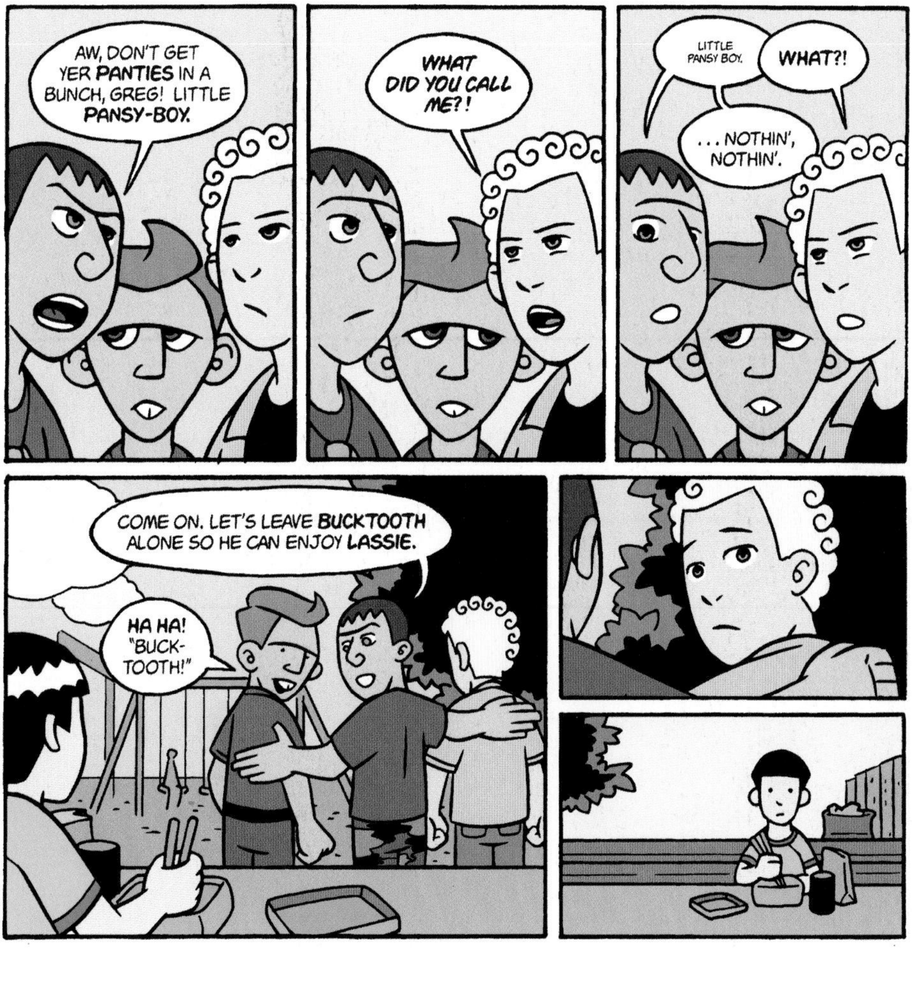
AW, DON'T GET YER PANTIES IN A BUNCH, GREG! LITTLE PANSY-BOY.
WHAT DID YOU CALL ME?!
LITTLE PANSY BOY.
WHAT?!
...NOTHIN', NOTHIN'.
COME ON. LET'S LEAVE BUCKTOOTH ALONE SO HE CAN ENJOY LASSIE.
HA HA! "BUCK-TOOTH!"

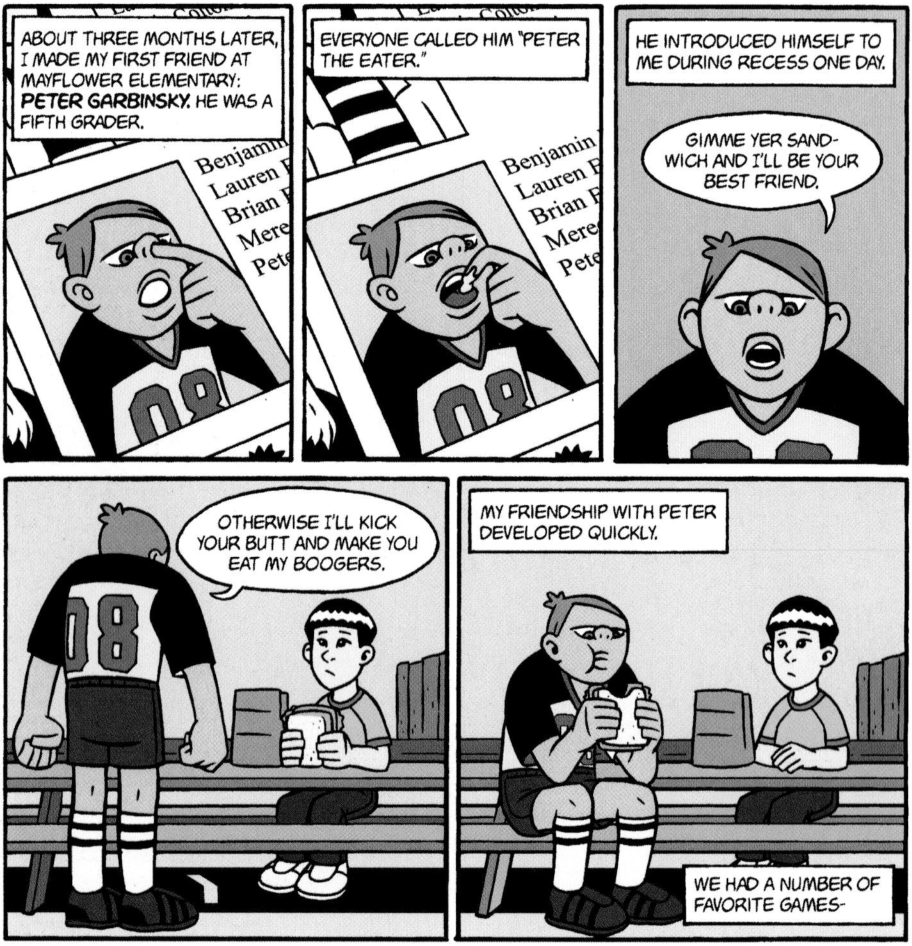
ABOUT THREE MONTHS LATER, I MADE MY FIRST FRIEND AT MAYFLOWER ELEMENTARY: **PETER GARBINSKY.** HE WAS A FIFTH GRADER.
EVERYONE CALLED HIM "PETER THE EATER."
HE INTRODUCED HIMSELF TO ME DURING RECESS ONE DAY.
GIMME YER SAND-WICH AND I'LL BE YOUR BEST FRIEND.
OTHERWISE I'LL KICK YOUR BUTT AND MAKE YOU EAT MY BOOGERS.
MY FRIENDSHIP WITH PETER DEVELOPED QUICKLY.
WE HAD A NUMBER OF FAVORITE GAMES-

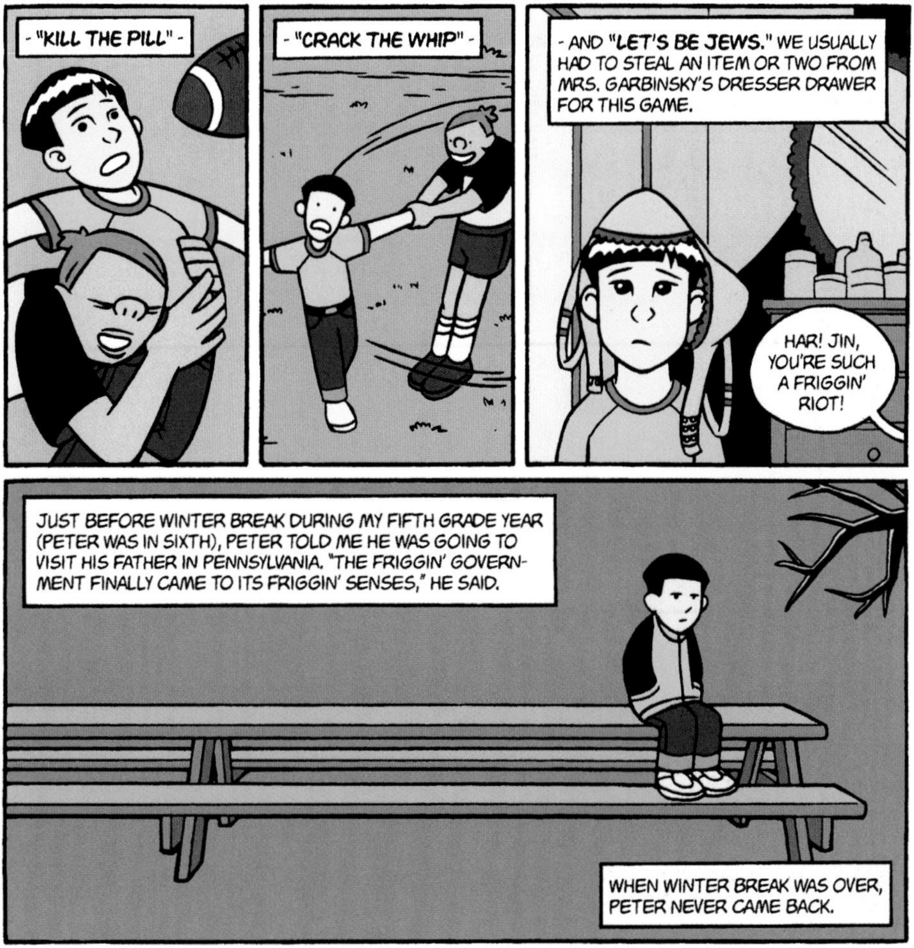

- "KILL THE PILL" -
- "CRACK THE WHIP" -
- AND "LET'S BE JEWS." WE USUALLY HAD TO STEAL AN ITEM OR TWO FROM MRS. GARBINSKY'S DRESSER DRAWER FOR THIS GAME.
HAR! JIN, YOU'RE SUCH A FRIGGIN' RIOT!
JUST BEFORE WINTER BREAK DURING MY FIFTH GRADE YEAR (PETER WAS IN SIXTH), PETER TOLD ME HE WAS GOING TO VISIT HIS FATHER IN PENNSYLVANIA. "THE FRIGGIN' GOVERNMENT FINALLY CAME TO ITS FRIGGIN' SENSES," HE SAID.
WHEN WINTER BREAK WAS OVER, PETER NEVER CAME BACK.

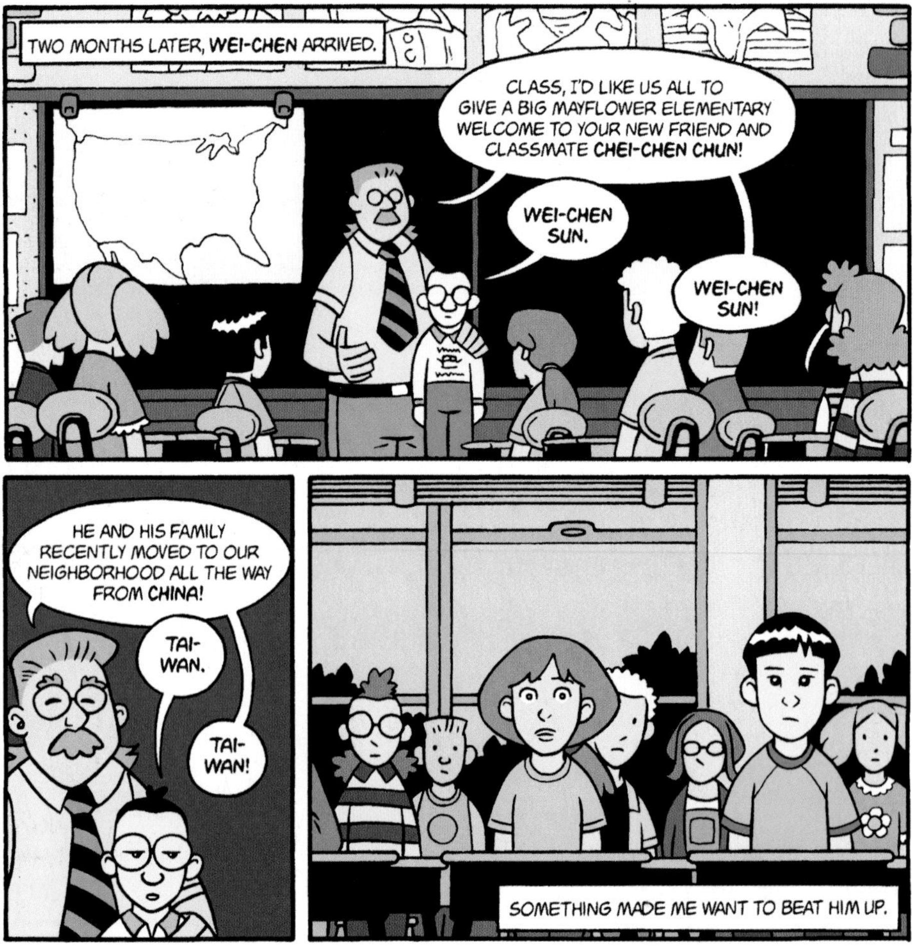
TWO MONTHS LATER, WEI-CHEN ARRIVED.
CLASS, I'D LIKE US ALL TO GIVE A BIG MAYFLOWER ELEMENTARY WELCOME TO YOUR NEW FRIEND AND CLASSMATE CHEI-CHEN CHUN!
WEI-CHEN SUN.
WEI-CHEN SUN!
HE AND HIS FAMILY RECENTLY MOVED TO OUR NEIGHBORHOOD ALL THE WAY FROM CHINA!
TAI-WAN.
TAI-WAN!
SOMETHING MADE ME WANT TO BEAT HIM UP.

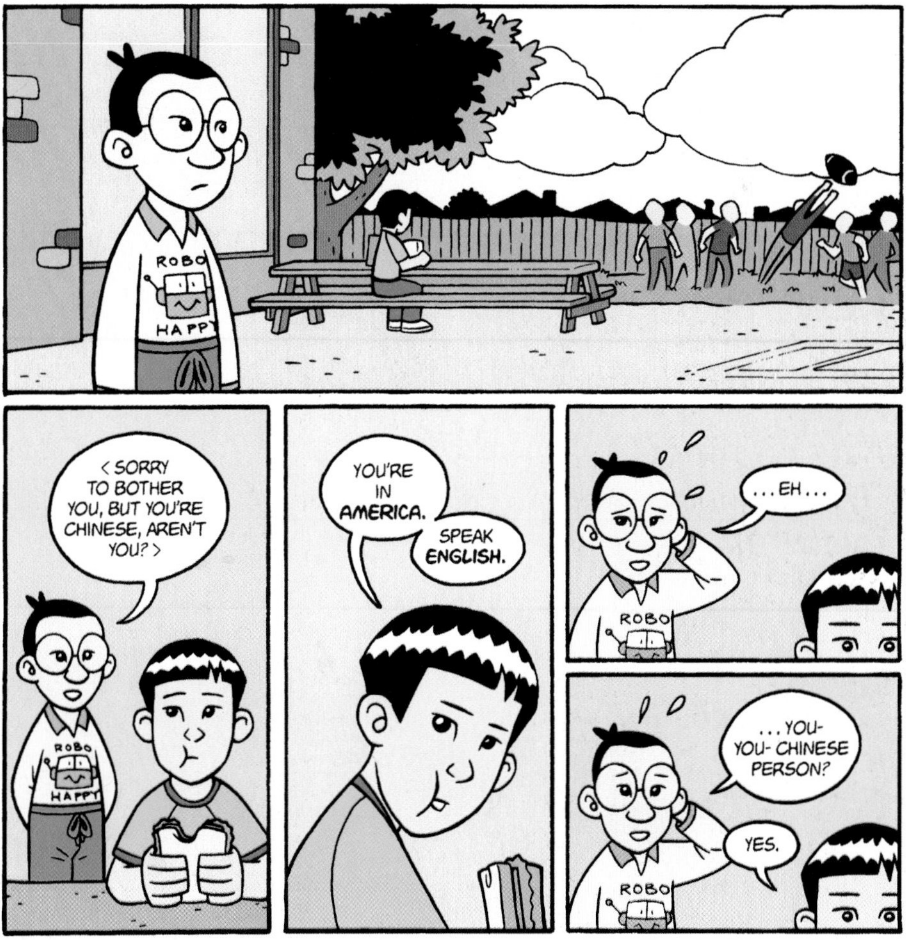
< SORRY TO BOTHER YOU, BUT YOU'RE CHINESE, AREN'T YOU? >
YOU'RE IN AMERICA.
SPEAK ENGLISH.
...EH...
...YOU- YOU- CHINESE PERSON?
YES.

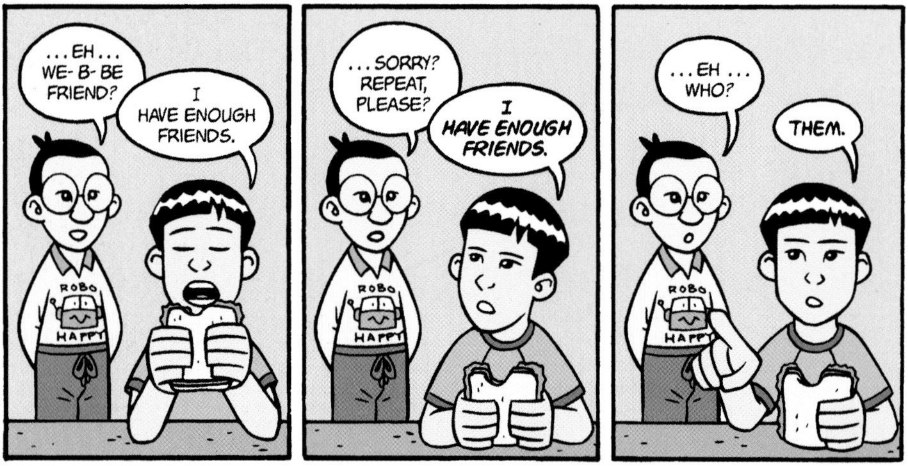
...EH...
WE- B- BE FRIEND?
I HAVE ENOUGH FRIENDS.
...SORRY? REPEAT, PLEASE?
I HAVE ENOUGH FRIENDS.
...EH ... WHO?
THEM.
OH.

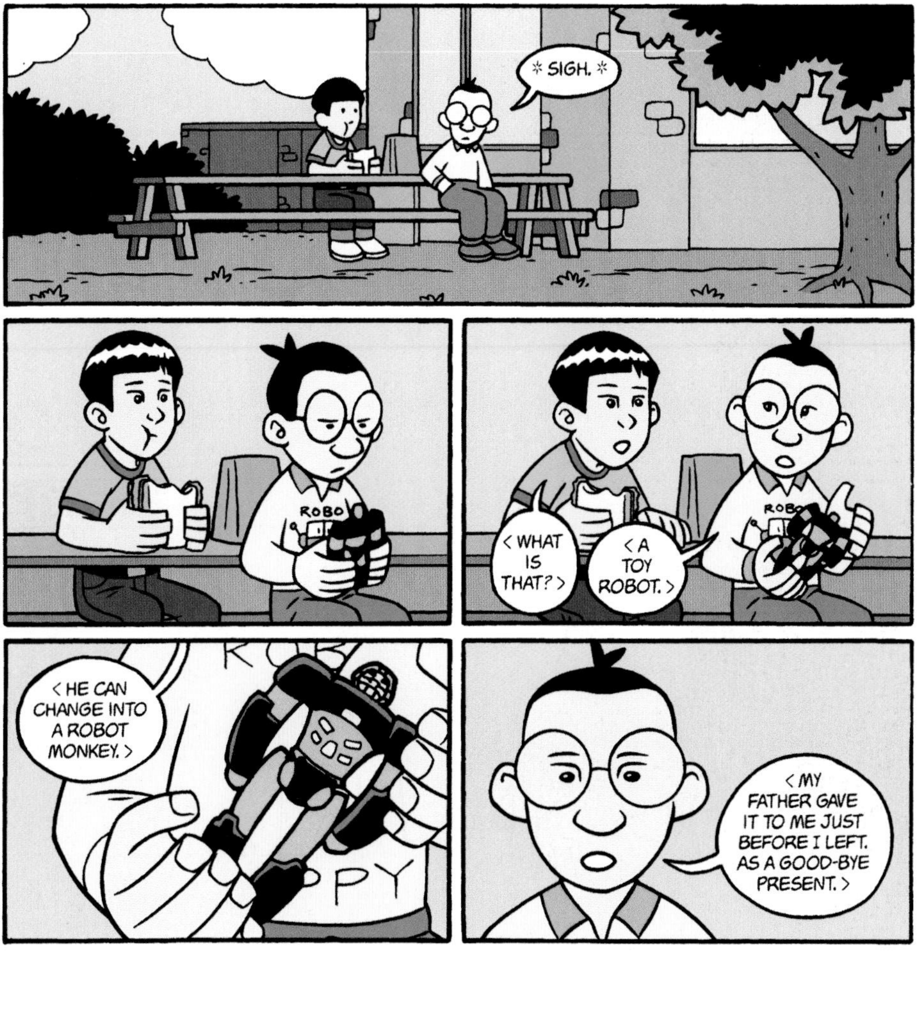
* SIGH. *
< WHAT IS THAT? >
< A TOY ROBOT. >
< HE CAN CHANGE INTO A ROBOT MONKEY. >
< MY FATHER GAVE IT TO ME JUST BEFORE I LEFT. AS A GOOD-BYE PRESENT. >

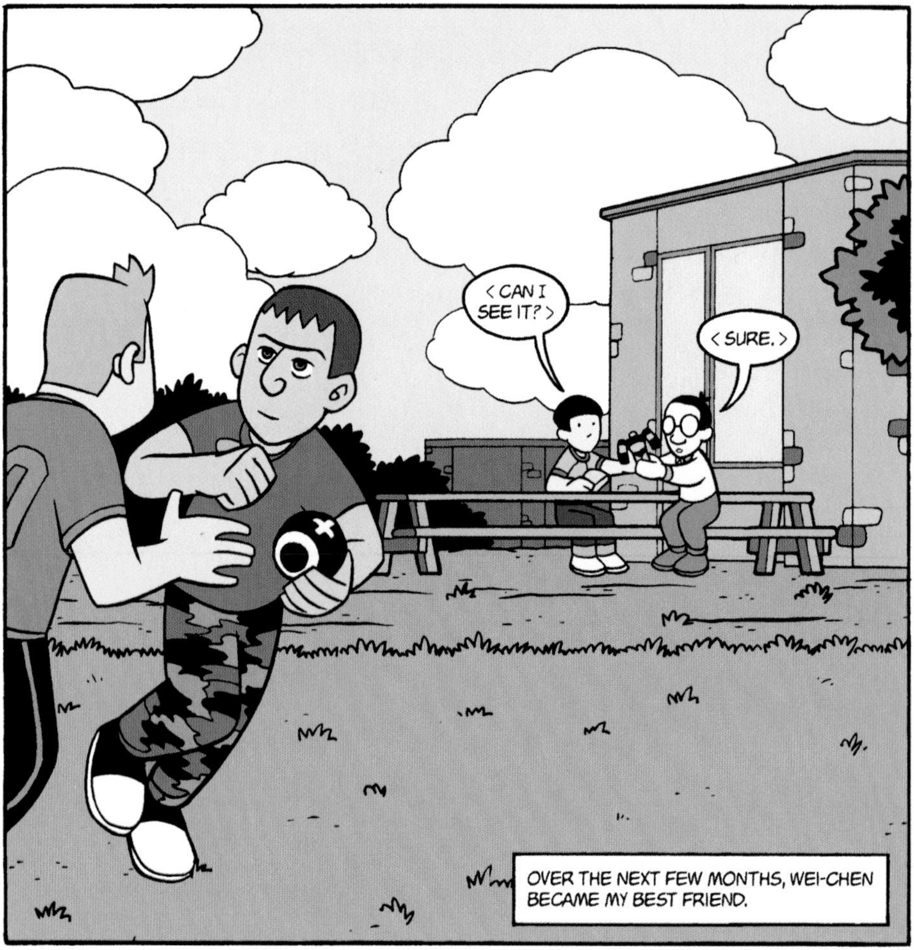
< CAN I SEE IT? >
< SURE. >
OVER THE NEXT FEW MONTHS, WEI-CHEN BECAME MY BEST FRIEND.

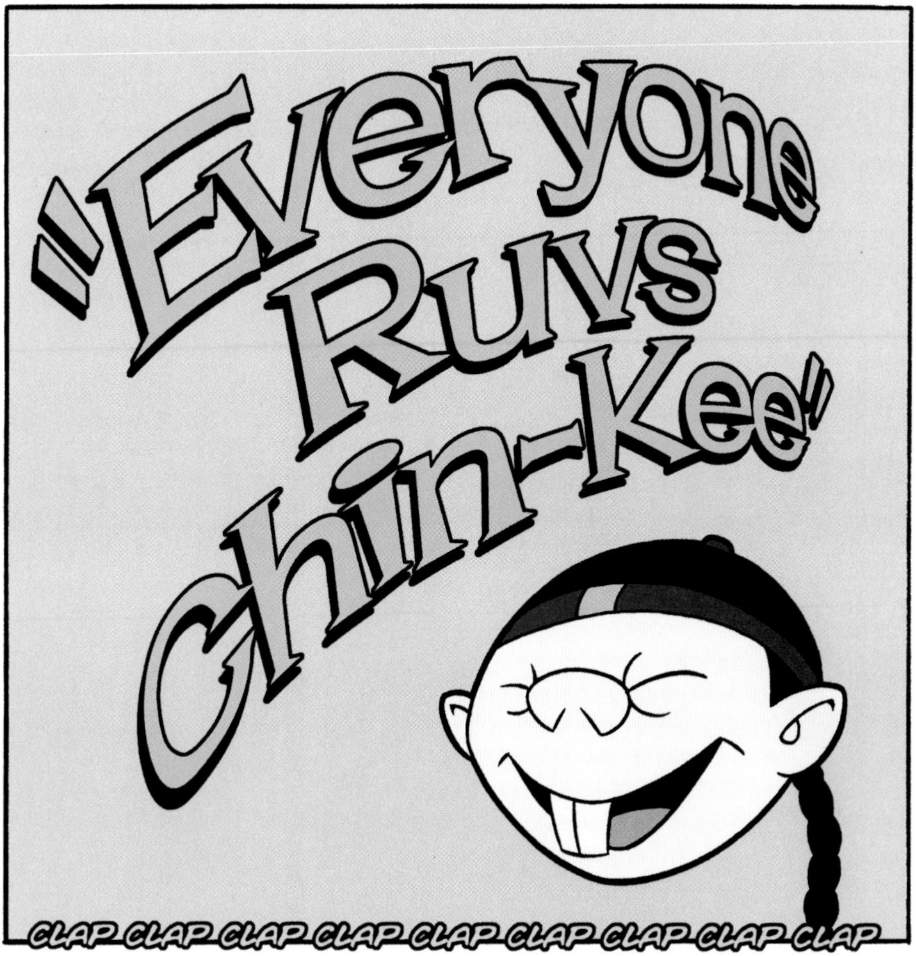
"Everyone Ruvs Chin-Kee"
CLAP CLAP CLAP CLAP CLAP CLAP CLAP CLAP CLAP

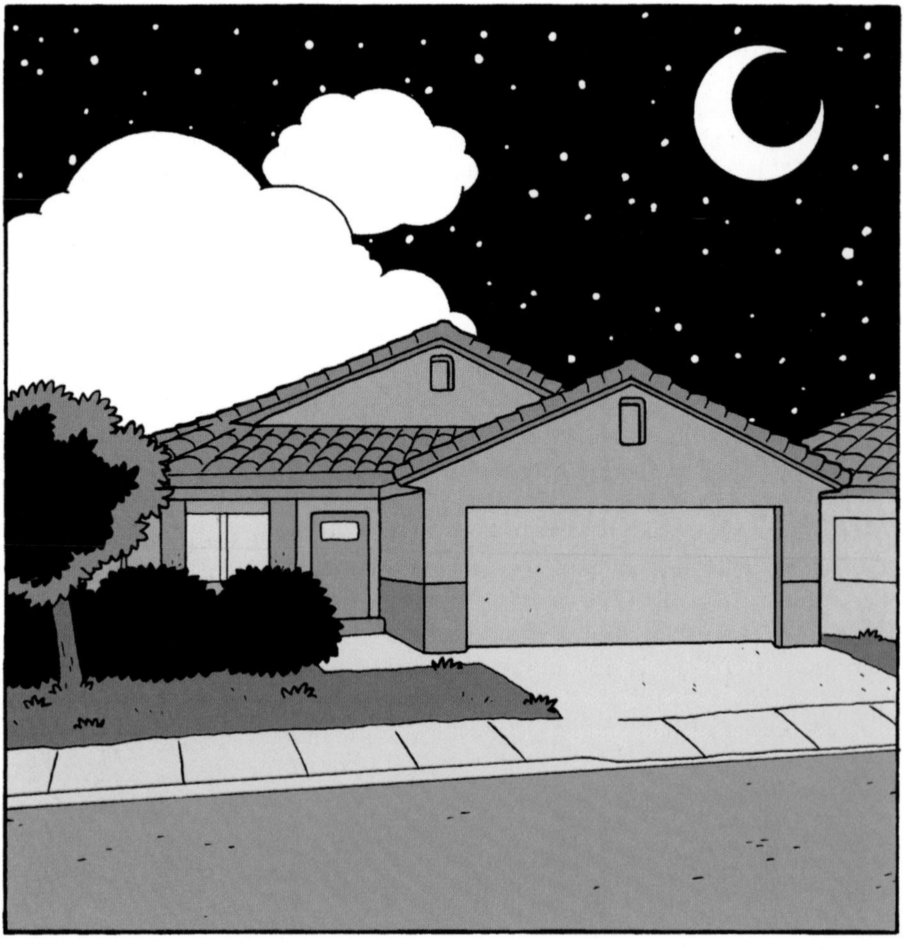

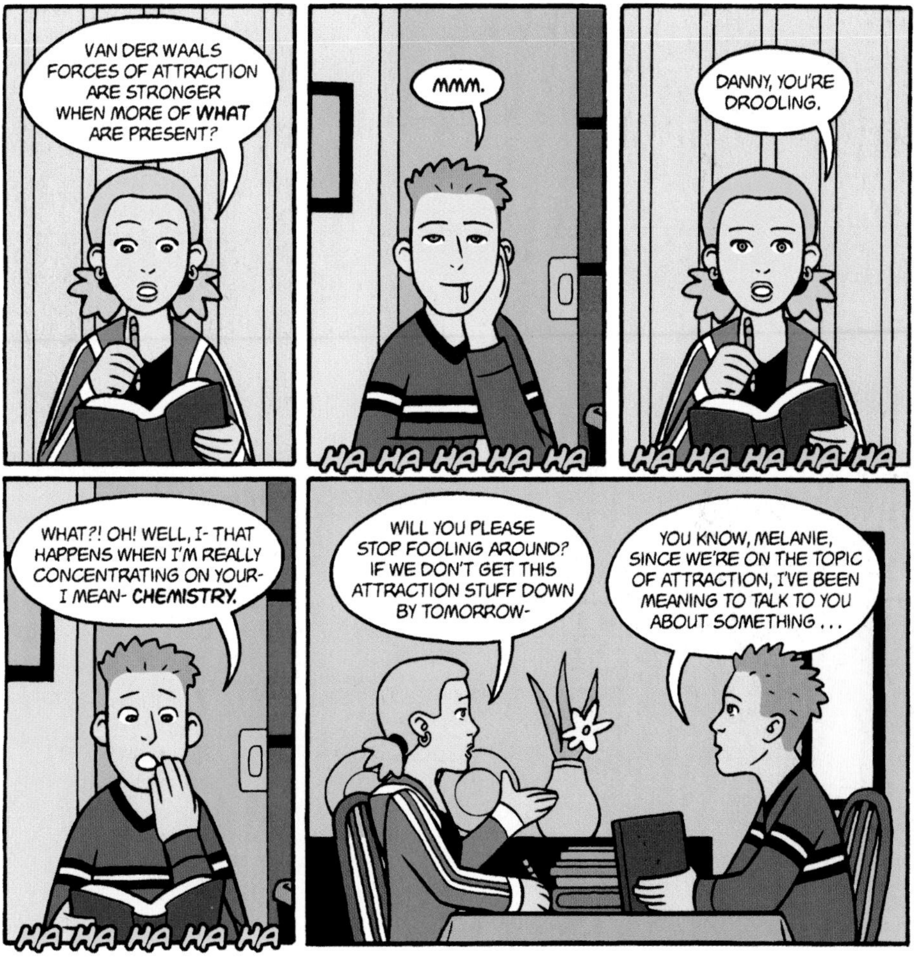
VAN DER WAALS FORCES OF ATTRACTION ARE STRONGER WHEN MORE OF **WHAT** ARE PRESENT?
MMM.
HA HA HA HA HA
DANNY, YOU'RE DROOLING.
HA HA HA HA HA
WHAT?! OH! WELL, I- THAT HAPPENS WHEN I'M REALLY CONCENTRATING ON YOUR- I MEAN- **CHEMISTRY.**
HA HA HA HA HA
WILL YOU PLEASE STOP FOOLING AROUND? IF WE DON'T GET THIS ATTRACTION STUFF DOWN BY TOMORROW-
YOU KNOW, MELANIE, SINCE WE'RE ON THE TOPIC OF ATTRACTION, I'VE BEEN MEANING TO TALK TO YOU ABOUT SOMETHING . . .

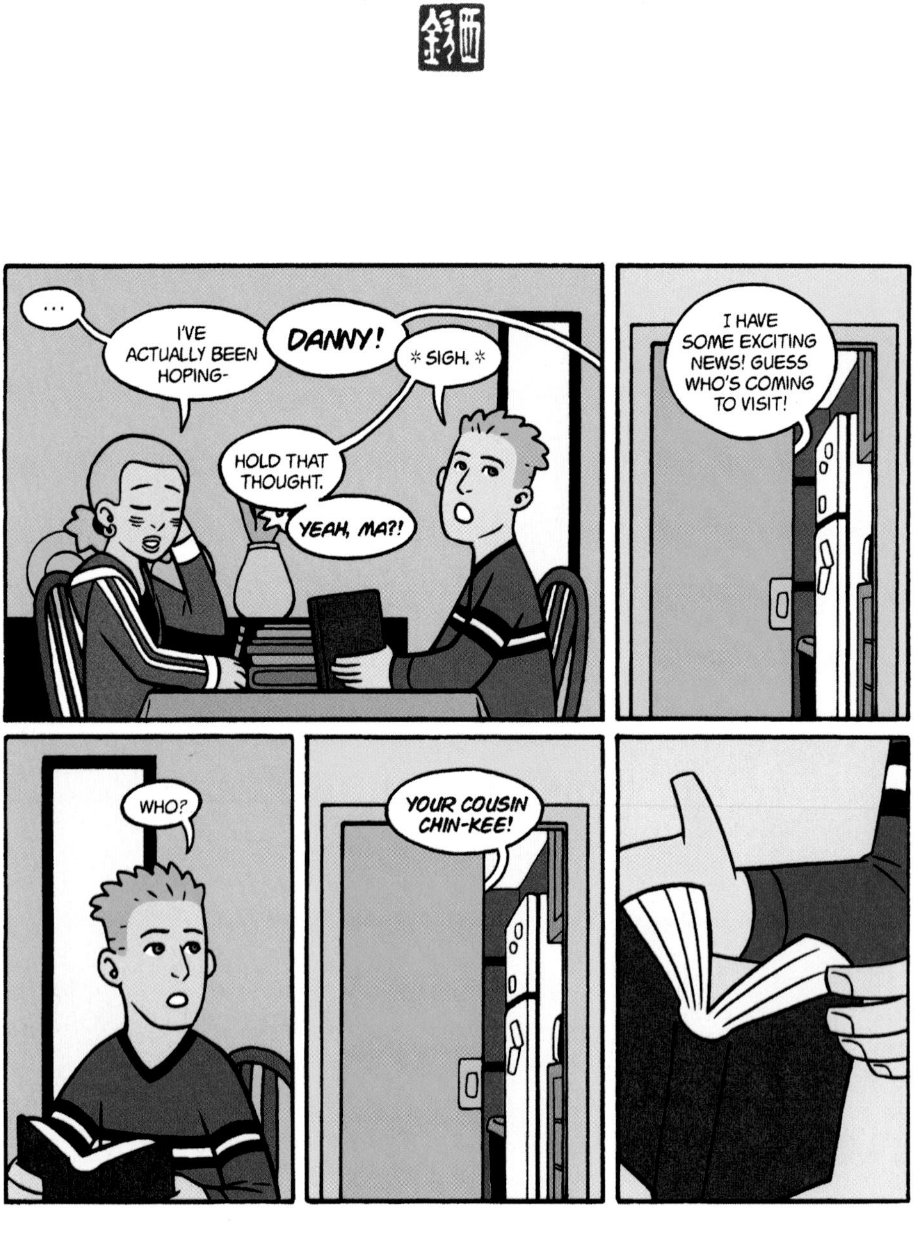
...
I'VE ACTUALLY BEEN HOPING-
DANNY!
✲ SIGH. ✲
HOLD THAT THOUGHT.
YEAH, MA?!
I HAVE SOME EXCITING NEWS! GUESS WHO'S COMING TO VISIT!
WHO?
YOUR COUSIN CHIN-KEE!

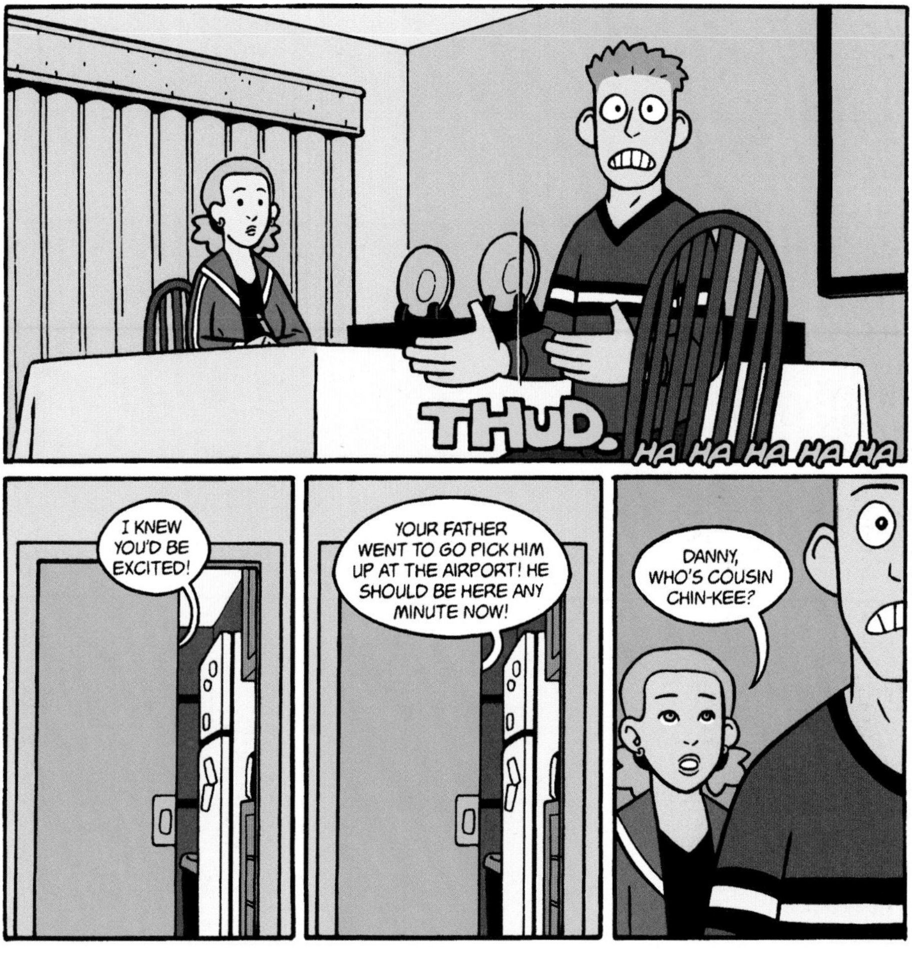
THUD.
HA HA HA HA HA
I KNEW YOU'D BE EXCITED!
YOUR FATHER WENT TO GO PICK HIM UP AT THE AIRPORT! HE SHOULD BE HERE ANY MINUTE NOW!
DANNY, WHO'S COUSIN CHIN-KEE?

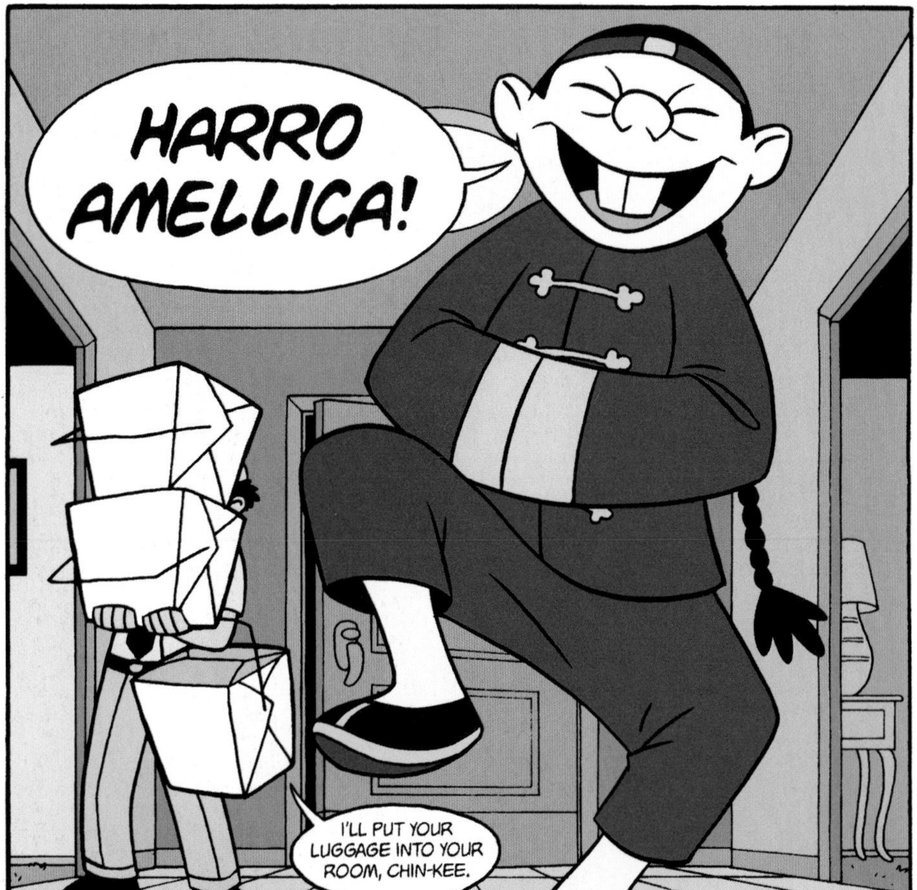
HARRO AMELLICA!
I'LL PUT YOUR LUGGAGE INTO YOUR ROOM, CHIN-KEE.
HA HA HA HA HA HA HA HA CLAP CLAP CLAP CLAP CLAP

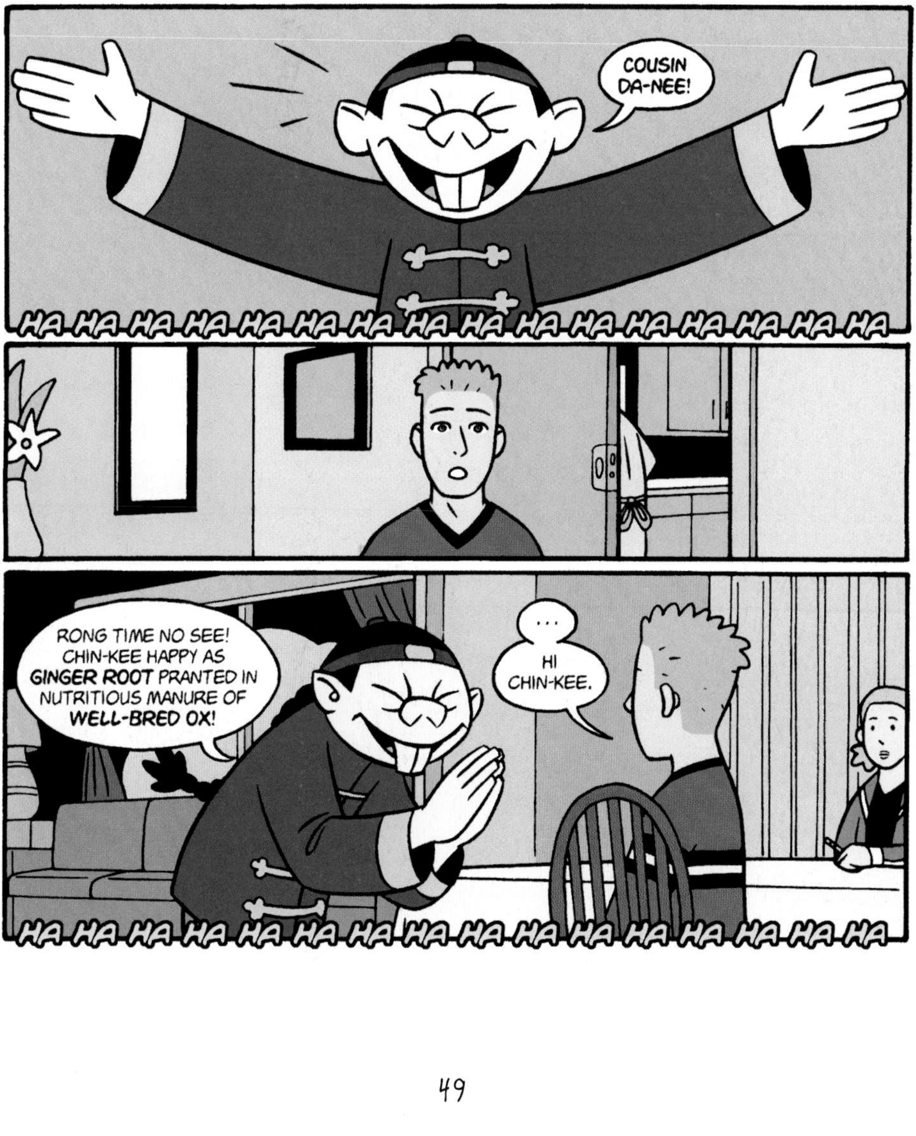
COUSIN DA-NEE!
HA HA HA HA HA HA HA HA HA HA HA HA HA HA HA HA
RONG TIME NO SEE! CHIN-KEE HAPPY AS **GINGER ROOT** PRANTED IN NUTRITIOUS MANURE OF **WELL-BRED OX!**
...
HI CHIN-KEE.
HA HA HA HA HA HA HA HA HA HA HA HA HA HA HA HA

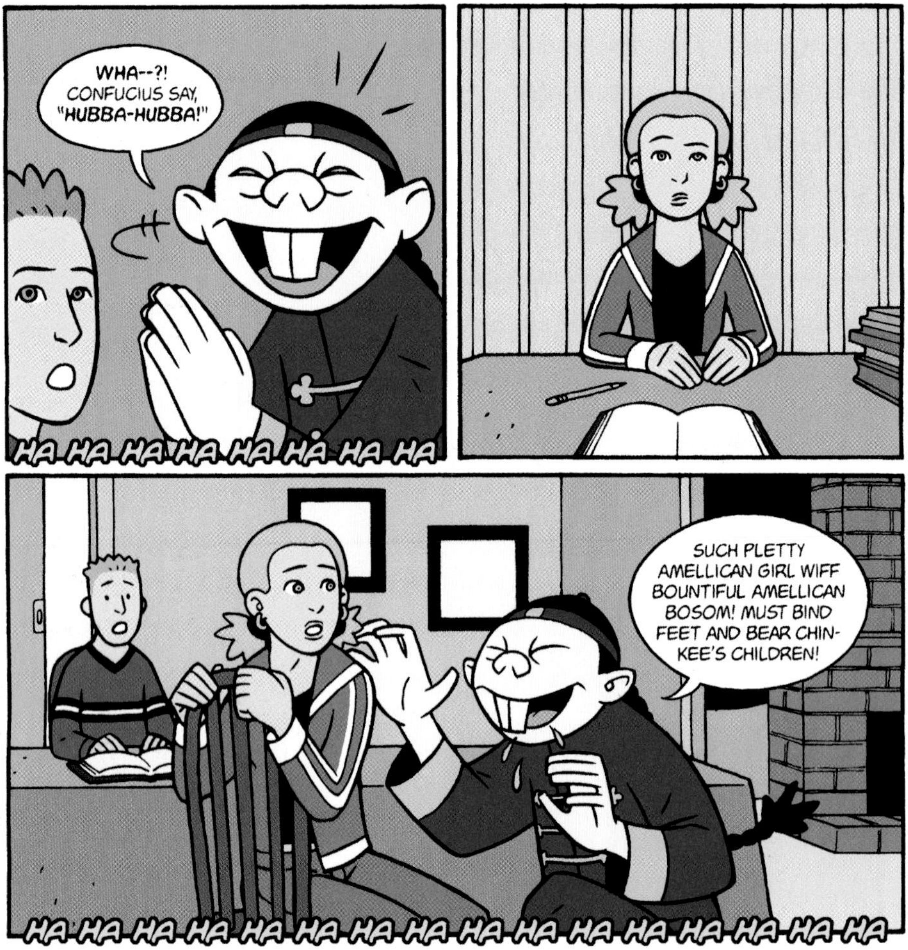
WHA--?! CONFUCIUS SAY, "HUBBA-HUBBA!"
HA HA HA HA HA HA HA HA HA
SUCH PLETTY AMELLICAN GIRL WIFF BOUNTIFUL AMELLICAN BOSOM! MUST BIND FEET AND BEAR CHIN-KEE'S CHILDREN!
HA HA HA HA HA HA HA HA HA HA HA HA HA HA HA HA

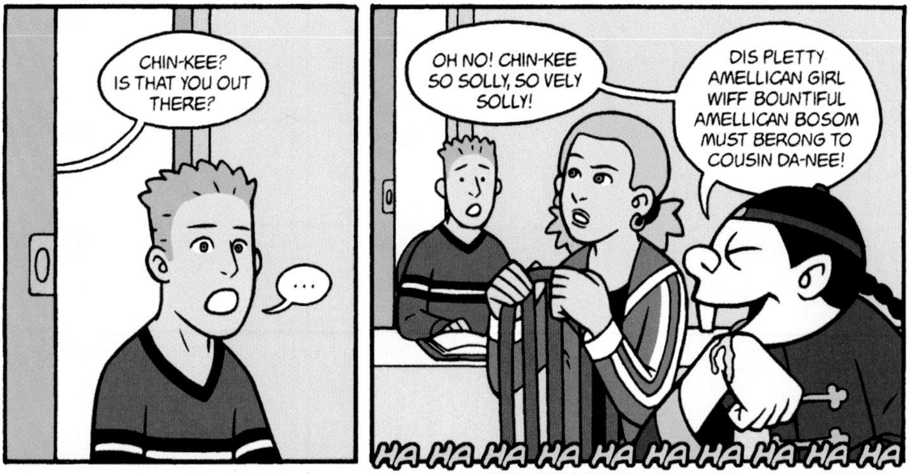
CHIN-KEE? IS THAT YOU OUT THERE?
...
OH NO! CHIN-KEE SO SOLLY, SO VELY SOLLY!
DIS PLETTY AMELLICAN GIRL WIFF BOUNTIFUL AMELLICAN BOSOM MUST BERONG TO COUSIN DA-NEE!
HA HA HA HA HA HA HA HA HA HA
PERHAPS CHIN-KEE CAN FIND PLETTY AMELLICAN GIRL FOR HISSELF WHEN HE ATTEND AMELLICAN SCHOOL TOMOLLOW WIFF COUSIN DA-NEE!
HA HA HA-HA HA
...?!
MA?!
OH, YOU TWO ARE GOING TO HAVE SO MUCH FUN TOGETHER!
HA HA HA HA HA

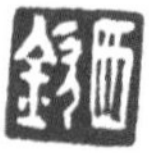

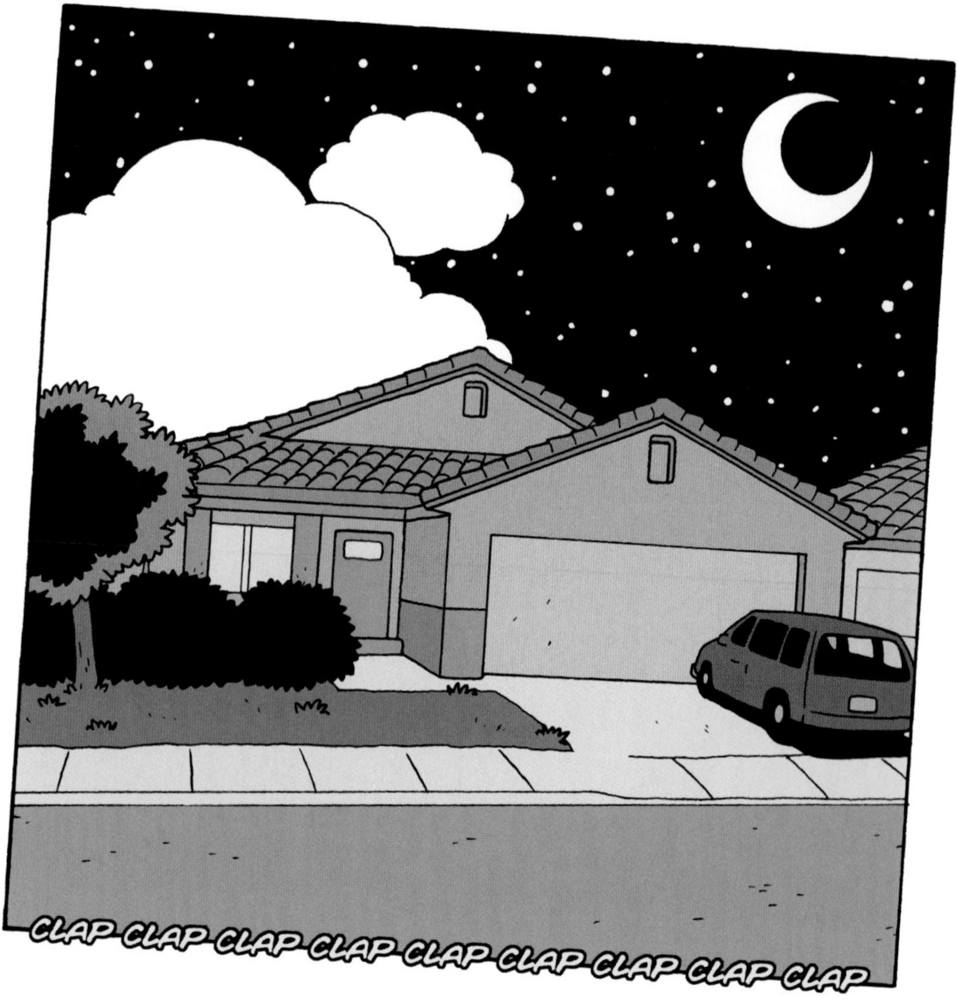
CLAP CLAP CLAP CLAP CLAP CLAP CLAP CLAP CLAP

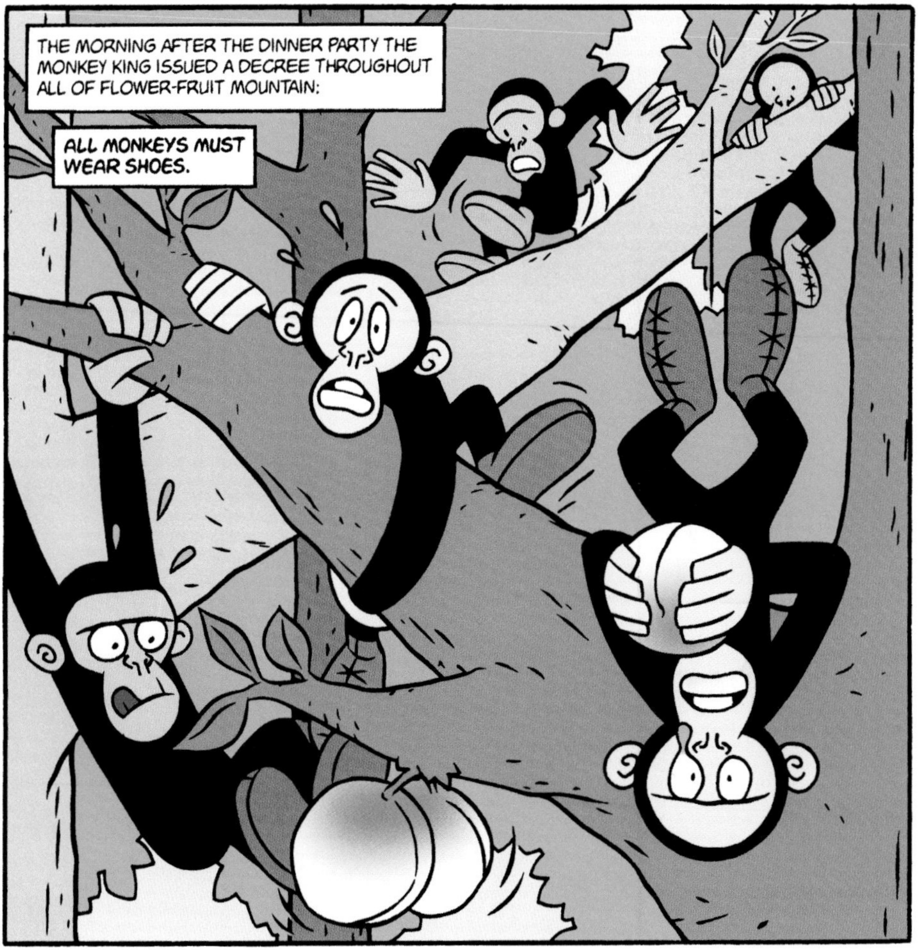
THE MORNING AFTER THE DINNER PARTY THE MONKEY KING ISSUED A DECREE THROUGHOUT ALL OF FLOWER-FRUIT MOUNTAIN:
ALL MONKEYS MUST WEAR SHOES.

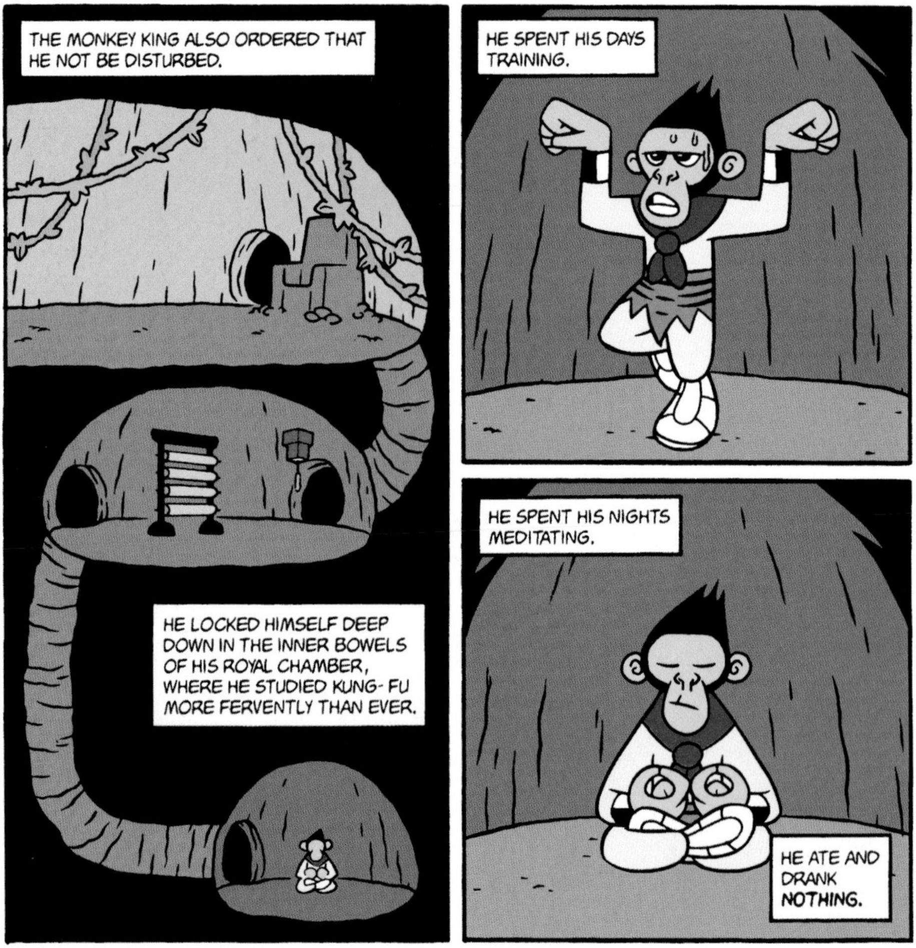
THE MONKEY KING ALSO ORDERED THAT HE NOT BE DISTURBED.
HE LOCKED HIMSELF DEEP DOWN IN THE INNER BOWELS OF HIS ROYAL CHAMBER, WHERE HE STUDIED KUNG- FU MORE FERVENTLY THAN EVER.
HE SPENT HIS DAYS TRAINING.
HE SPENT HIS NIGHTS MEDITATING.
HE ATE AND DRANK **NOTHING.**

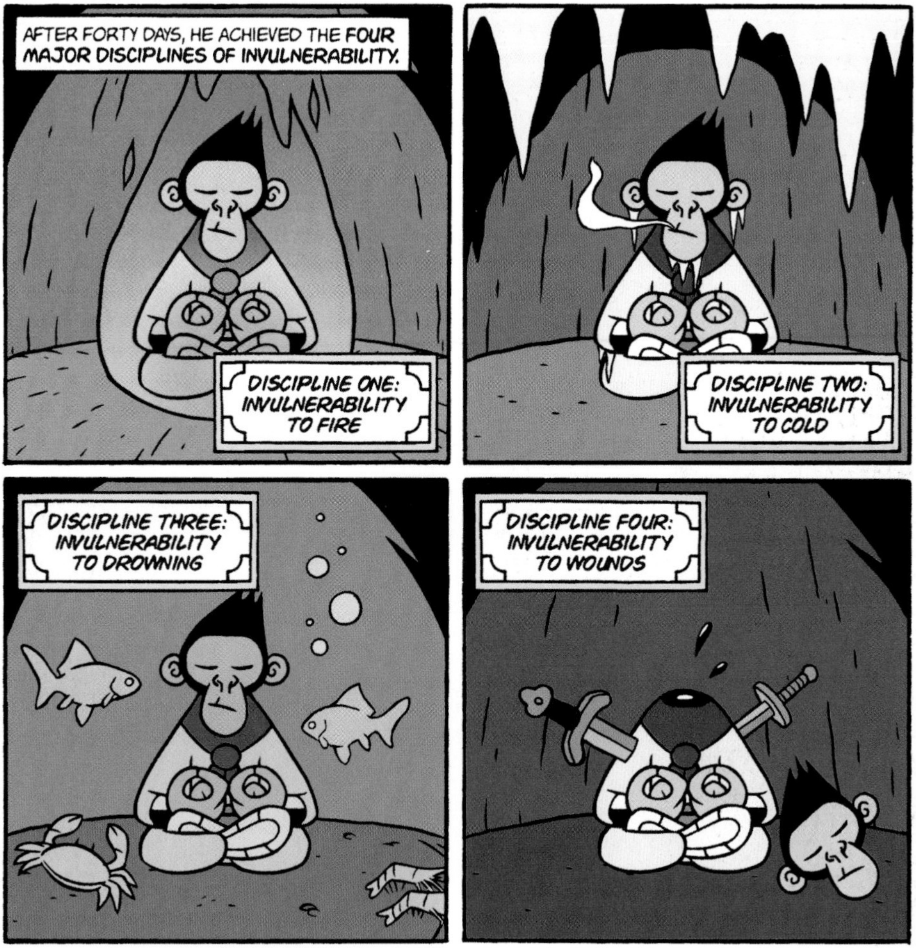

AFTER FORTY DAYS, HE ACHIEVED THE FOUR MAJOR DISCIPLINES OF INVULNERABILITY.
DISCIPLINE ONE: INVULNERABILITY TO FIRE
DISCIPLINE TWO: INVULNERABILITY TO COLD
DISCIPLINE THREE: INVULNERABILITY TO DROWNING
DISCIPLINE FOUR: INVULNERABILITY TO WOUNDS

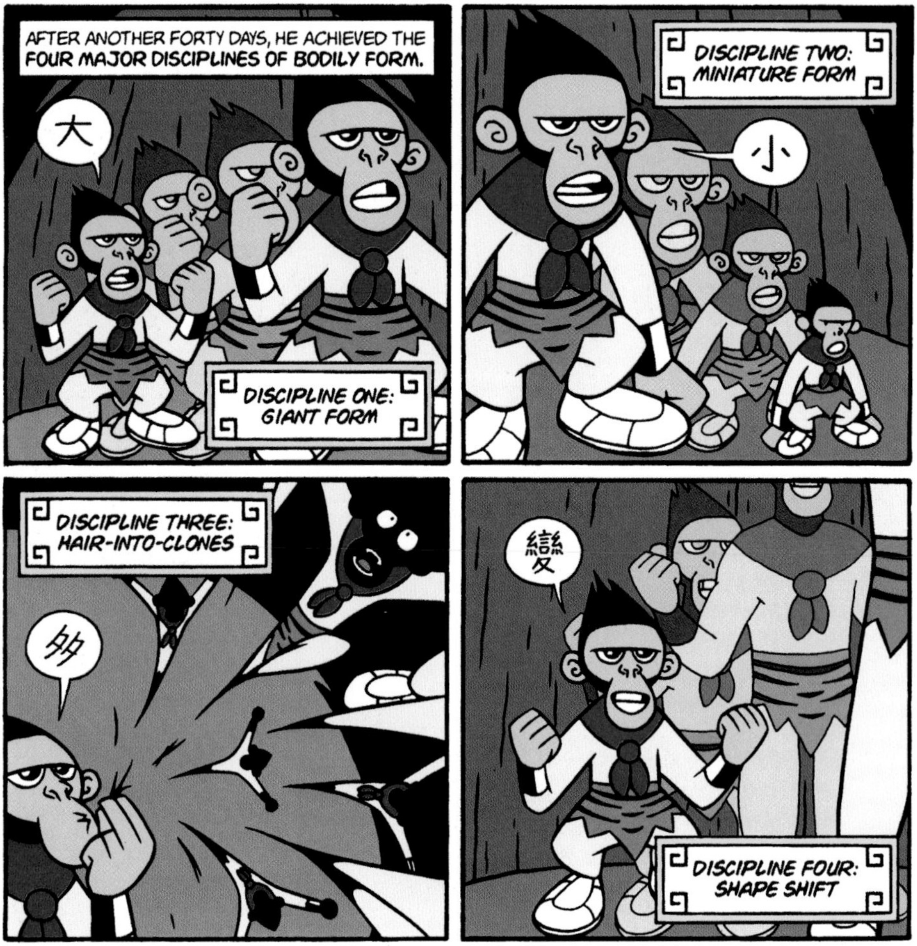
AFTER ANOTHER FORTY DAYS, HE ACHIEVED THE FOUR MAJOR DISCIPLINES OF BODILY FORM.
大
DISCIPLINE ONE: GIANT FORM
DISCIPLINE TWO: MINIATURE FORM
小
DISCIPLINE THREE: HAIR-INTO-CLONES
多
變
DISCIPLINE FOUR: SHAPE SHIFT

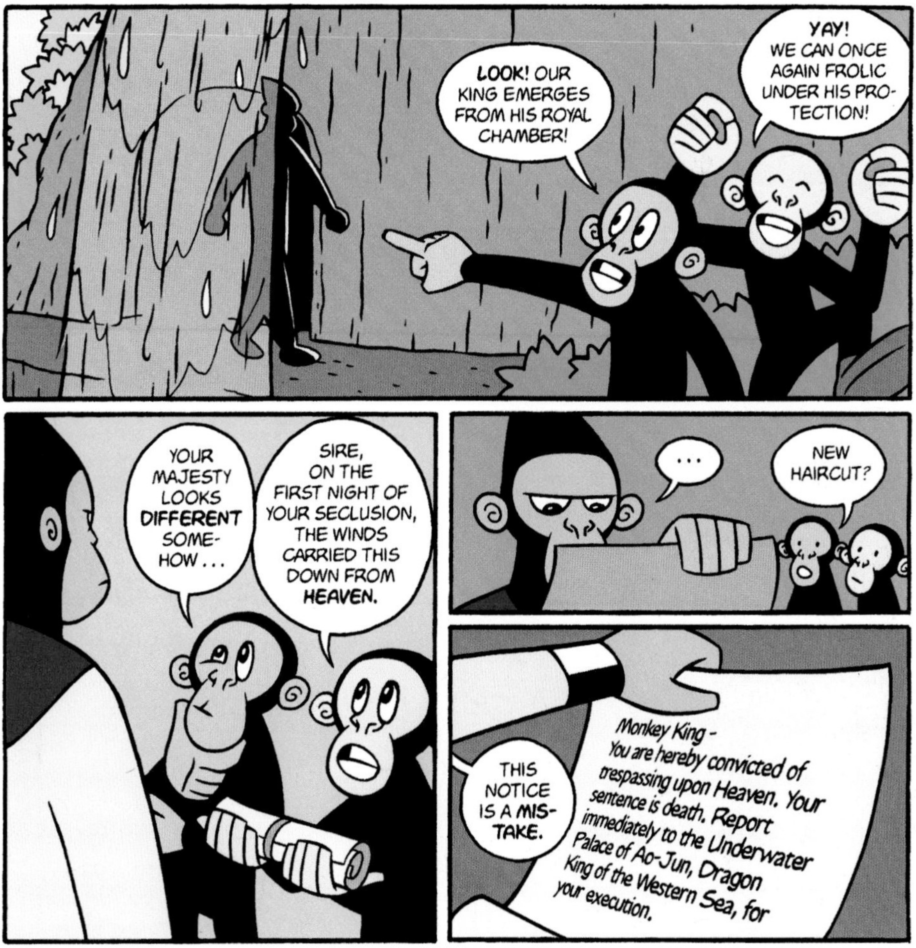
LOOK! OUR KING EMERGES FROM HIS ROYAL CHAMBER!
YAY! WE CAN ONCE AGAIN FROLIC UNDER HIS PROTECTION!
YOUR MAJESTY LOOKS DIFFERENT SOMEHOW . . .
SIRE, ON THE FIRST NIGHT OF YOUR SECLUSION, THE WINDS CARRIED THIS DOWN FROM HEAVEN.
. . .
NEW HAIRCUT?
Monkey King - You are hereby convicted of trespassing upon Heaven. Your sentence is death. Report immediately to the Underwater Palace of Ao-Jun, Dragon King of the Western Sea, for your execution.
THIS NOTICE IS A MISTAKE.

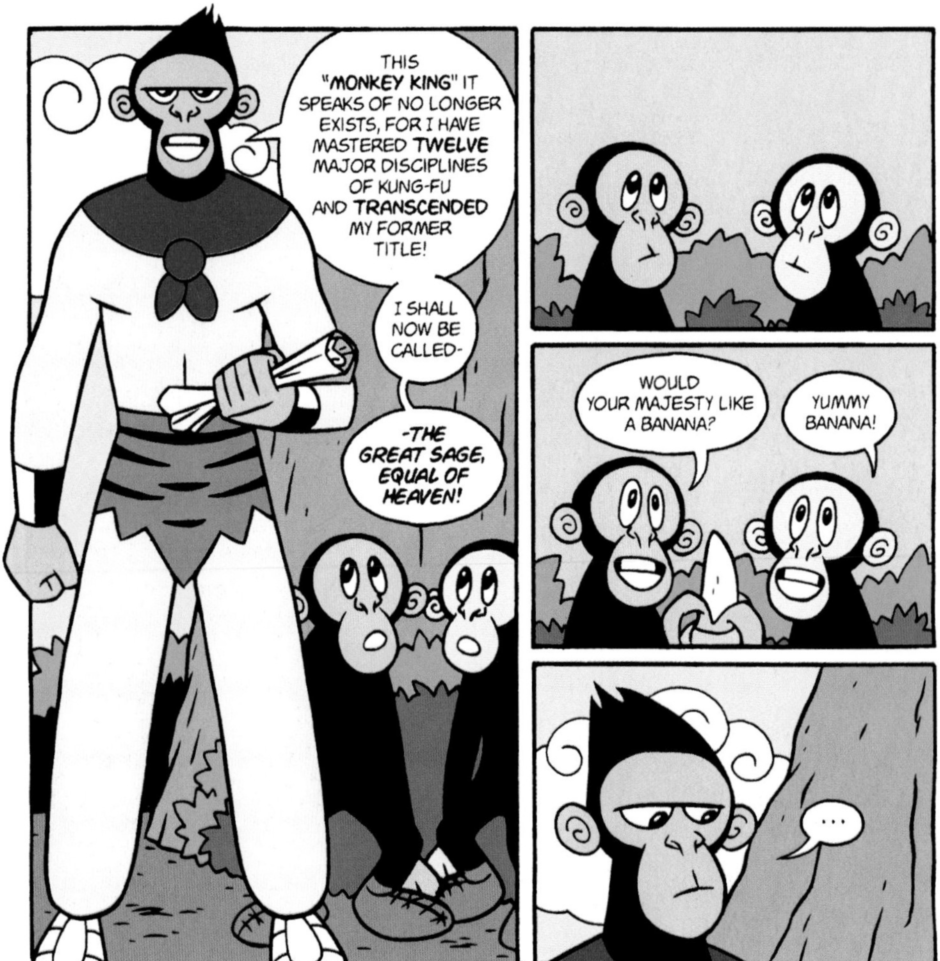
THIS "MONKEY KING" IT SPEAKS OF NO LONGER EXISTS, FOR I HAVE MASTERED TWELVE MAJOR DISCIPLINES OF KUNG-FU AND TRANSCENDED MY FORMER TITLE!
I SHALL NOW BE CALLED-
-THE GREAT SAGE, EQUAL OF HEAVEN!
WOULD YOUR MAJESTY LIKE A BANANA?
YUMMY BANANA!
...

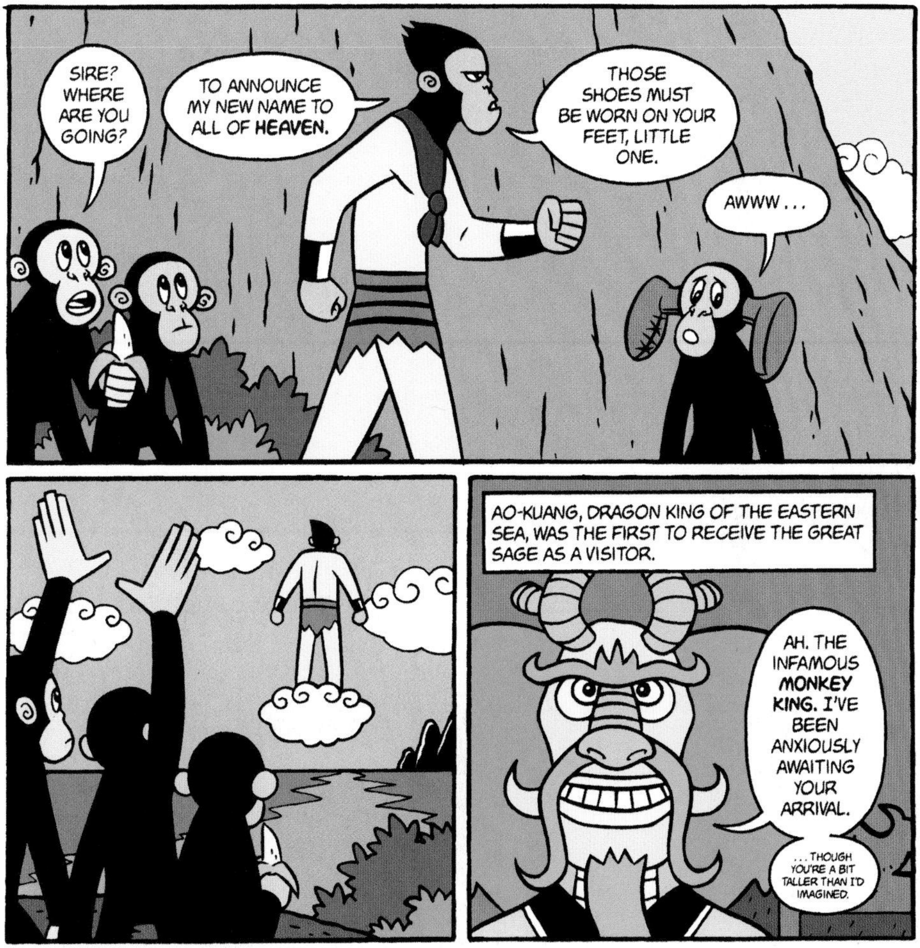
SIRE? WHERE ARE YOU GOING?
TO ANNOUNCE MY NEW NAME TO ALL OF **HEAVEN.**
THOSE SHOES MUST BE WORN ON YOUR FEET, LITTLE ONE.
AWWW . . .
AO-KUANG, DRAGON KING OF THE EASTERN SEA, WAS THE FIRST TO RECEIVE THE GREAT SAGE AS A VISITOR.
AH. THE INFAMOUS **MONKEY KING.** I'VE BEEN ANXIOUSLY AWAITING YOUR ARRIVAL.
. . . THOUGH YOU'RE A BIT TALLER THAN I'D IMAGINED.

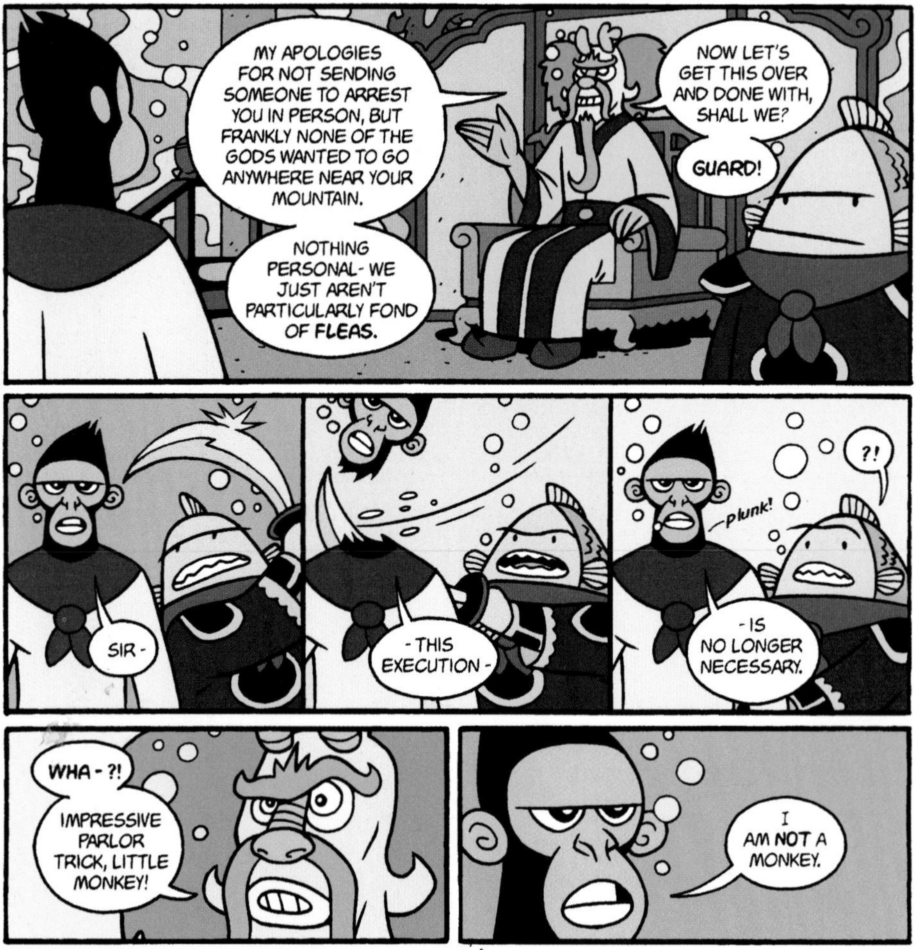
MY APOLOGIES FOR NOT SENDING SOMEONE TO ARREST YOU IN PERSON, BUT FRANKLY NONE OF THE GODS WANTED TO GO ANYWHERE NEAR YOUR MOUNTAIN.
NOTHING PERSONAL- WE JUST AREN'T PARTICULARLY FOND OF FLEAS.
NOW LET'S GET THIS OVER AND DONE WITH, SHALL WE?
GUARD!
SIR -
- THIS EXECUTION -
-plunk!
?!
- IS NO LONGER NECESSARY.
WHA - ?!
IMPRESSIVE PARLOR TRICK, LITTLE MONKEY!
I AM NOT A MONKEY.

HEH HEH. YOU'RE - HEH - NOT A MONKEY?
HEE HEE!
I HAVE MASTERED TWELVE DISCIPLINES OF KUNG-FU. I AM NOW THE GREAT SAGE, EQUAL OF HEAVEN.
HA HA HA!
BWA HA HA!
THE DRAGON KING NEEDED SOME CONVINCING.

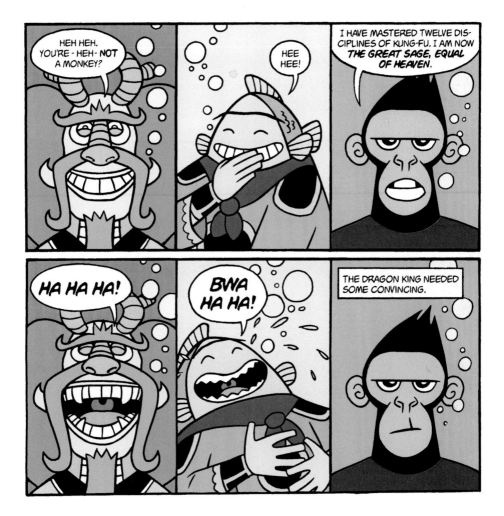

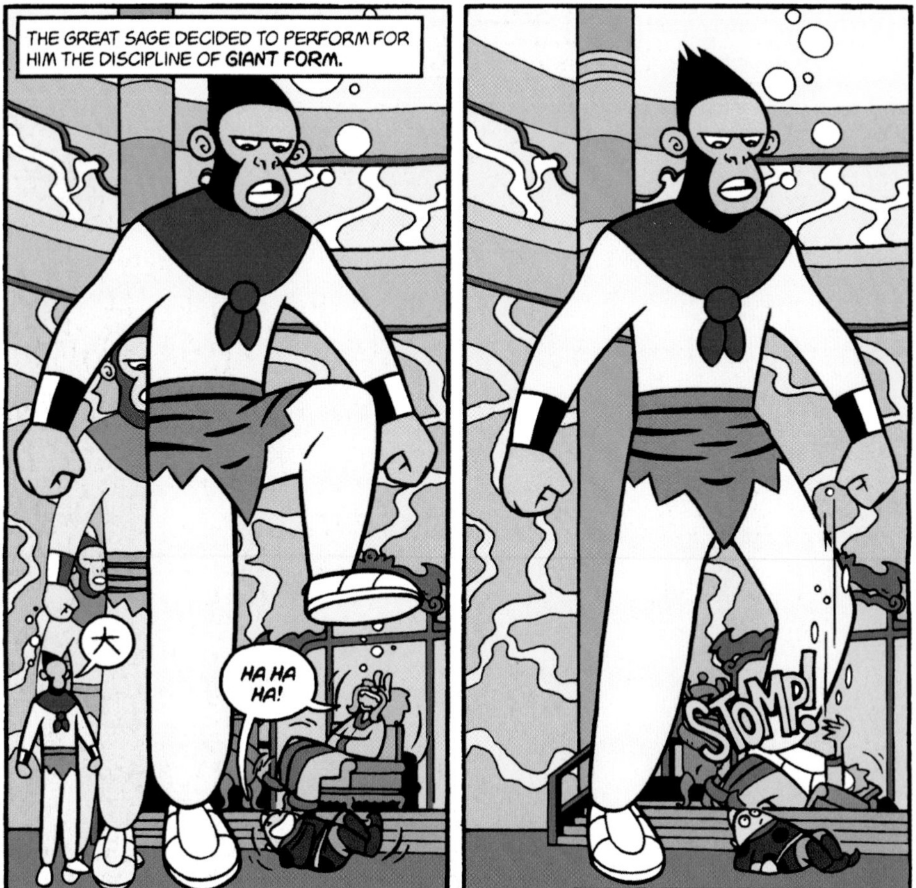
THE GREAT SAGE DECIDED TO PERFORM FOR HIM THE DISCIPLINE OF **GIANT FORM.**
大
HA HA HA!
STOMP!
THE DRAGON KING WAS CONVINCED.

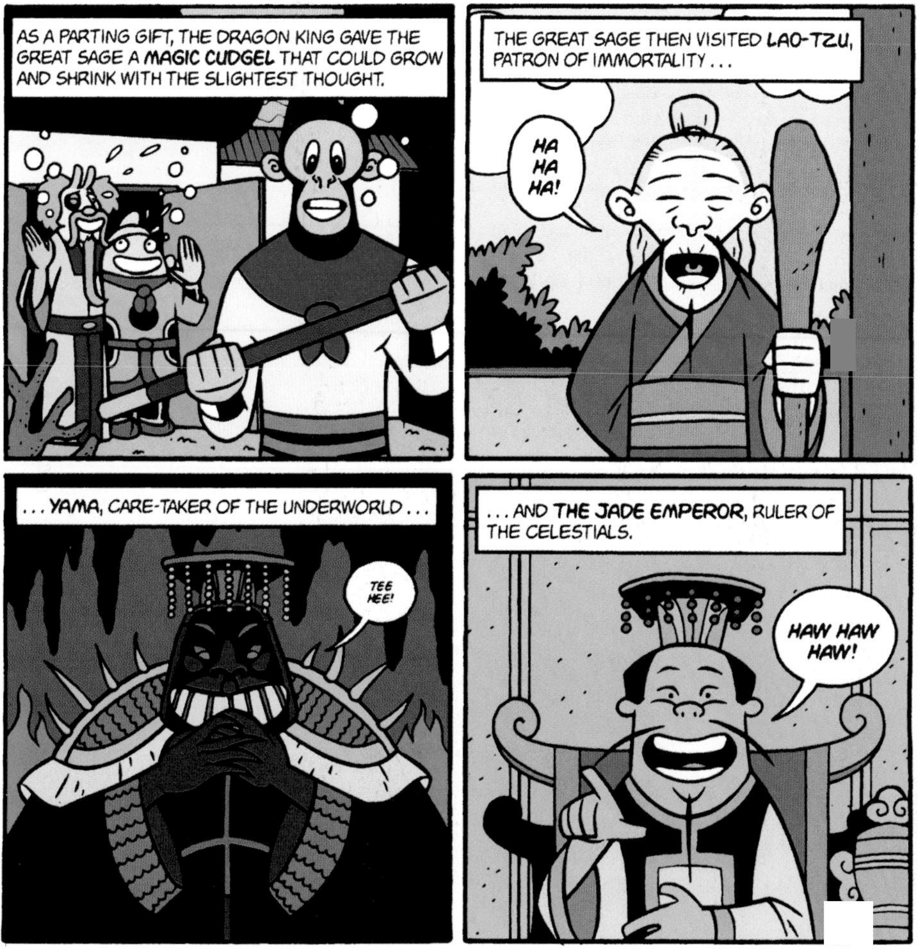
AS A PARTING GIFT, THE DRAGON KING GAVE THE GREAT SAGE A MAGIC CUDGEL THAT COULD GROW AND SHRINK WITH THE SLIGHTEST THOUGHT.
THE GREAT SAGE THEN VISITED LAO-TZU, PATRON OF IMMORTALITY . . .
HA HA HA!
. . . YAMA, CARE-TAKER OF THE UNDERWORLD . . .
TEE HEE!
. . . AND THE JADE EMPEROR, RULER OF THE CELESTIALS.
HAW HAW HAW!

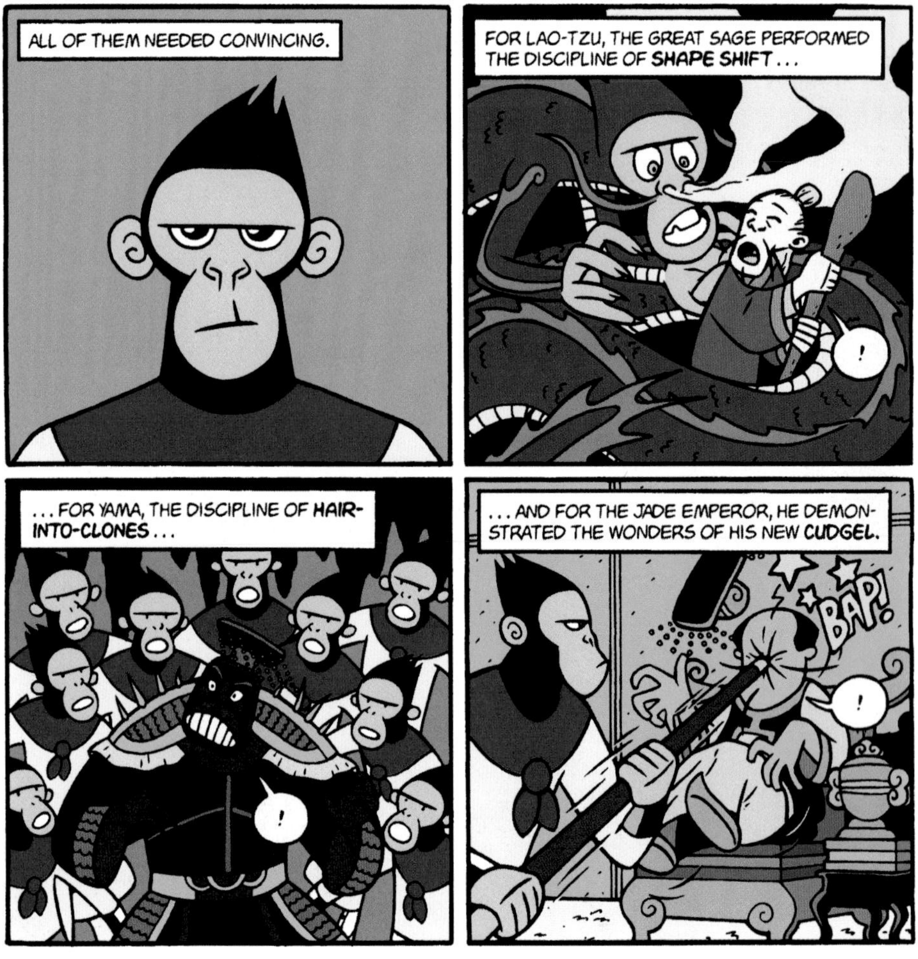
ALL OF THEM NEEDED CONVINCING.
FOR LAO-TZU, THE GREAT SAGE PERFORMED THE DISCIPLINE OF **SHAPE SHIFT** . . .
!
. . . FOR YAMA, THE DISCIPLINE OF **HAIR-INTO-CLONES** . . .
!
. . . AND FOR THE JADE EMPEROR, HE DEMONSTRATED THE WONDERS OF HIS NEW **CUDGEL.**
BAP!
!

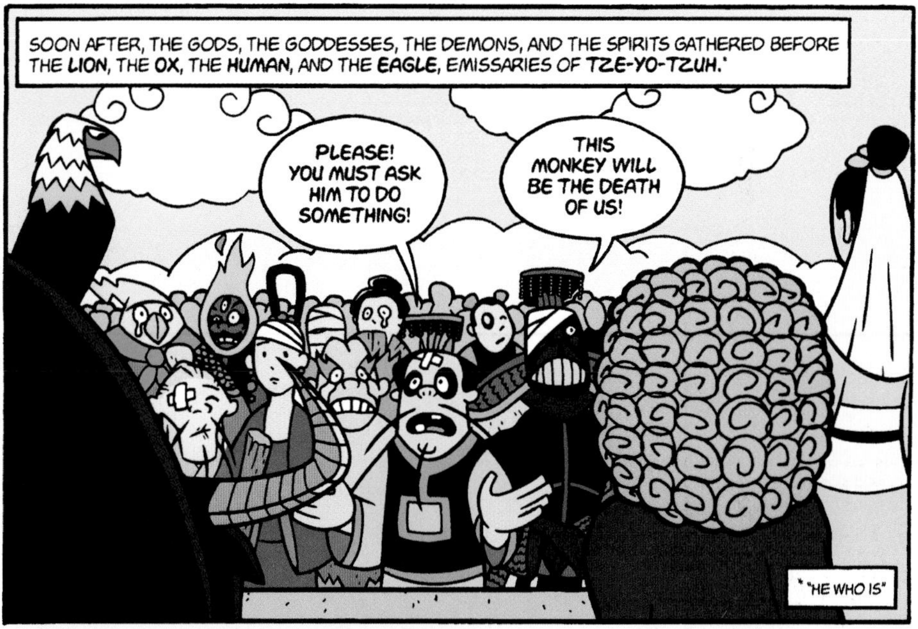
SOON AFTER, THE GODS, THE GODDESSES, THE DEMONS, AND THE SPIRITS GATHERED BEFORE THE **LION**, THE **OX**, THE **HUMAN**, AND THE **EAGLE**, EMISSARIES OF **TZE-YO-TZUH**.*
PLEASE! YOU MUST ASK HIM TO DO SOMETHING!
THIS MONKEY WILL BE THE DEATH OF US!
* "HE WHO IS"

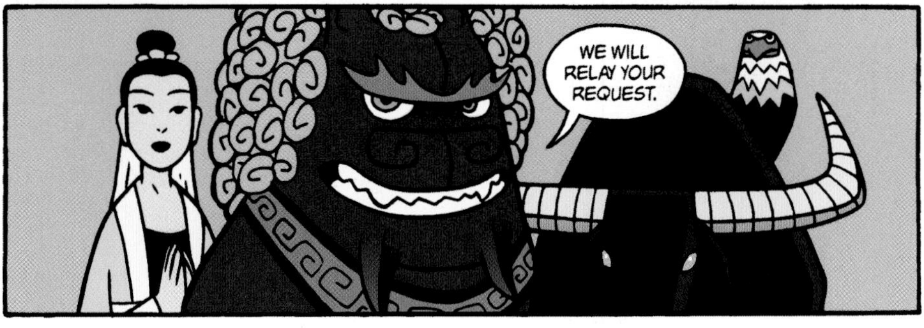
WE WILL RELAY YOUR REQUEST.

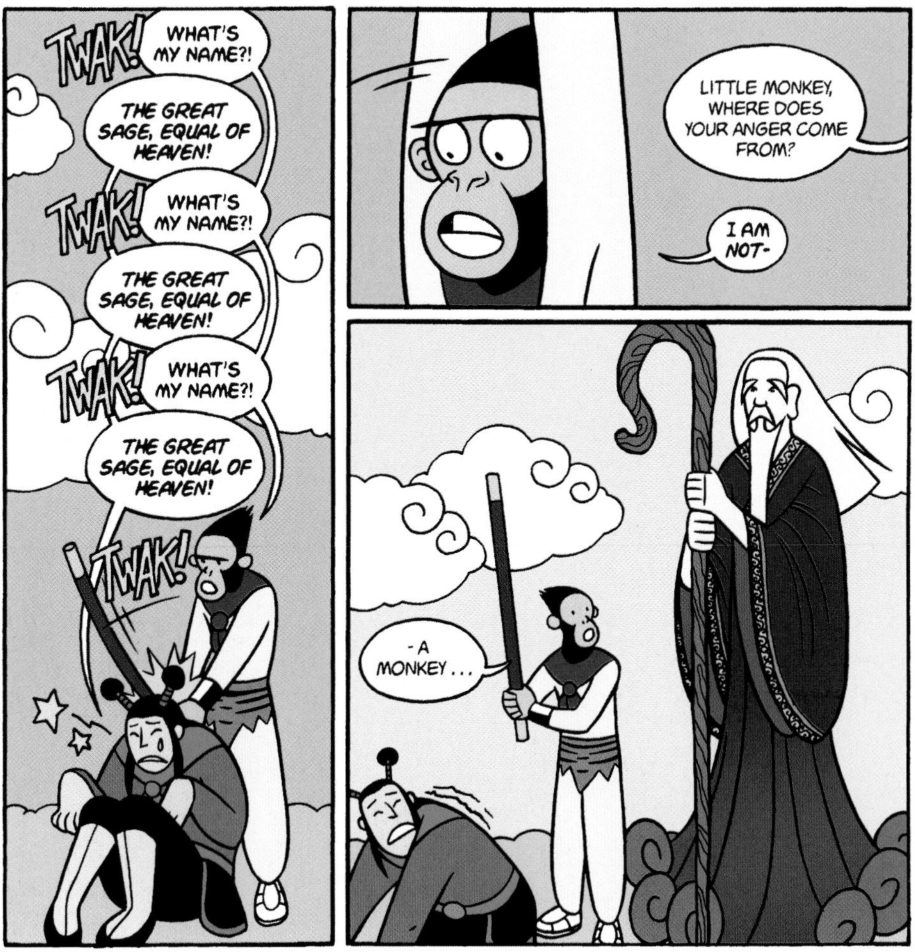
TWAK!
WHAT'S MY NAME?!
THE GREAT SAGE, EQUAL OF HEAVEN!
TWAK!
WHAT'S MY NAME?!
THE GREAT SAGE, EQUAL OF HEAVEN!
TWAK!
WHAT'S MY NAME?!
THE GREAT SAGE, EQUAL OF HEAVEN!
TWAK!
LITTLE MONKEY, WHERE DOES YOUR ANGER COME FROM?
I AM NOT-
-A MONKEY...

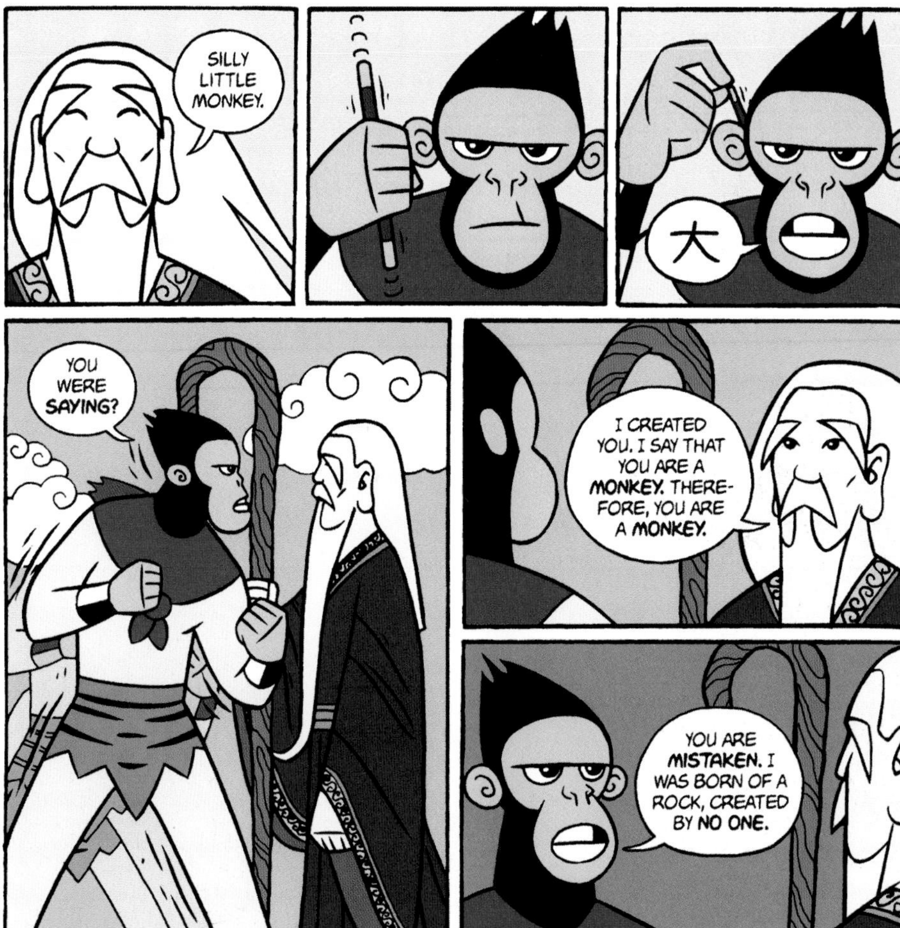
SILLY LITTLE MONKEY.
大
YOU WERE SAYING?
I CREATED YOU. I SAY THAT YOU ARE A MONKEY. THEREFORE, YOU ARE A MONKEY.
YOU ARE MISTAKEN. I WAS BORN OF A ROCK, CREATED BY NO ONE.

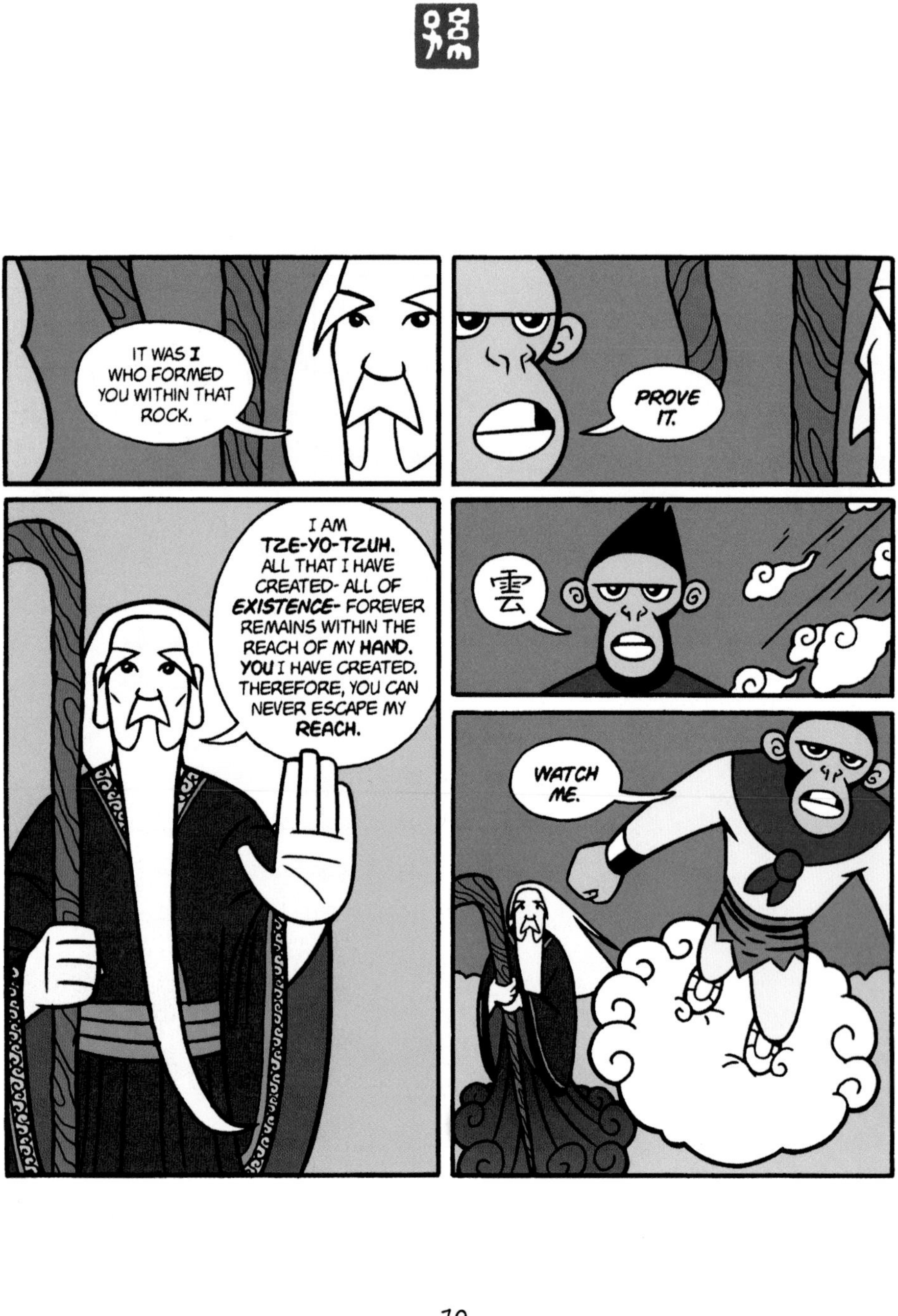
IT WAS I WHO FORMED YOU WITHIN THAT ROCK.
PROVE IT.
I AM TZE-YO-TZUH. ALL THAT I HAVE CREATED- ALL OF EXISTENCE- FOREVER REMAINS WITHIN THE REACH OF MY HAND. YOU I HAVE CREATED. THEREFORE, YOU CAN NEVER ESCAPE MY REACH.
雲
WATCH ME.

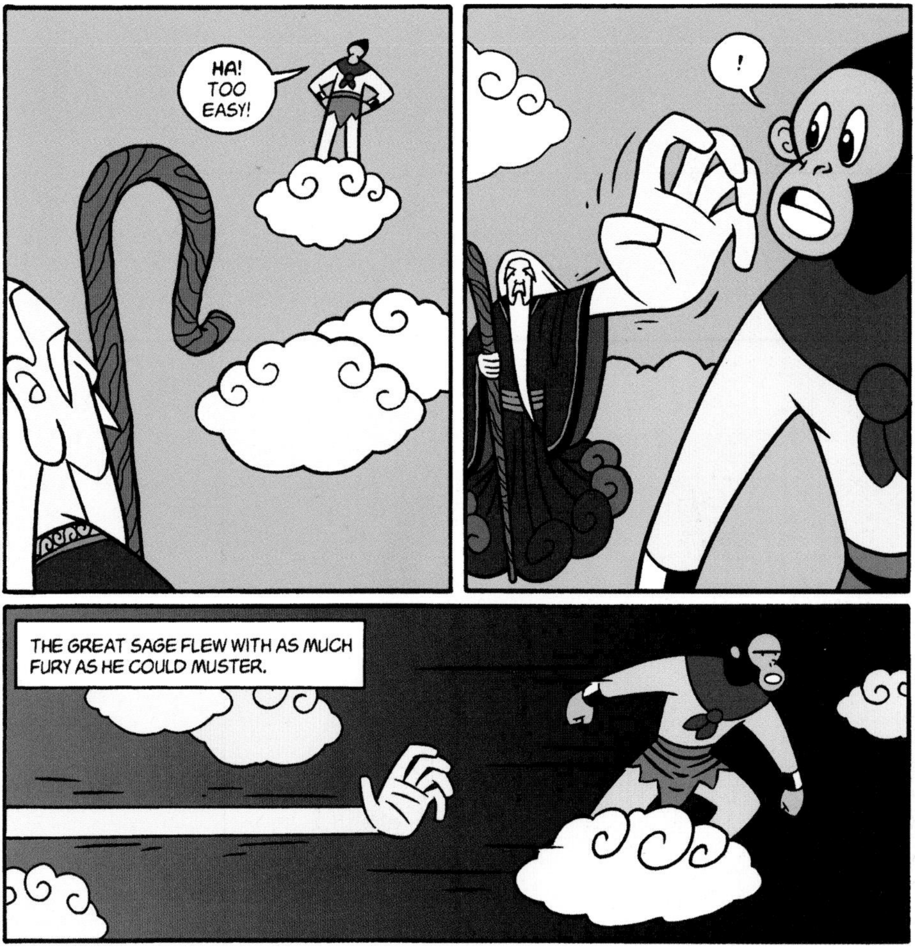
HA! TOO EASY!
!
THE GREAT SAGE FLEW WITH AS MUCH FURY AS HE COULD MUSTER.

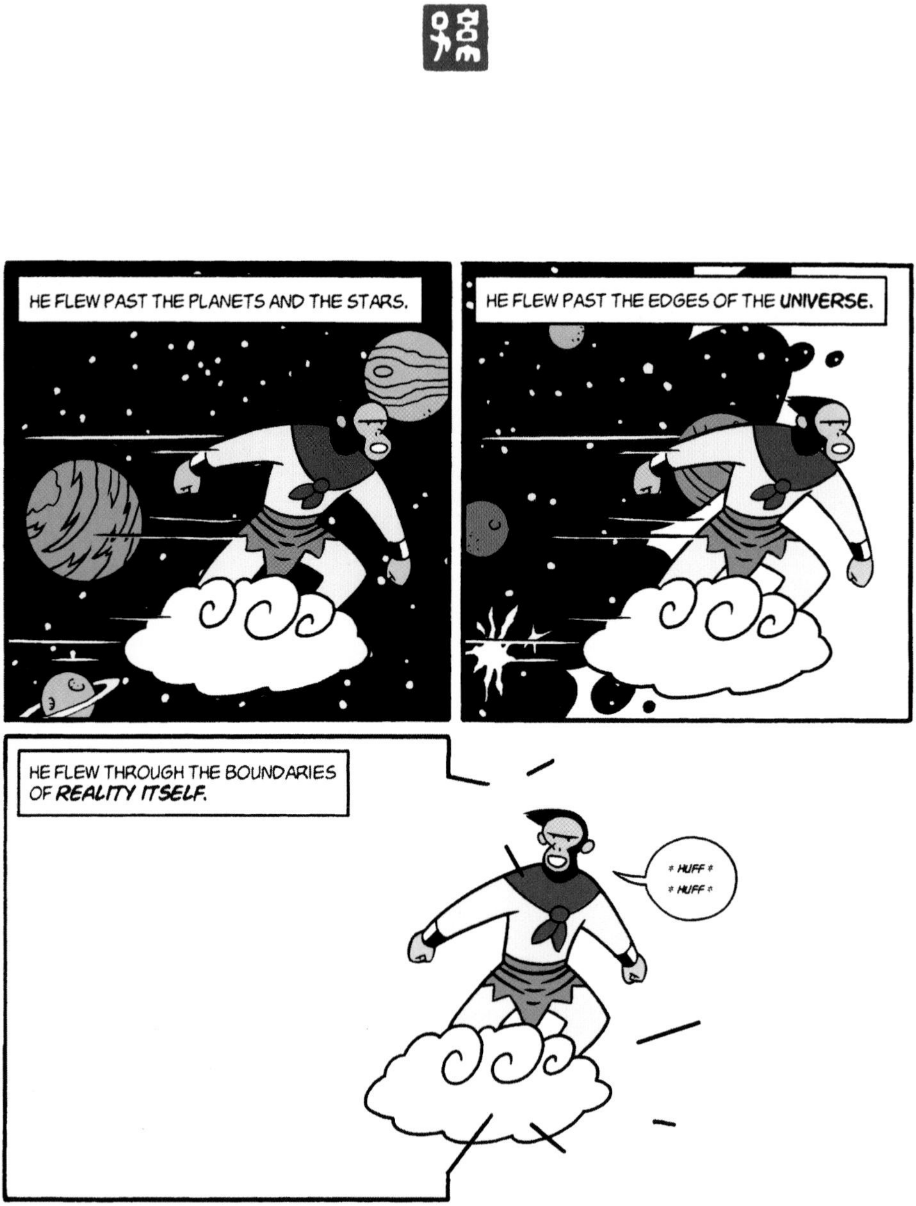
HE FLEW PAST THE PLANETS AND THE STARS.
HE FLEW PAST THE EDGES OF THE UNIVERSE.
HE FLEW THROUGH THE BOUNDARIES OF REALITY ITSELF.
* HUFF *
* HUFF *

THERE, AT THE END OF ALL THAT IS, THE GREAT SAGE CAME UPON **FIVE PILLARS OF GOLD.**

NEVER ONE TO MISS OUT ON A CHANCE FOR RECOGNITION, THE GREAT SAGE CARVED HIS NAME INTO ONE OF THE PILLARS.

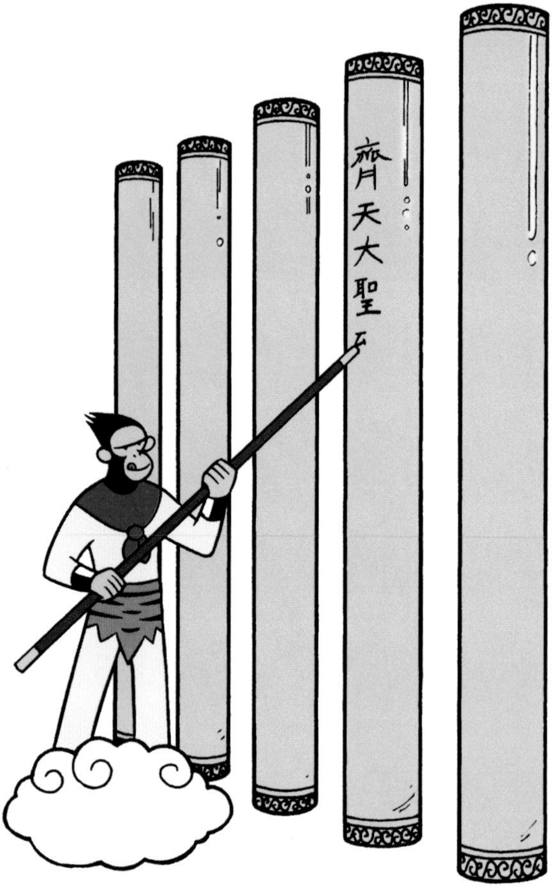
齊天大聖

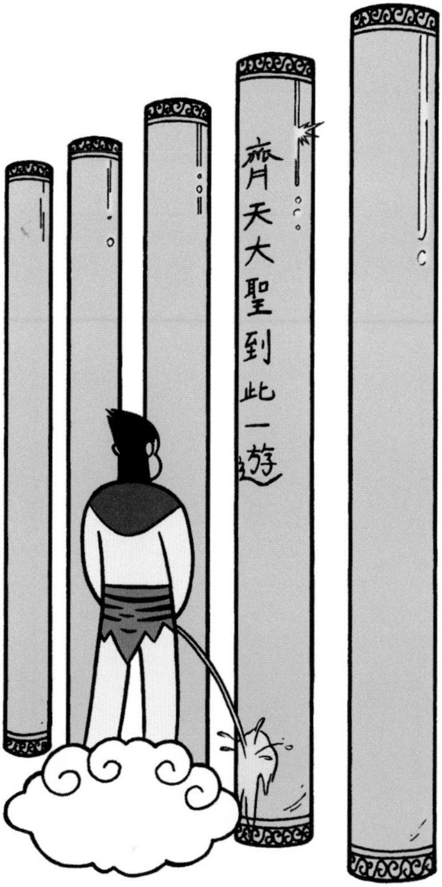
THEN HE RELIEVED HIMSELF. (IT HAD BEEN AN AWFULLY LONG TRIP.)
齊天大聖到此一遊

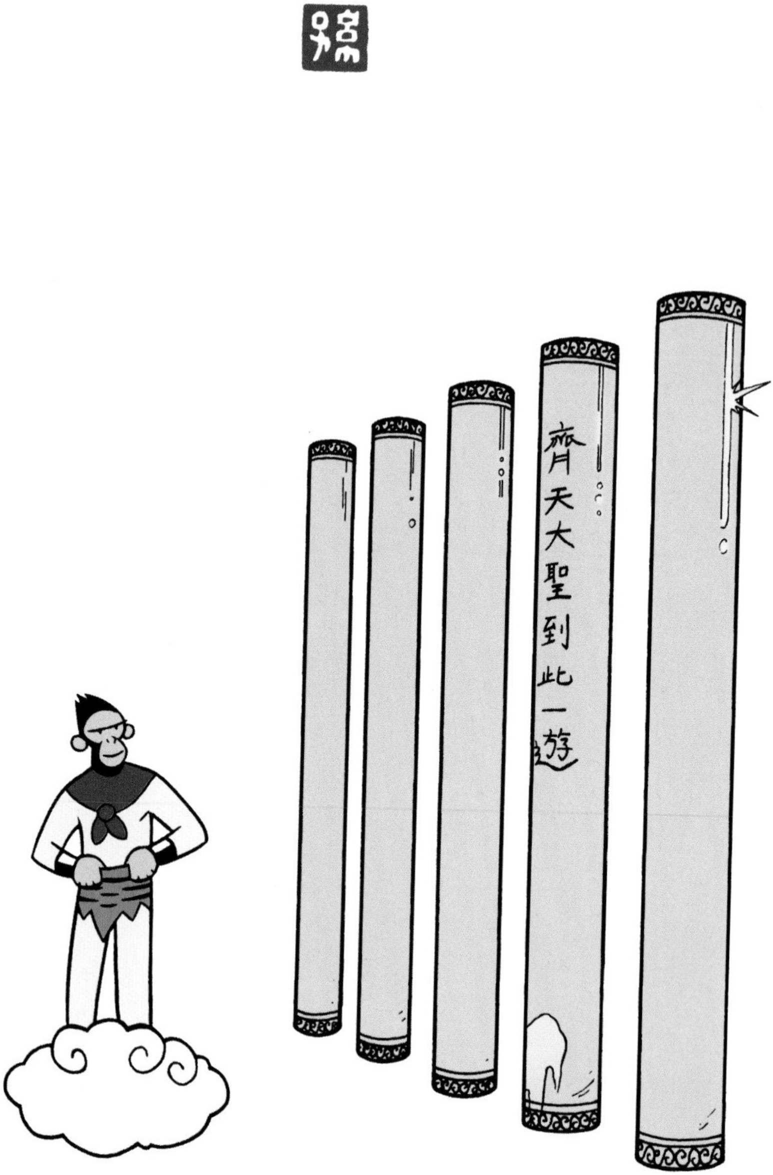
齊天大聖到此一遊

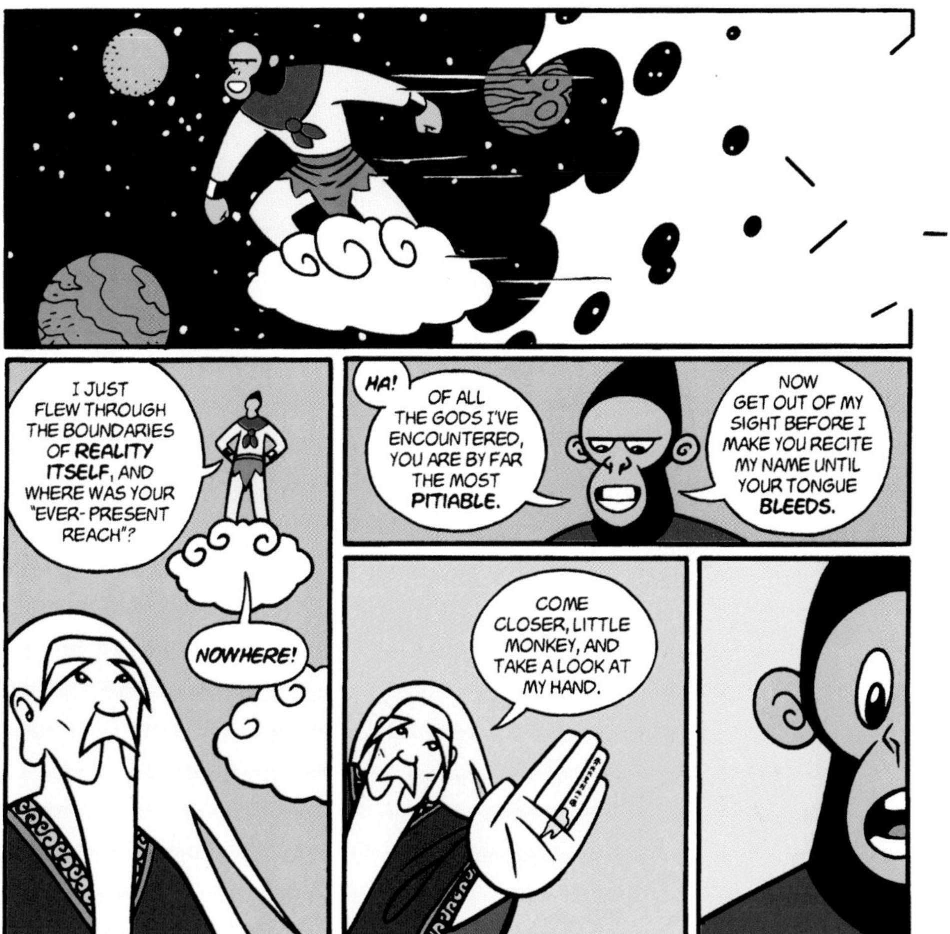
I JUST FLEW THROUGH THE BOUNDARIES OF REALITY ITSELF, AND WHERE WAS YOUR "EVER-PRESENT REACH"?
NOWHERE!
HA!
OF ALL THE GODS I'VE ENCOUNTERED, YOU ARE BY FAR THE MOST PITIABLE.
NOW GET OUT OF MY SIGHT BEFORE I MAKE YOU RECITE MY NAME UNTIL YOUR TONGUE BLEEDS.
COME CLOSER, LITTLE MONKEY, AND TAKE A LOOK AT MY HAND.

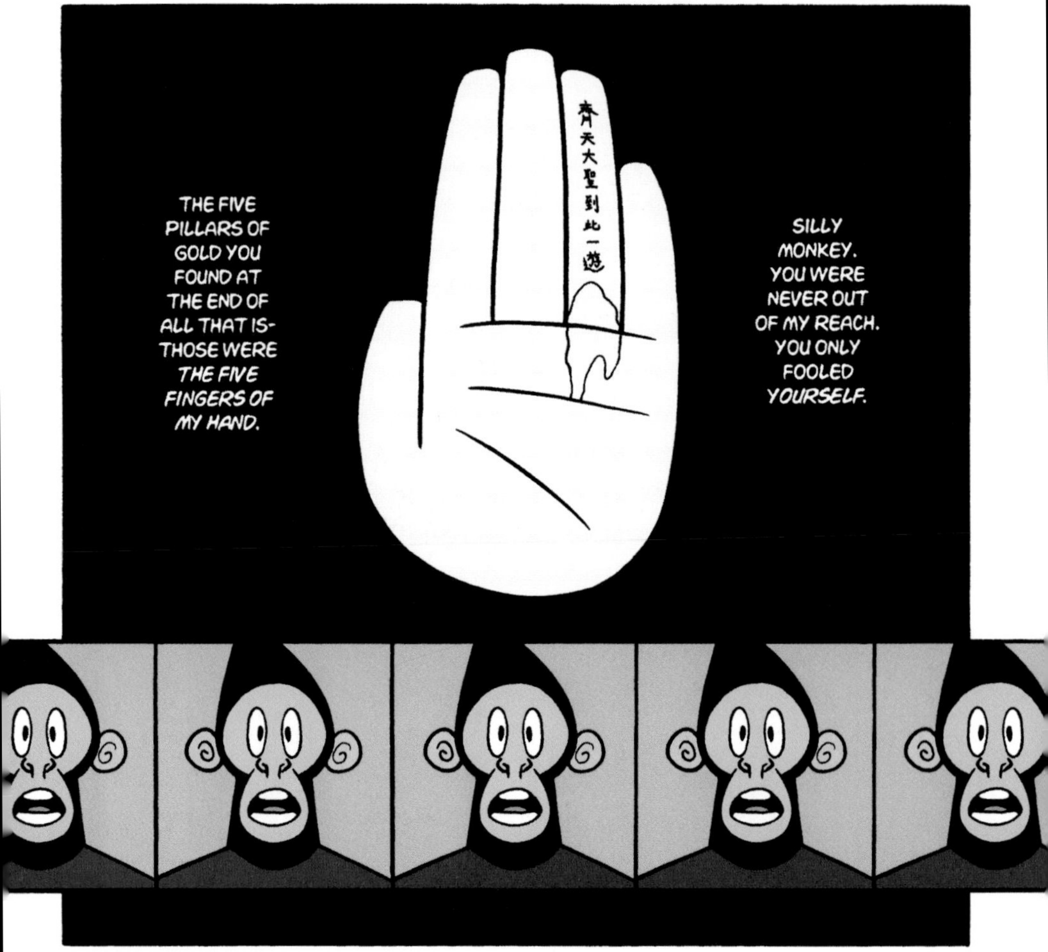
THE FIVE PILLARS OF GOLD YOU FOUND AT THE END OF ALL THAT IS- THOSE WERE *THE FIVE FINGERS OF MY HAND.*
齊天大聖到此一遊
SILLY MONKEY. YOU WERE NEVER OUT OF MY REACH. YOU ONLY FOOLED *YOURSELF.*

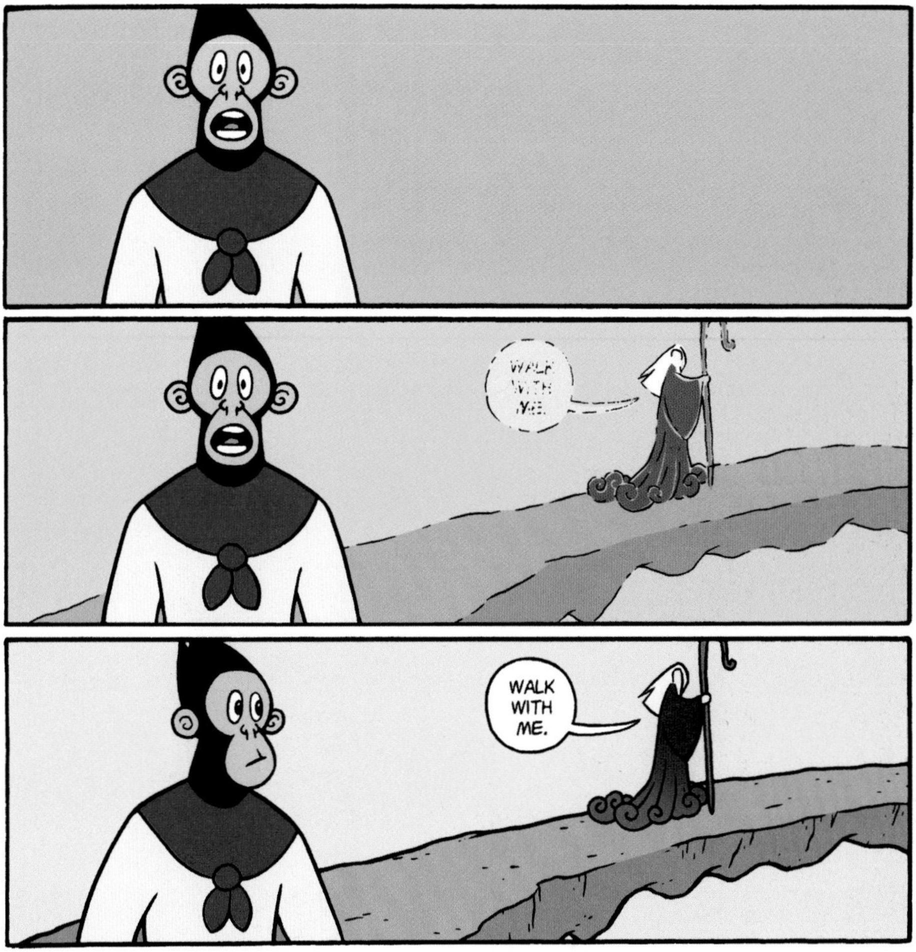
WALK WITH ME.
WALK WITH ME.

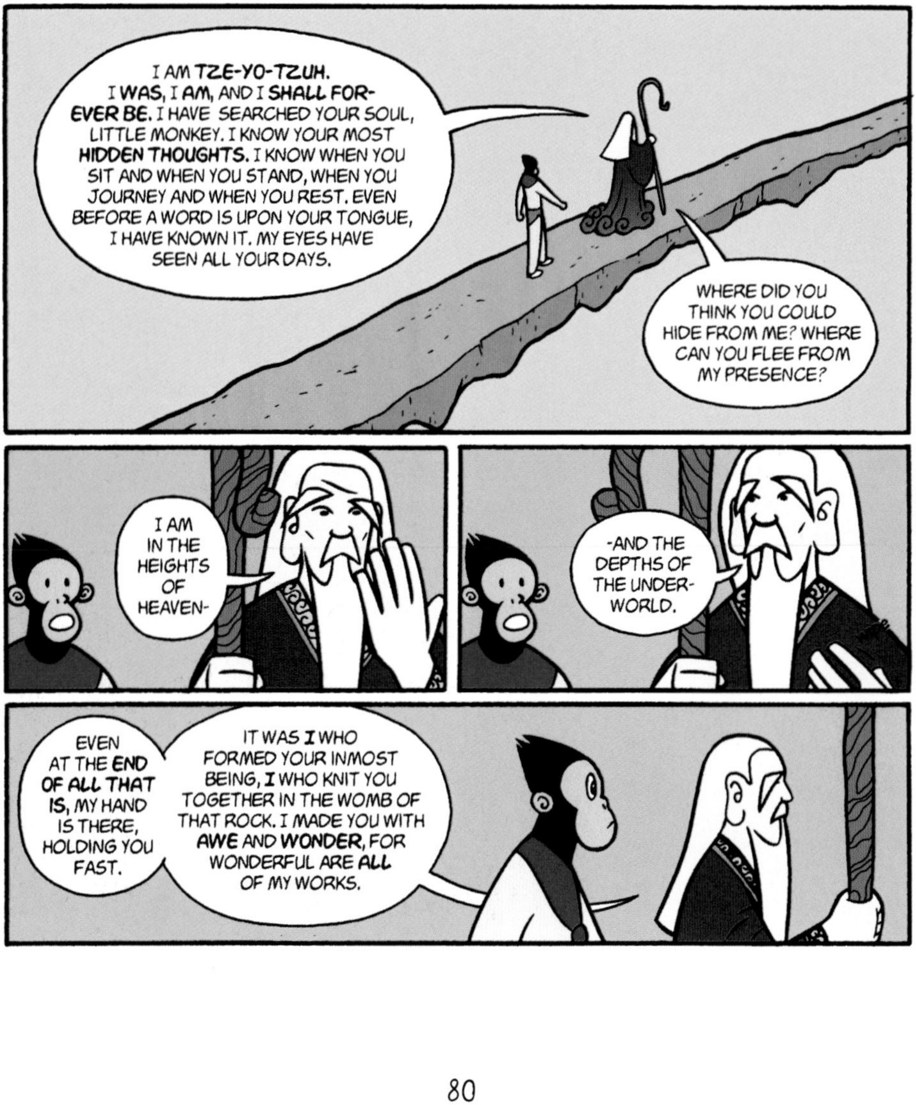
I AM TZE-YO-TZUH. I WAS, I AM, AND I SHALL FOREVER BE. I HAVE SEARCHED YOUR SOUL, LITTLE MONKEY. I KNOW YOUR MOST HIDDEN THOUGHTS. I KNOW WHEN YOU SIT AND WHEN YOU STAND, WHEN YOU JOURNEY AND WHEN YOU REST. EVEN BEFORE A WORD IS UPON YOUR TONGUE, I HAVE KNOWN IT. MY EYES HAVE SEEN ALL YOUR DAYS.
WHERE DID YOU THINK YOU COULD HIDE FROM ME? WHERE CAN YOU FLEE FROM MY PRESENCE?
I AM IN THE HEIGHTS OF HEAVEN-
-AND THE DEPTHS OF THE UNDERWORLD.
EVEN AT THE END OF ALL THAT IS, MY HAND IS THERE, HOLDING YOU FAST.
IT WAS I WHO FORMED YOUR INMOST BEING, I WHO KNIT YOU TOGETHER IN THE WOMB OF THAT ROCK. I MADE YOU WITH AWE AND WONDER, FOR WONDERFUL ARE ALL OF MY WORKS.

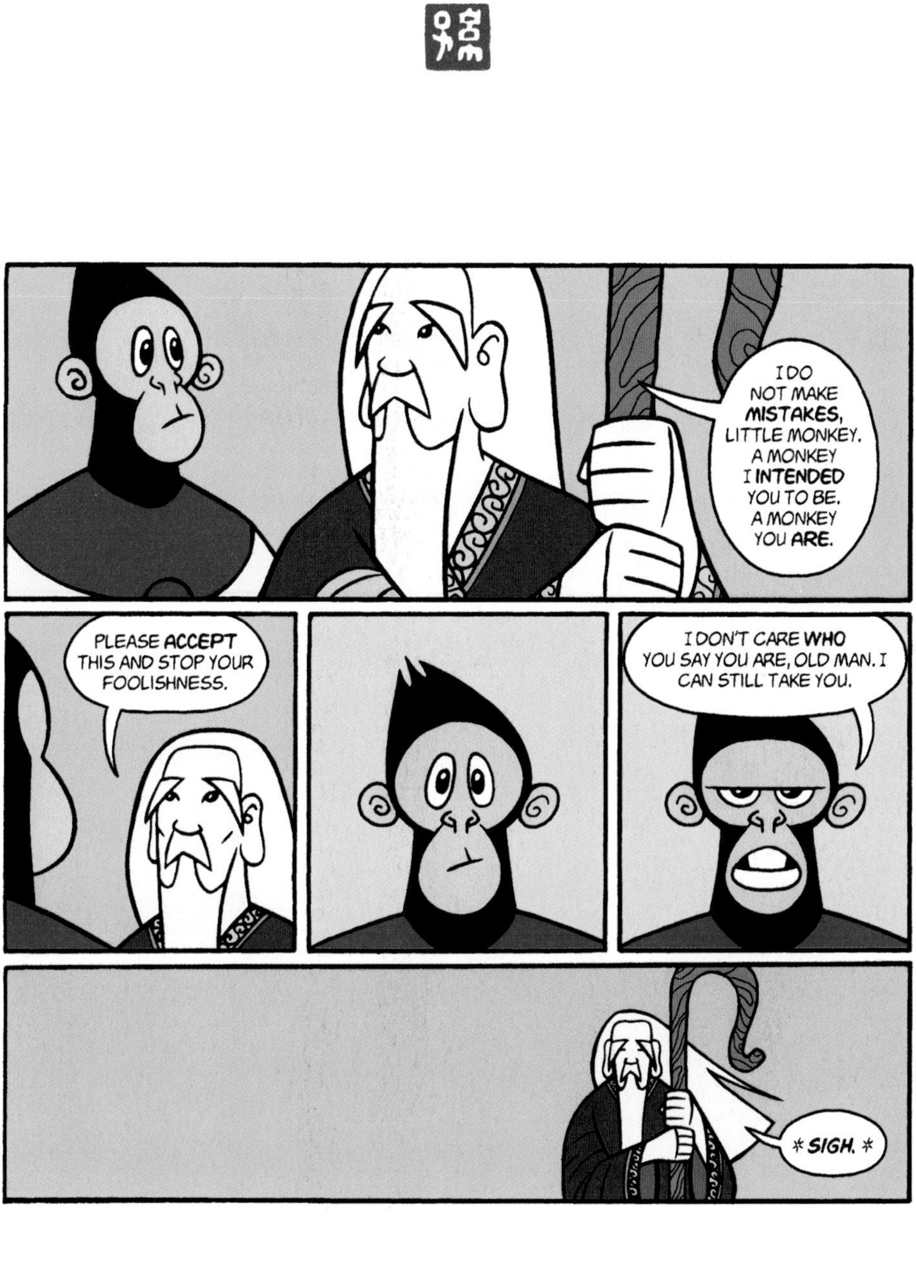
I DO NOT MAKE MISTAKES, LITTLE MONKEY. A MONKEY I INTENDED YOU TO BE. A MONKEY YOU ARE.
PLEASE ACCEPT THIS AND STOP YOUR FOOLISHNESS.
I DON'T CARE WHO YOU SAY YOU ARE, OLD MAN. I CAN STILL TAKE YOU.
* SIGH. *

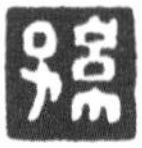

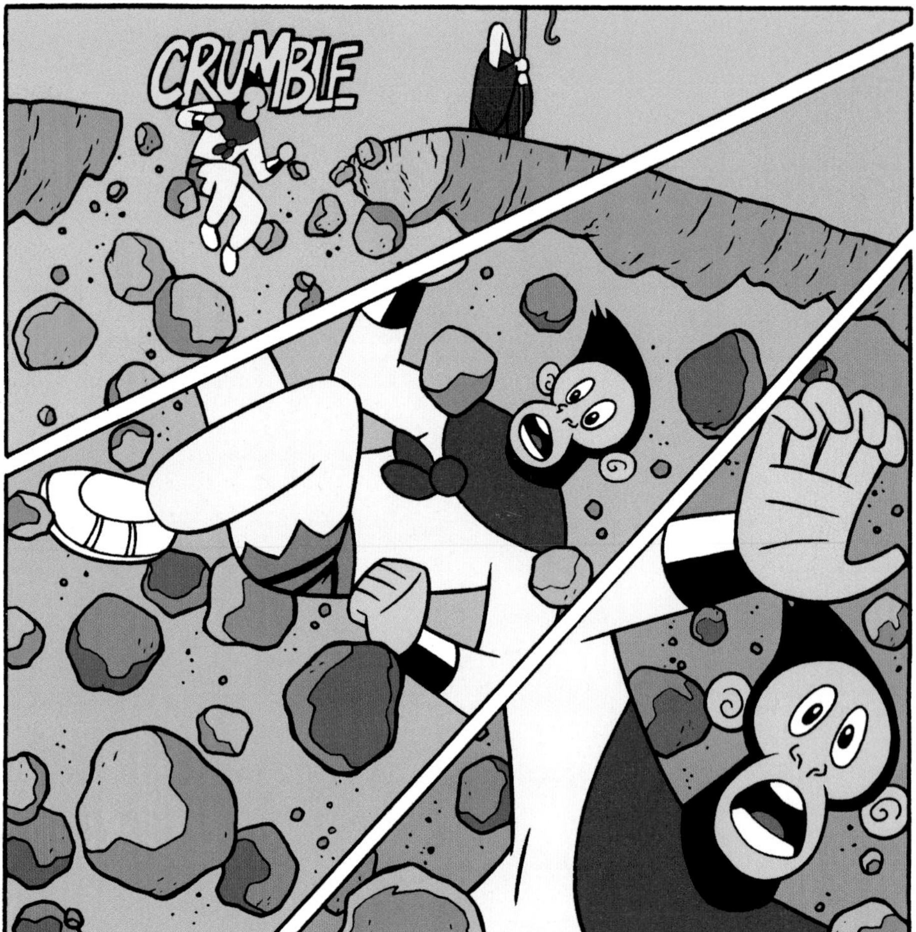
CRUMBLE

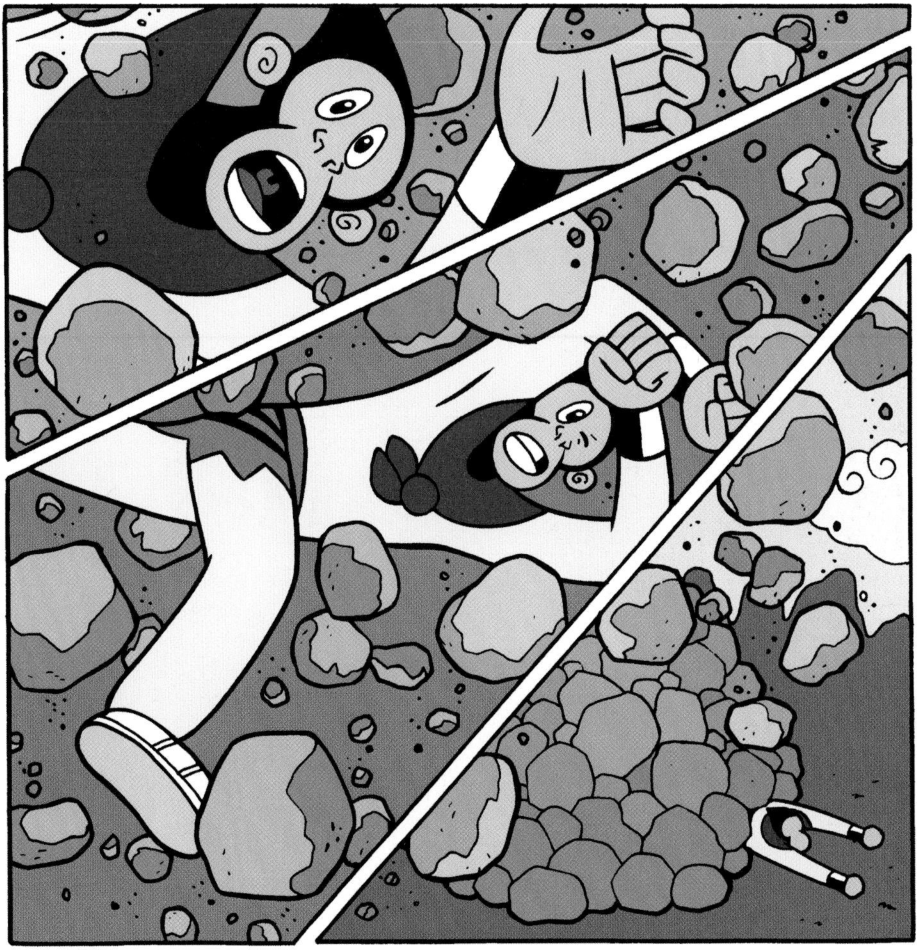

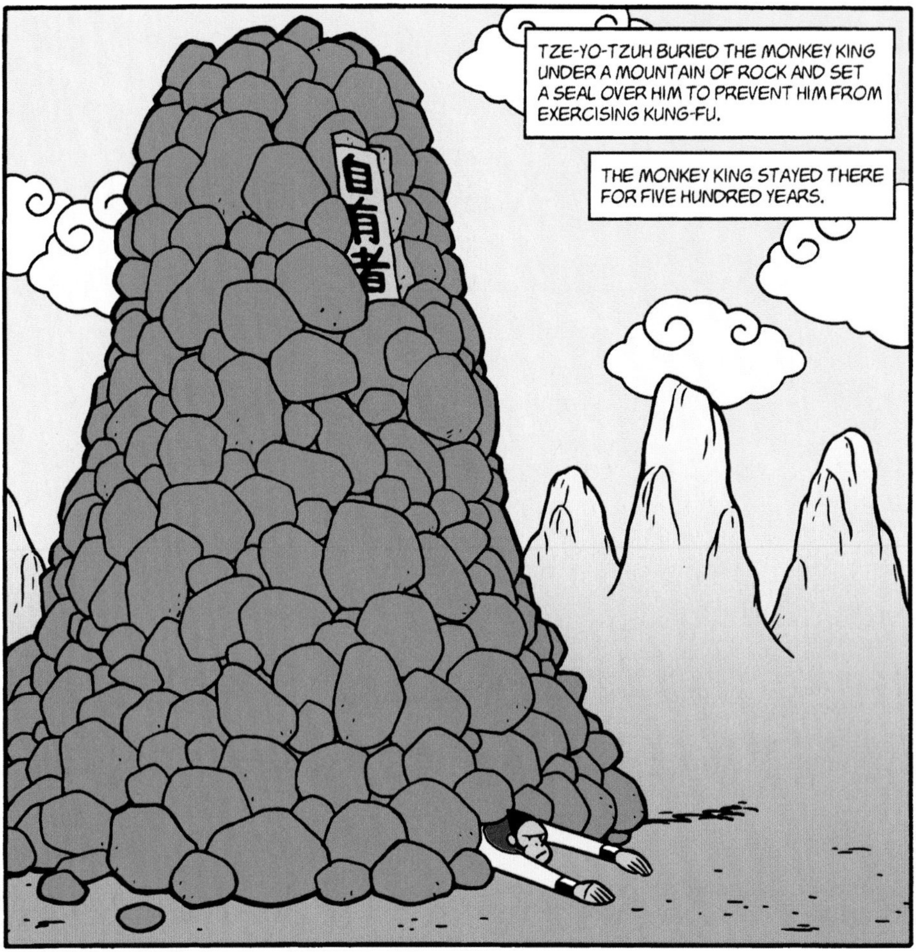
TZE-YO-TZUH BURIED THE MONKEY KING UNDER A MOUNTAIN OF ROCK AND SET A SEAL OVER HIM TO PREVENT HIM FROM EXERCISING KUNG-FU.
THE MONKEY KING STAYED THERE FOR FIVE HUNDRED YEARS.

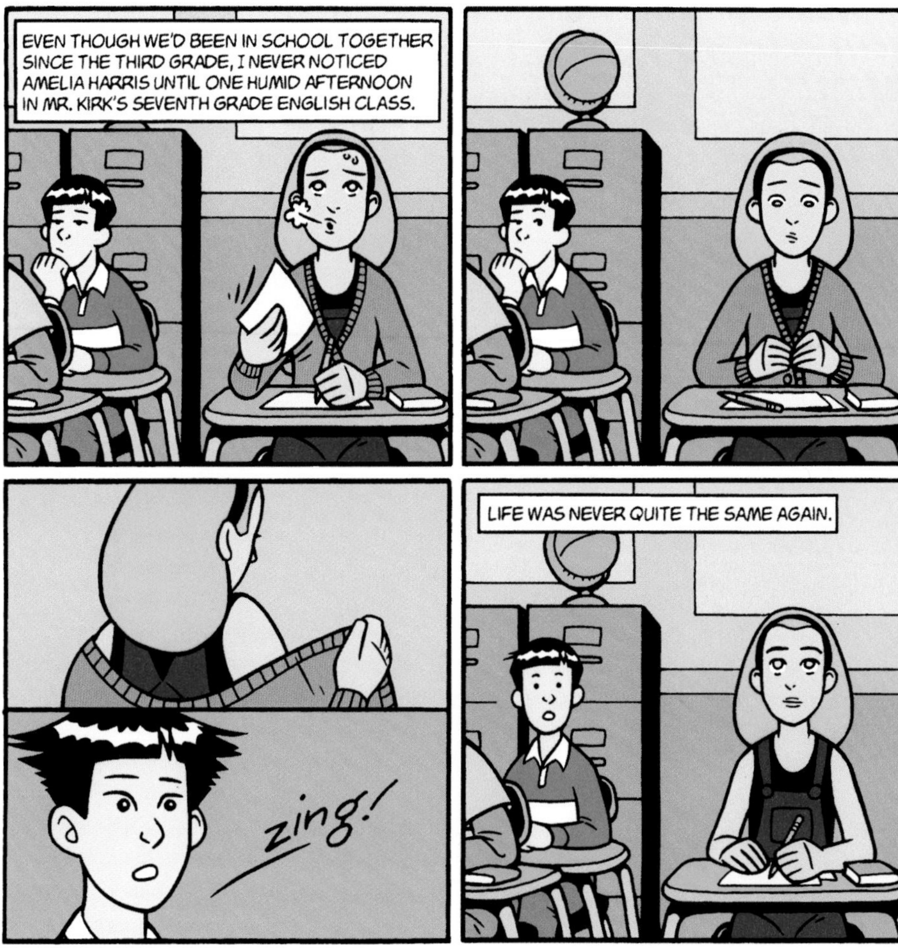
EVEN THOUGH WE'D BEEN IN SCHOOL TOGETHER SINCE THE THIRD GRADE, I NEVER NOTICED AMELIA HARRIS UNTIL ONE HUMID AFTERNOON IN MR. KIRK'S SEVENTH GRADE ENGLISH CLASS.
zing!
LIFE WAS NEVER QUITE THE SAME AGAIN.

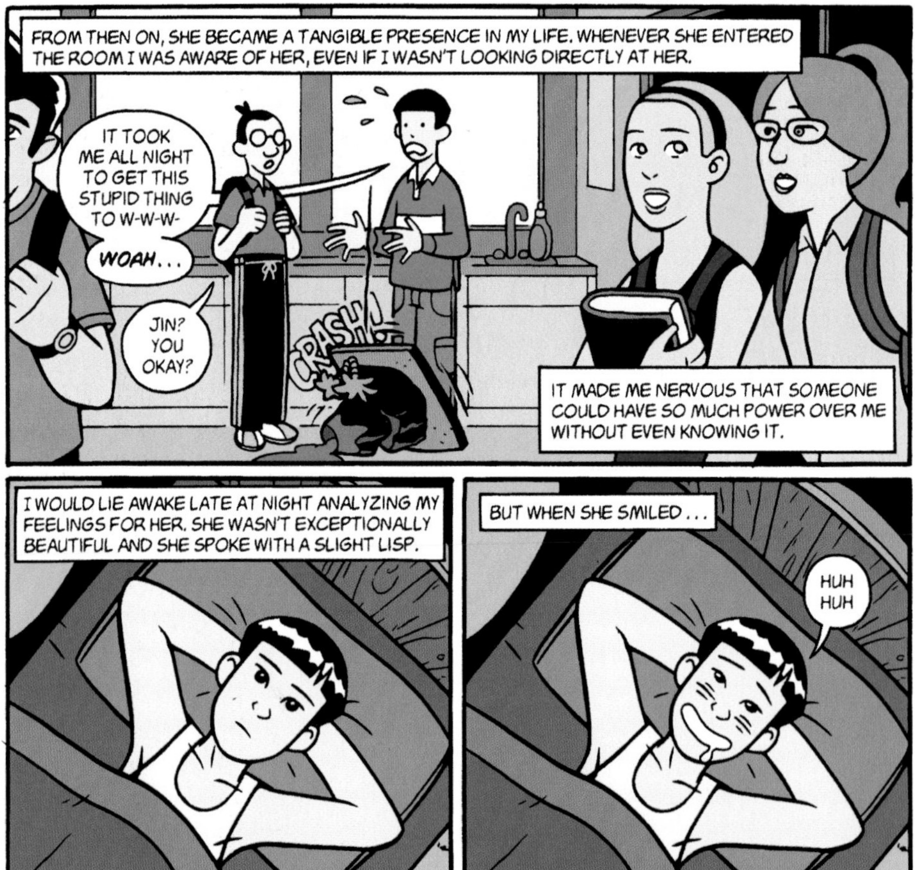
FROM THEN ON, SHE BECAME A TANGIBLE PRESENCE IN MY LIFE. WHENEVER SHE ENTERED THE ROOM I WAS AWARE OF HER, EVEN IF I WASN'T LOOKING DIRECTLY AT HER.
IT TOOK ME ALL NIGHT TO GET THIS STUPID THING TO W-W-W-
WOAH . . .
JIN? YOU OKAY?
CRASH!
IT MADE ME NERVOUS THAT SOMEONE COULD HAVE SO MUCH POWER OVER ME WITHOUT EVEN KNOWING IT.
I WOULD LIE AWAKE LATE AT NIGHT ANALYZING MY FEELINGS FOR HER. SHE WASN'T EXCEPTIONALLY BEAUTIFUL AND SHE SPOKE WITH A SLIGHT LISP.
I'D EVEN SEEN A FLAKE OR TWO OF DANDRUFF WHEN I GOT CLOSE ENOUGH.
BUT WHEN SHE SMILED . . .
HUH HUH

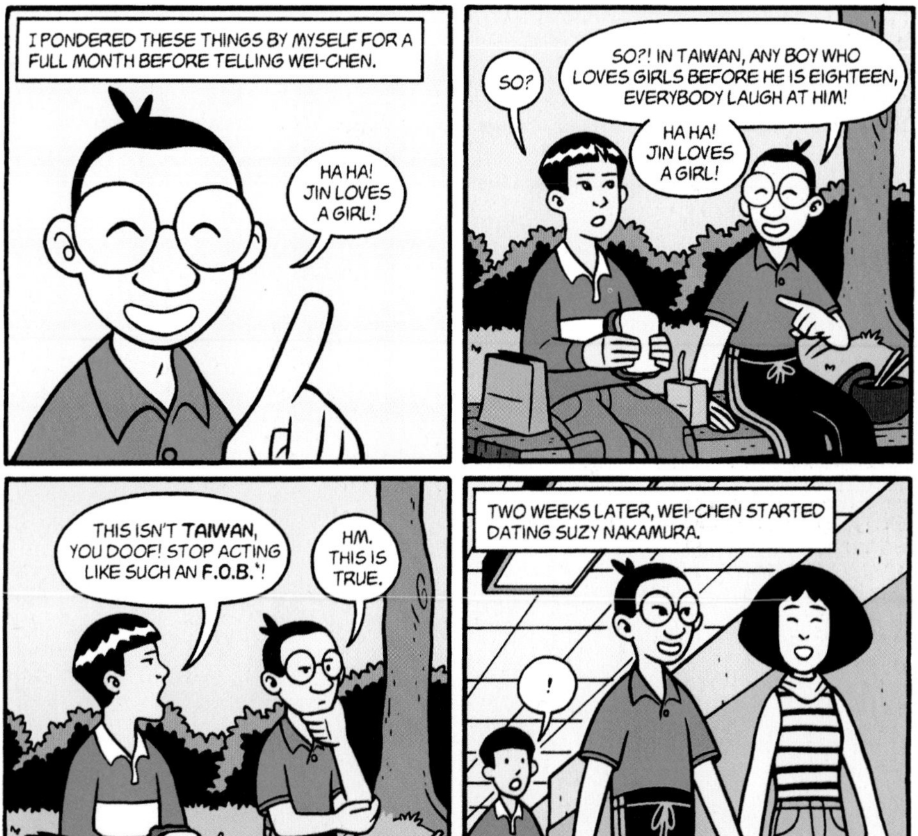
I PONDERED THESE THINGS BY MYSELF FOR A FULL MONTH BEFORE TELLING WEI-CHEN.
HA HA! JIN LOVES A GIRL!
SO?
SO?! IN TAIWAN, ANY BOY WHO LOVES GIRLS BEFORE HE IS EIGHTEEN, EVERYBODY LAUGH AT HIM!
HA HA! JIN LOVES A GIRL!
THIS ISN'T TAIWAN, YOU DOOF! STOP ACTING LIKE SUCH AN F.O.B.*!
HM. THIS IS TRUE.
* FRESH OFF THE BOAT
TWO WEEKS LATER, WEI-CHEN STARTED DATING SUZY NAKAMURA.
!

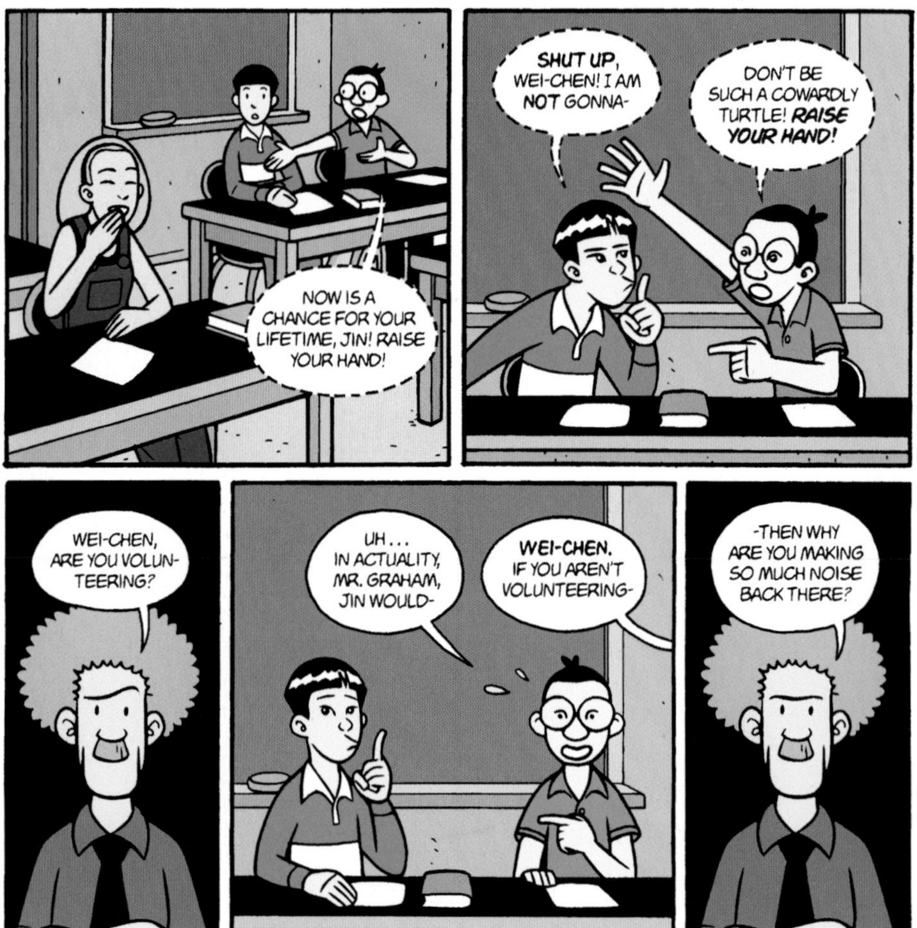
NOW IS A CHANCE FOR YOUR LIFETIME, JIN! RAISE YOUR HAND!
SHUT UP, WEI-CHEN! I AM NOT GONNA-
DON'T BE SUCH A COWARDLY TURTLE! RAISE YOUR HAND!
WEI-CHEN, ARE YOU VOLUNTEERING?
UH... IN ACTUALITY, MR. GRAHAM, JIN WOULD-
WEI-CHEN. IF YOU AREN'T VOLUNTEERING-
-THEN WHY ARE YOU MAKING SO MUCH NOISE BACK THERE?

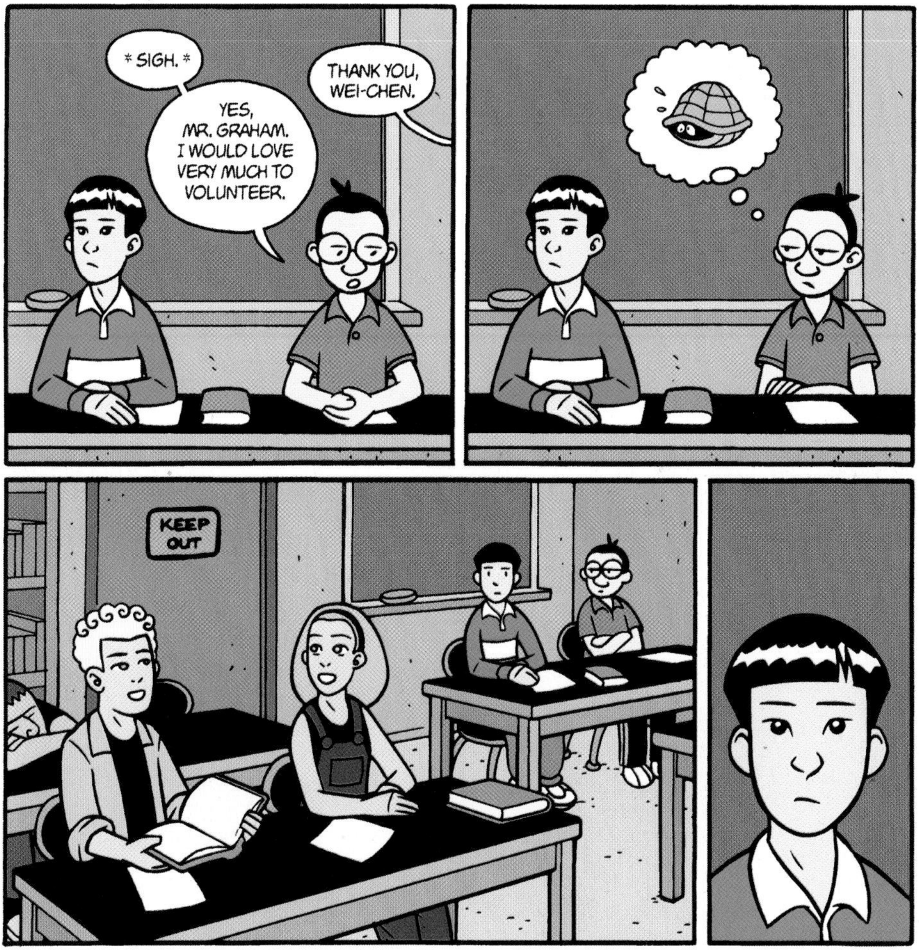
* SIGH. *
YES, MR. GRAHAM. I WOULD LOVE VERY MUCH TO VOLUNTEER.
THANK YOU, WEI-CHEN.
KEEP OUT

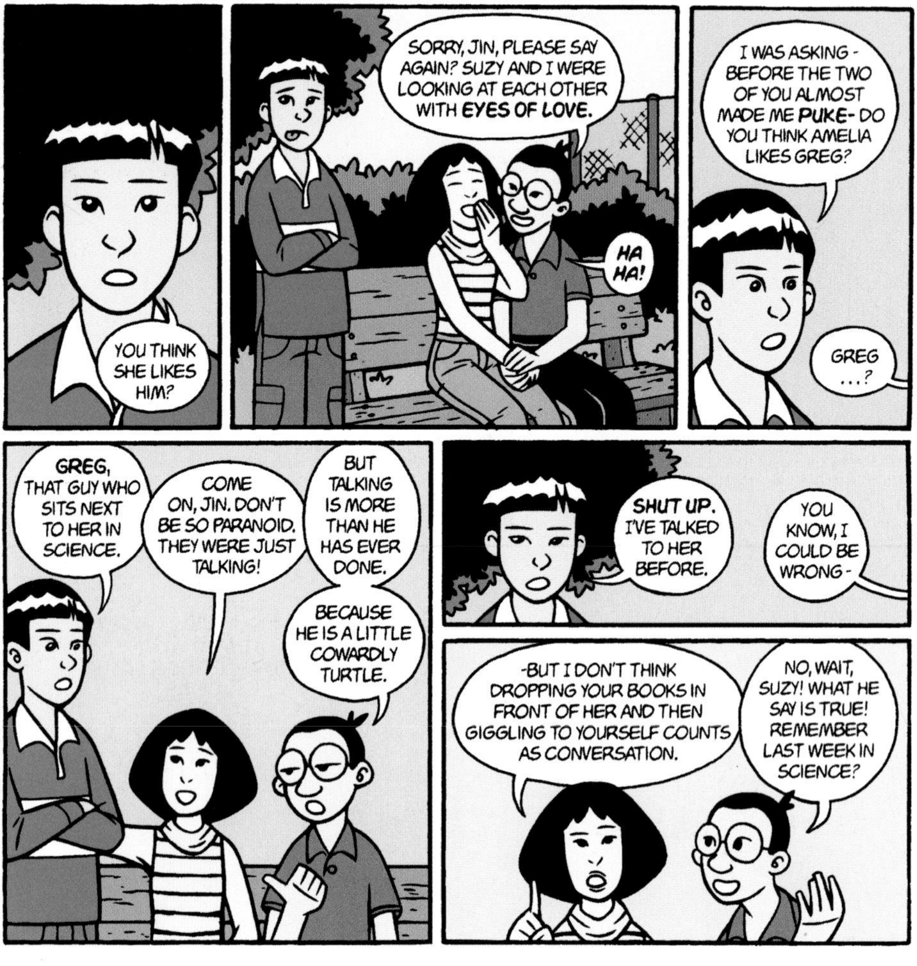
YOU THINK SHE LIKES HIM?
SORRY, JIN, PLEASE SAY AGAIN? SUZY AND I WERE LOOKING AT EACH OTHER WITH EYES OF LOVE.
HA HA!
I WAS ASKING - BEFORE THE TWO OF YOU ALMOST MADE ME PUKE- DO YOU THINK AMELIA LIKES GREG?
GREG ...?
GREG, THAT GUY WHO SITS NEXT TO HER IN SCIENCE.
COME ON, JIN. DON'T BE SO PARANOID. THEY WERE JUST TALKING!
BUT TALKING IS MORE THAN HE HAS EVER DONE.
BECAUSE HE IS A LITTLE COWARDLY TURTLE.
SHUT UP. I'VE TALKED TO HER BEFORE.
YOU KNOW, I COULD BE WRONG -
-BUT I DON'T THINK DROPPING YOUR BOOKS IN FRONT OF HER AND THEN GIGGLING TO YOURSELF COUNTS AS CONVERSATION.
NO, WAIT, SUZY! WHAT HE SAY IS TRUE! REMEMBER LAST WEEK IN SCIENCE?

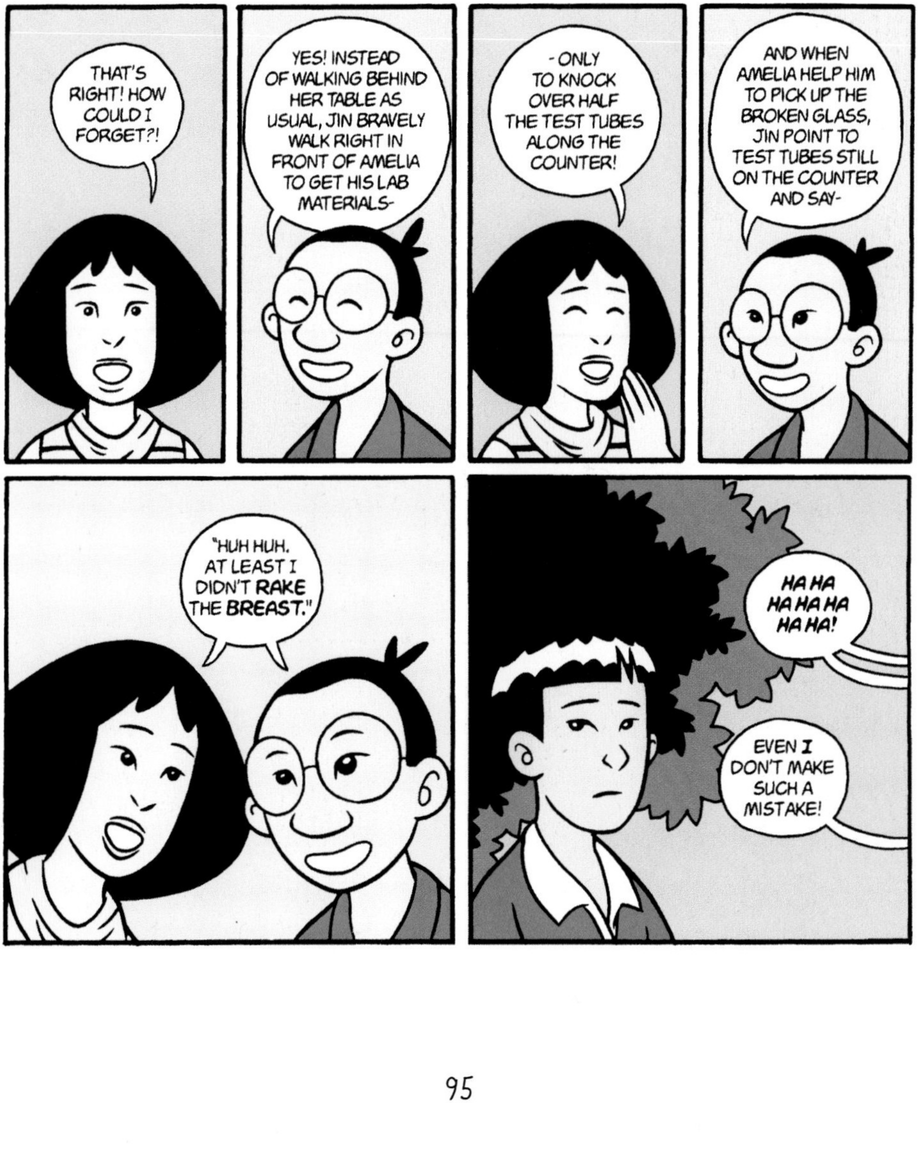
THAT'S RIGHT! HOW COULD I FORGET?!
YES! INSTEAD OF WALKING BEHIND HER TABLE AS USUAL, JIN BRAVELY WALK RIGHT IN FRONT OF AMELIA TO GET HIS LAB MATERIALS-
-ONLY TO KNOCK OVER HALF THE TEST TUBES ALONG THE COUNTER!
AND WHEN AMELIA HELP HIM TO PICK UP THE BROKEN GLASS, JIN POINT TO TEST TUBES STILL ON THE COUNTER AND SAY-
"HUH HUH. AT LEAST I DIDN'T RAKE THE BREAST."
HA HA HA HA HA HA HA!
EVEN I DON'T MAKE SUCH A MISTAKE!

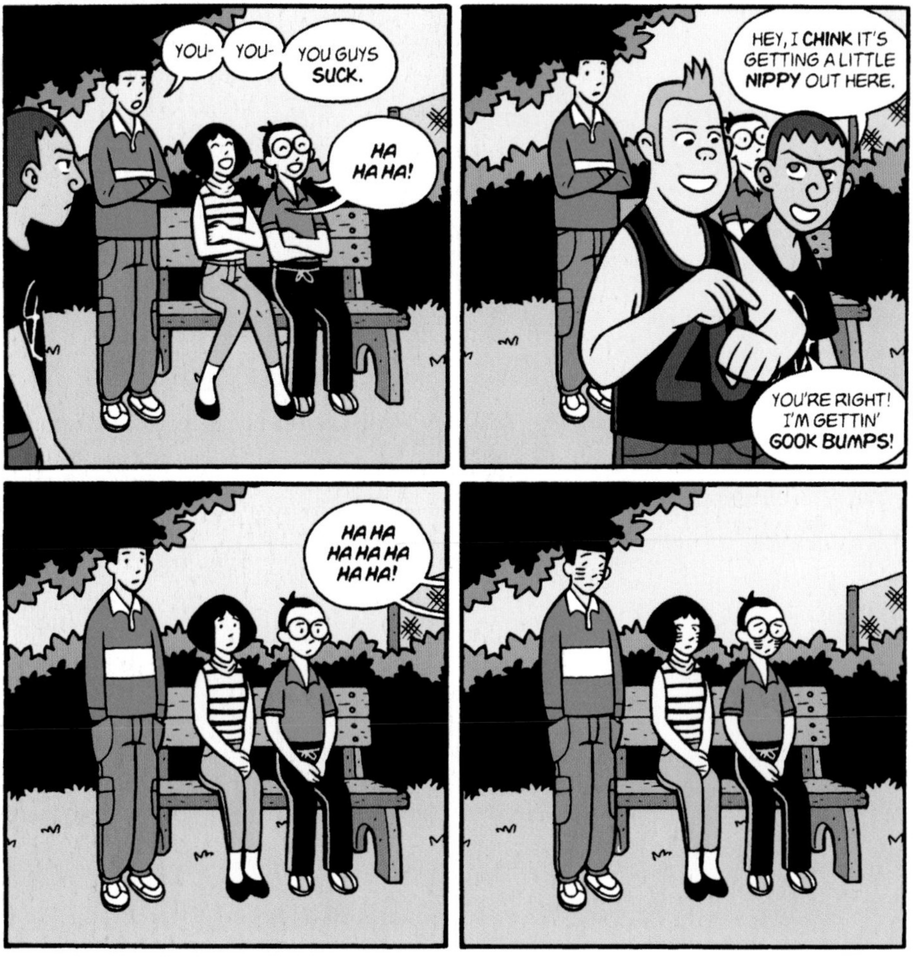
YOU-
YOU-
YOU GUYS **SUCK.**
HA HA HA!
HEY, I **CHINK** IT'S GETTING A LITTLE **NIPPY** OUT HERE.
YOU'RE RIGHT! I'M GETTIN' **GOOK BUMPS!**
HA HA HA HA HA HA HA!

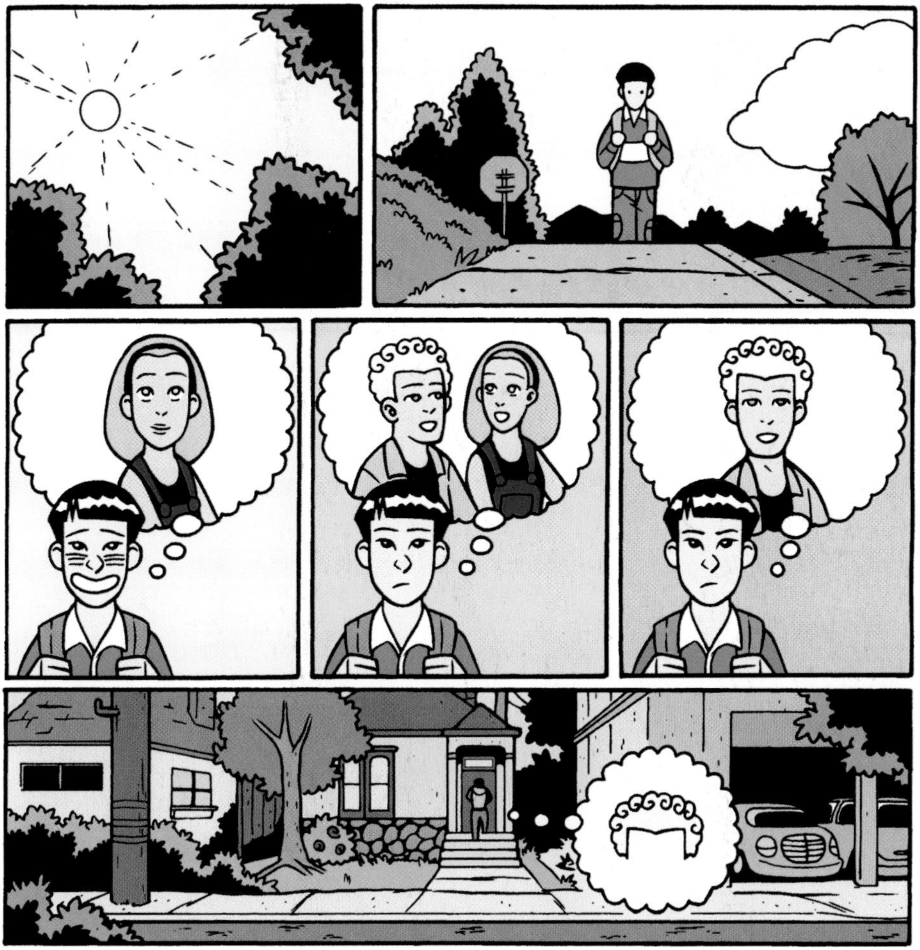

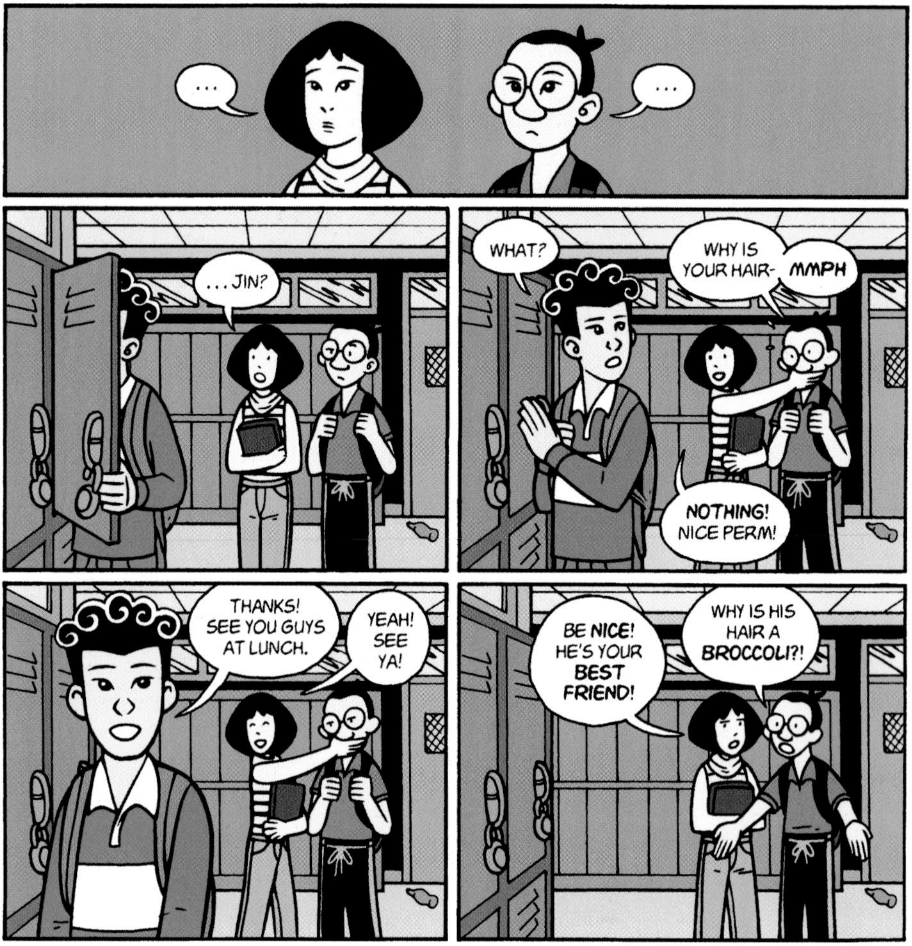
...
...
...JIN?
WHAT?
WHY IS YOUR HAIR- MMPH
NOTHING! NICE PERM!
THANKS! SEE YOU GUYS AT LUNCH.
YEAH! SEE YA!
BE NICE! HE'S YOUR BEST FRIEND!
WHY IS HIS HAIR A BROCCOLI?!

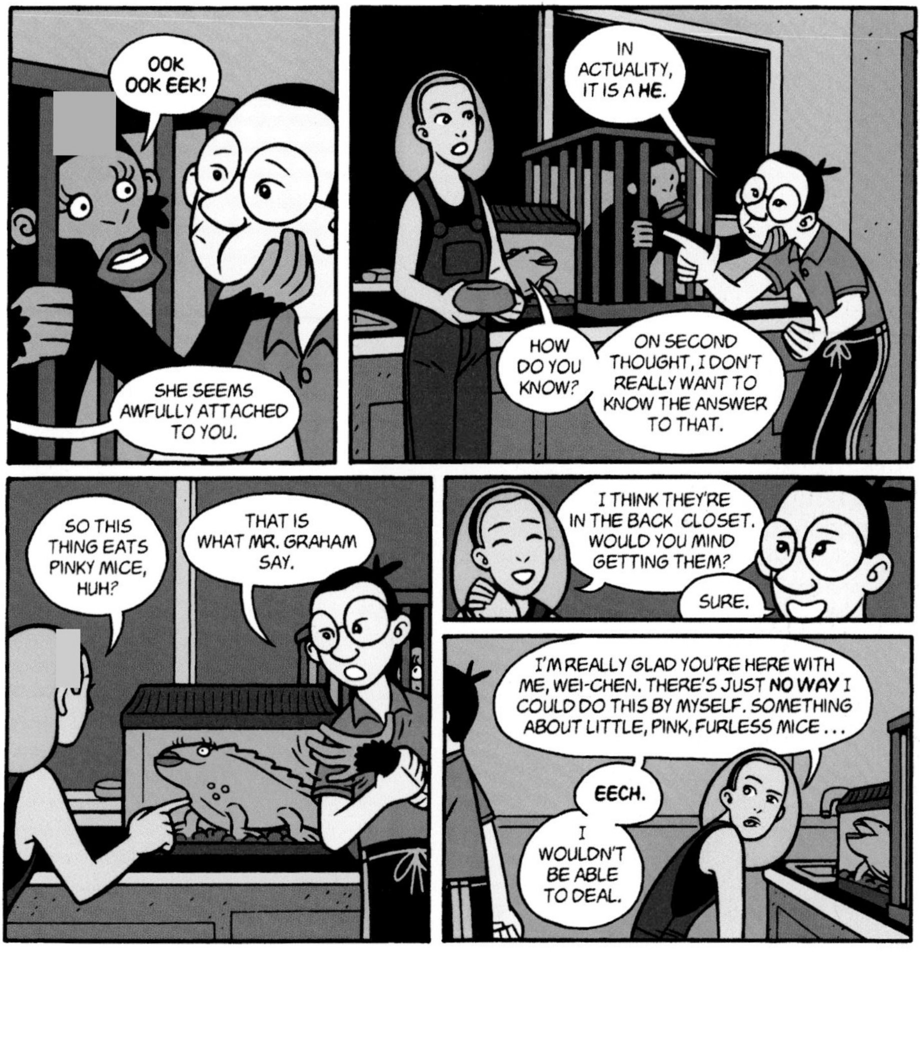
OOK OOK EEK!
SHE SEEMS AWFULLY ATTACHED TO YOU.
IN ACTUALITY, IT IS A **HE**.
HOW DO YOU KNOW?
ON SECOND THOUGHT, I DON'T REALLY WANT TO KNOW THE ANSWER TO THAT.
SO THIS THING EATS PINKY MICE, HUH?
THAT IS WHAT MR. GRAHAM SAY.
I THINK THEY'RE IN THE BACK CLOSET. WOULD YOU MIND GETTING THEM?
SURE.
I'M REALLY GLAD YOU'RE HERE WITH ME, WEI-CHEN. THERE'S JUST **NO WAY** I COULD DO THIS BY MYSELF. SOMETHING ABOUT LITTLE, PINK, FURLESS MICE . . .
EECH.
I WOULDN'T BE ABLE TO DEAL.

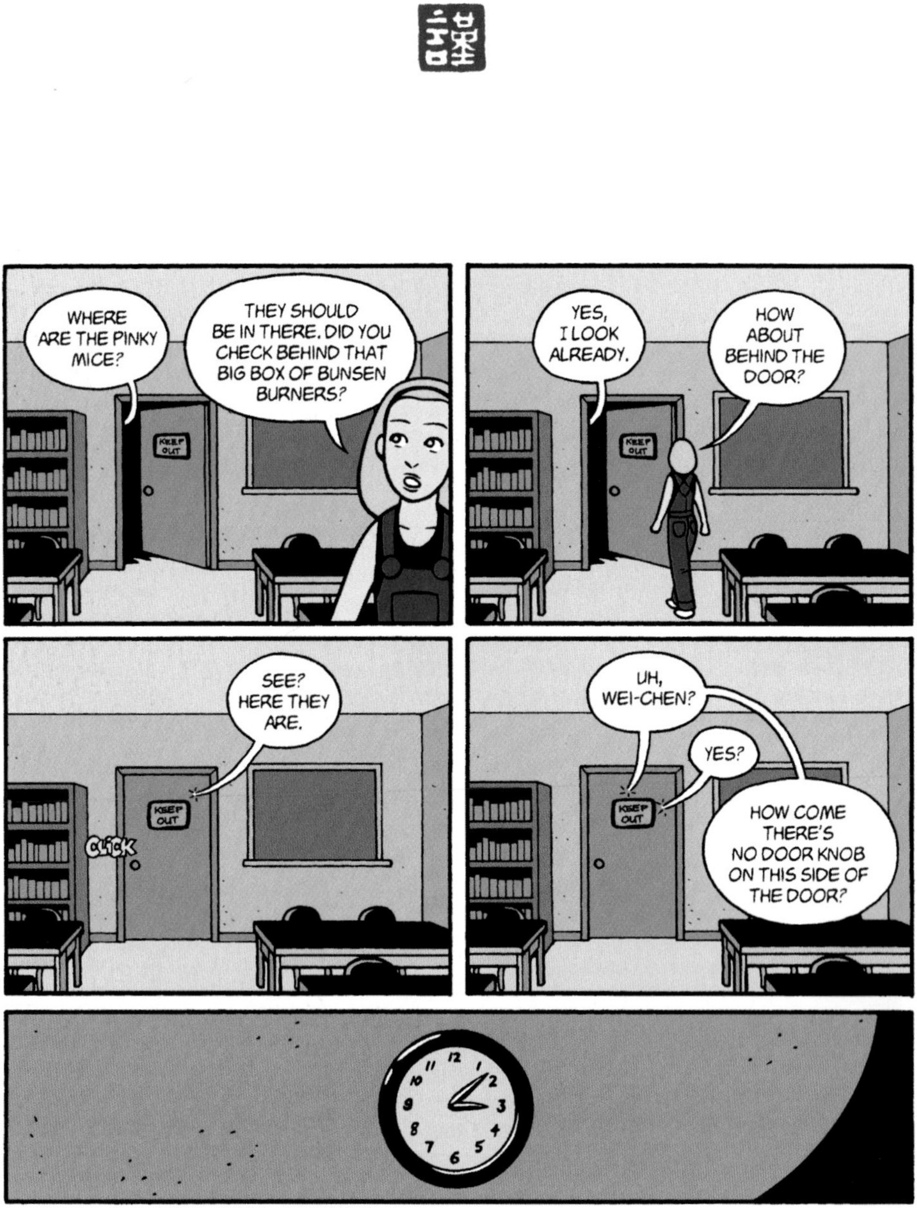
WHERE ARE THE PINKY MICE?
THEY SHOULD BE IN THERE. DID YOU CHECK BEHIND THAT BIG BOX OF BUNSEN BURNERS?
KEEP OUT
YES, I LOOK ALREADY.
HOW ABOUT BEHIND THE DOOR?
SEE? HERE THEY ARE.
CLICK
UH, WEI-CHEN?
YES?
HOW COME THERE'S NO DOOR KNOB ON THIS SIDE OF THE DOOR?

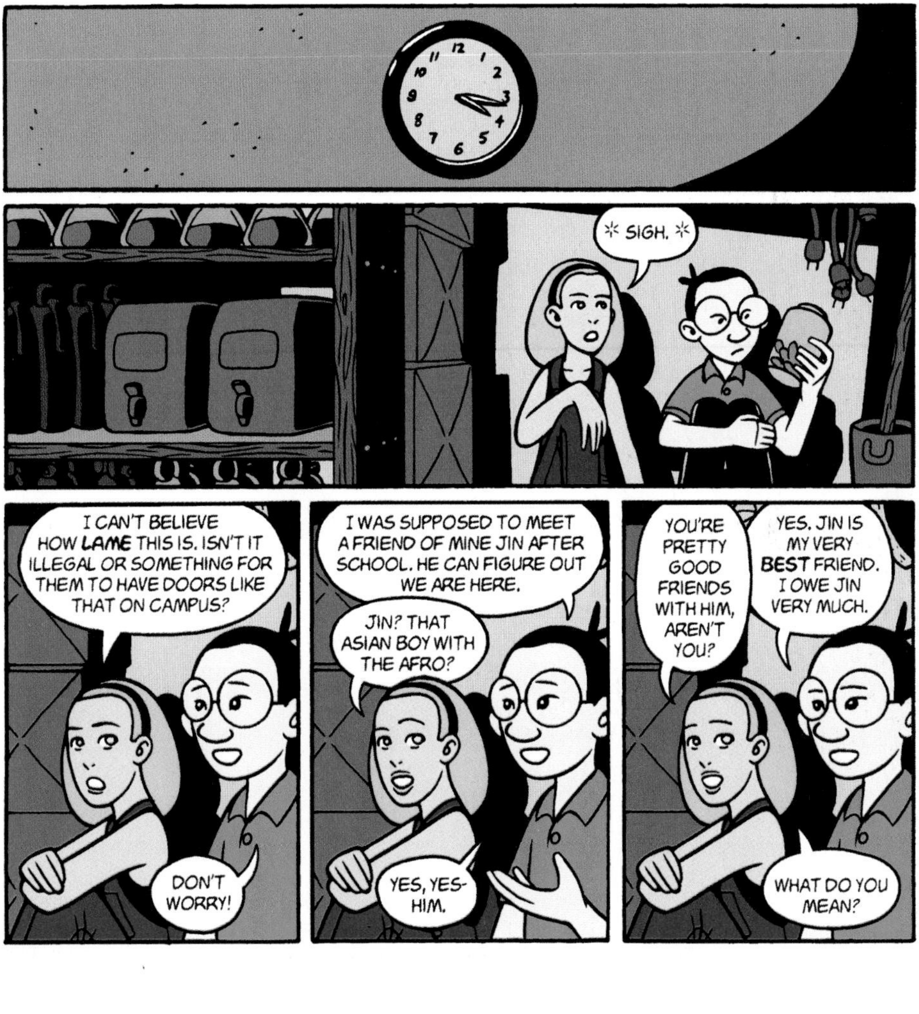
* SIGH. *
I CAN'T BELIEVE HOW **LAME** THIS IS. ISN'T IT ILLEGAL OR SOMETHING FOR THEM TO HAVE DOORS LIKE THAT ON CAMPUS?
DON'T WORRY!
I WAS SUPPOSED TO MEET A FRIEND OF MINE JIN AFTER SCHOOL. HE CAN FIGURE OUT WE ARE HERE.
JIN? THAT ASIAN BOY WITH THE AFRO?
YES, YES- HIM.
YOU'RE PRETTY GOOD FRIENDS WITH HIM, AREN'T YOU?
YES. JIN IS MY VERY **BEST** FRIEND. I OWE JIN VERY MUCH.
WHAT DO YOU MEAN?

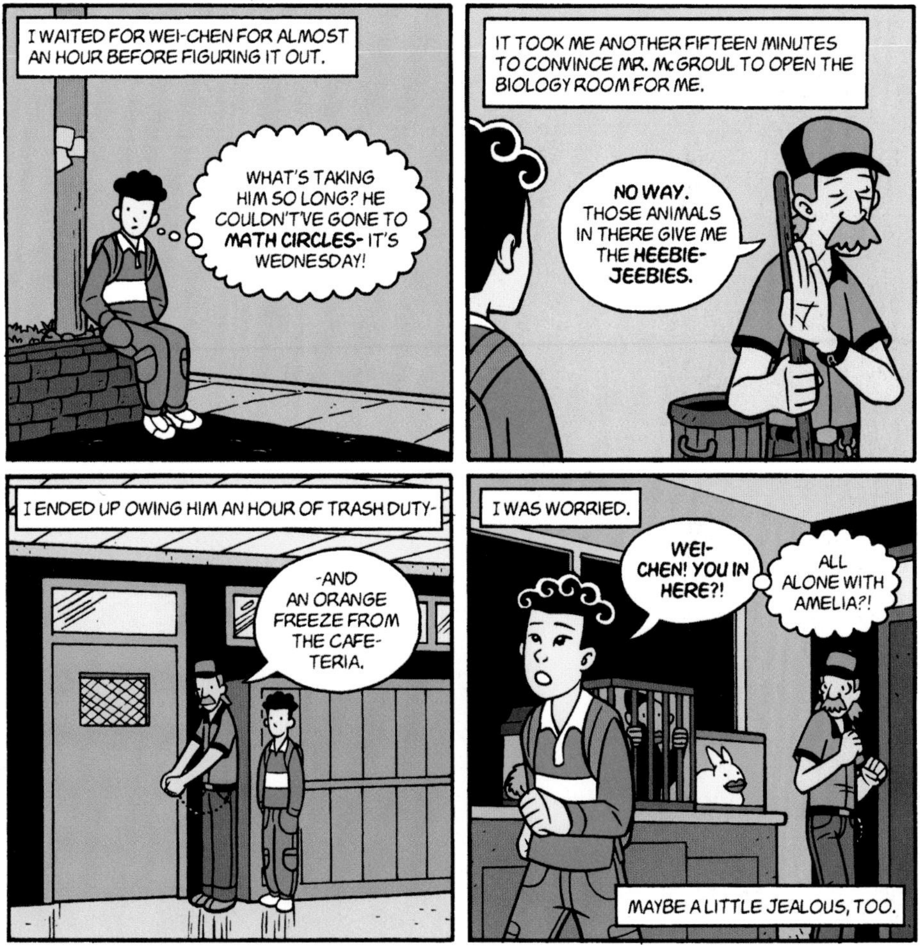
I WAITED FOR WEI-CHEN FOR ALMOST AN HOUR BEFORE FIGURING IT OUT.
WHAT'S TAKING HIM SO LONG? HE COULDN'T'VE GONE TO MATH CIRCLES- IT'S WEDNESDAY!
IT TOOK ME ANOTHER FIFTEEN MINUTES TO CONVINCE MR. McGROUL TO OPEN THE BIOLOGY ROOM FOR ME.
NO WAY. THOSE ANIMALS IN THERE GIVE ME THE HEEBIE-JEEBIES.
I ENDED UP OWING HIM AN HOUR OF TRASH DUTY-
-AND AN ORANGE FREEZE FROM THE CAFETERIA.
I WAS WORRIED.
WEI-CHEN! YOU IN HERE?!
ALL ALONE WITH AMELIA?!
MAYBE A LITTLE JEALOUS, TOO.

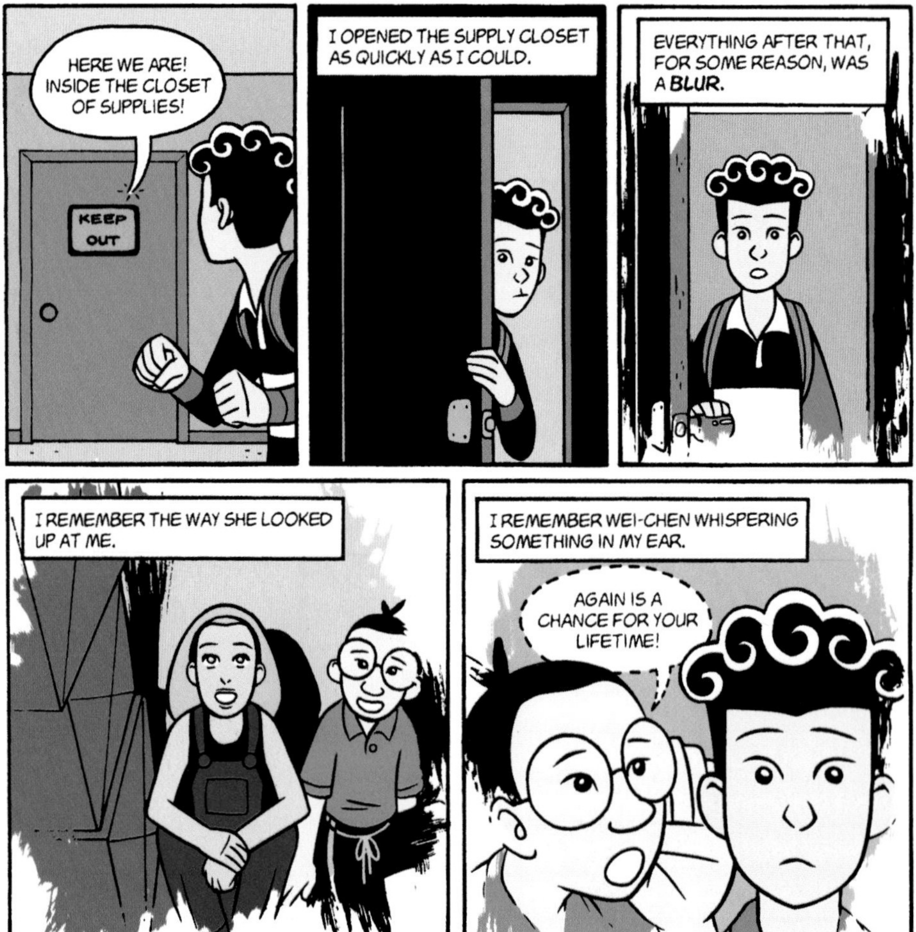
HERE WE ARE! INSIDE THE CLOSET OF SUPPLIES!
KEEP OUT
I OPENED THE SUPPLY CLOSET AS QUICKLY AS I COULD.
EVERYTHING AFTER THAT, FOR SOME REASON, WAS A **BLUR**.
I REMEMBER THE WAY SHE LOOKED UP AT ME.
I REMEMBER WEI-CHEN WHISPERING SOMETHING IN MY EAR.
AGAIN IS A CHANCE FOR YOUR LIFETIME!

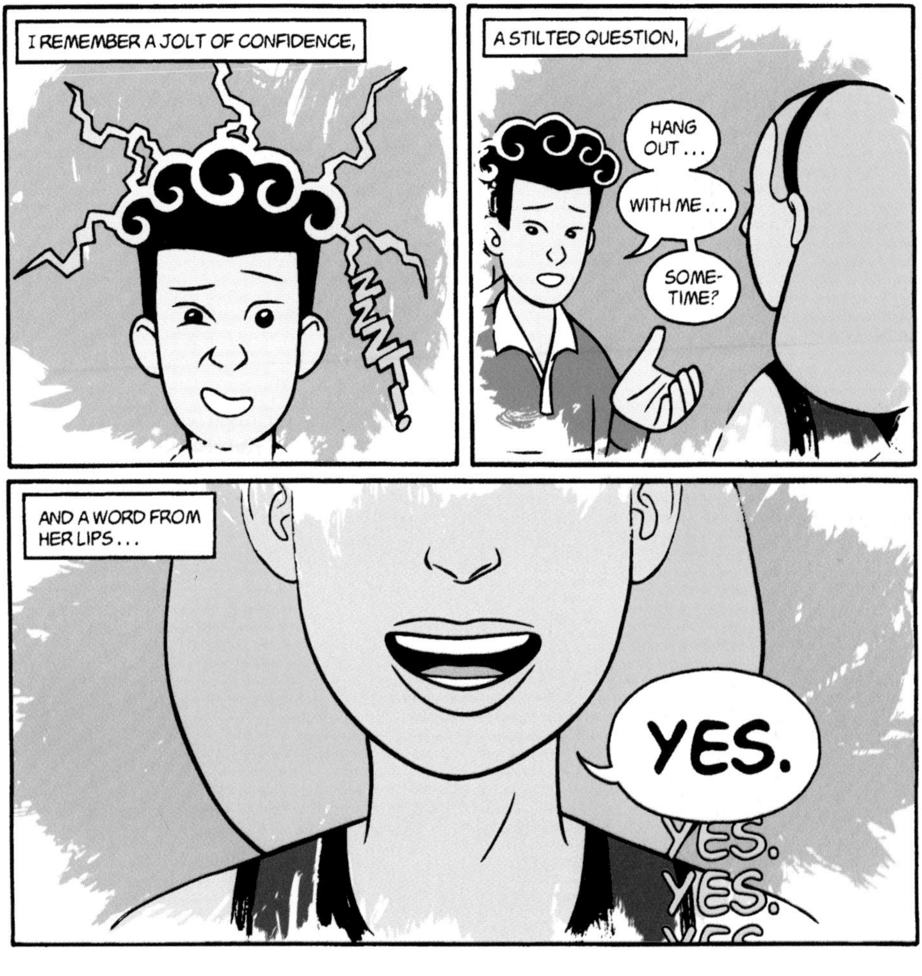
I REMEMBER A JOLT OF CONFIDENCE,
ZZZT!
A STILTED QUESTION,
HANG OUT . . .
WITH ME . . .
SOME-TIME?
AND A WORD FROM HER LIPS . . .
YES.
YES.
YES.

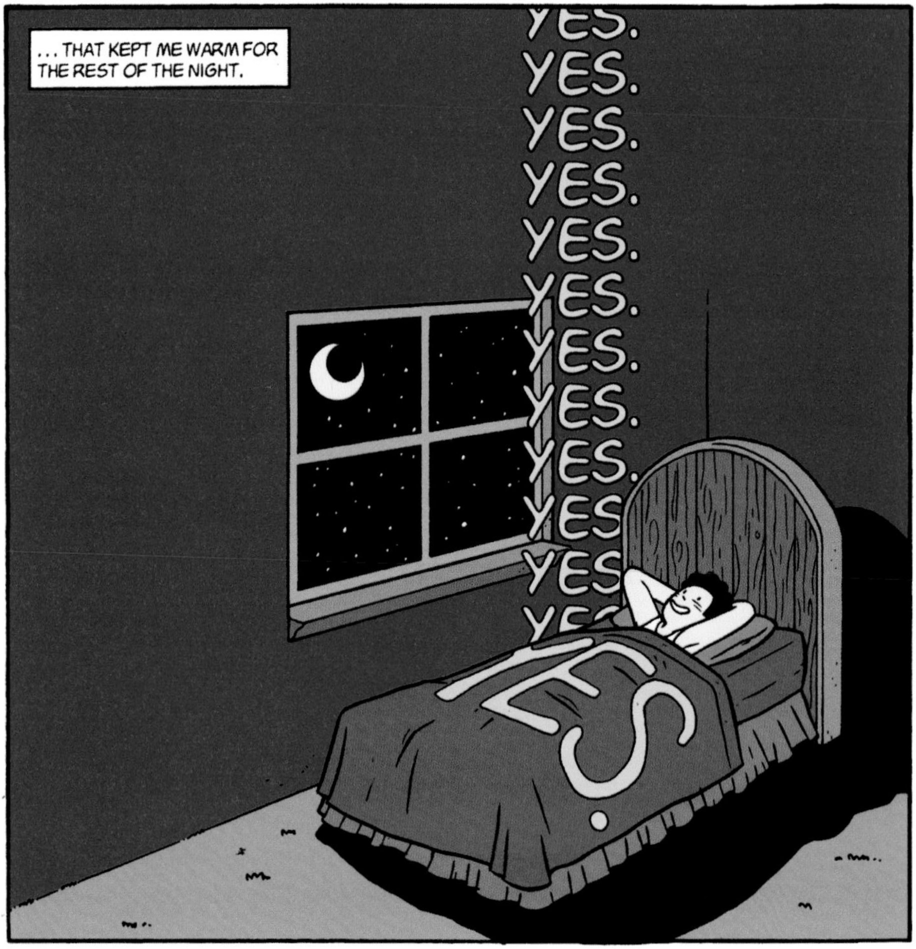
...THAT KEPT ME WARM FOR THE REST OF THE NIGHT.
YES.
YES.
YES.
YES.
YES.
YES.
YES.
YES.
YES.
YES.
YES.

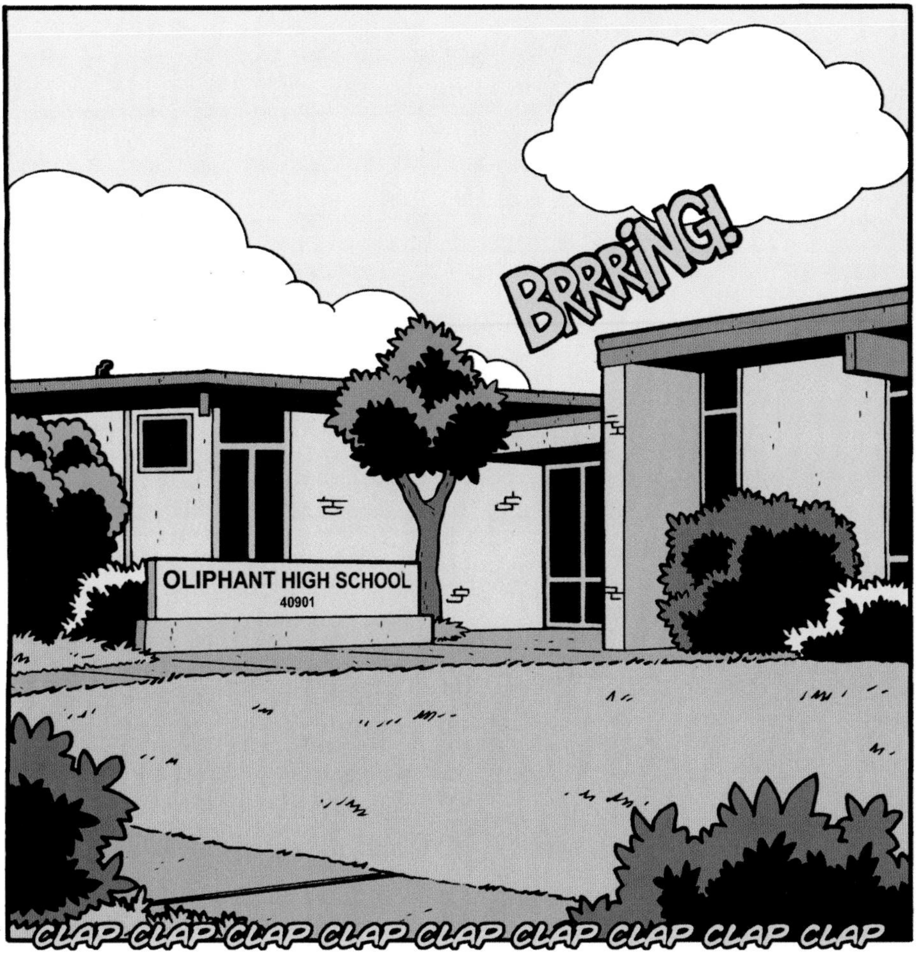
BRRRING!
OLIPHANT HIGH SCHOOL
40901
CLAP CLAP CLAP CLAP CLAP CLAP CLAP CLAP CLAP

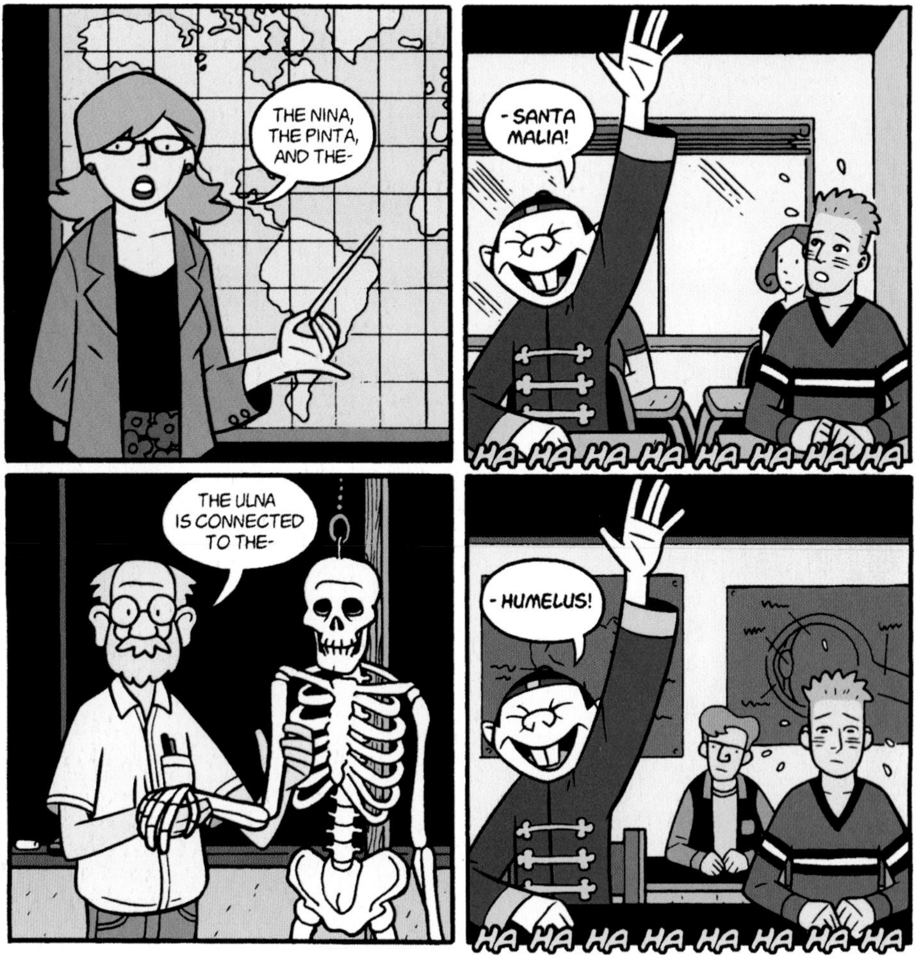
THE NINA, THE PINTA, AND THE-
- SANTA MALIA!
HA HA HA HA HA HA HA HA
THE ULNA IS CONNECTED TO THE-
- HUMELUS!
HA HA HA HA HA HA HA HA

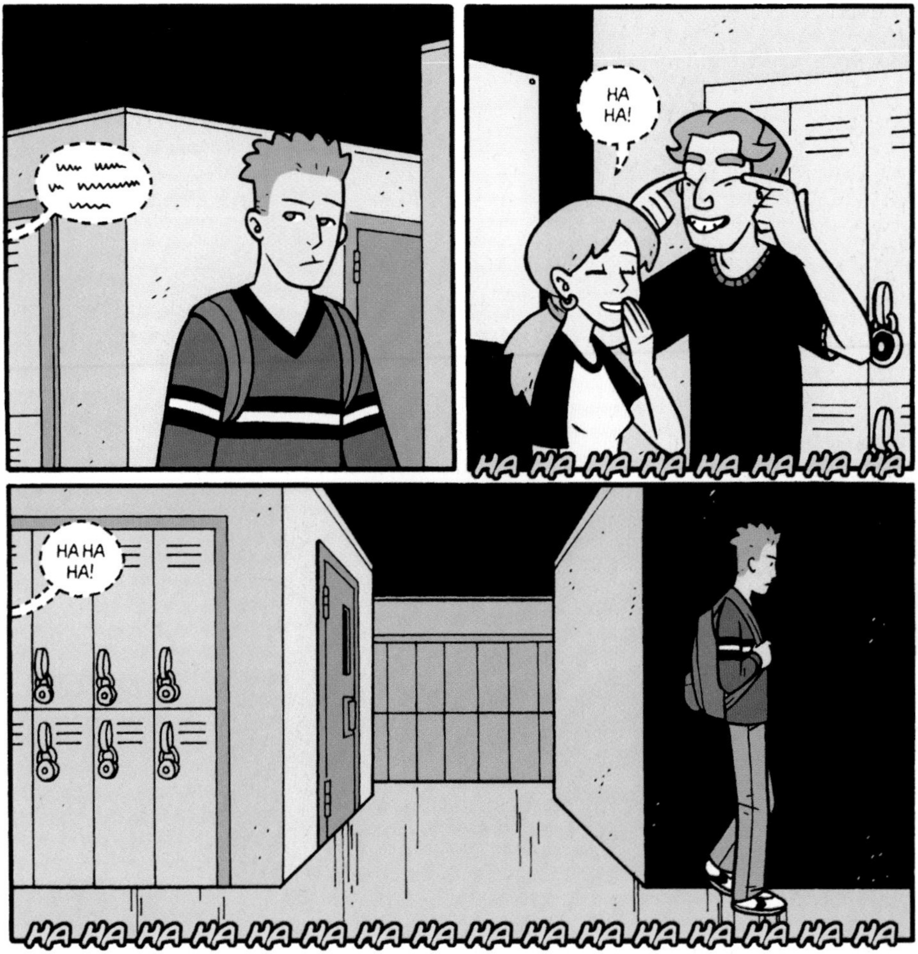
HA HA!
HA HA HA HA HA HA HA HA
HA HA HA!
HA HA HA HA HA HA HA HA HA HA HA HA HA HA HA HA

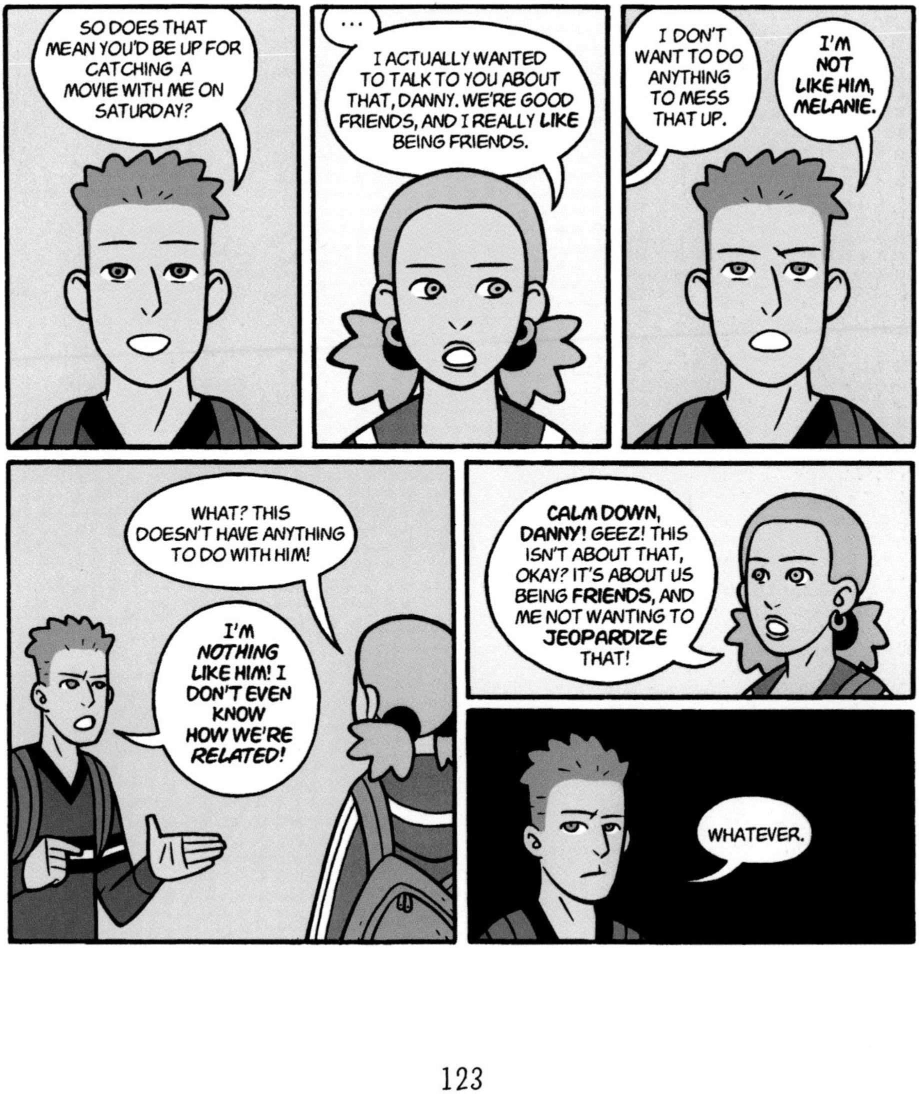
SO DOES THAT MEAN YOU'D BE UP FOR CATCHING A MOVIE WITH ME ON SATURDAY?
...
I ACTUALLY WANTED TO TALK TO YOU ABOUT THAT, DANNY. WE'RE GOOD FRIENDS, AND I REALLY LIKE BEING FRIENDS.
I DON'T WANT TO DO ANYTHING TO MESS THAT UP.
I'M NOT LIKE HIM, MELANIE.
WHAT? THIS DOESN'T HAVE ANYTHING TO DO WITH HIM!
I'M NOTHING LIKE HIM! I DON'T EVEN KNOW HOW WE'RE RELATED!
CALM DOWN, DANNY! GEEZ! THIS ISN'T ABOUT THAT, OKAY? IT'S ABOUT US BEING FRIENDS, AND ME NOT WANTING TO JEOPARDIZE THAT!
WHATEVER.

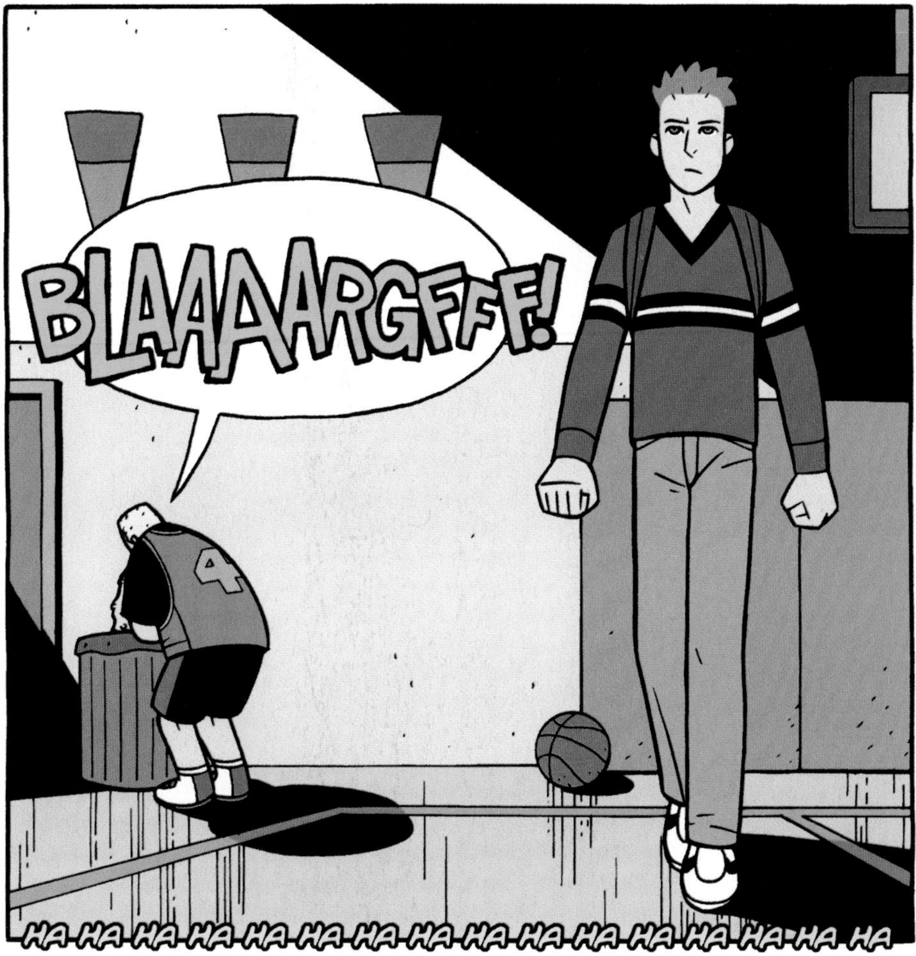
BLAAAARGFFF!
HA HA HA HA HA HA HA HA HA HA HA HA HA HA HA HA

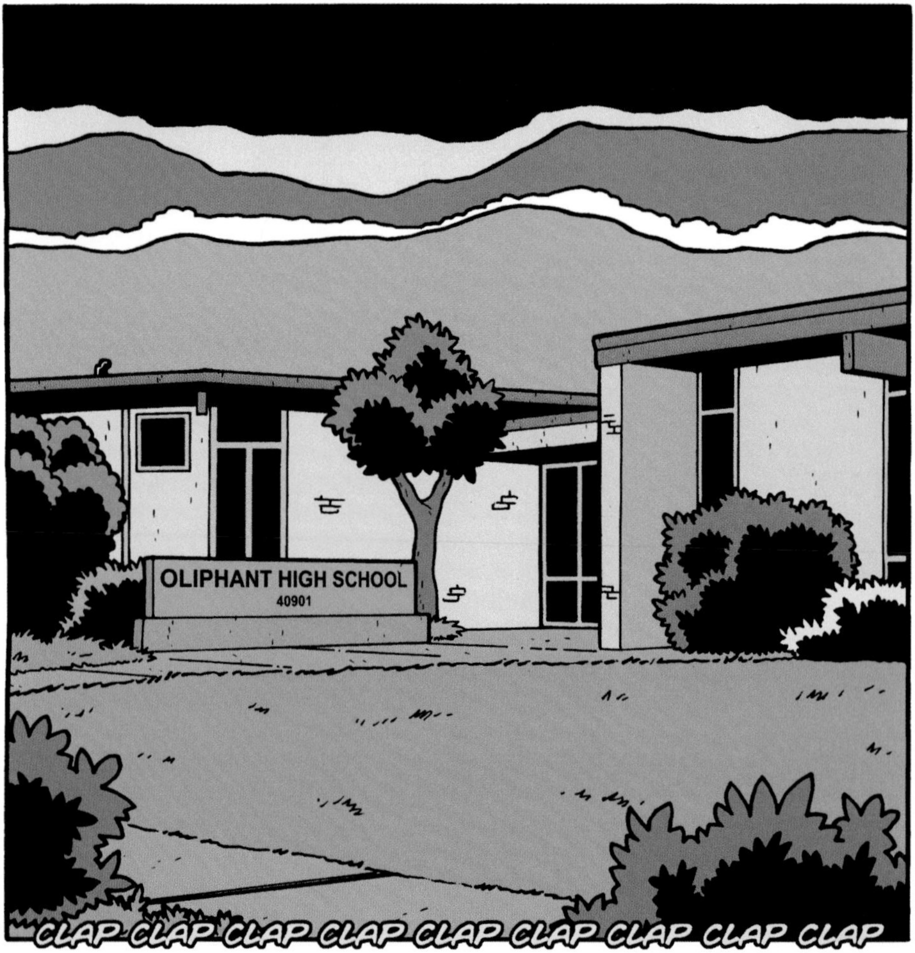
OLIPHANT HIGH SCHOOL
40901
CLAP CLAP CLAP CLAP CLAP CLAP CLAP CLAP CLAP

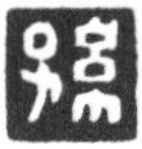

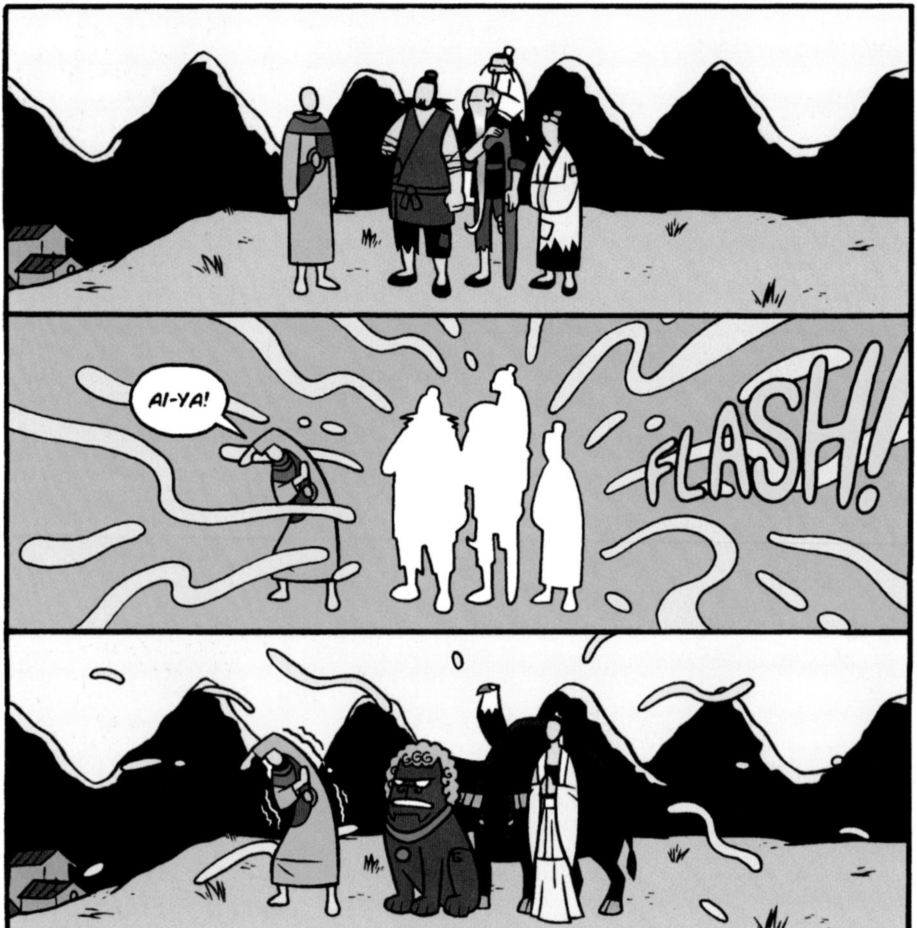
AI-YA!
FLASH!

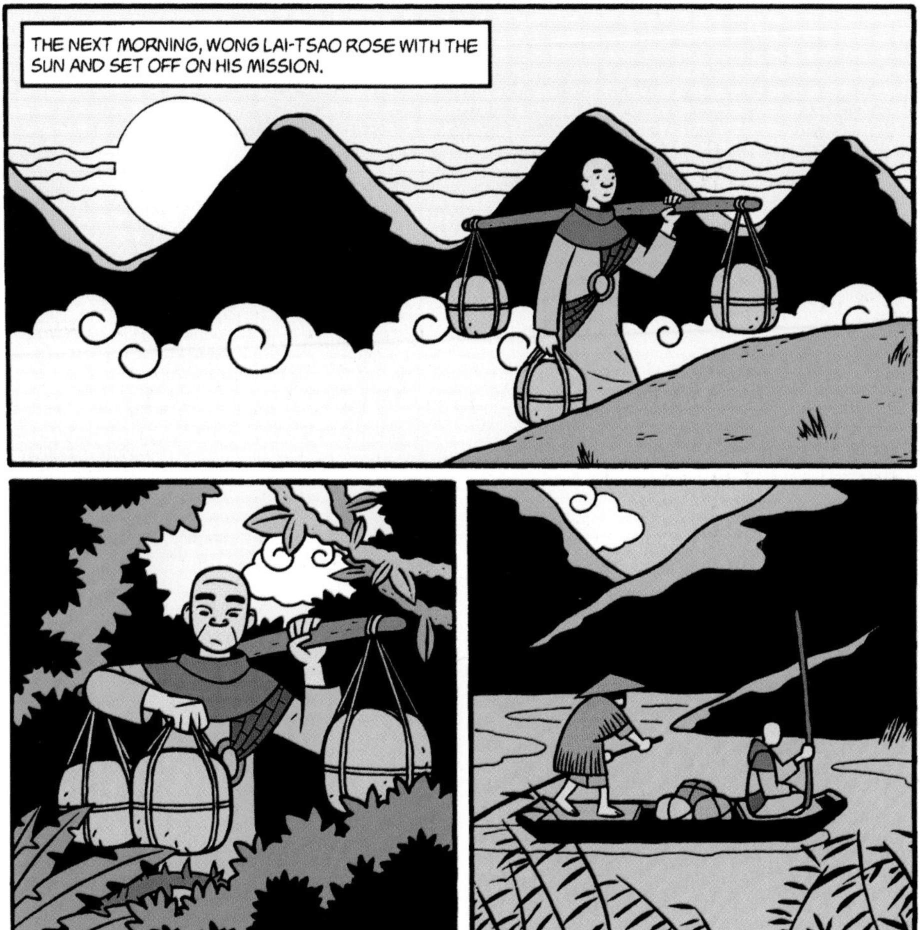
THE NEXT MORNING, WONG LAI-TSAO ROSE WITH THE SUN AND SET OFF ON HIS MISSION.

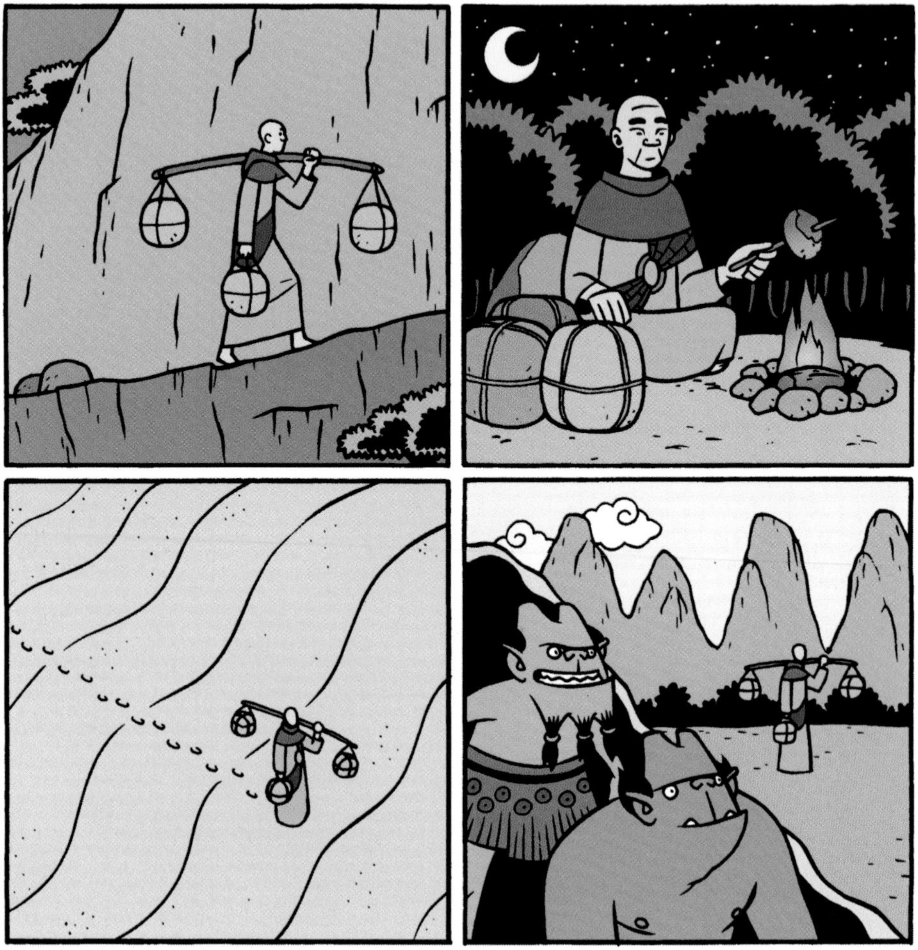

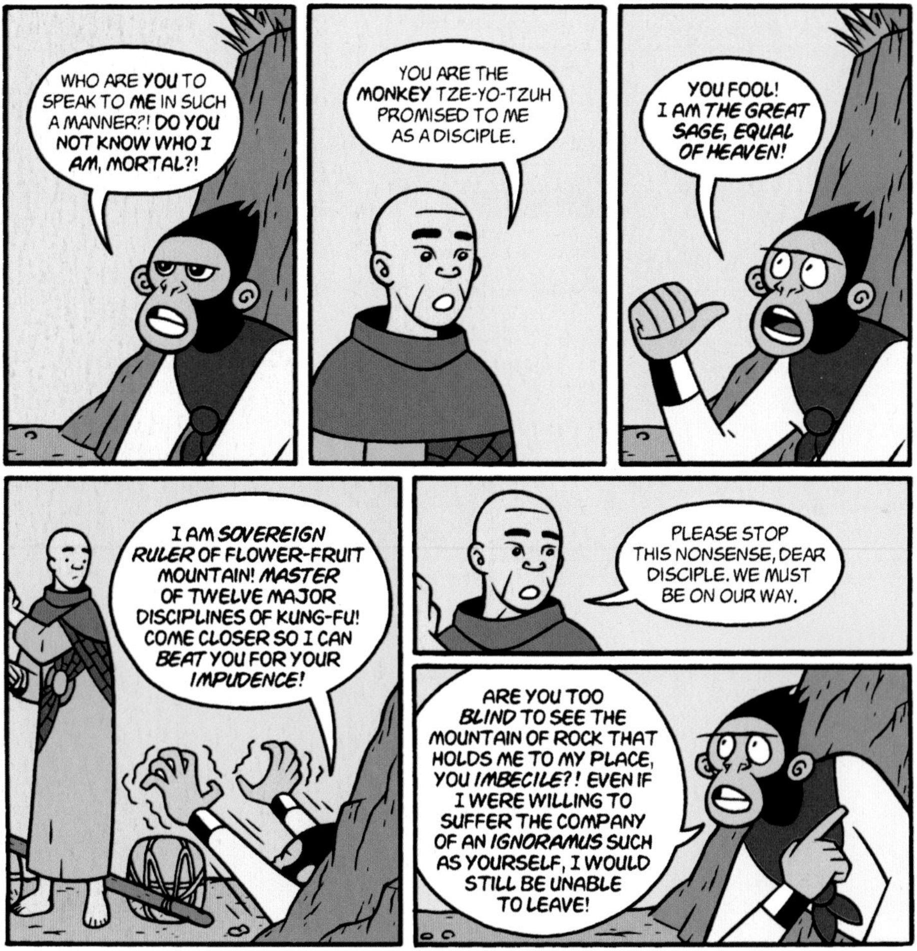
WHO ARE YOU TO SPEAK TO ME IN SUCH A MANNER?! DO YOU NOT KNOW WHO I AM, MORTAL?!
YOU ARE THE MONKEY TZE-YO-TZUH PROMISED TO ME AS A DISCIPLE.
YOU FOOL! I AM THE GREAT SAGE, EQUAL OF HEAVEN!
I AM SOVEREIGN RULER OF FLOWER-FRUIT MOUNTAIN! MASTER OF TWELVE MAJOR DISCIPLINES OF KUNG-FU! COME CLOSER SO I CAN BEAT YOU FOR YOUR IMPUDENCE!
PLEASE STOP THIS NONSENSE, DEAR DISCIPLE. WE MUST BE ON OUR WAY.
ARE YOU TOO BLIND TO SEE THE MOUNTAIN OF ROCK THAT HOLDS ME TO MY PLACE, YOU IMBECILE?! EVEN IF I WERE WILLING TO SUFFER THE COMPANY OF AN IGNORAMUS SUCH AS YOURSELF, I WOULD STILL BE UNABLE TO LEAVE!

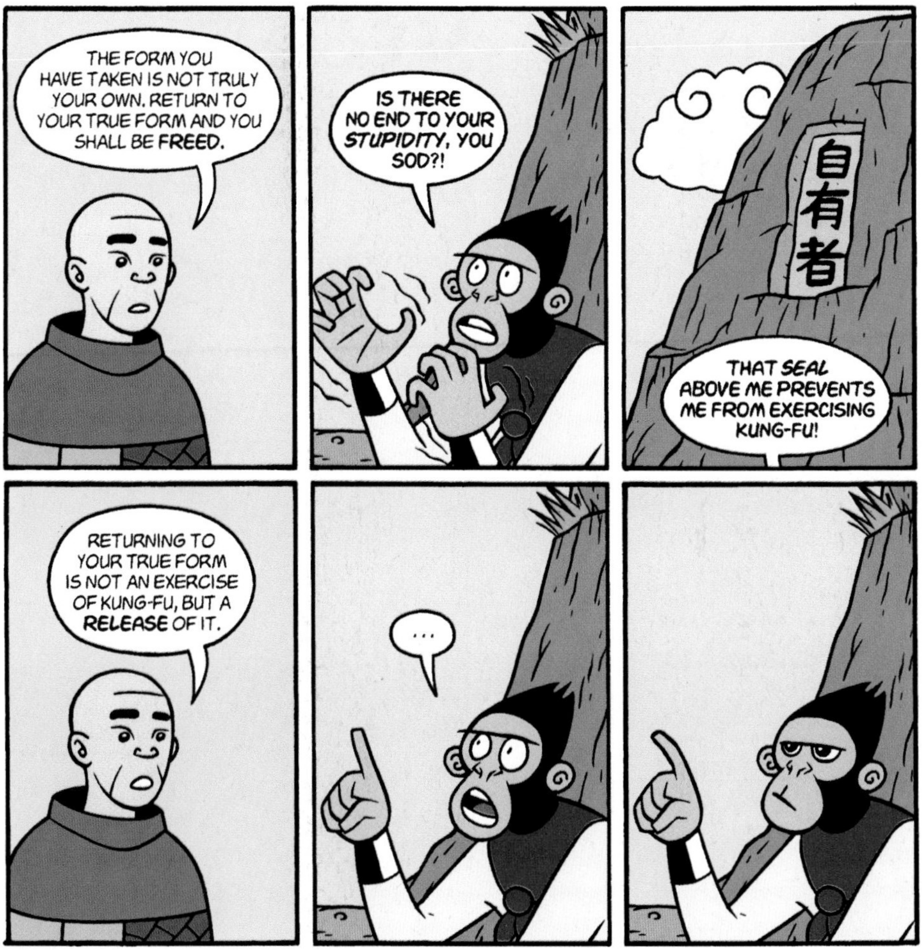
THE FORM YOU HAVE TAKEN IS NOT TRULY YOUR OWN. RETURN TO YOUR TRUE FORM AND YOU SHALL BE FREED.
IS THERE NO END TO YOUR STUPIDITY, YOU SOD?!
自有者
THAT SEAL ABOVE ME PREVENTS ME FROM EXERCISING KUNG-FU!
RETURNING TO YOUR TRUE FORM IS NOT AN EXERCISE OF KUNG-FU, BUT A RELEASE OF IT.
...

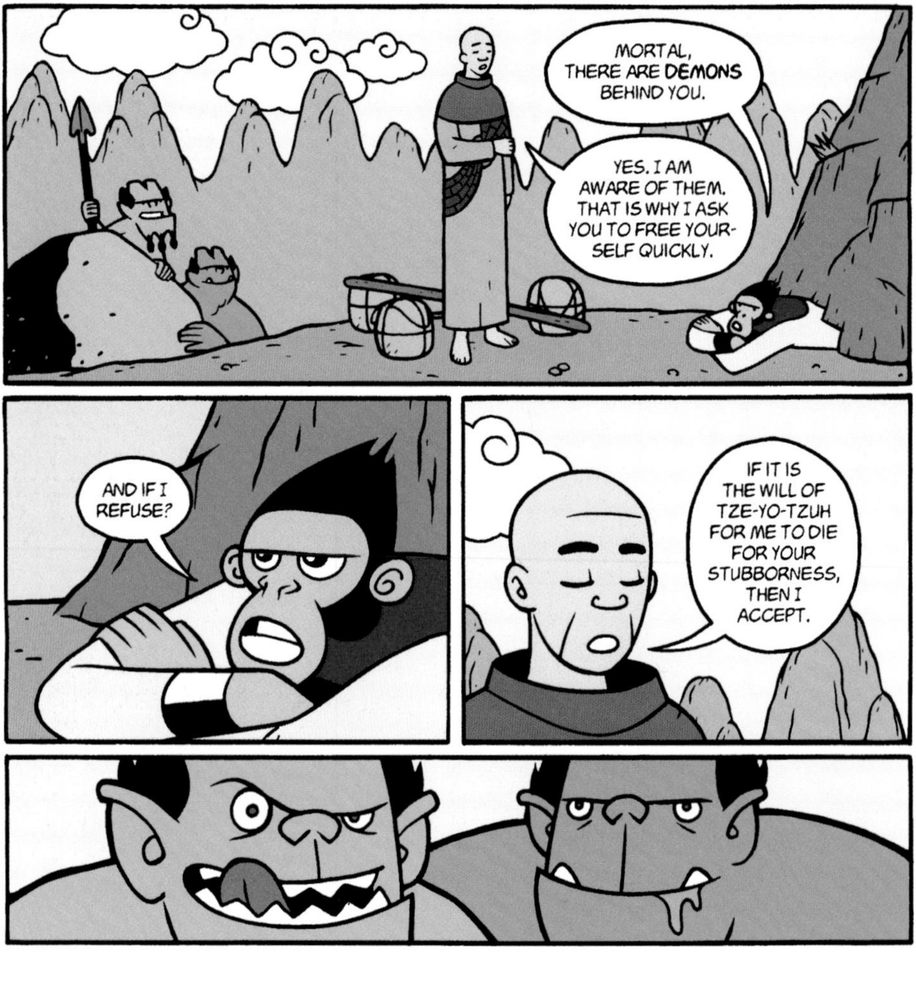
MORTAL, THERE ARE **DEMONS** BEHIND YOU.
YES. I AM AWARE OF THEM. THAT IS WHY I ASK YOU TO FREE YOURSELF QUICKLY.
AND IF I REFUSE?
IF IT IS THE WILL OF TZE-YO-TZUH FOR ME TO DIE FOR YOUR STUBBORNESS, THEN I ACCEPT.

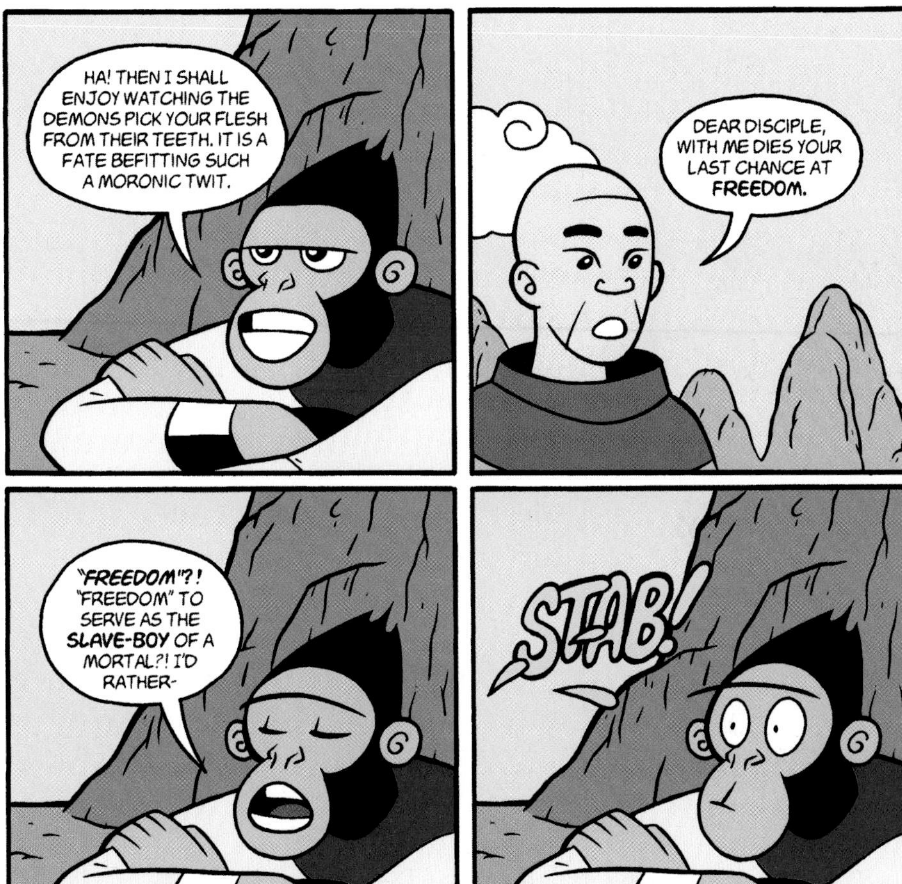
HA! THEN I SHALL ENJOY WATCHING THE DEMONS PICK YOUR FLESH FROM THEIR TEETH. IT IS A FATE BEFITTING SUCH A MORONIC TWIT.
DEAR DISCIPLE, WITH ME DIES YOUR LAST CHANCE AT **FREEDOM.**
"***FREEDOM***"?! "FREEDOM" TO SERVE AS THE **SLAVE-BOY** OF A MORTAL?! I'D RATHER-
STAB!

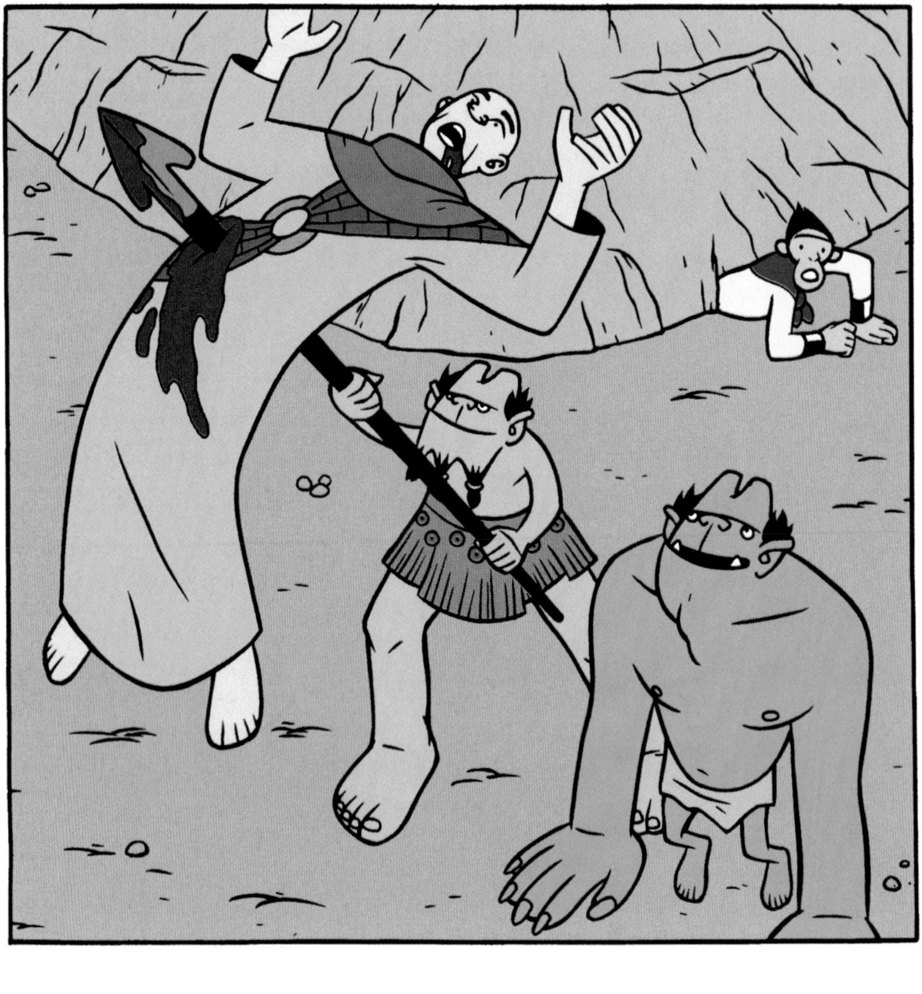

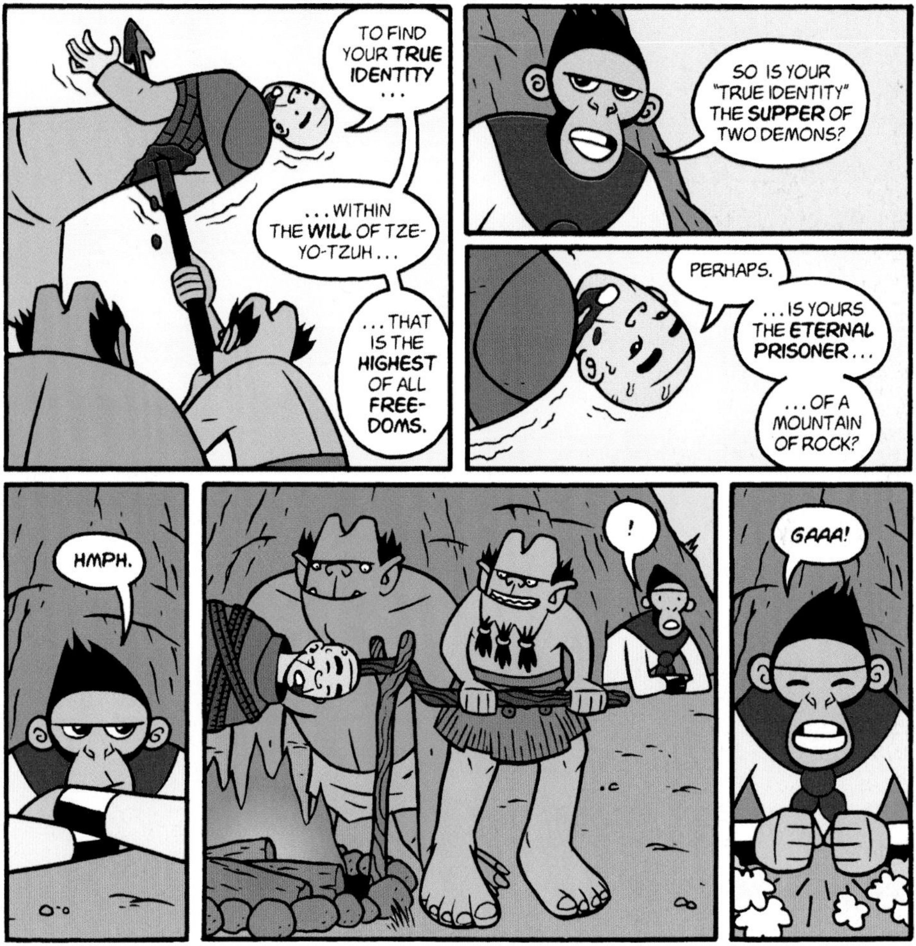
TO FIND YOUR **TRUE IDENTITY** . . .
. . . WITHIN THE **WILL** OF TZE-YO-TZUH . . .
. . . THAT IS THE **HIGHEST** OF ALL **FREE-DOMS.**
SO IS YOUR "TRUE IDENTITY" THE **SUPPER** OF TWO DEMONS?
PERHAPS.
. . . IS YOURS THE **ETERNAL PRISONER** . . .
. . . OF A MOUNTAIN OF ROCK?
HMPH.
!
GAAA!

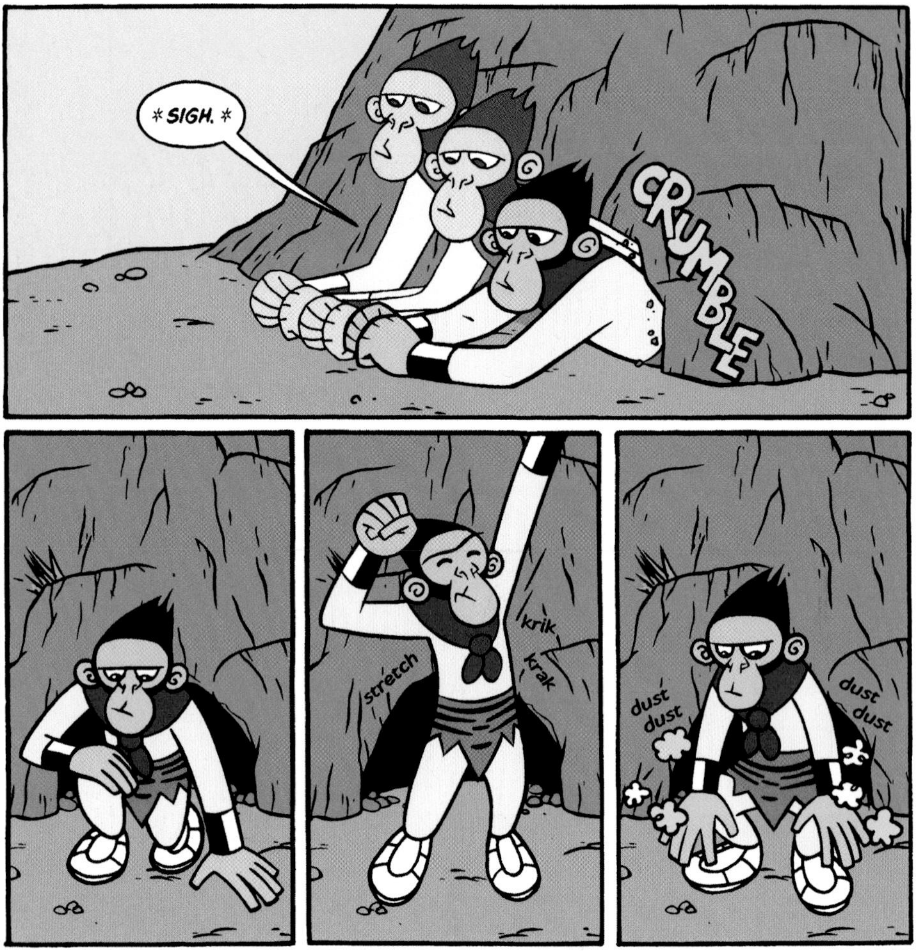
* SIGH. *
CRUMBLE
stretch
krik
krak
dust
dust
dust
dust

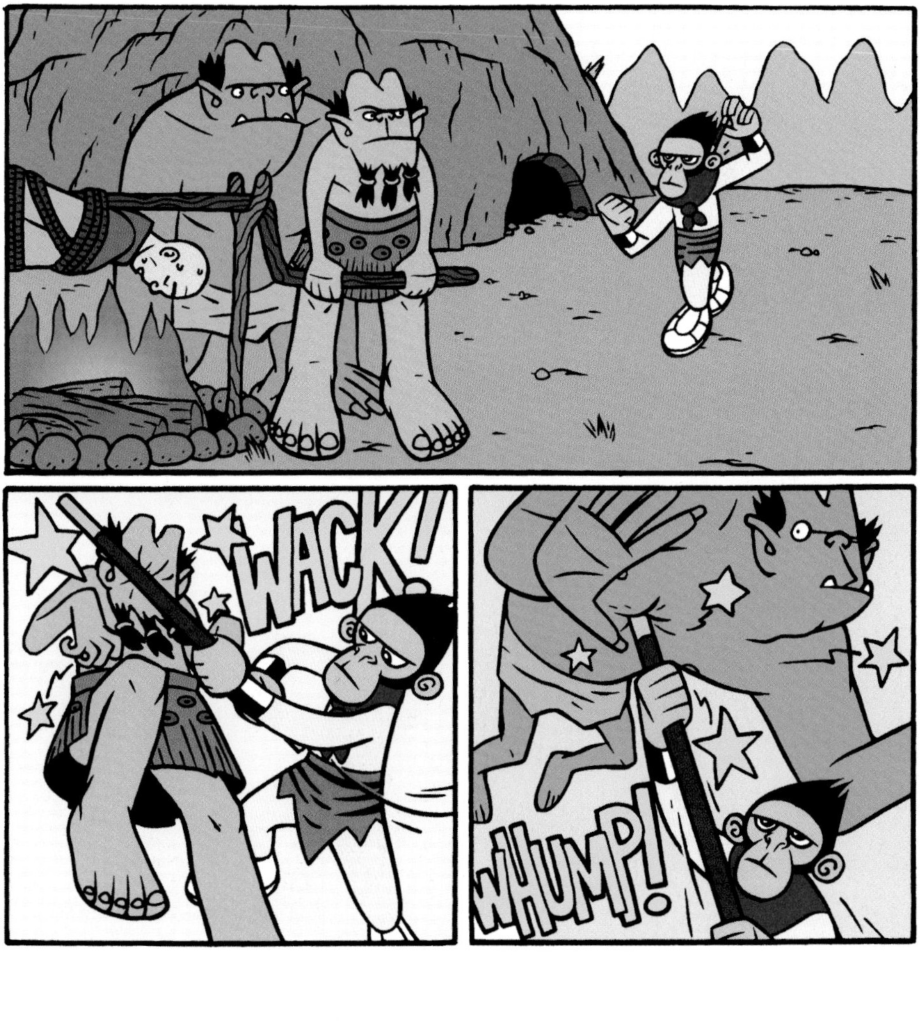
WACK!
WHUMP!

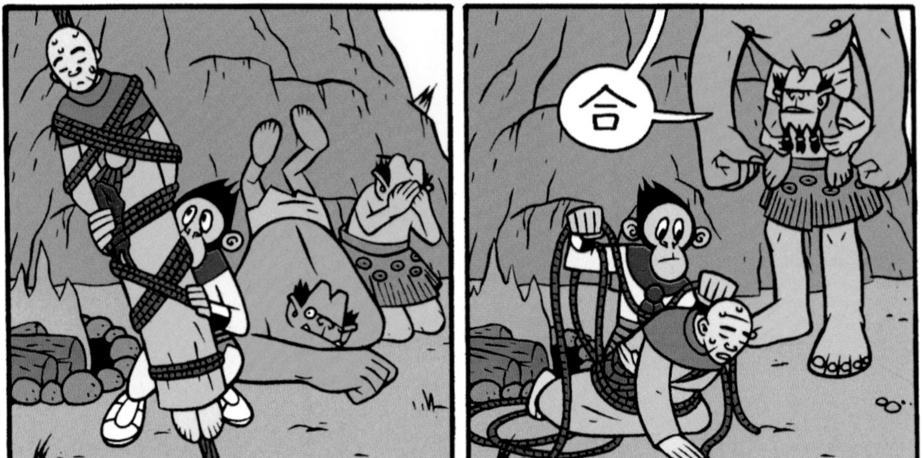
合
?!

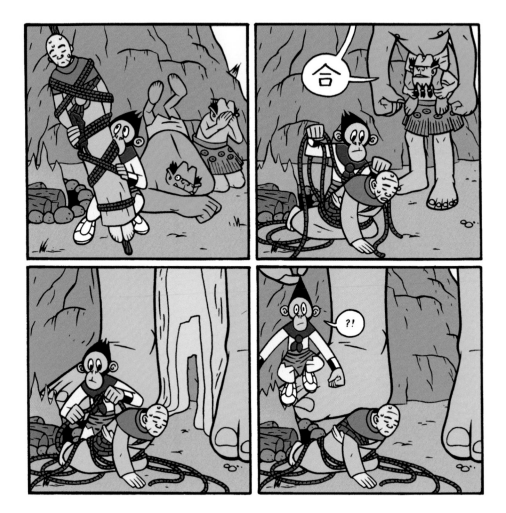

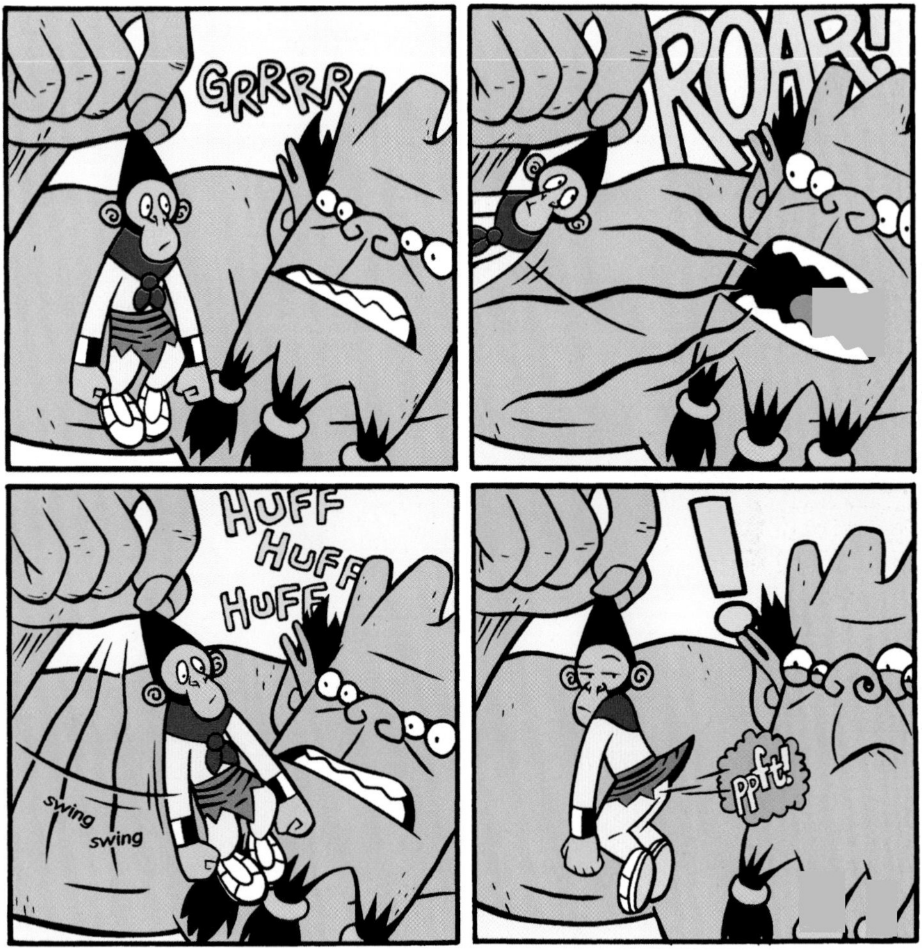
GRRRR
ROAR!
HUFF
HUFF
HUFF
swing
swing
!
ppft!

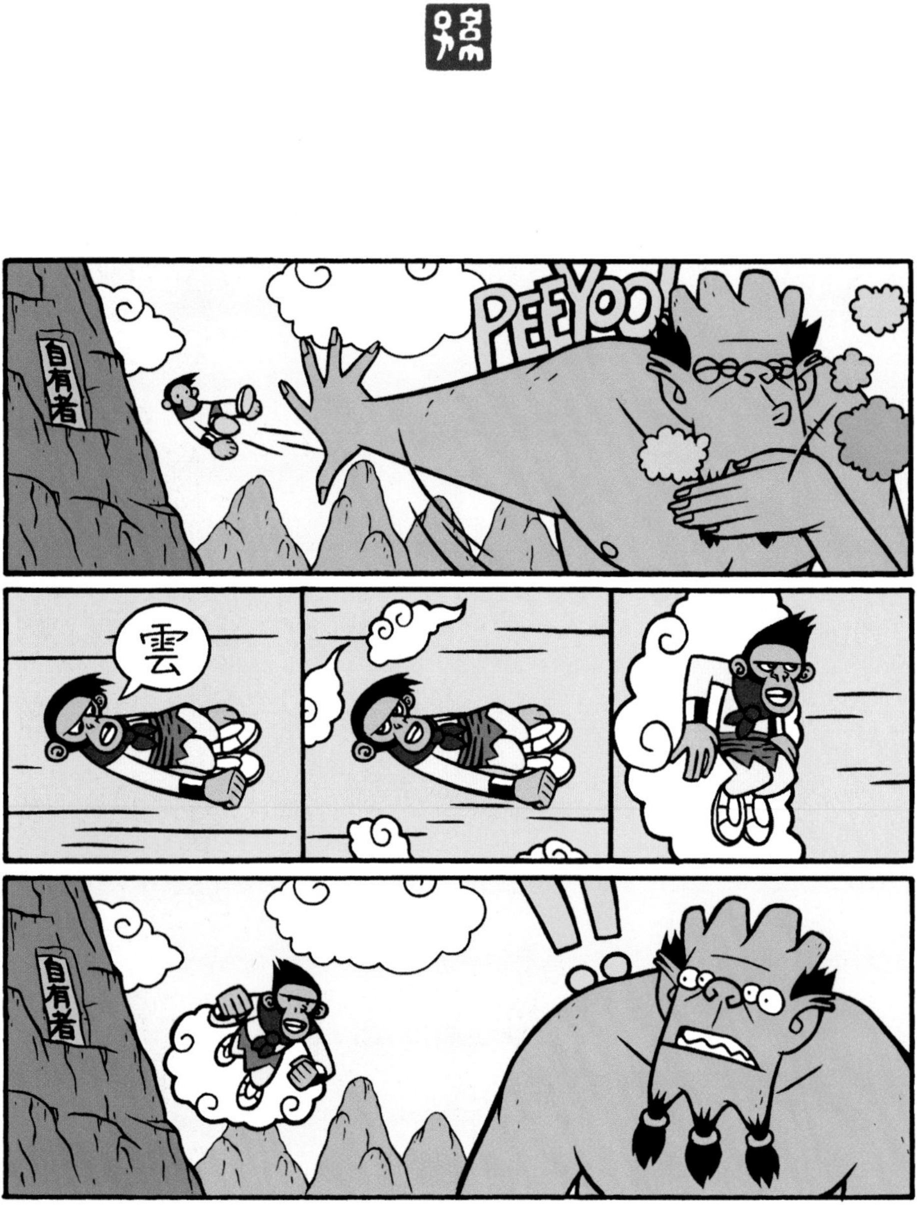
自有者
PEEYOO!
雲
自有者

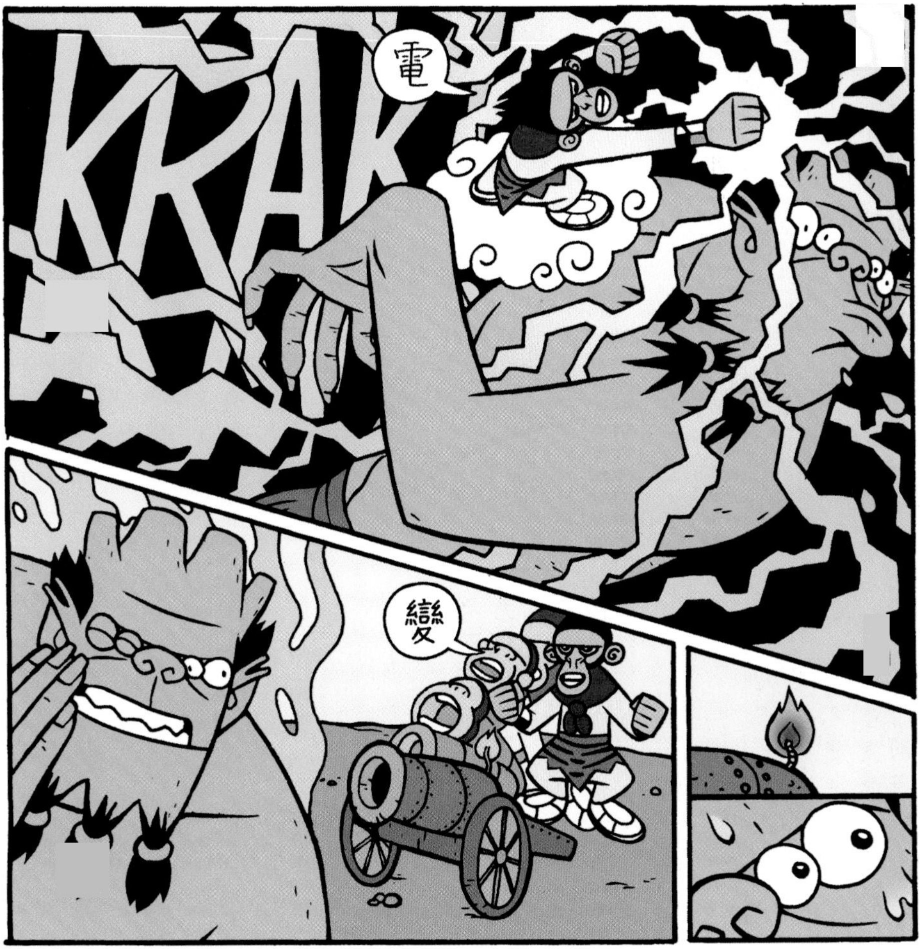
KRAK
電
變

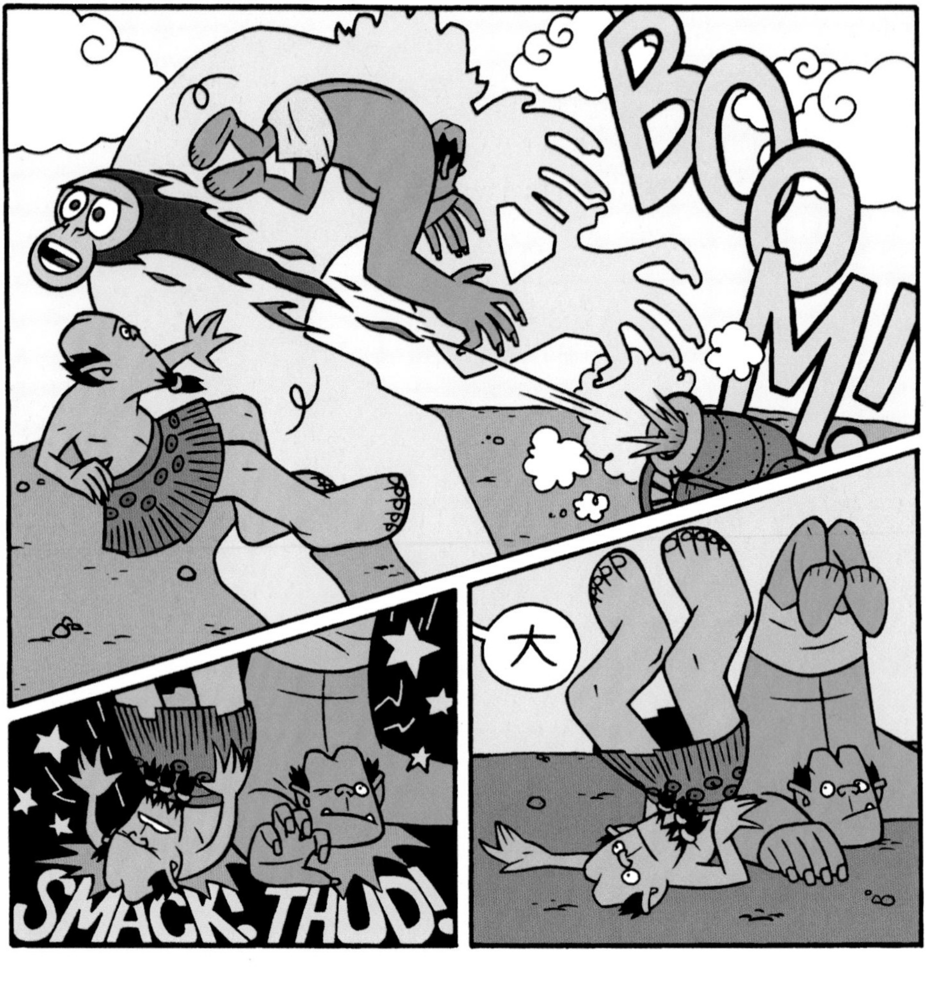
BOOM!
SMACK! THUD!
大

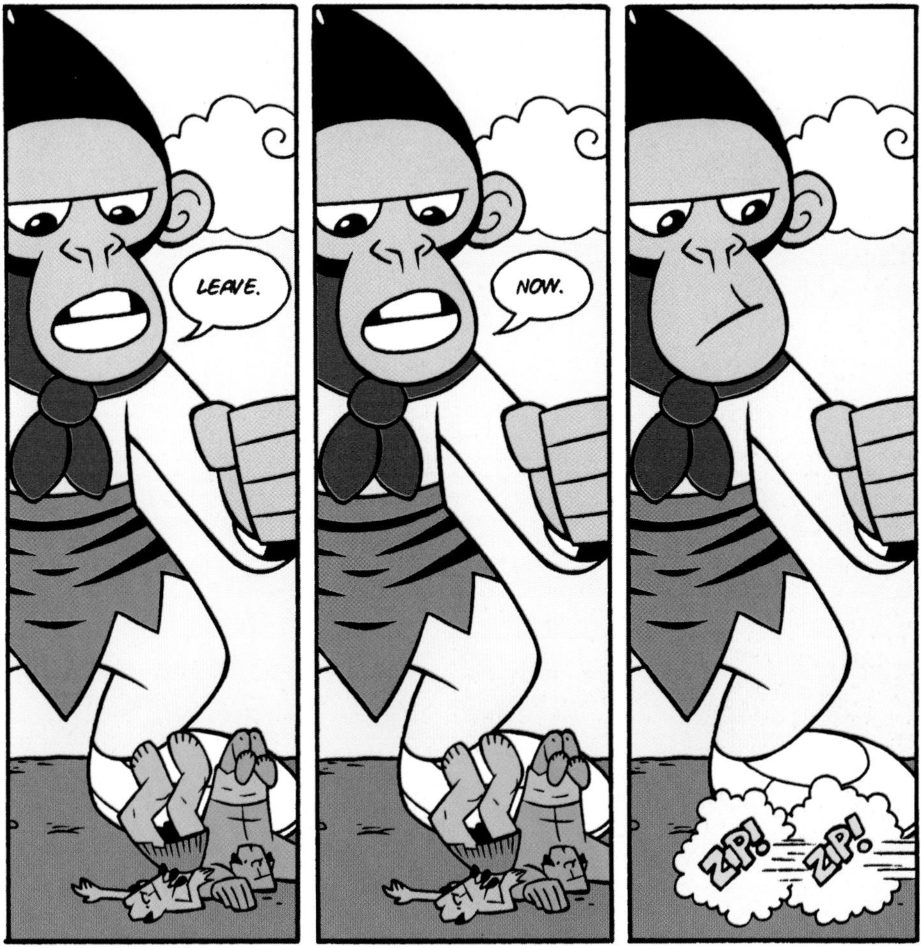
LEAVE.
NOW.
ZIP!
ZIP!

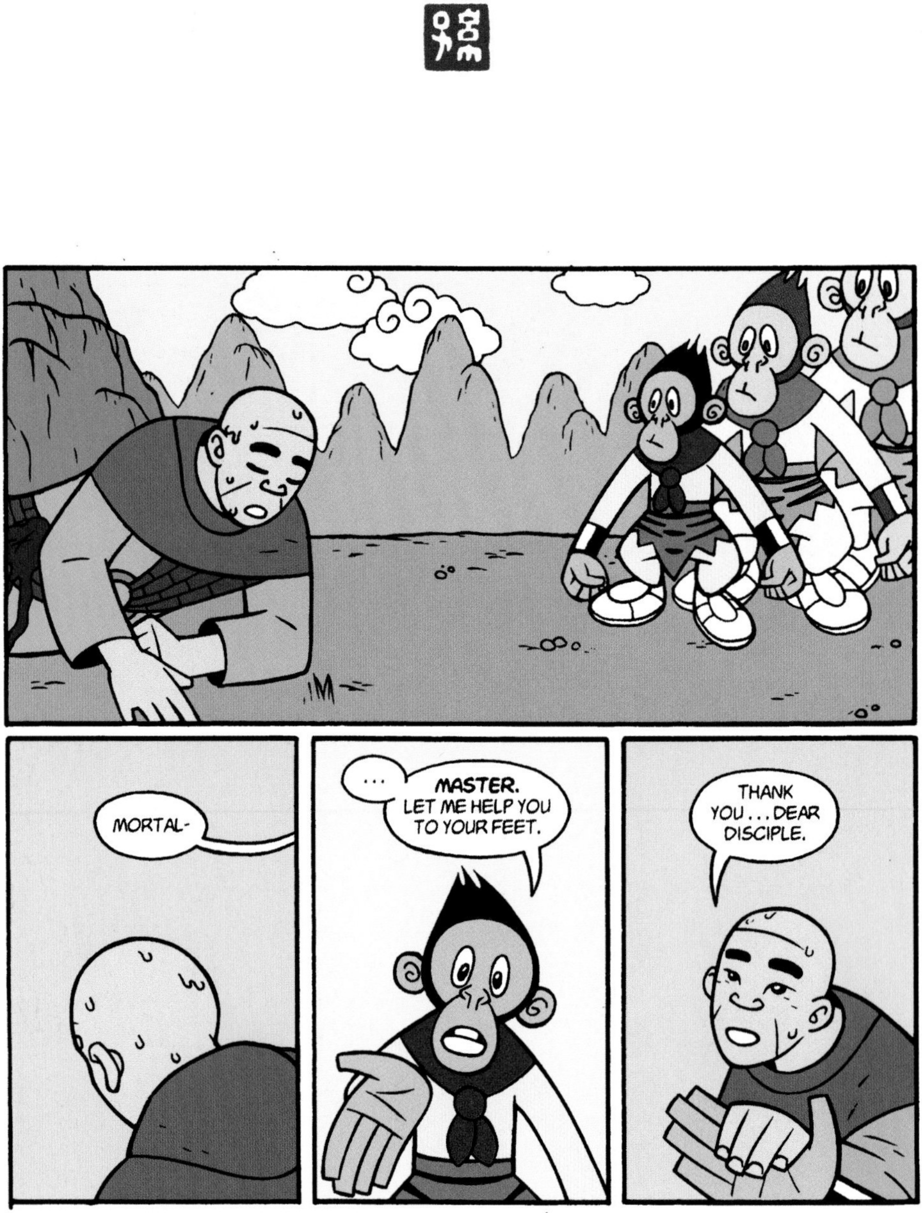
MORTAL-
...
MASTER. LET ME HELP YOU TO YOUR FEET.
THANK YOU... DEAR DISCIPLE.

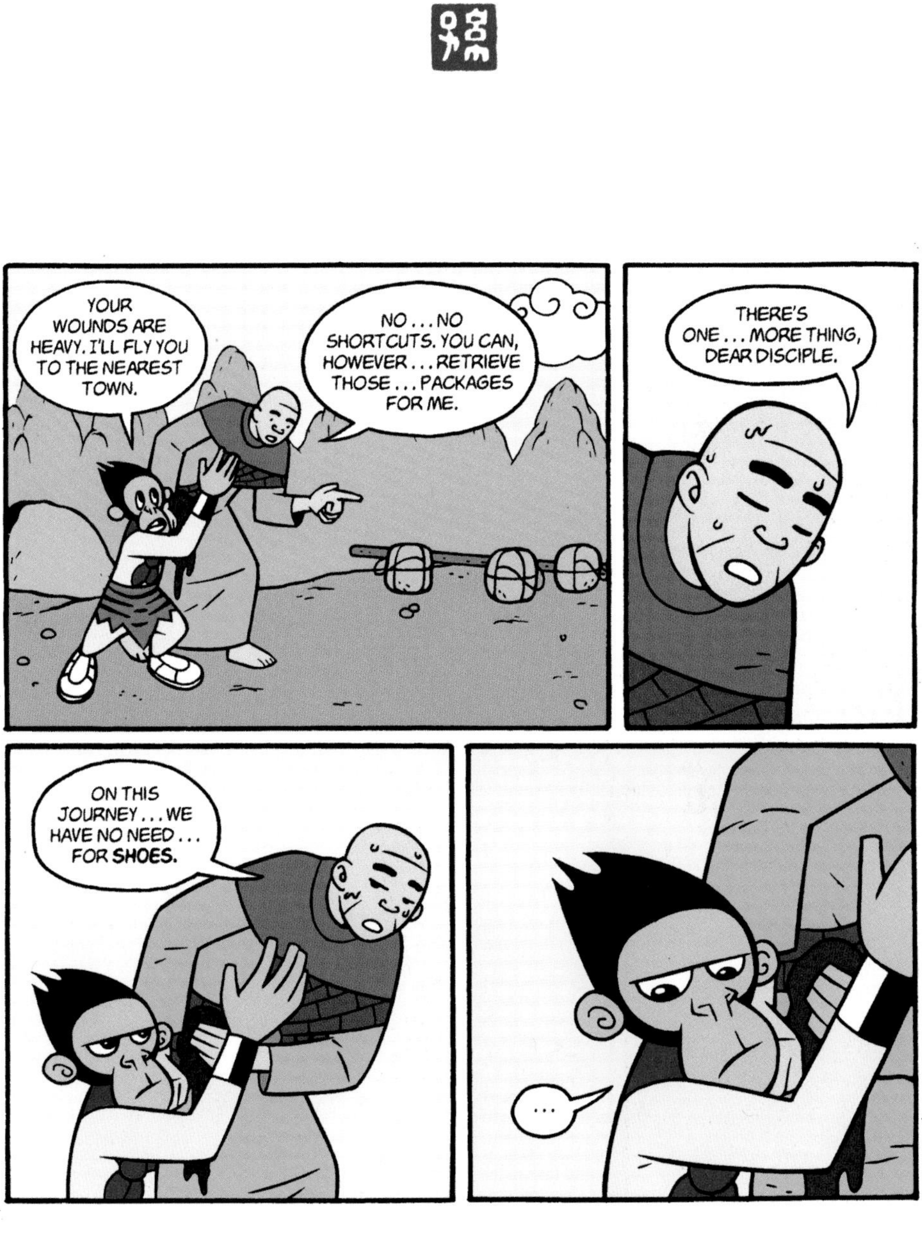
YOUR WOUNDS ARE HEAVY. I'LL FLY YOU TO THE NEAREST TOWN.
NO . . . NO SHORTCUTS. YOU CAN, HOWEVER . . . RETRIEVE THOSE . . . PACKAGES FOR ME.
THERE'S ONE . . . MORE THING, DEAR DISCIPLE.
ON THIS JOURNEY . . . WE HAVE NO NEED . . . FOR **SHOES.**
. . .

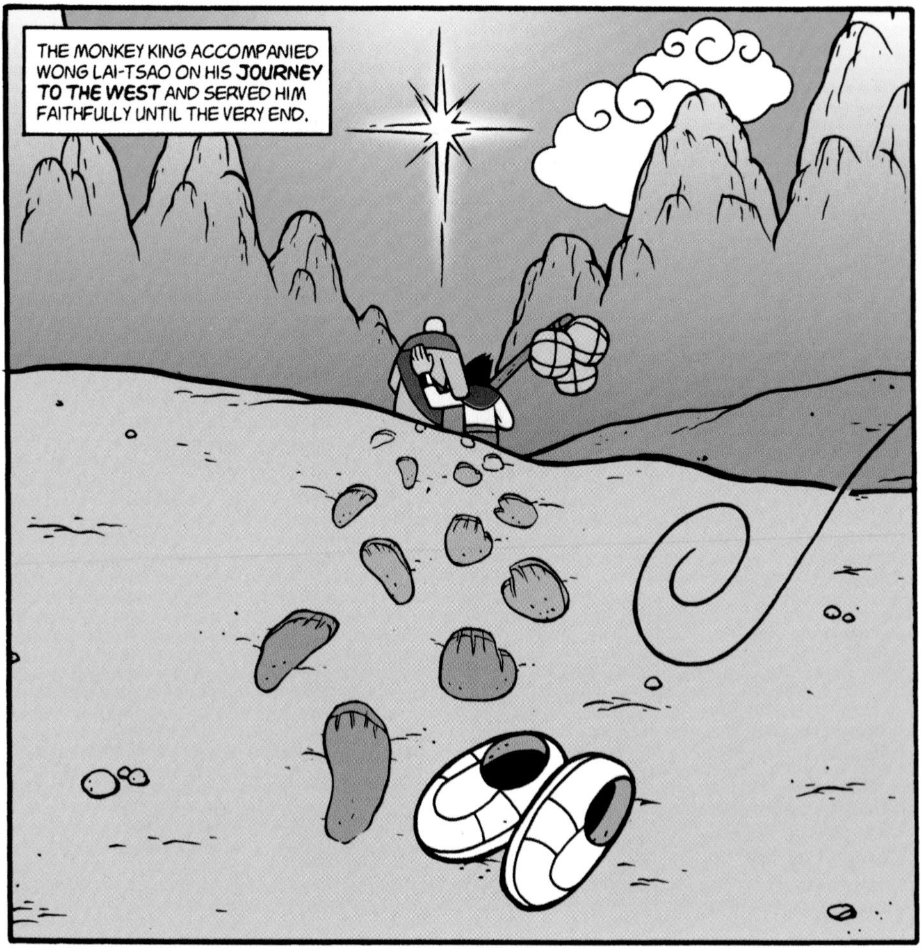
THE MONKEY KING ACCOMPANIED WONG LAI-TSAO ON HIS **JOURNEY TO THE WEST** AND SERVED HIM FAITHFULLY UNTIL THE VERY END.

謹

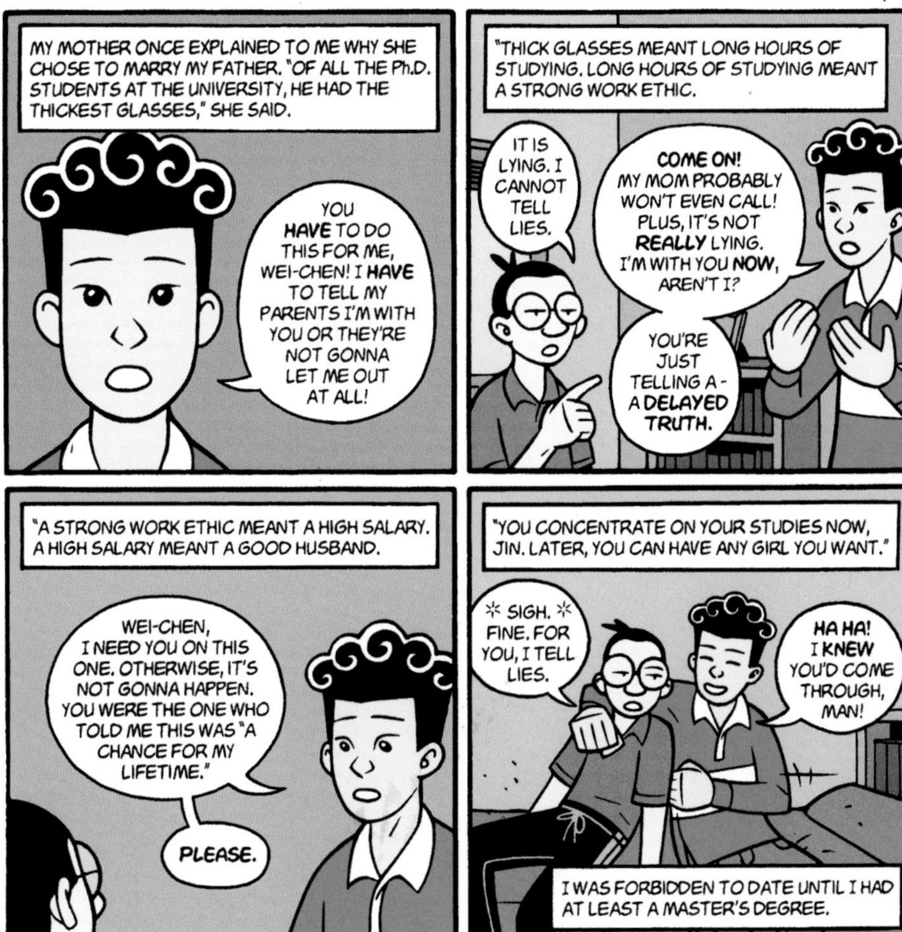
MY MOTHER ONCE EXPLAINED TO ME WHY SHE CHOSE TO MARRY MY FATHER. "OF ALL THE Ph.D. STUDENTS AT THE UNIVERSITY, HE HAD THE THICKEST GLASSES," SHE SAID.
YOU HAVE TO DO THIS FOR ME, WEI-CHEN! I HAVE TO TELL MY PARENTS I'M WITH YOU OR THEY'RE NOT GONNA LET ME OUT AT ALL!
"THICK GLASSES MEANT LONG HOURS OF STUDYING. LONG HOURS OF STUDYING MEANT A STRONG WORK ETHIC.
IT IS LYING. I CANNOT TELL LIES.
COME ON! MY MOM PROBABLY WON'T EVEN CALL! PLUS, IT'S NOT REALLY LYING. I'M WITH YOU NOW, AREN'T I?
YOU'RE JUST TELLING A - A DELAYED TRUTH.
"A STRONG WORK ETHIC MEANT A HIGH SALARY. A HIGH SALARY MEANT A GOOD HUSBAND.
WEI-CHEN, I NEED YOU ON THIS ONE. OTHERWISE, IT'S NOT GONNA HAPPEN. YOU WERE THE ONE WHO TOLD ME THIS WAS "A CHANCE FOR MY LIFETIME."
PLEASE.
"YOU CONCENTRATE ON YOUR STUDIES NOW, JIN. LATER, YOU CAN HAVE ANY GIRL YOU WANT."
SIGH. FINE. FOR YOU, I TELL LIES.
HA HA! I KNEW YOU'D COME THROUGH, MAN!
I WAS FORBIDDEN TO DATE UNTIL I HAD AT LEAST A MASTER'S DEGREE.

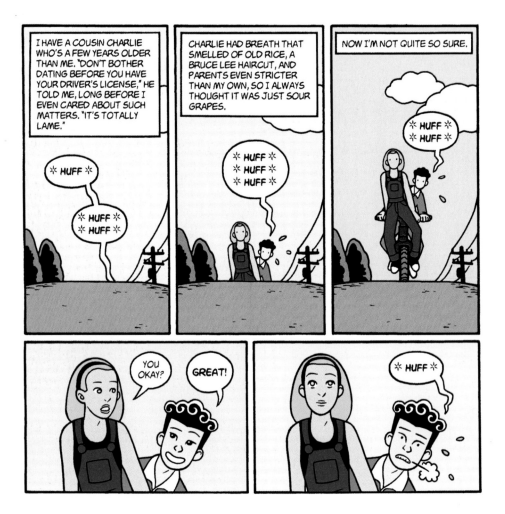

I HAVE A COUSIN CHARLIE WHO'S A FEW YEARS OLDER THAN ME. "DON'T BOTHER DATING BEFORE YOU HAVE YOUR DRIVER'S LICENSE," HE TOLD ME, LONG BEFORE I EVEN CARED ABOUT SUCH MATTERS. "IT'S TOTALLY LAME."

✳ HUFF ✳

✳ HUFF ✳
✳ HUFF ✳

CHARLIE HAD BREATH THAT SMELLED OF OLD RICE, A BRUCE LEE HAIRCUT, AND PARENTS EVEN STRICTER THAN MY OWN, SO I ALWAYS THOUGHT IT WAS JUST SOUR GRAPES.

✳ HUFF ✳
✳ HUFF ✳
✳ HUFF ✳

NOW I'M NOT QUITE SO SURE.

✳ HUFF ✳
✳ HUFF ✳

YOU OKAY?

GREAT!

✳ HUFF ✳

164

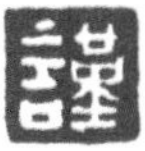

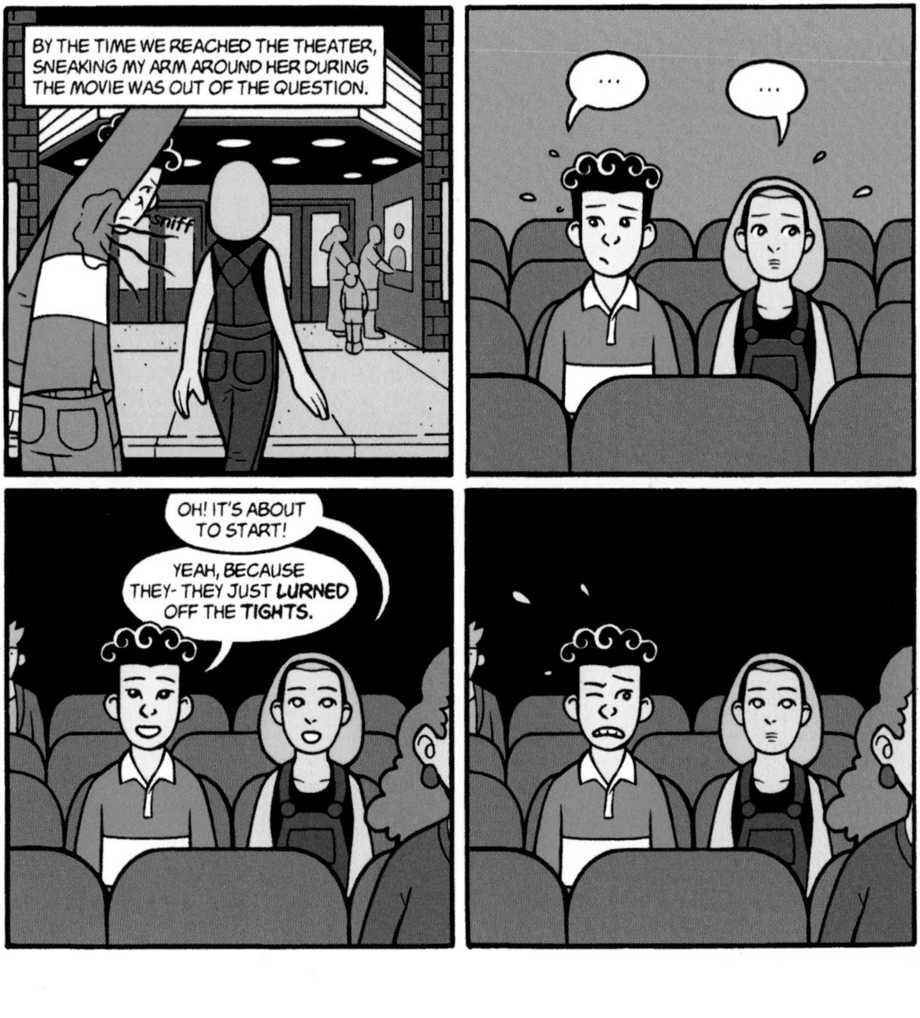
BY THE TIME WE REACHED THE THEATER, SNEAKING MY ARM AROUND HER DURING THE MOVIE WAS OUT OF THE QUESTION.
sniff
...
...
OH! IT'S ABOUT TO START!
YEAH, BECAUSE THEY- THEY JUST **LURNED** OFF THE **TIGHTS.**

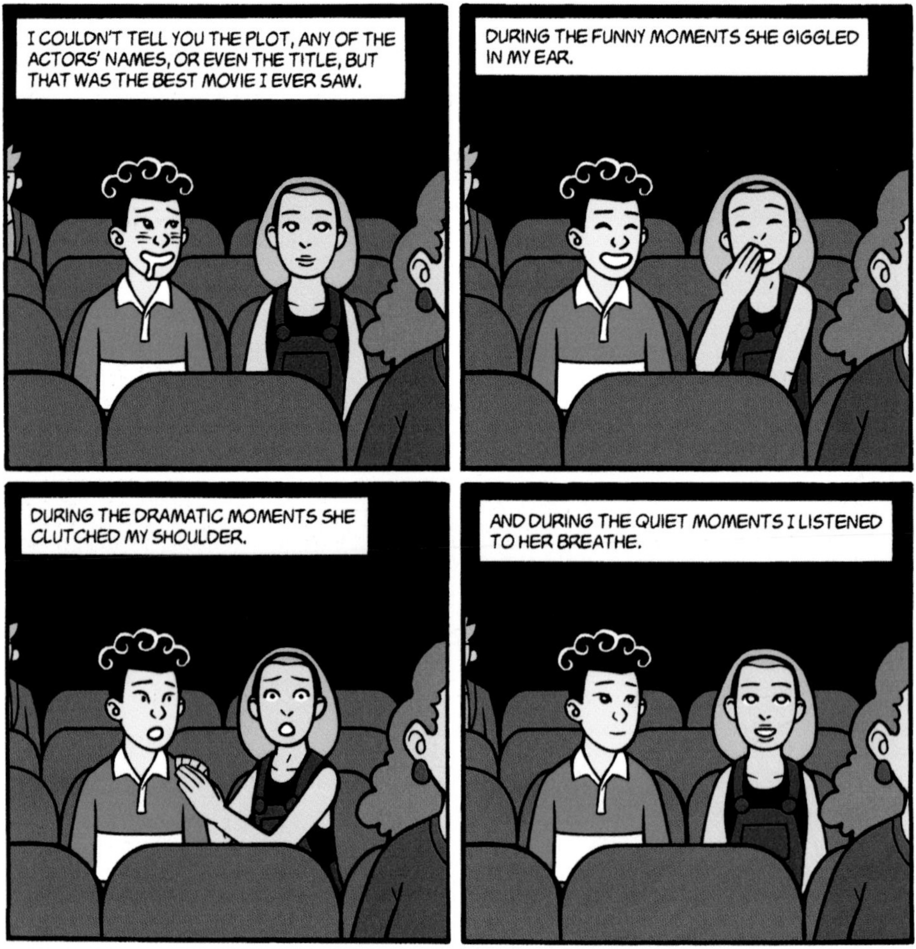
I COULDN'T TELL YOU THE PLOT, ANY OF THE ACTORS' NAMES, OR EVEN THE TITLE, BUT THAT WAS THE BEST MOVIE I EVER SAW.
DURING THE FUNNY MOMENTS SHE GIGGLED IN MY EAR.
DURING THE DRAMATIC MOMENTS SHE CLUTCHED MY SHOULDER.
AND DURING THE QUIET MOMENTS I LISTENED TO HER BREATHE.

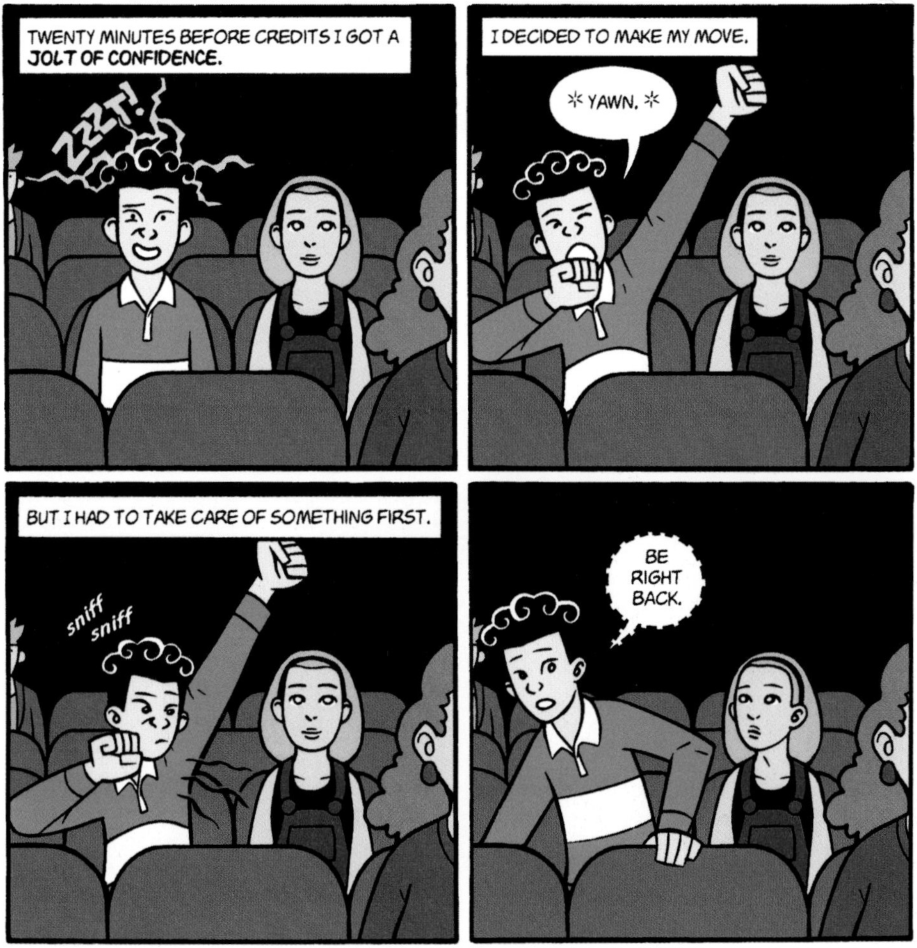
TWENTY MINUTES BEFORE CREDITS I GOT A **JOLT OF CONFIDENCE.**
ZZZT!
I DECIDED TO MAKE MY MOVE.
YAWN.
BUT I HAD TO TAKE CARE OF SOMETHING FIRST.
sniff sniff
BE RIGHT BACK.

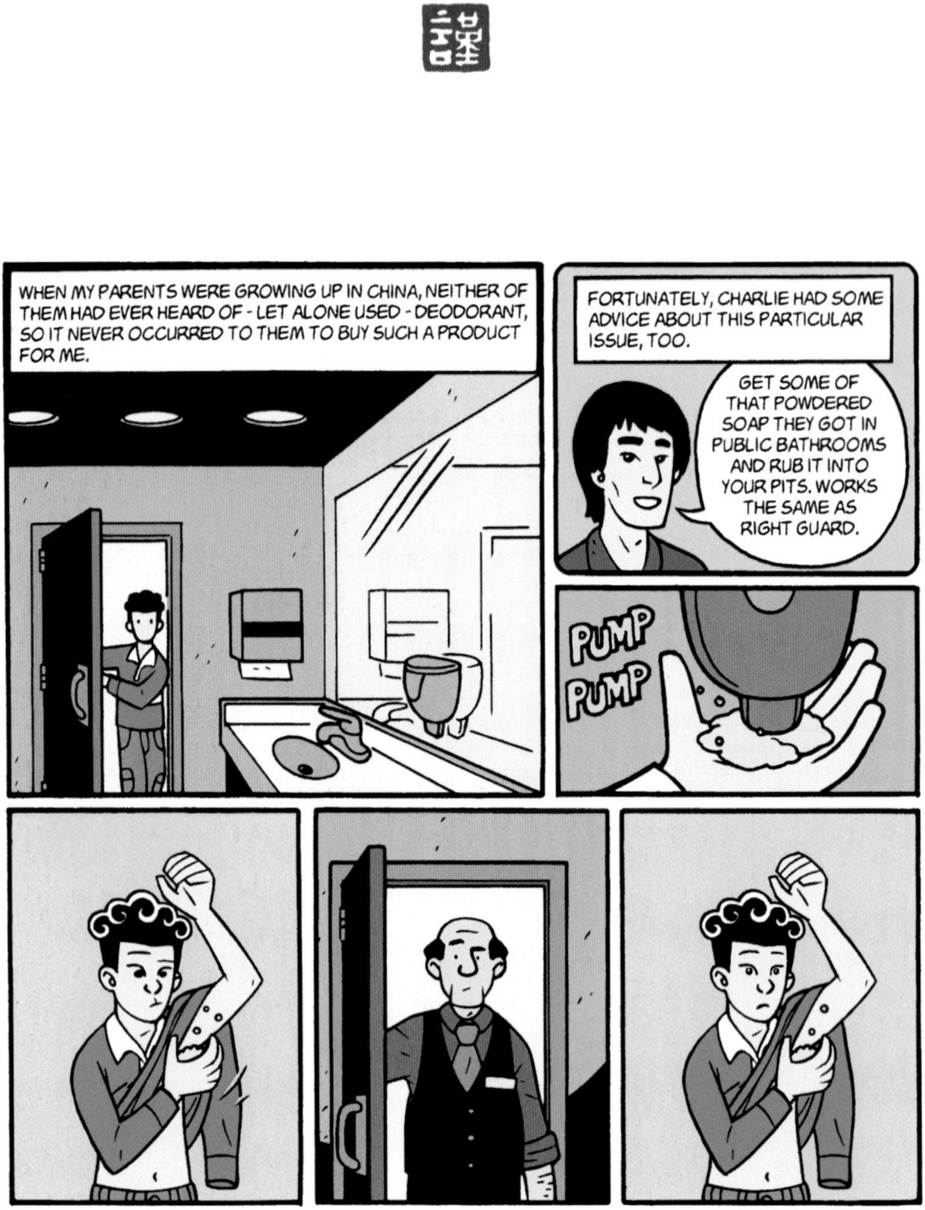
WHEN MY PARENTS WERE GROWING UP IN CHINA, NEITHER OF THEM HAD EVER HEARD OF - LET ALONE USED - DEODORANT, SO IT NEVER OCCURRED TO THEM TO BUY SUCH A PRODUCT FOR ME.
FORTUNATELY, CHARLIE HAD SOME ADVICE ABOUT THIS PARTICULAR ISSUE, TOO.
GET SOME OF THAT POWDERED SOAP THEY GOT IN PUBLIC BATHROOMS AND RUB IT INTO YOUR PITS. WORKS THE SAME AS RIGHT GUARD.
PUMP
PUMP

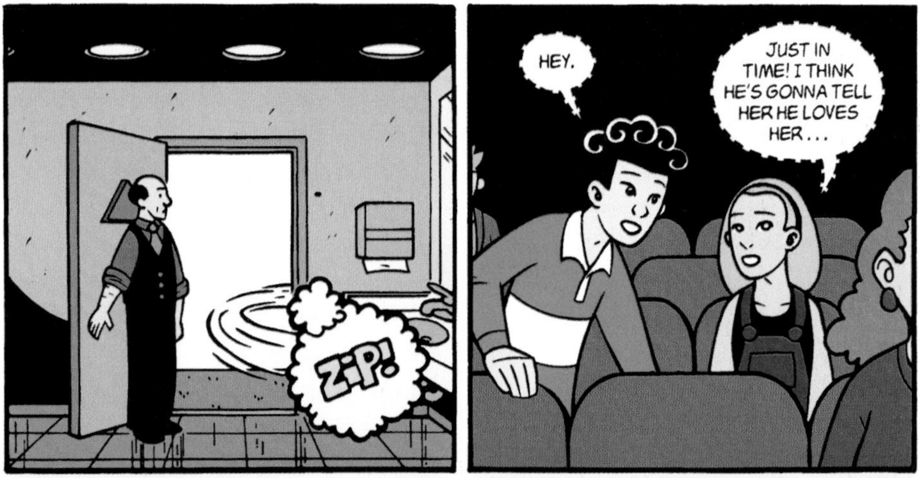
ZiP!
HEY.
JUST IN TIME! I THINK HE'S GONNA TELL HER HE LOVES HER...
ZZZT!
AWWW...

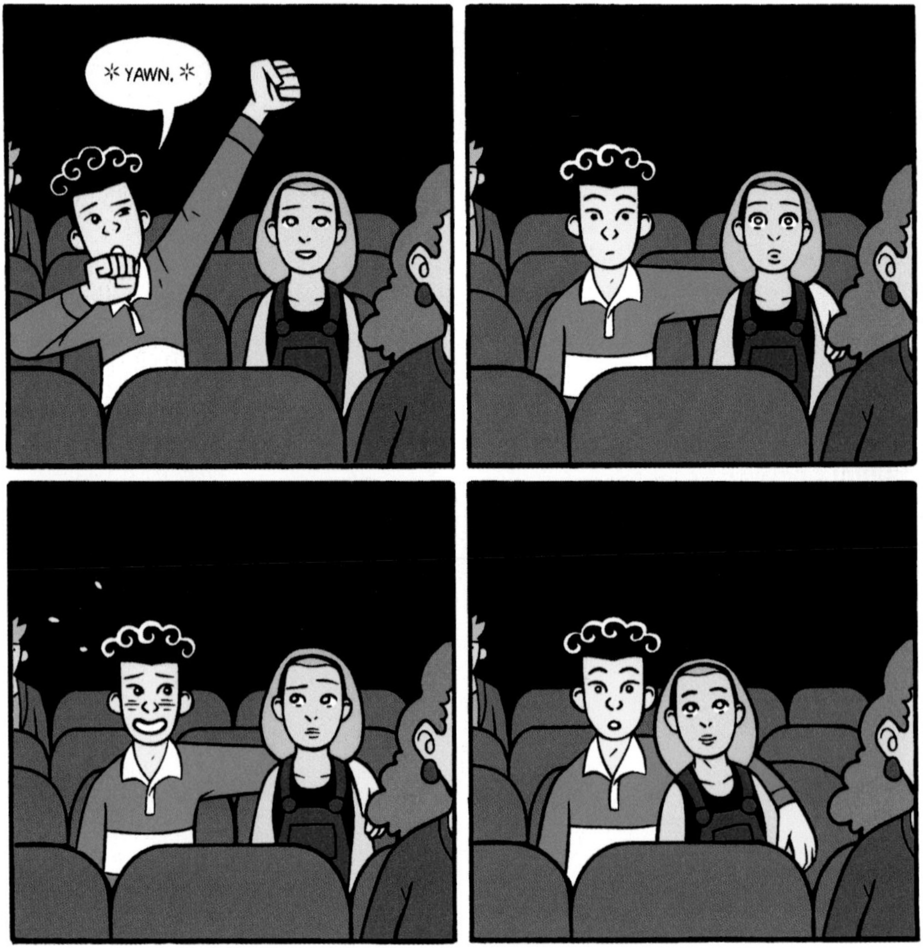
* YAWN. *

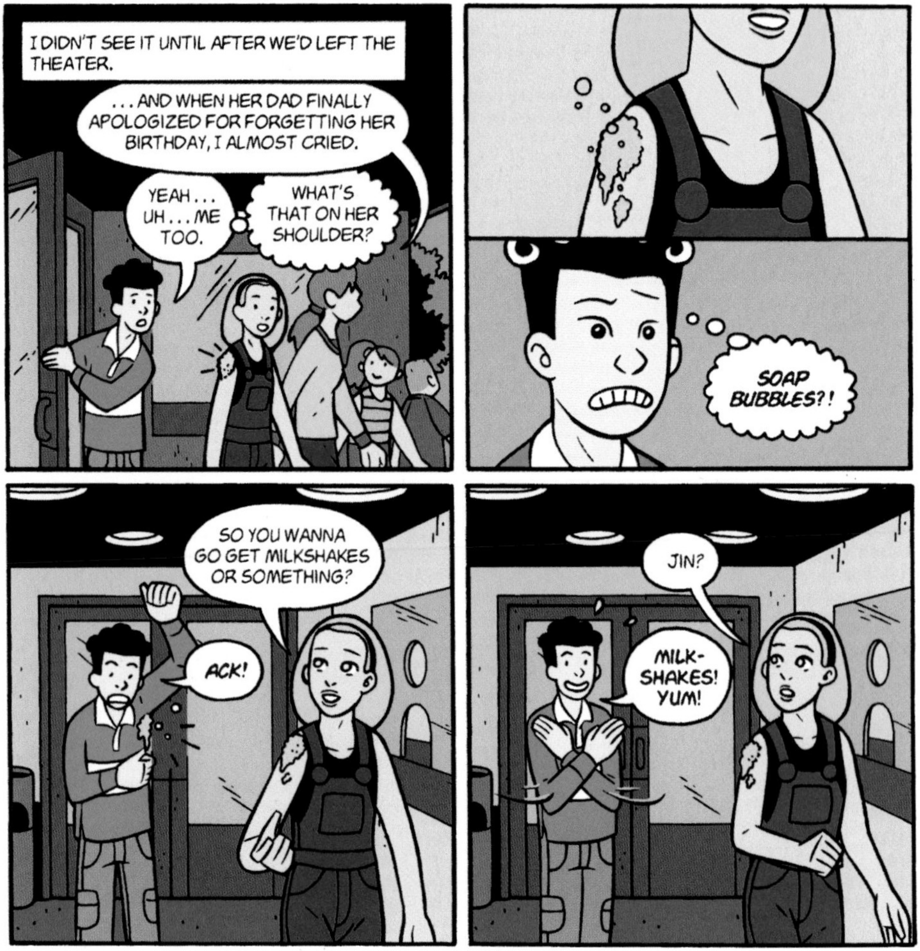
I DIDN'T SEE IT UNTIL AFTER WE'D LEFT THE THEATER.
...AND WHEN HER DAD FINALLY APOLOGIZED FOR FORGETTING HER BIRTHDAY, I ALMOST CRIED.
YEAH... UH... ME TOO.
WHAT'S THAT ON HER SHOULDER?
SOAP BUBBLES?!
SO YOU WANNA GO GET MILKSHAKES OR SOMETHING?
ACK!
JIN?
MILK-SHAKES! YUM!

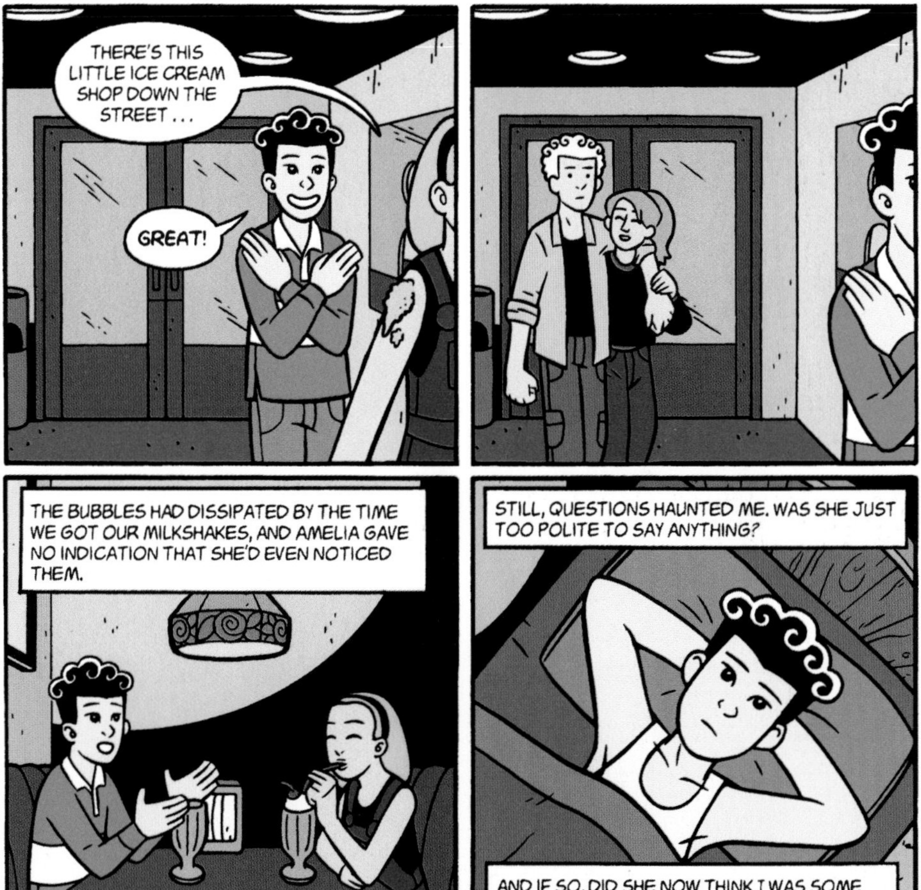
THERE'S THIS LITTLE ICE CREAM SHOP DOWN THE STREET . . .
GREAT!
THE BUBBLES HAD DISSIPATED BY THE TIME WE GOT OUR MILKSHAKES, AND AMELIA GAVE NO INDICATION THAT SHE'D EVEN NOTICED THEM.
STILL, QUESTIONS HAUNTED ME. WAS SHE JUST TOO POLITE TO SAY ANYTHING?
AND IF SO, DID SHE NOW THINK I WAS SOME SORT OF FREAK WITH BUBBLY ARMPIT SWEAT?

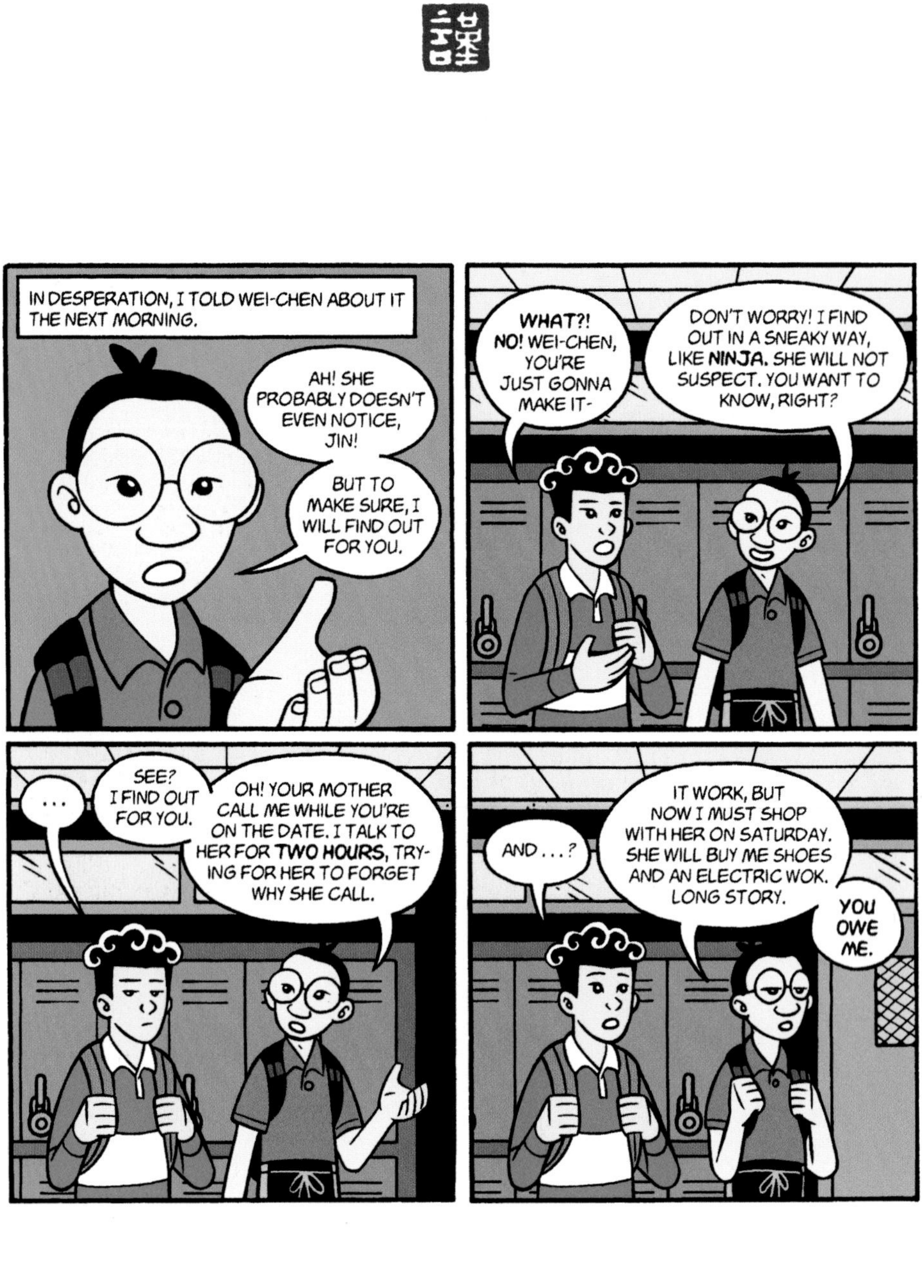
IN DESPERATION, I TOLD WEI-CHEN ABOUT IT THE NEXT MORNING.
AH! SHE PROBABLY DOESN'T EVEN NOTICE, JIN!
BUT TO MAKE SURE, I WILL FIND OUT FOR YOU.
WHAT?! NO! WEI-CHEN, YOU'RE JUST GONNA MAKE IT-
DON'T WORRY! I FIND OUT IN A SNEAKY WAY, LIKE NINJA. SHE WILL NOT SUSPECT. YOU WANT TO KNOW, RIGHT?
...
SEE? I FIND OUT FOR YOU.
OH! YOUR MOTHER CALL ME WHILE YOU'RE ON THE DATE. I TALK TO HER FOR TWO HOURS, TRYING FOR HER TO FORGET WHY SHE CALL.
AND ...?
IT WORK, BUT NOW I MUST SHOP WITH HER ON SATURDAY. SHE WILL BUY ME SHOES AND AN ELECTRIC WOK. LONG STORY.
YOU OWE ME.

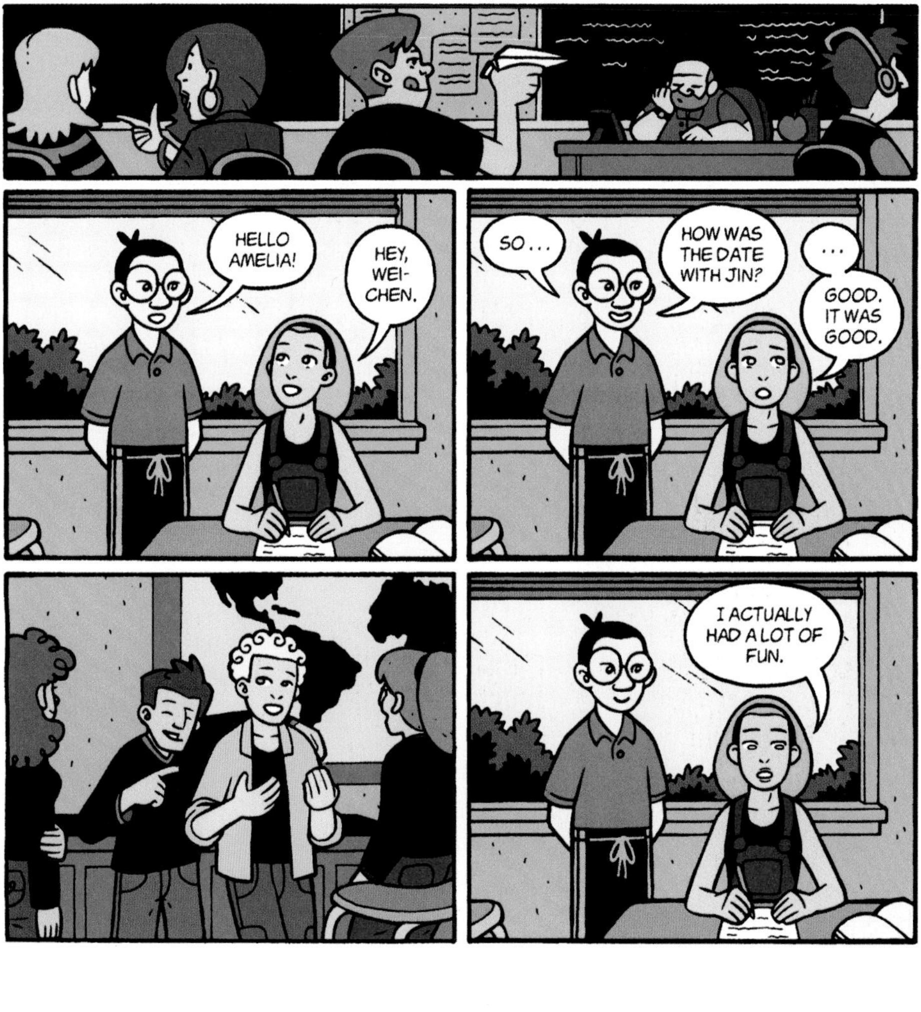
HELLO AMELIA!
HEY, WEI-CHEN.
SO...
HOW WAS THE DATE WITH JIN?
...
GOOD. IT WAS GOOD.
I ACTUALLY HAD A LOT OF FUN.

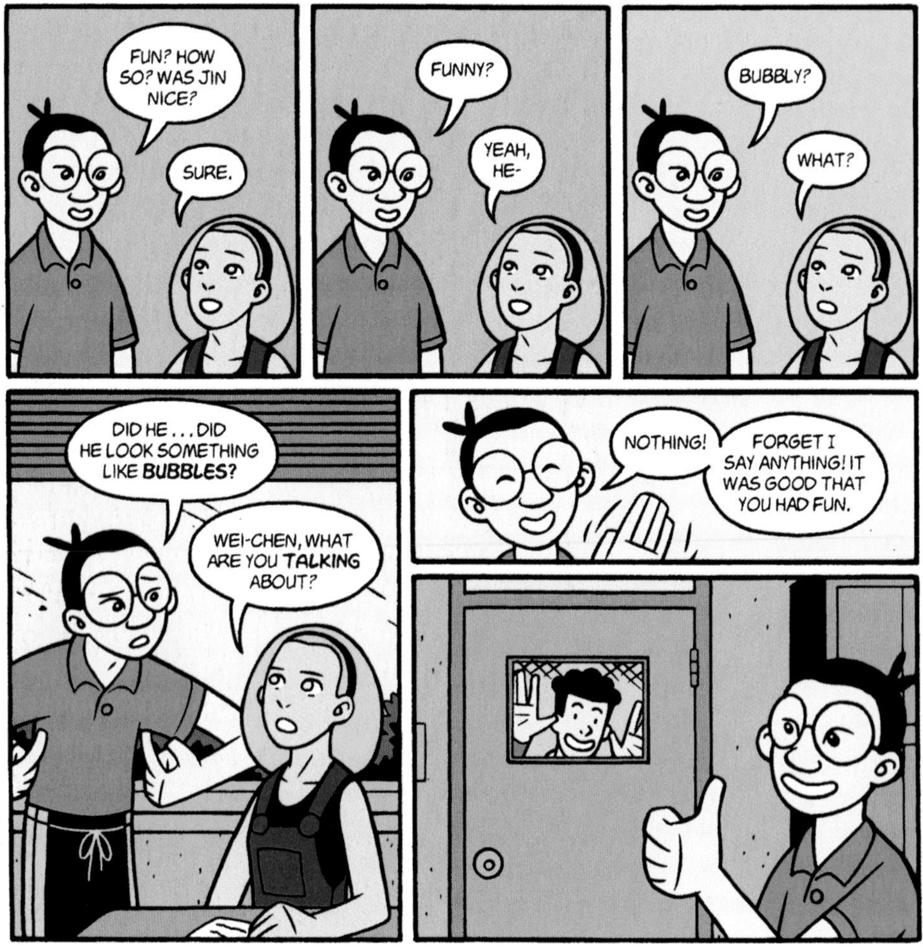
FUN? HOW SO? WAS JIN NICE?
SURE.
FUNNY?
YEAH, HE-
BUBBLY?
WHAT?
DID HE . . . DID HE LOOK SOMETHING LIKE **BUBBLES?**
WEI-CHEN, WHAT ARE YOU **TALKING** ABOUT?
NOTHING!
FORGET I SAY ANYTHING! IT WAS GOOD THAT YOU HAD FUN.

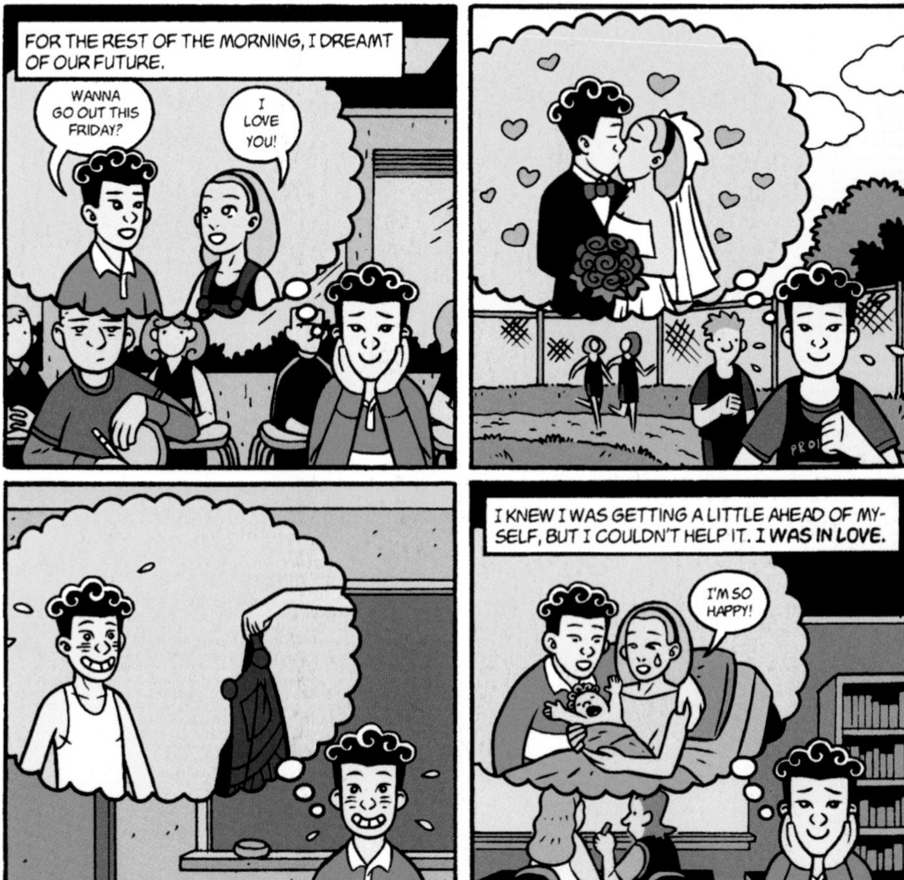
FOR THE REST OF THE MORNING, I DREAMT OF OUR FUTURE.
WANNA GO OUT THIS FRIDAY?
I LOVE YOU!
I KNEW I WAS GETTING A LITTLE AHEAD OF MY-SELF, BUT I COULDN'T HELP IT. **I WAS IN LOVE.**
I'M SO HAPPY!

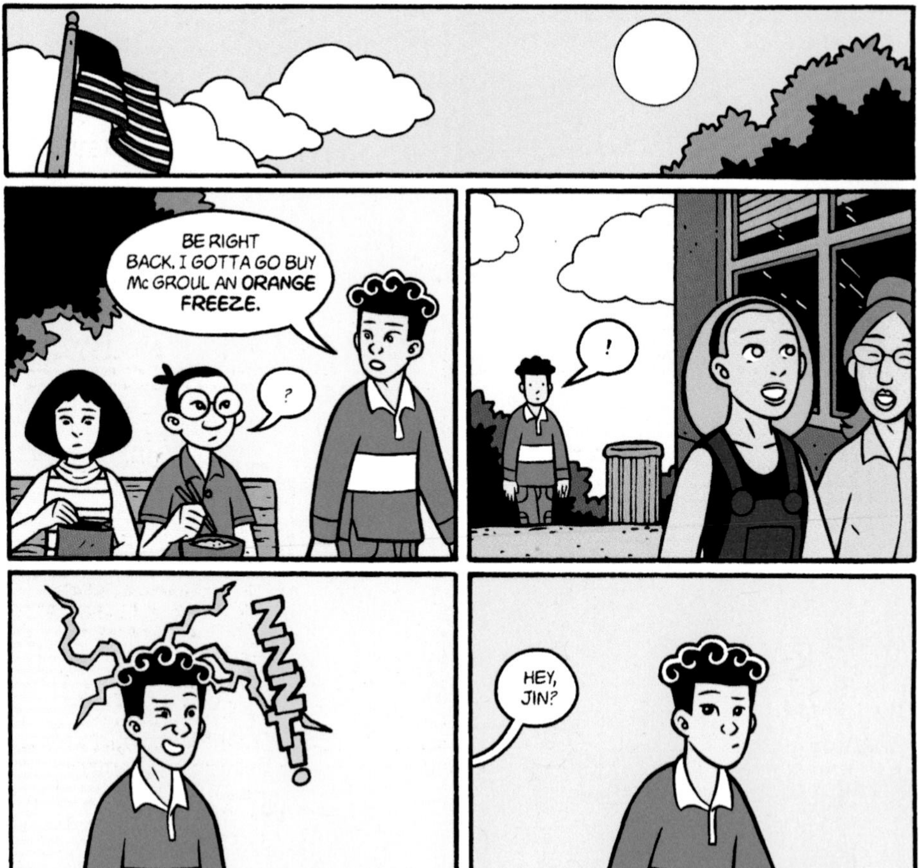
BE RIGHT BACK. I GOTTA GO BUY Mc GROUL AN ORANGE FREEZE.
?
!
ZZZT!
HEY, JIN?

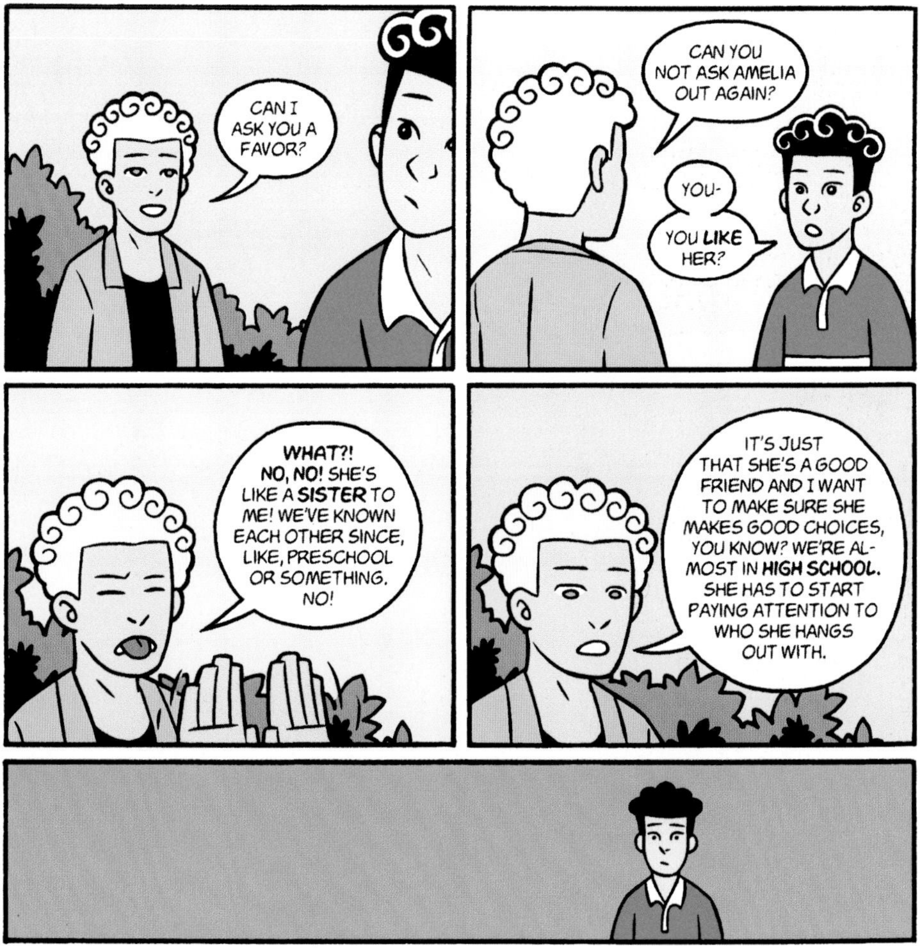
CAN I ASK YOU A FAVOR?
CAN YOU NOT ASK AMELIA OUT AGAIN?
YOU-
YOU **LIKE** HER?
WHAT?! NO, NO! SHE'S LIKE A **SISTER** TO ME! WE'VE KNOWN EACH OTHER SINCE, LIKE, PRESCHOOL OR SOMETHING. NO!
IT'S JUST THAT SHE'S A GOOD FRIEND AND I WANT TO MAKE SURE SHE MAKES GOOD CHOICES, YOU KNOW? WE'RE AL-MOST IN **HIGH SCHOOL.** SHE HAS TO START PAYING ATTENTION TO WHO SHE HANGS OUT WITH.

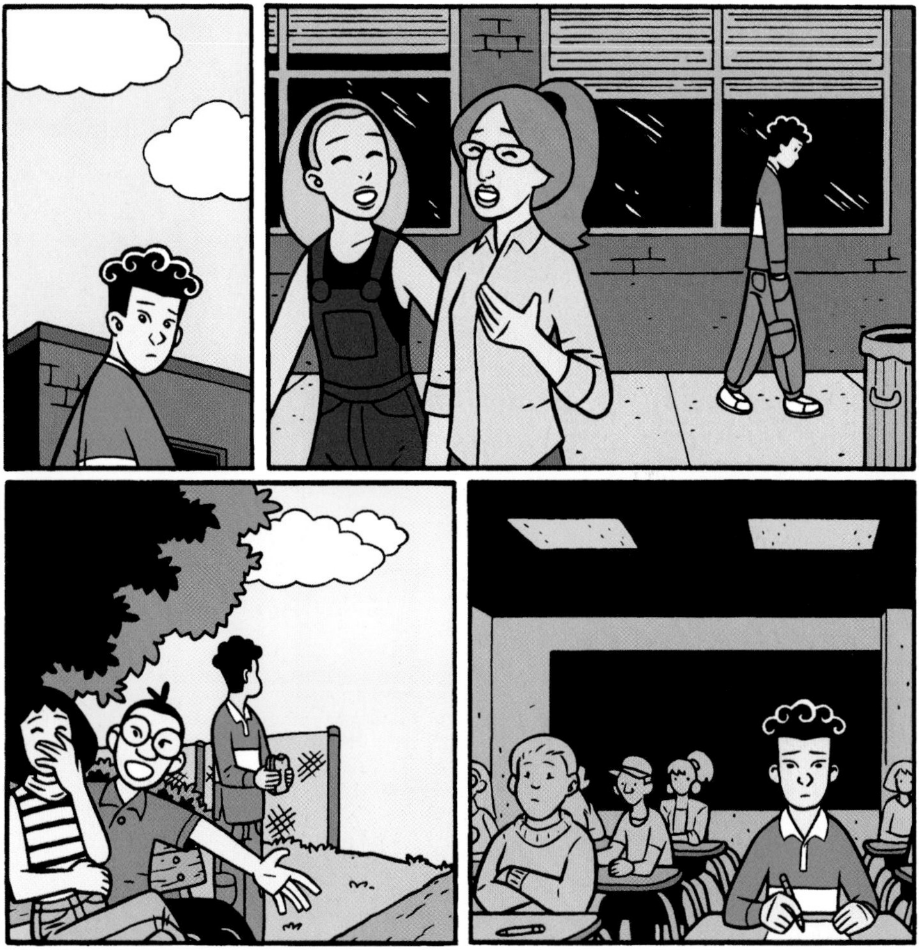

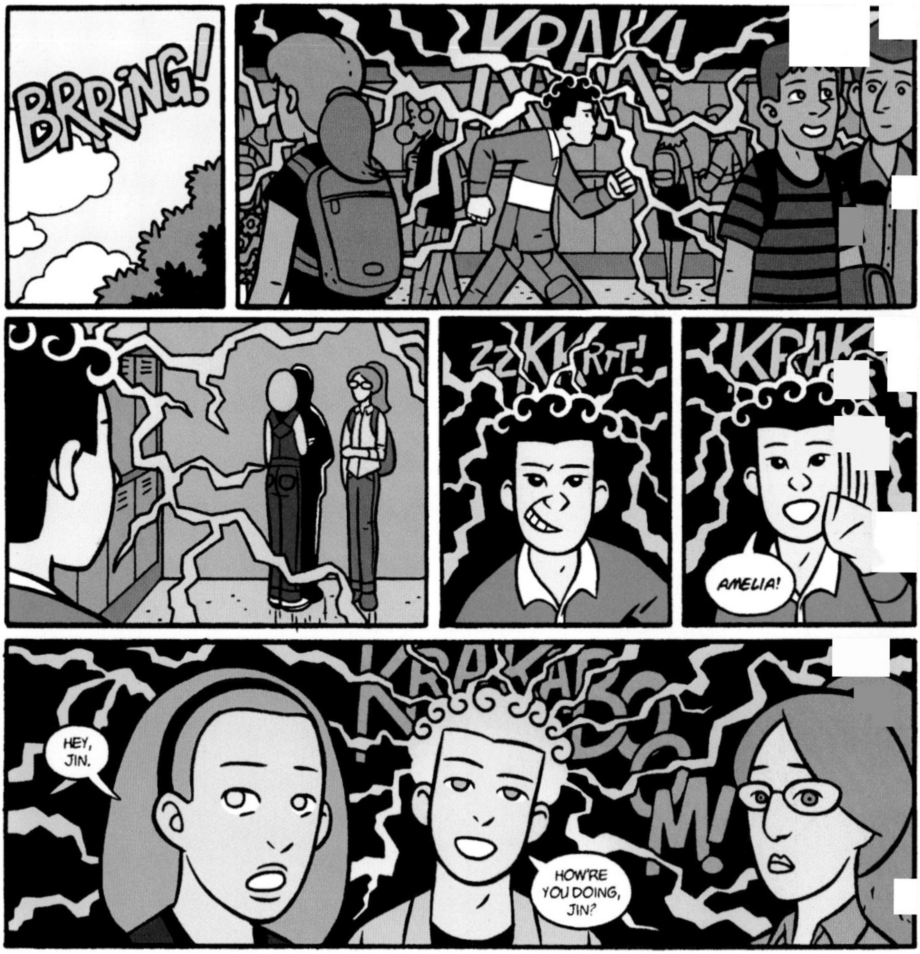
BRRING!
ZZKKRTT!
AMELIA!
HEY, JIN.
HOW'RE YOU DOING, JIN?

I HAD TROUBLE FALLING ASLEEP THAT NIGHT. I REPLAYED THE DAY'S EVENTS OVER AND OVER AGAIN IN MY MIND.

AND AT AROUND THREE IN THE MORNING, I FINALLY **BELIEVED** MYSELF.

EACH TIME I REACHED THE SAME CONCLUSION: WEI-CHEN NEEDED TO HEAR WHAT I HAD TO SAY. IT WAS, AFTER ALL, THE **TRUTH.**

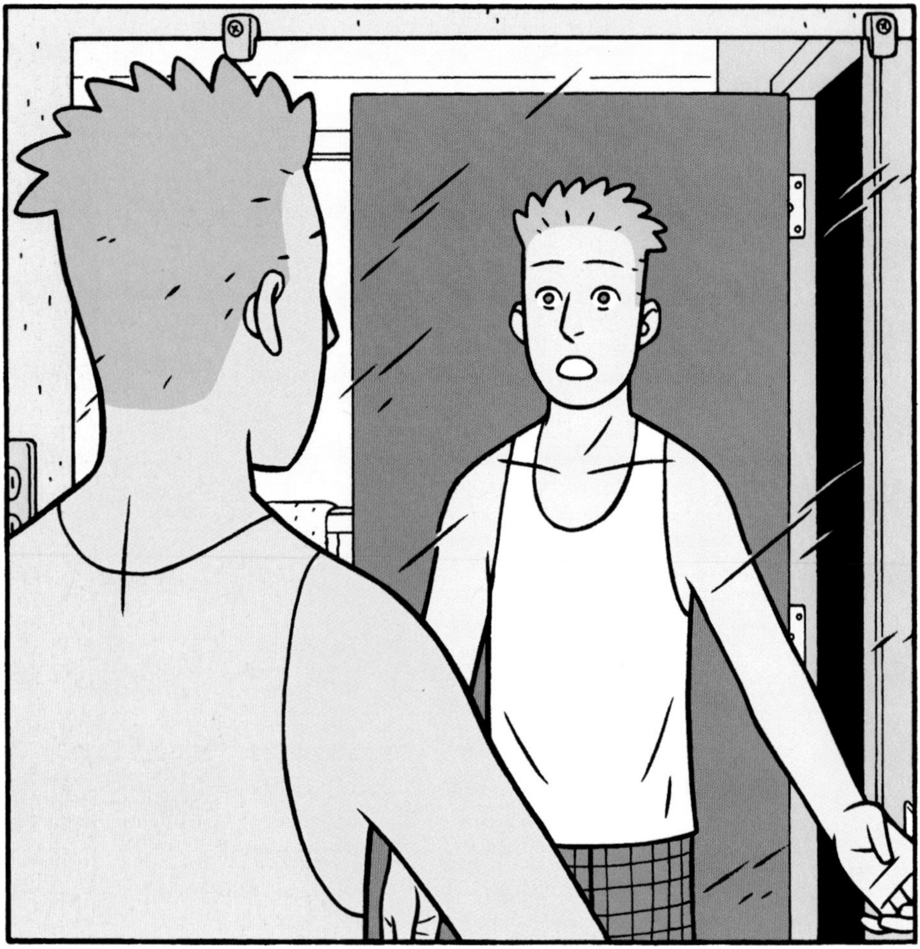

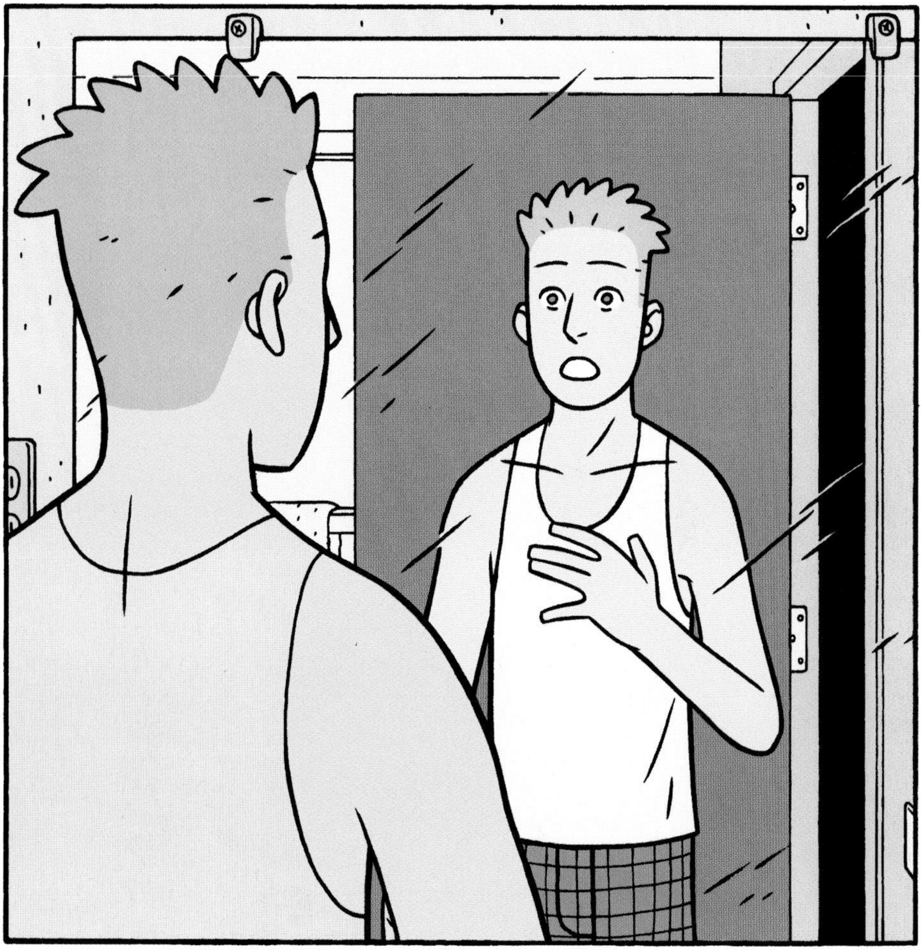

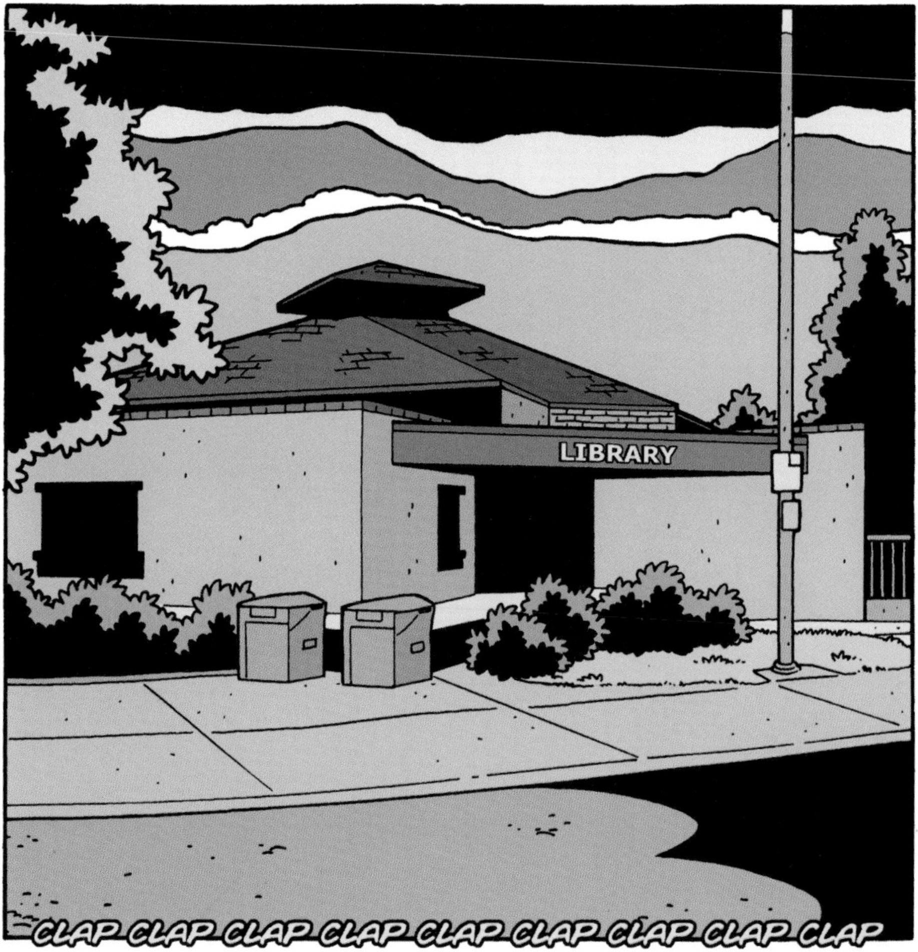
LIBRARY
CLAP CLAP CLAP CLAP CLAP CLAP CLAP CLAP CLAP

210

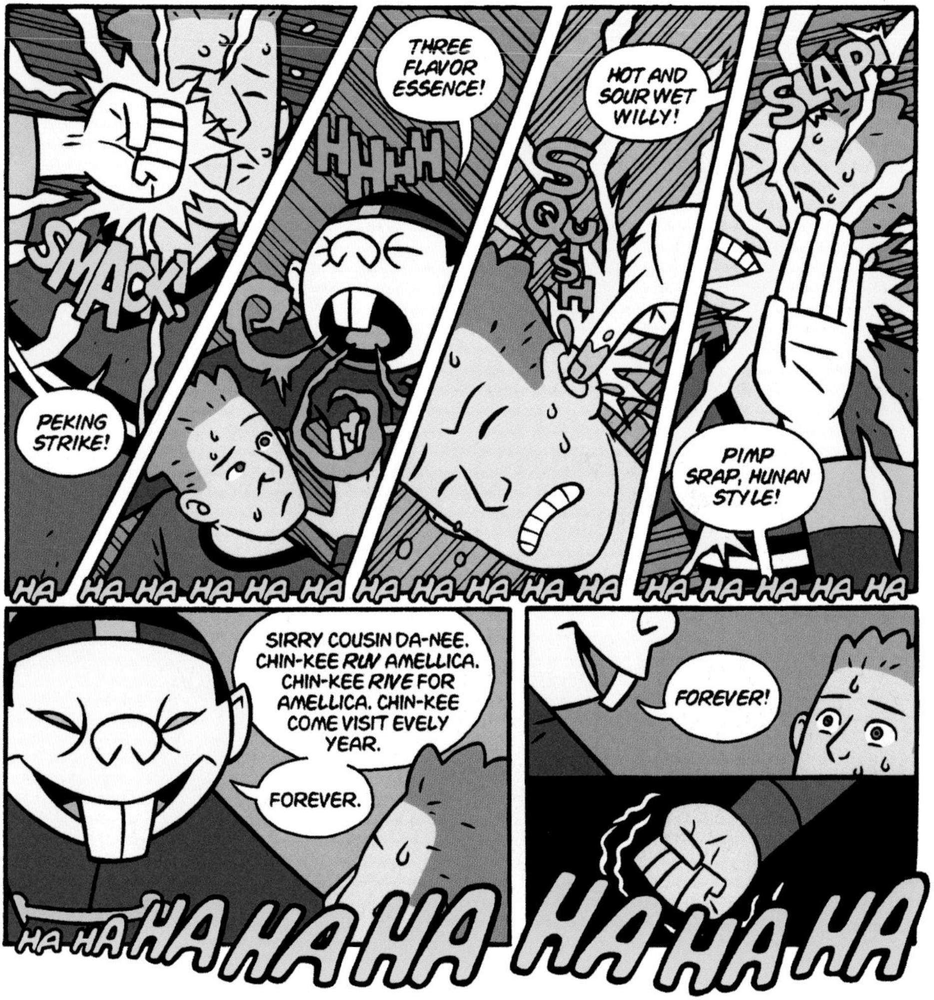

SMACK!
PEKING STRIKE!
HA
THREE FLAVOR ESSENCE!
HHHHH
HA HA HA HA HA
HOT AND SOUR WET WILLY!
SQUISH
HA HA HA HA HA
SLAP!
PIMP SRAP, HUNAN STYLE!
HA HA HA HA HA
SIRRY COUSIN DA-NEE. CHIN-KEE *RUN* AMELLICA. CHIN-KEE *RIVE* FOR AMELLICA. CHIN-KEE COME VISIT EVELY YEAR.
FOREVER.
FOREVER!
HA HA HA HA HA HA HA HA HA

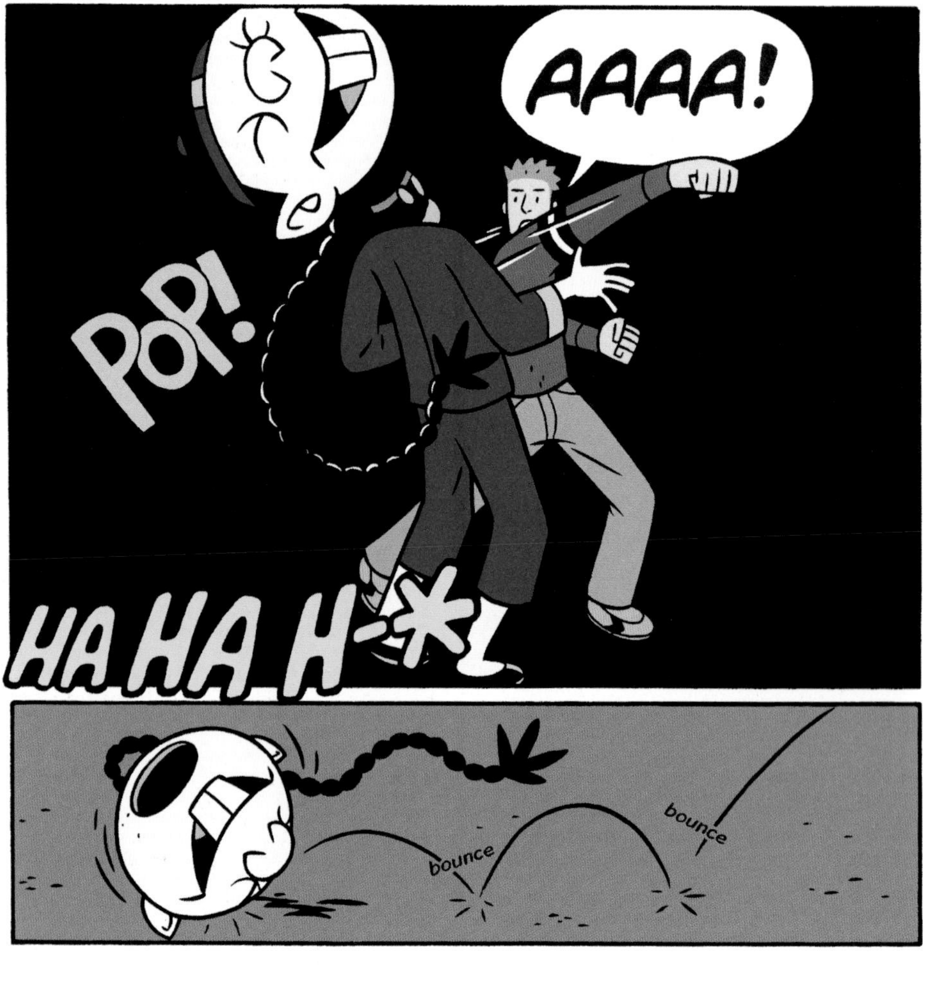
AAAA!
POP!
HA HA H-
bounce
bounce

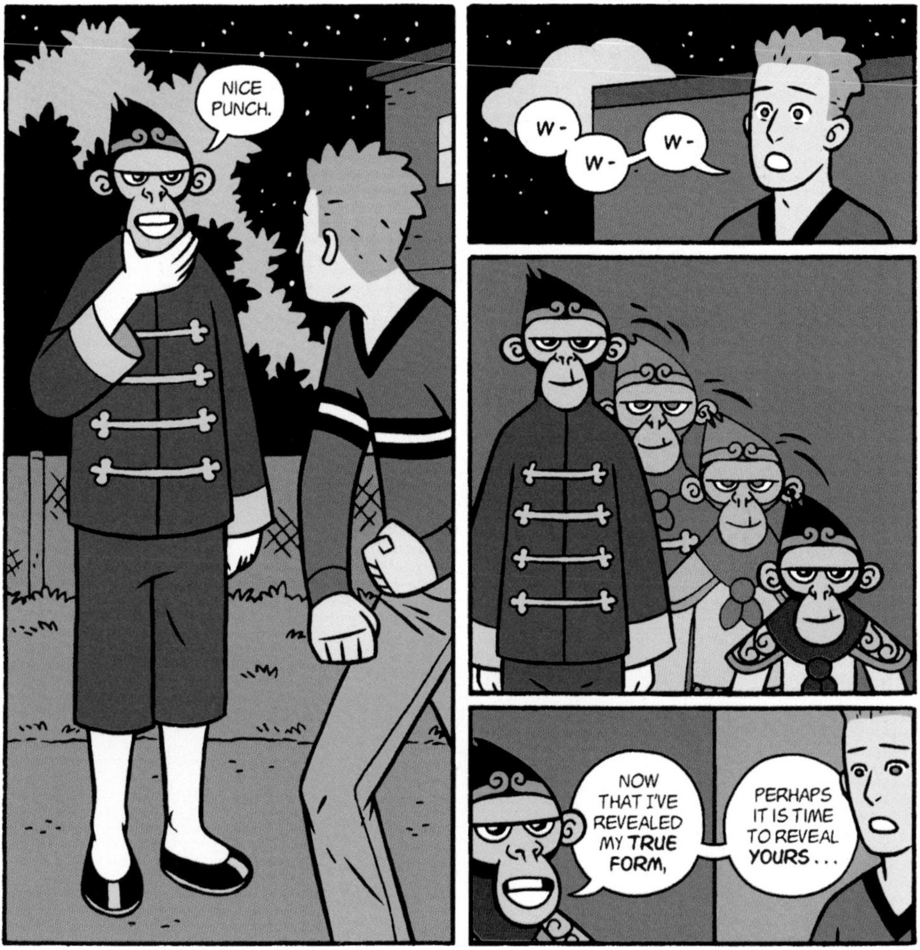
NICE PUNCH.
W-
W-
W-
NOW THAT I'VE REVEALED MY **TRUE FORM**,
PERHAPS IT IS TIME TO REVEAL **YOURS**...

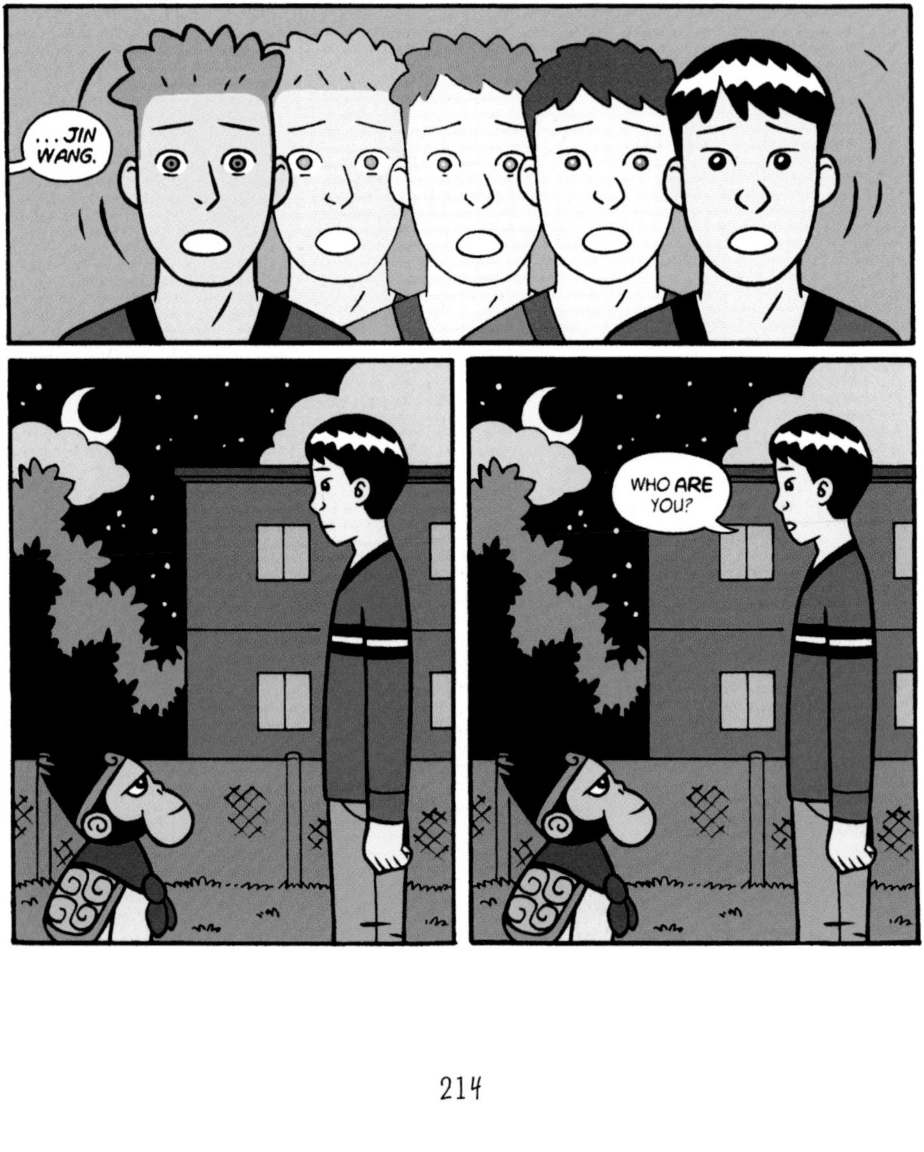
...JIN WANG.
WHO ARE YOU?

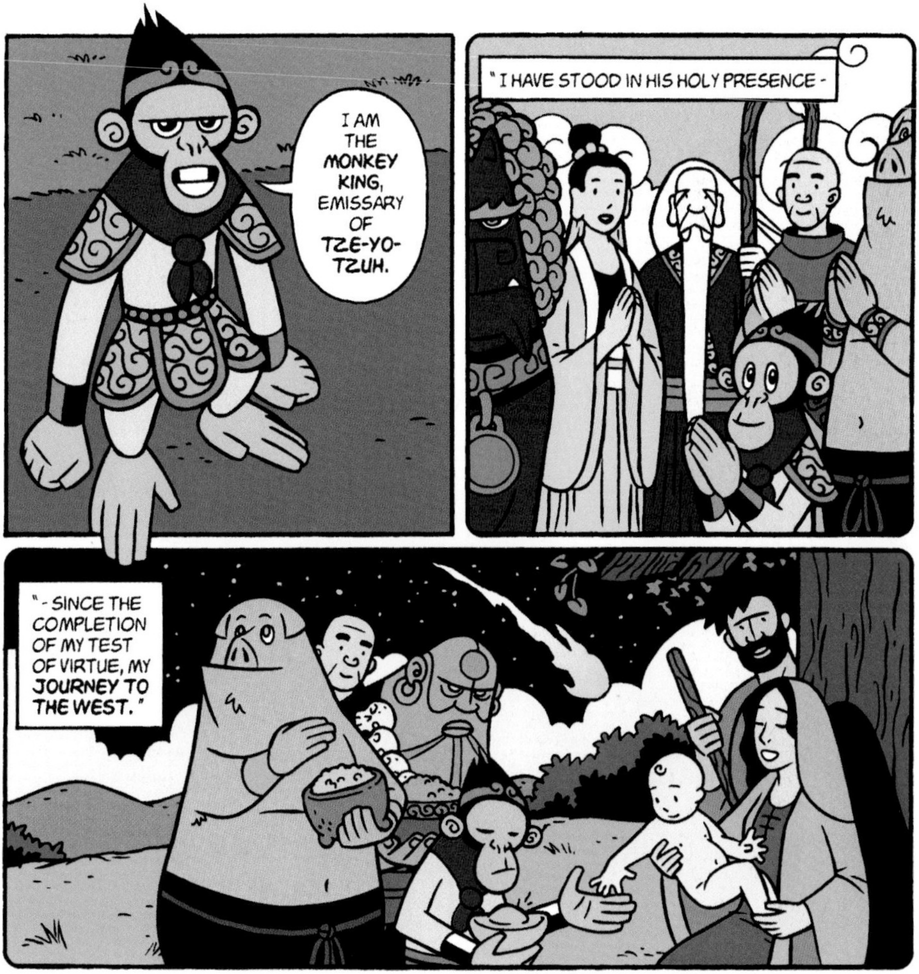
I AM THE MONKEY KING, EMISSARY OF TZE-YO-TZUH.
"I HAVE STOOD IN HIS HOLY PRESENCE -
"- SINCE THE COMPLETION OF MY TEST OF VIRTUE, MY JOURNEY TO THE WEST."

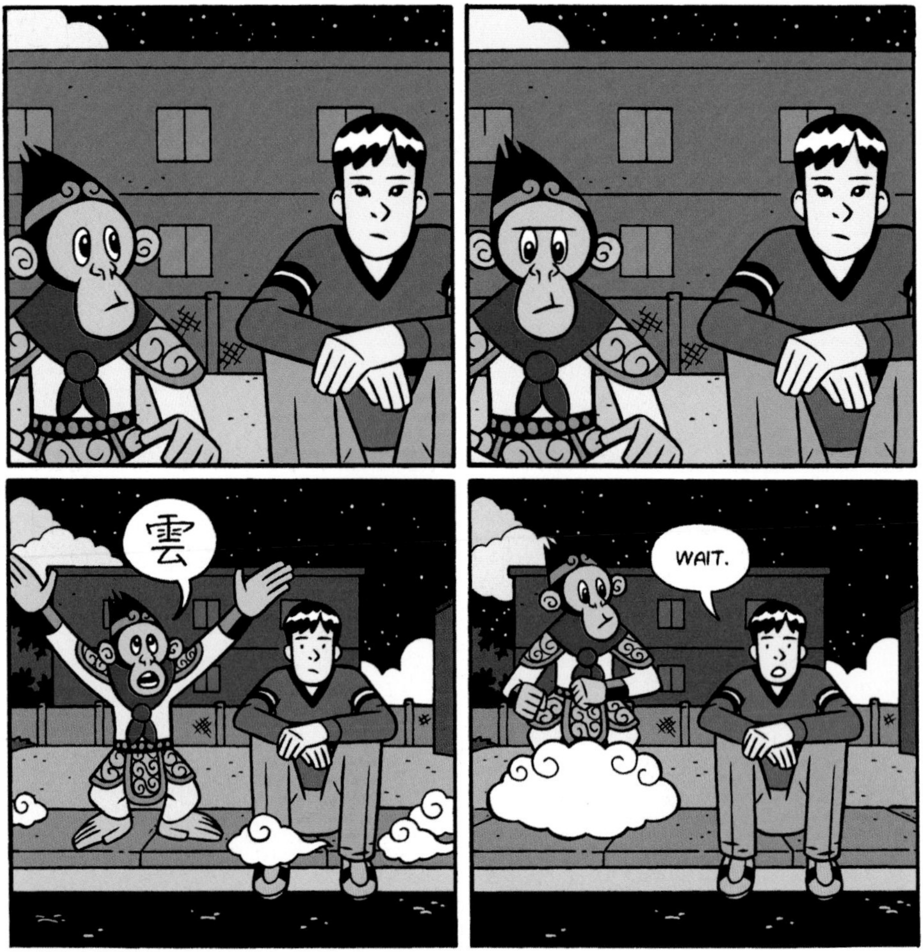
雲
WAIT.

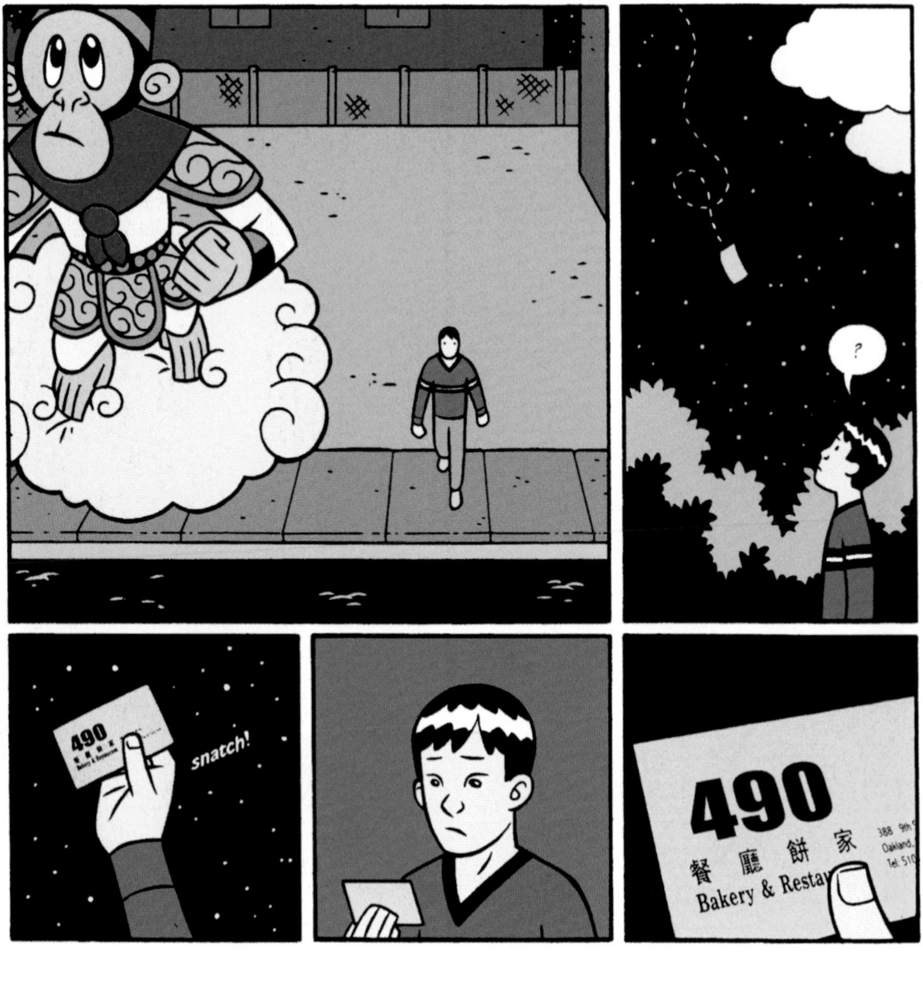
?
snatch!
490
餐 廳 餅 家

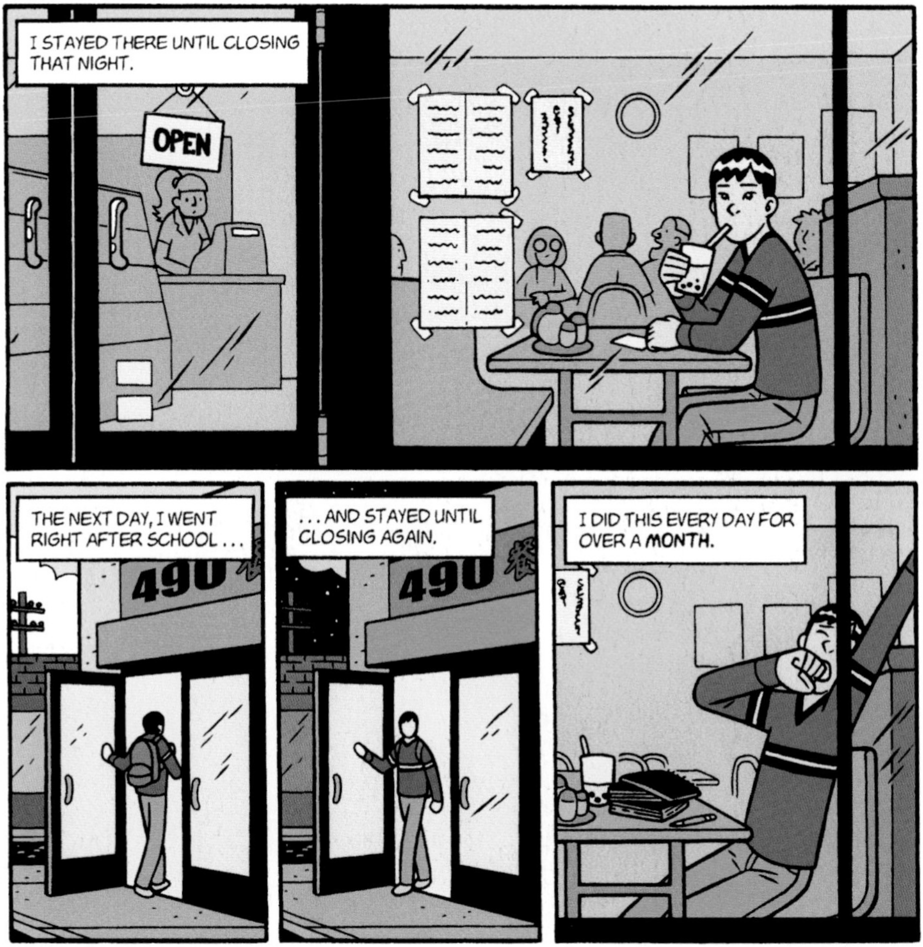
I STAYED THERE UNTIL CLOSING THAT NIGHT.
OPEN
THE NEXT DAY, I WENT RIGHT AFTER SCHOOL . . .
490
. . . AND STAYED UNTIL CLOSING AGAIN.
490
I DID THIS EVERY DAY FOR OVER A MONTH.

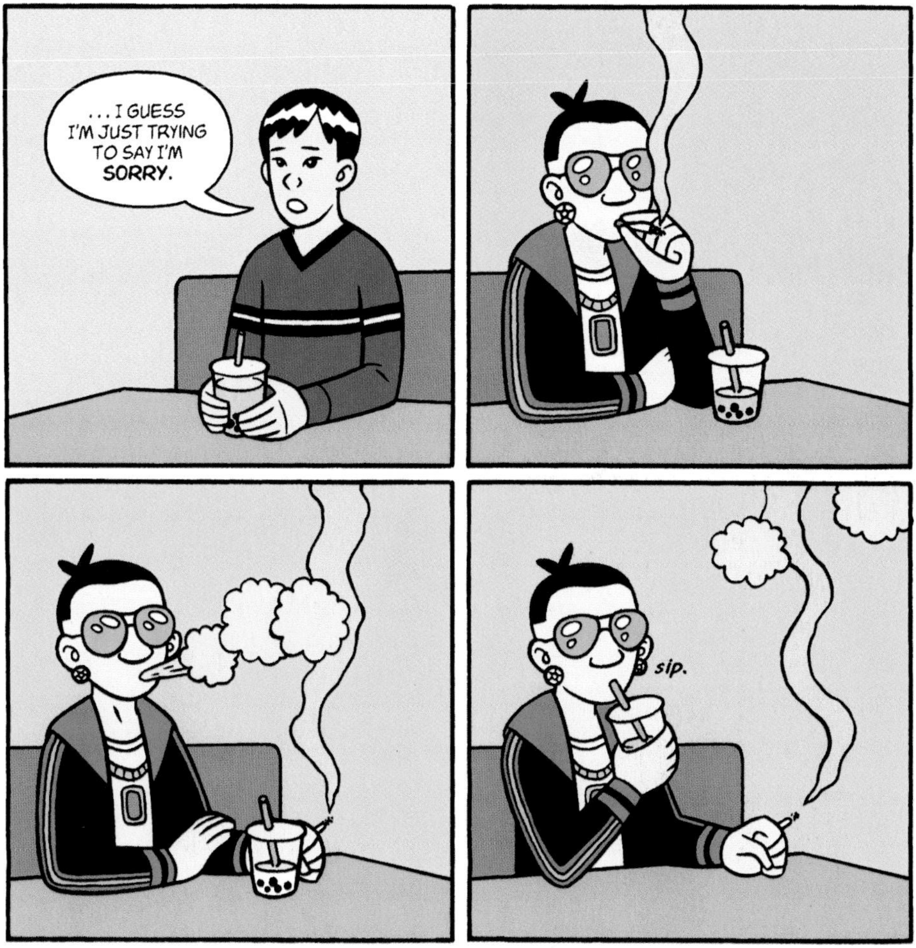
...I GUESS I'M JUST TRYING TO SAY I'M **SORRY**.
sip.

The End

:01
First Second

New York & London

Published by First Second
First Second is an imprint of Roaring Brook Press, a division of Holtzbrinck Publishing Holdings
Limited Partnership
175 Fifth Avenue, New York, NY 10010

Distributed in Canada by H. B. Fenn and Company Ltd.
Distributed in the United Kingdom by Macmillan Children's Books, a division of Pan Macmillan.

Design by Danica Novgorodoff
Chinese chops by Guo Ming Chen

She Bangs
By Afanasieff & Child
© 2000 Sony/ATV Tunes LLC, Wallyworld Music, Desmundo Music, Warner
Tamerlane Pub. Corp., A Phantom Vox Publishing. All rights on behalf of
Sony/ATV Tunes LLC, Wallyworld Music and Desmundo Music, administered by
Sony/ATV Music Publishing, 8 Music Square West, Nashville, TN 37203. All
rights reserved. Used by permission.

Library of Congress Cataloging-in-Publication Data

Yang, Gene.
American born Chinese / Gene Yang ; coloring by Lark Pien
p. cm.
Summary: Alternates three interrelated stories about the problems of young Chinese Americans
trying to participate in the popular culture. Presented in comic book format.
ISBN-13: 978-159643-152-2
ISBN-10: 1-59643-152-0
COLLECTOR'S EDITION
ISBN-13: 978-1-59643-208-6
ISBN-10: 1-59643-208-X

[1.Chinese Americans—Juvenile Fiction. 2. Chinese Americans—Fiction. 3. Identity—Fiction. 4.
Schools—Fiction. 5. Cartoons and comics.] I. Title
PZ7.K678337 Am 2006
[Fic] dc22
2005058105

First Second books are available for special promotions and premiums.
For details, contact: Director of Special Markets, Holtzbrinck Publishers.

FIRST
EDITION

First Edition September 2006

Printed in the USA

Paperback: 10 9 8 7   Hardcover: 10 9 8 7 6 5 4 3

Thank You

Theresa Kim Yang
Kolbe Kim Yang
Jon Yang
Derek Kirk Kim
Lark Pien
Mark Siegel
Judy Hansen
Danica Novgorodoff
Thien Pham
Jesse Hamm
Jason Shiga
Jesse Reklaw
Andy Hartzell
Joey Manley
Alan Davis
Rory Root
Albert Olson Hong
Shauna Olson Hong
Hank Lee
Pin Chou
Jacon Chun
Jonathan Crawford
Jess Delegencia
Susi Jensen

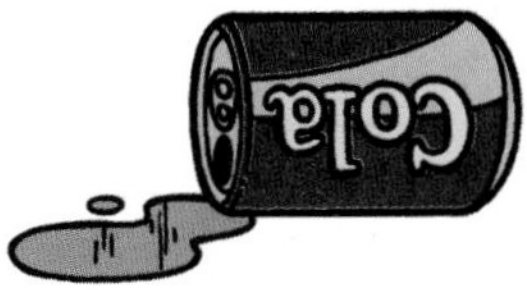
Cola

Also By Gene Yang

Gordon Yamamoto and the King of the Geeks

Loyola Chin and the San Peligran Order

The Rosary Comic Book

The Motherless One

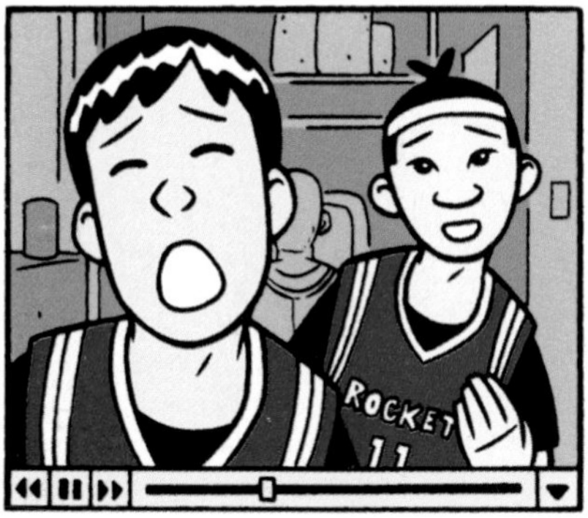
ROCKET
11